AGNES SHARP AND THE TRIP OF A LIFETIME

By Leonie Swann

The Sunset Years of Agnes Sharp
Agnes Sharp and the Trip of a Lifetime

AGNES SHARP AND THE TRIP OF A LIFETIME

LEONIE SWANN

Translated from the German by Amy Bojang

Allison & Busby Limited
11 Wardour Mews
London W1F 8AN
allisonandbusby.com

First published in Germany as *Miss Sharp macht Urlaub* in 2022.
First published in Great Britain by Allison & Busby in 2024.

Published by arrangement with Soho Press, New York, with the
assistance of Rights People, London.

First Edition

ISBN 978-0-7490-3150-3

Typeset in 11/16pt Sabon LT Pro by
Allison & Busby Ltd.

By choosing this product, you help take care of the world's forests.
Learn more: www.fsc.org.

FSC
www.fsc.org
MIX
Paper from
responsible sources
FSC® C020471

Printed and bound by
CPI Group (UK) Ltd, Croydon, CR0 4YY

DRAMATIS PERSONAE

THE RESIDENTS OF SUNSET HALL

AGNES — Used to be in the police, and still has a sharp eye for law and order, both in the house share and in life.

EDWINA — Does yoga and other crazy things, likes animals, and used to be in the Secret Service.

CHARLIE — Is chic, elegant and always up for a gin and tonic.

WINSTON — Uses a wheelchair and is a pretty shrewd operator – Sunset Hall's rock.

BERNADETTE — Blind and direct, with clothes as colourful as her past.

MARSHALL — Forgetful, but still dashing; has a thing for Agnes.

BREXIT — Charlie's wolfhound, not allowed to go with them on holiday.

LILLITH — Former housemate, dead and in a tin, but still very much a member of Sunset Hall.

HETTIE — Pet tortoise, hibernating in the fridge.

HETTIE II — Inflatable tortoise.

DRAMATIS PERSONAE

AT THE HOTEL

MOJO	Whippersnapper with green fingernails and an internet following.
HELEN	Efficient hotel manager.
TRUDY	Ravenous member of the detox group.
THE WHITE WIDOW	Shifty woman in white whose husband died in mysterious circumstances.
MAX	Barman with a side hustle.
LILAC	Masseuse.
HOWARD HOPE	Charmer with round red glasses.
JACK	A man from Bernadette's past.
EVE ASHWOOD	Hotel guest on honeymoon, potential murder victim.
FRANK ASHWOOD	Eve's husband.
OBERON	White boa constrictor in exile.
MRS MEYER-BRINKS	Hotel guest, bookworm.
WALTER ROSS	Hotel guest with a penchant for pastels.

SERPENT

I've never been in a club like this before. Clubs like this aren't meant for people like me. Nevertheless, it was ridiculously easy to get in.

Private function? Not if you know the world of hotels, bars, back streets and staff entrances like I do. A smelly alleyway. A steel door, a narrow corridor, past champagne crates, then a velvet curtain.

Peeling back the layers of an onion to enter the rotting heart.

As expected, the heart is dark, and I slip into the shadows. Points of light flit across the floor, but they don't get me. I look out for a hiding place, but it's hardly necessary. Nobody here sees me. Nobody wants to see me. I might just as well be invisible.

All eyes are on the little stage at the other end of the room.

They're dancing on it.

Eve.

And the serpent.

Long legs, topless, a sparkly little thing round her hips, the reptile draped over her shoulders.

It should look obscene, but on her it seems strangely

innocent. Childlike even. A scene from paradise.

Obviously, I don't buy the whole innocent act. She ought to know better. I'm not quite sure of all the things a bride has to do before her wedding, but definitely not this. Not this shameless making-a-show-of-yourself. She feels so safe. She's mistaken. Oh, she'll soon realise just how mistaken she is!

A champagne cork pops and Eve cheers. She hops off the stage and jumps into the lap of the man who opened the champagne. He passes her a glass and she laughs, throwing her head back, curls like a waterfall.

Everyone laughs.

If you think about it, they're laughing at me.

Eve shakes her hair, and it's like snow. She's so blonde. Pale as a piece of wood that's been left in the sun. Suddenly I wish she weren't so blonde. Does she think she's beautiful? Do other people think she's beautiful? I can't gauge it anymore. At home she wears flowing silk dresses in misty hues, and she moves gracefully, but now there is something akin to shattered glass in her voice.

Suddenly I'm struggling to suppress a laugh too.

Now I've got her, trapped forever more as if she were in a glittering snow globe. There is no escape for her, no matter how loud she laughs, no matter how much champagne she drinks. I raise my phone and quickly take two, three photos, almost surprised at how easy everything is all of a sudden.

How clear.

How cold.

As I'm taking photos, the pale snake frees itself from

Eve's shoulders, lunges forward, with a swinging motion and flicks its rosy tongue at me.

A grin steals across my face.

I have to admit I'm looking forward to the honeymoon.

1

BELLS

Agnes Sharp opened the village quack's door and poked her nose outside. A cold wind blew in her face, tugged at her scarf and instantly seeped into her limbs. Ugh, yuck!

For a moment she toyed with the idea of calling a taxi. Then she cast another glance back to the waiting room, where a crowd of people seemed to be damn happy to finally see the back of her. At least as happy as she was to be able to give her back to those petty-minded fuddy-duddies. There had been some unpleasant scenes and even a bit of a tussle over a dog-eared magazine, and when the receptionist noticed Agnes looking, her brow furrowed with concern.

Back to the waiting room? No way!

Onwards!

Agnes fished her walking stick out of the umbrella stand and stepped pluckily onto the pavement. At least the air out there was fresh, not as stale as in the surgery, and a bit of exercise had never hurt anyone.

Except her hip maybe.

Leaning heavily on her walking stick, off she strode.

Clack-clack-clack.

Like a strange three-legged animal.

It only occurred to Agnes two houses down the road how dark it was already.

Not even five o'clock and dark already. Pitch-black, in fact.

It was enough to give her the heebie-jeebies . . .

Her village had only ventured into the modern day ten or twenty years ago and installed a couple of streetlamps, islands of light in the night. There weren't many of them. Agnes spotted the bus stop at the other end of the road, in a pool of light. Full of promise.

That's where she was heading.

But first she had to struggle past the church, which, shrouded by the graveyard, lay in thick, soupy darkness.

Agnes clutched her walking stick. Her biggest fear was not noticing some kind of obstacle in the darkness, having a fall, not being able to get back on her feet and then being found and rescued by the waiting room clowns, let alone by the snooty receptionist who had taken the magazine from her before.

The scandal. The shame. The snide remarks.

It didn't bear thinking about!

So, she proceeded even more slowly and used her stick to feel in front of her for trip hazards in the dark. Nothing. To top it all, the church bells suddenly started up, all at once, as if they were poking fun at her. Agnes winced. Up until very recently, she wouldn't really have noticed the ringing, a muffled background noise like so many others, but now, with the hearing aid, each chime of the bell went through her like a little shock. Pretty stressful things, these hearing aids!

Agnes limped stubbornly on.

But once she had almost made it to the beam of light at the bus stop, something made her stop. It took a while for her to realise what it was exactly.

The bells.

Or to be precise, the bell.

All the other church bells had fallen silent, but one was still chiming, getting quicker and quicker, and quicker again. In her long life, Agnes had spent a lot of time near these bells, but she'd never heard them ringing like that. So erratic, panicked almost. Something wasn't right.

She looked back at the church, which still lay in deep darkness, then over at the bus stop, where a bus could appear at any moment.

Curiosity finally got the better of her.

While the bell began a hectic finale, Agnes turned around with a sigh and groped her way back towards the church using her tried-and-tested three-legged technique.

By the time she had reached the graveyard and was following the dully shimmering strip of gravel path, the bell had long since stilled.

She got to the church door, felt for the knob with her free hand, turned and pushed. The door opened with a bloodcurdling creak, a scream almost.

Inside it felt even colder than outside, if that was possible. She looked around. A light was flickering on the altar, but she wasn't interested in that. Another light caught her attention, a narrow strip peeking out from beneath the door to the belfry.

In there, then.

Before Agnes set off again, she took a moment to listen.

Outside, the wind was howling at the top of its lungs. It had been a long time since she had last really heard the wind.

But in here, nothing.

Or almost nothing.

Thanks to the hearing aid, she could hear something like a gentle dragging, like something soft against stone or wood. Agnes wasn't sure. She didn't quite trust the new hearing aid as far as she could throw it, and she obviously didn't trust her own ears in the slightest.

There was only one way to clear it up, Agnes dragged herself towards the chink of light. She tried the door, discovered it was open, and she was suddenly bathed in yellow light. Awaiting her was a medium-sized room with an unimaginatively carpeted floor and a row of narrow benches and stools along the walls. One of the stools had tipped over. A sign on the wall pointed out the importance of washing your hands, exactly like one she'd seen before at the doctor's.

The unusual thing was the ropes.

The space at the foot of the bell tower was dominated by six thick ropes, which disappeared into the ceiling and presumably led up to the bells, tonnes and tonnes of singing bronze, centuries old.

Five of the thick ropes were each neatly knotted in loose loops at the end and were swinging gently back and forth.

The verger was hanging from the sixth.

He wasn't completely dead yet. His fingertips were still twitching. But the strange angle of his head and neck told Agnes that he was beyond help.

Broken neck.

Nothing could be done.

The body was hanging in an unusual, half-kneeling position, his head in a loop at the end of the rope. Not just hanged then, the rope wasn't hanging high enough for that. The verger would only have had to stretch out his legs to free himself from the rope. Curious.

Agnes stepped closer and carefully prodded the body with her stick. The verger swung gently back and forth, an expression of infinite surprise in his fixed eyes.

'You probably imagined your Friday evening a bit differently, didn't you?' she murmured. 'Me too!'

Agnes had always had a somewhat relaxed relationship with the dead – after all, they didn't make any stupid comments, they were discreet and polite, albeit not always hygienic. Panting, she sat down on one of the stools – to think, but also because her hip really was fed up now.

She knew that bell ringing wasn't an altogether risk-free endeavour. Once the huge bronze bells up there were in motion, nothing and nobody could stop them. She had heard of cases where a distracted bell-ringer got his foot caught in one of the loops and was then yanked several feet up in the air by the corresponding bell, only to land back on the ground again with broken bones and back injuries.

If a neck were to get caught in the loop instead of a foot . . .

Agnes looked at the dead verger, whose fingertips had now stopped twitching, and noticed that one of his legs was also sticking out at an unhealthy angle.

Aha! That's what must have happened! But how did you manage to get your head caught in a loop, especially after the ringing, when all of the other ropes were already neatly rolled up? An accident was out of the question, unless the verger was crawling through the room on all fours, drunk as a lord.

She sniffed but couldn't smell any alcohol.

Suicide?

She hadn't known the verger personally, but from afar he had made a rather reserved impression. Not the sort to dramatically break his neck with several tonnes of bronze. Aside from that, the man looked far too surprised for that to be the case.

Still murder then.

Murder in Duck End.

Again!

Agnes sighed and clambered to her feet. The murderer must have set the bell in motion and then quickly put the loop around his neck. The verger had been dragged upwards, and the bell had broken his neck instantly. That explained the surprised look on his face.

Then the bell had jingled itself out, getting quicker and quicker, while the murderer – that's a point, where had he got to?

Agnes wasn't the fastest on her feet. It was quite possible that the killer had slipped outside before she arrived. Maybe he was outside crouching behind one of the pitch-black headstones, waiting for her to leave. Or he was hiding in the church.

Or . . .

Agnes suddenly felt overwhelmed by the situation. For years, she had fought against getting a hearing aid, and now that she had one in her ear, everything seemed loud to her.

Even the silence.

And then there was the body . . . It was too much aggravation for one day. She was an old woman with a bit of plastic in her ear. Who was interested in what she thought, anyway? What was she doing there? And what was she hoping to achieve?

She realised she had no desire to do her civic duty and call the police. They would take her to the station and scream in her ear – and the rest of the day was sure to be a write-off. Apart from that, the local police were good for nothing. Complete waste of time. She decided to make her way back to the bus stop. Life was hard enough; there was no sense in letting the dead verger spoil her evening. Maybe she could call the police from home, anonymously of course, then they could deal with the dead body and the corresponding criminal. It was nothing to do with her and she was too old for this squit. She was looking forward to a cosy evening by the fire – maybe a nice cup of tea and some music on the radio.

Or just an early night, with a bulging hot water bottle and a good book, but definitely not a murder mystery.

Agnes Sharp hobbled back to the inviting glow of the bus stop, by some kind of miracle caught her bus, and was soon on her way home.

To Sunset Hall.

But eager anticipation turned to unease as the bus ambled its way through the village, and Agnes stared out of the window, only able to see her own reflection, complete with cold-reddened nose. A few years ago, she had turned her home into a house share for senior citizens, and living together had lots of advantages – if you were in a bad mood, there was usually someone there you could take it out on, but there were also disadvantages. Not much got past the residents of Sunset Hall. Today they would be waiting for her full of curiosity – with some sort of warmed-up dinner and a whole host of awkward questions. They were dying to test out Agnes's new hearing aid.

Charlie, Bernadette, Winston, Brexit, Marshall and, of course, Edwina. Individually they were each good eggs, but when something as exciting as a doctor's appointment took place, they transformed into a mob and wanted to know exactly how it went.

It had gone badly, and Agnes had no desire to let her housemates in on the embarrassing details. The bad thing about a hearing aid was that you heard things that you could really do without. The words 'hippies' and 'antisocial,' for example. And if a hefty magazine happened to be at hand . . . At least she would be able to distract her housemates with the story of the dead verger. With a bit of luck, it would keep them busy for long enough to facilitate her escape up to bed.

With a bit of luck – because just lately a murder in Duck End was no great shakes anymore.

The bus stopped at the village square, where they'd recently fished the pharmacist out of the pond. It passed where the chairman of the pigeon fanciers' club had been found dead in a bush – not a mark on him, but there was definitely something fishy about it – and hurtled purposefully along the road towards Sunset Hall.

As a heater blew warm air up her skirt, Agnes's face flushed hot and red, and her mood got darker and darker.

What was going on in Duck End, her home village?

Things like this didn't used to happen there.

Any conflict in the village had traditionally always been solved in a civil fashion. People had spread nasty rumours, shaved cats, hammered copper nails into neighbouring apple trees or, at a pinch, written poisonous anonymous letters in to the village rag, but as a rule, murder was frowned upon.

Until now, that is.

Now it looked as if the residents of Duck End were suddenly making up for all of the murders that they had suppressed over the last twenty years.

And of course, the trend had started back in the autumn with Agnes's friends Lillith and Mildred. Thanks to Agnes, those cases had been solved, but that didn't seem to stop the villagers from merrily murdering away.

Agnes did not approve.

Was she expected to somehow clear up all the mess in the village? They'd be waiting a long time. After all, she'd been retired for so long, she could hardly remember exactly what she used to do in the police. There had been lots of files, and every now and then someone had brought scones into the office, that much she was certain of. The rest was a bit hazy.

She stared gloomily at her reflection, which was getting more and more red in the face, until the bus finally spat her out in front of Sunset Hall.

Agnes hobbled up the garden path, her house in front of her managing to look cosy even in the inhospitable winter months. Rose hips flashed on bare branches, ivy snuggled up to the walls like a green blanket, warm light illuminated the windows and the welcoming, and recently painted, coral red front door. Like a picture-postcard. Then Agnes spotted her housemates through one of the illuminated windows. As expected, they had assembled in the lounge, even Brexit the wolfhound was there, and they were lying in wait, ready to pump Agnes for information about her doctor's appointment.

She took a deep breath, opened the door, hung her stick on the hall stand and wriggled out of her coat.

Then she entered the lounge, ready to do battle, the story of the dead verger on the tip of her tongue.

'You'll never believe what happened to me tod—'

She fell silent because it dawned on her that nobody was interested in what had happened to her in the village, today, yesterday, the day after tomorrow or any other time for that matter. Brexit briefly but politely wagged his tail, but the others' attention was focused on a letter resting on the coffee table, harmless, white and rectangular.

'What's that?' Agnes asked, suddenly offended by the general disinterest. After all, she had got a hearing aid at the behest of her housemates – and now nobody gave two hoots about it!

'A letter,' Charlie murmured. She was their new arrival and far too glamorous for Agnes's tastes, but she did make outstanding pancakes.

'I can see that!' Agnes hissed. It was a mystery to her how a letter could be more interesting than her story about the verger.

'It's for *Edwina*!' Bernadette added gravely. Bernadette was blind and fat and cynical. Behind her dark glasses, she could be gloomy like no other.

Oh!

Agnes had to sit down. A letter for Edwina really was something to write home about!

Edwina was what some people would refer to as 'not all there.' Such people didn't understand how unbelievably 'there' Edwina could be when you lived with her. Yoga, dancing, games, antics with Hettie the tortoise. Apart from that, she baked the hardest biscuits for miles around. Superb missiles. Practically indestructible, like Edwina herself.

Only, she was by no means a likely correspondent. In all their years of living together, Agnes couldn't remember ever having seen a letter addressed to Edwina – not even junk mail. But today was the day.

She looked more closely. The letter seemed official, with a little plastic window you could see the address through. Agnes put on her reading glasses and gingerly fished the missive off the table. Edwina's name was clearly written on it. And, Sunset Hall.

She sighed.

'We thought we'd wait for you to open it,' Marshall explained. He used to be in the military, and as a general rule waited for Agnes in crisis situations, whether she liked it or not.

By the look of it, they had already formed factions. The first, anti-letter faction consisted of Bernadette, Winston, Marshall and Charlie. The other faction was Edwina, who had adopted the warrior yoga pose. Not a good sign.

Winston manoeuvred himself next to Agnes in his wheelchair. 'We even wondered if we should just burn it,' he whispered to her. Winston was responsible for peace and logic in the house. A controversial suggestion like that wasn't like him at all.

'It's *my* letter! No way!' screeched Edwina, who still had good ears. Good ears, good eyes, good bones, a good figure. It was only soft and woolly inside her head. Edwina snatched the letter out of Agnes's hand and made to open it.

'Maybe it's a bomb!' Charlie warned.

That gave them all food for thought. Edwina used to work in the Secret Service, and taking into account all of the facts, a letter bomb seemed a great deal more likely than a straight-forward letter.

'It *is* not!' Edwina objected, but stopped in her tracks regardless.

In a daring manoeuvre that almost cost Agnes her balance, she managed to bring the letter back under her control.

She thought for a moment.

'Let's open it,' she decided finally. 'We can still burn it afterwards.'

It took a while for Agnes to poke open the envelope with the help of a knitting needle – she didn't really believe in the thing about the letter bomb, but better to be safe than sorry. The letter consisted of a single sheet of paper. Agnes unfolded it and adjusted her reading glasses.

'Dear Edwina Singh,' she read.

'That's me!' Edwina beamed.

The rest of the household was hanging on Agnes's every word, a rare occurrence.

'I am delighted to inform you that you are the winner of our grand prize draw!' Agnes read.

'Hurrah!' Edwina cheered.

* * *

Later on, it took them quite a while to ascertain how it had come about that Edwina was able to even take part in a prize draw, let alone win the thing. Normally they made a concerted effort to make sure Edwina had as little contact with the outside world as possible. It was better that way.

Above all, for the outside world's sake.

Strictly speaking, Marshall was to blame. The mistake happened about a month ago, when, worn down by hours of pestering, he had let Edwina on the internet so she could look at tortoise videos.

Then he had gone to the loo and subsequently got a bit side-tracked.

In the fifteen minutes of internet time that she got out of it, Edwina had managed not only to watch videos of mating tortoises, order a heat lamp for reptiles and register Marshall for a dating agency, but she had obviously also taken part in a prize draw – and won!

Now they were getting their just deserts!

'And *what* has she won?' Charlie asked gingerly.

'A . . .' Agnes read on, speechless.

Then she read it a second time.

And a third time just to be sure.

It was all far worse than she had feared!

2

PANCAKES

Agnes was sitting in bed, wide awake and absolutely livid. She had got out the big guns, the hot water bottle was bulging, hot tea was steaming in her mug, music was tinkling from the radio, and a good book was lying open on her lap.

Not a murder mystery, obviously. Something with a bit of class.

Despite everything, the cosy atmosphere she had imagined in beautiful technicolour detail didn't quite come to fruition. The heating had stopped working again and the hot water bottle was no match for the arctic room temperature. Her tea was cooling rapidly. 'Jingle Bells' was booming mercilessly from the radio, bringing back unpleasant memories of the verger.

And on top of that, there was the matter of the holiday too.

As ill luck would have it, Edwina really had gone and won a holiday on the internet. A romantic getaway, no less! For two. To the coast. To a high-end luxury eco-conscious hotel. *Romantic!* Edwina! And instead of trying to talk her out of it, as would be right and proper, her housemates were busy sucking up to Edwina to win the second guest's place.

The whole thing was completely out of the question, of course. None of them was in any position to keep Edwina in check on their own. No way. And in a romantic hotel, even little mishaps could have dire consequences. Apart from that, Agnes found the 'eco' in the hotel's name unsettling. Carrots could be eco-friendly, couldn't they? And were then mostly a bit wrinkly. But a hotel? It didn't make sense . . .

She realised she wasn't remotely interested in her book, whether it had a bit of class or not, and threw it out of bed in annoyance. Her tea was cold, the hot water bottle was gurgling mockingly, the radio switched to an untimely rendition of 'The Little Drummer Boy.'

Parumpumpum-pum.

Agnes flicked the switch on the radio, then the reading light.

Then she lay in the dark and fretted herself to sleep.

When she entered the kitchen the next morning, wrapped in three cardigans and still stiff with cold, the rest of the household was already sitting down to breakfast. Highly unusual, normally Agnes was the first to the table. Winston was swaddled in a garish wool blanket and with his bald head, he looked alarmingly like a giant baby; Marshall was wearing a scarf and military hat to keep out the cold; Bernadette had just brought her duvet to the table; Edwina was wearing a down jacket, and a tea cosy as a head covering; and a fabulous fur hat sat atop Charlie's head.

Brexit's breath was steaming.

Agnes sniffed. It smelt good. Of coffee and . . .

Charlie had made her famous pancakes, and Edwina had already stacked four of them on her plate. Eyes bigger than her stomach, again, but nobody said a word. Of course they didn't.

'Good morning,' Agnes murmured.

Marshall leapt up and pulled up a chair for her. Then he poured her some lukewarm coffee. At least that was still working.

Other than that, her housemates were good for nothing this morning. Becapped and bundled up, they sat there watching as Edwina stuffed one pancake after another into her mouth.

At least nobody had uttered the stupid 'holiday' word.

But once Edwina was finished – she left one partially eaten pancake, just as Agnes had feared – Winston plucked up the courage.

'So, Edwina,' he said gently. 'Have you had any thoughts?'

Agnes resolutely swallowed down a bit of pancake and attempted a distraction tactic.

'We need a plumber!' she said loudly. 'I've had a look at the boiler. It's not just on the blink. It's completely broken! Again!'

This news would normally have prompted widespread consternation, but today they all did their best to ignore Agnes. It was outrageous!

'Thoughts about what?' Edwina asked after a while, poking around with her fork at the spurned pancake.

'Well,' Charlie murmured. 'Who you'd like to take . . .'

'On the holiday,' Bernadette added, as if there could be any doubt.

Marshall looked as if he wanted to throw his hat in the ring too, but he noticed the look on Agnes's face and loyally kept his mouth shut.

Edwina nodded. 'I have. Of course I have.'

She rolled the partially eaten pancake up and held it up to her eye like a telescope. Then she looked from one of them to the other.

Charlie, Marshall, Brexit, Bernadette, Winston, Agnes. Agnes, Winston, Bernadette, Brexit, Marshall, Charlie. Charlie . . .

Was Agnes seeing things, or did her housemates really sit up straighter when Edwina turned her pancake telescope on them?

'So?' Bernadette asked finally. 'Who are you taking?'

'Lillith!' Edwina beamed.

Bernadette groaned, Charlie rolled her eyes, Marshall put his hand to his forehead, and Winston slumped down a bit beneath his garish blanket. Agnes felt a hysterical laugh rising in her throat but managed to pull herself together.

Edwina, seeming to sense the general resistance, plopped her pancake back on her plate. 'Lillith is my best friend,' she explained. 'And she doesn't get out much.'

'No way!' Agnes belligerently sipped her coffee. 'You can't go to a hotel like that on your own. Someone has to take care of you!'

'And someone has to take care of the hotel,' Bernadette muttered.

'Lillith can look after me!' Edwina wasn't giving in without a fight.

Agnes finally exploded. 'Lillith is dead and in a tin!' she hissed.

Unfortunately, their friend Lillith had fallen prey to a bullet a few months ago and had resided in a coffee tin in the flower window ever since. Did Edwina really prefer the company of a tin of human ashes to theirs? That really did speak volumes!

Edwina did finally look a bit guilty. 'Obviously, I would prefer to take Hettie, but Charlie said we shouldn't break the cold chain,' she explained sensibly.

Hettie was Sunset Hall's pet tortoise; she spent the cold months hibernating reptile-style in the fridge.

'What about Brexit?' Agnes asked sarcastically.

The wolfhound heard his name and optimistically turned his attention to the last pancake.

Edwina shook her head earnestly. It was obvious that she had already considered it. 'Brexit's too big. He can't come!' With that, she apologetically pushed her pancake towards the dog, and Brexit chowed down.

Agnes noticed she was holding her breath. Now Edwina had run out of non-human companions, and things were heating up again. To her great consternation, Agnes realised that even she was beginning to find the thought of a holiday quite attractive. Sure, whoever the chosen one was would have Edwina on their hands – not exactly fun – but a well-heated hotel room alone seemed like a luxury at the moment, and there would probably be lots of good food and maybe even an entertainment programme.

Apart from that, she wouldn't have to grapple with the dead verger. She had this vague feeling that sooner or later the thing would be pinned on her, incompetent as the local police generally were.

But if she were to just pack her case . . .

She wrestled with an excitement of sorts and stood up.

'I'm going to call the plumber!' she announced and stalked out of the kitchen. Suck up to Edwina?

As if!

When Agnes returned with crushing news, the mood had shifted. Before, they had all been trying to curry favour with Edwina, now all eyes turned optimistically to Agnes.

Odd.

'The plumber has vanished,' she declared gloomily. Presumably also murdered, as was the current trend in Duck End. Or fled. Maybe he was the killer? Or he'd just run away with his mistress? Agnes didn't really care. What was for certain was that he would not be repairing their boiler, and the plumber from the next small town along had, by his own admission, a waiting list as long as his arm.

'Won't get to you for another three weeks at least!' Three weeks without hot water. Three weeks huddled together in the lounge, the only room with a functioning fireplace. If only she hadn't let herself be persuaded to convert to central heating in the eighties! Why had she thrown the baby out with the bathwater? Although there could, of course, be no real talk of baths for the foreseeable future. Short cold showers – and then shivering into an even colder bed. Maybe it would be better just to lapse into hibernation like Hettie – the temperature was ripe for it after all!

Agnes looked from one of them to the other, but

somehow her news didn't seem to be getting through to them.

'Oh,' Marshall said sympathetically, but Agnes could tell he wasn't quite with it.

She crossed her arms. What was going on here? They should at least stick together when it came to the boiler!

Winston cleared his throat. 'Charlie's had an idea,' he said gingerly.

Beneath her fur hat, Charlie looked a bit like Catherine the Great, but also a bit mischievous at the same time. She smiled cautiously, then she spread her arms wide, as elegant as it was dramatic. The tassels on her dressing gown jiggled.

'Why don't we just *all* go?'

Later on, Agnes was in the lounge brooding, sitting as close to the fire as was physically possible without singeing her cardigan.

Obviously, there were a hundred and one valid reasons why they couldn't all go away at the same time.

Money, for example.

Or rather, lack of money.

She didn't know exactly how much was currently in the household kitty, or how much a group holiday like that would cost, but she was certain that the two figures were not compatible.

Apart from that, Brexit had to be taken out.

And somebody had to be on the ground to call the plumber now responsible for fixing the boiler, and put the fear of God into him. If not, at this rate they'd be waiting until spring for warm water.

Apart from that . . .

'Have you had any thoughts?' Marshall asked sheepishly next to her.

'There's nothing to think about!' Agnes snapped and tried to shift away from him with her armchair. But it didn't work, because Bernadette was sitting on the other side of her, Charlie next to her, and then Winston, so tightly packed, that a sheet of paper barely would have fit between them, never mind an angry Agnes. Brexit was lying in front of her, snoring and reeking of wet dog, and from behind, the cold was clawing at her back with its long, greedy fingers. Agnes was trapped.

She groaned and closed her eyes. Her housemates had ganged up against her and all wanted to go away together. And they actually had some pretty reasonable arguments!

What a nightmare!

In moments like these she would have preferred to sulk in her room, but things being as they were, it was simply too cold for lone sulking. She was trapped in the lounge, and if she showed even the slightest sign of weakness, sooner or later they would grind her down.

Edwina was the only one not sitting with them by the fire. Still wrapped up in her down jacket, she had already started packing.

Yoga mat.

Pocketknife.

Reptile heat lamp.

Lillith in her tin.

Remote control.

'We won't be needing a remote control at the hotel.' Agnes snarled.

Then she was even more annoyed at what she had let slip. The triumphant looks that Charlie and Winston were giving each other did not escape her attention.

Now the matter was practically settled.

Generally speaking, Agnes was against changes she hadn't suggested herself. As a matter of principle. And a trip like this was a huge change. On the other hand, it would solve the warmth issue – at least temporarily. Apart from that, unlike in Duck End there would be no murder and mayhem in a chic hotel, and the household kitty was also safe, because Charlie had offered to pay for them all. A generous gesture – Agnes had had no idea her housemate was so well-heeled.

Charlie had promised Brexit could stay at her grandson's; Marshall had hired a house-sitter on the internet for the house plants and promised to bug the plumber via email. Winston had ordered a new, extra-compact, foldable travel wheelchair for the occasion; and Bernadette had started to plan all of the things she would eat while she was away, a lot, that was for sure.

Agnes realised that even she was humming away to herself, albeit discreetly. She was still against this crazy holiday, of course, but she had secretly also already started to look forward to the trip.

She would see the sea for the first time in a long while.

There was bound to be staff, central heating and food, and surely they were attuned to elderly guests.

What could go wrong?

She glanced at Edwina, who was trying to get Lillith's big garden shears in her suitcase, and sighed.

* * *

At lunchtime they sat in the kitchen next to the oven, which was doing its level best to heat up a frozen pizza, and listened to Charlie on her mobile tearing strips off someone at the hotel until they had sorted out all of the rooms for her.

'I don't care *how*!' Charlie shouted, rolling her eyes, although the person on the other end definitely couldn't see. 'The question is *when*!'

It seemed like they were trying to get a word in, but instantly being rebuffed by Charlie.

'As soon as possible, of course!' she shouted. 'What's that? Thursday? Newquay? No problem at all! We're *flying*! *Of course*, we've all got passports! Fabulous!'

Thursday rolled round really quickly, mainly thanks to the frantic and time-consuming search for the passports. When they weren't searching or packing or squabbling about the best route to the airport, they were glued to the fire, passing a thermos of hot tea around and planning their trip.

'There will be canapés,' Bernadette said happily. 'Loads of canapés.'

'And champagne!' added Charlie. 'Don't forget the champagne!'

'Cakes and scones and biscuits,' Bernadette responded.

'Gin and tonic.' Charlie sighed.

'And tortoises,' Edwina said dreamily. 'Exotic tortoises, who never hibernate! Not to eat, of course. For company!'

Nobody had the heart to tell her that the tortoise thing was rather unlikely, even at a luxury eco hotel.

'There's bound to be yoga,' said Charlie, who was the

most au fait with luxury because one of her many ex-husbands had had some success on the markets at some point. 'And massages. A sauna. Maybe even a little boogie.'

Agnes swallowed a barbed remark and decided to join in with the general excitement. 'The boiler there will work flawlessly,' she said optimistically. 'And it will be peaceful. So peaceful. No murder and mayhem!' For a moment she thought about the dead verger, hanging in the ropes. What had happened, had she actually called the . . . ? Apparently, in all the excitement about Edwina's letter, she'd forgotten to call them, but he was bound to have been found in the meantime, and ultimately it wasn't her problem.

She felt a pang of guilt, then she pushed the image of the dangling verger out of her mind. Her case was packed, and with the finest clothes her wardrobe had to offer, to boot. On top of that, she was planning on investing in a new lipstick at the airport and maybe trying out a beauty treatment at the hotel. See how good the treatments really were . . .

'We can finally all relax!' Winston declared. That was, however, unlikely because they were very good at mutually preventing one another from relaxing. But maybe a harmony of sorts would materialise at the hotel, lubricated as they would be by canapés and champagne?

'I want to look out to sea and feel the wind on my face,' Marshall announced. Since it had become evident that the holiday was to a seaside hotel, he had started to play the sea dog a bit, and yet, as far as Agnes knew, during his time in the military he hadn't been in the Marines, he'd been stationed in the desert.

'We'll meet new people.' Winston beamed. 'Like-minded people.'

Hopefully it wouldn't come to that. Agnes tried to imagine like-minded people and shuddered.

'It'll be sunny!' Bernadette said, as if Cornwall were somewhere in the Caribbean and not just a few hours away from Duck End.

'Inspiring!' shouted Charlie, so fervently that her fur hat slipped.

'And elegant,' said Edwina and pirouetted. 'Exceedingly elegant!'

Once the others had gone to bed the night before they were due to depart, unusually early, in readiness for the threatened early start, Edwina got up again and padded downstairs into the lounge, barefoot, despite the cold.

The others mustn't hear her.

She stood downstairs, motionless for a moment, felt the cold stone floor beneath her bare feet and listened. It was exceptionally still in Sunset Hall. Brexit had already been picked up by Charlie's good-looking grandson yesterday, they hadn't heard a peep from the boiler for days, and Hettie was sleeping in the fridge, so deeply that none of Edwina's thoughts could ever reach her, so deeply that her heart only beat every now and then, subdued, incidentally.

Edwina had no desire to think about Hettie's sporadic heartbeat. As soon as she was certain she wouldn't be surprised, she opened her case once more, to check her kit.

Pocketknife.

Garden shears.

Notebook and pen.

Lighter.

Corkscrew.

Remote control.

Heat lamp.

Wig.

Homemade biscuits.

Inflatable tortoise for the pool.

Lillith.

Somewhere, there was also a swimsuit, a comb, some underwear, one or two tracksuits and a blue dress that Agnes had practically forced her to take, but that didn't matter.

Unlike the others, Edwina hadn't let herself be fooled by the spurious story about the prize draw for a second. Of course she hadn't. The holiday wasn't just a holiday.

It was a *mission*.

She, Edwina, on Her Majesty's Secret Service, had finally been called out of her own long, cold period of hibernation to complete an assignment. She could feel her heart beating, not sluggishly like Hettie's, but expectantly, decisively.

The fact that she had no idea what her mission could entail didn't worry Edwina. She would find out soon enough, via a mysterious phone call perhaps, a note secretly left in her coat pocket with a telephone number on it, or maybe via a card brought to her room hidden inside a box of chocolates. (She was secretly hoping for the method with the box of chocolates.)

Now, she just had to be ready. She eyed the contents of her suitcase critically. Did she need more underwear? Had she packed enough biscuits? Was Lillith stowed safely?

It worried her a bit that she couldn't take any real weapons with her, not on a plane, but a pair of garden shears or a corkscrew could cause a fair bit of damage if necessary. Now, she just had to make sure nobody was onto her.

Edwina decided not to leave the inflatable tortoise in her suitcase, but to carry it in her hand luggage, a distraction tactic, as it were. She started to blow. As the rubber tortoise, which she'd already christened 'Hettie II,' slowly took shape, Lillith's ashes seemed to be eyeing her critically.

Edwina briefly stopped puffing. 'Don't worry, Lillith,' she said quietly. 'I'll take good care of myself. And the others. And you, in any case.'

Lillith seemed reassured, and Edwina was happy to have her friend in her luggage. The others were good eggs, but they could sometimes be a bit unworldly. Lillith was the only one who you could have really good conversations with, forge plans, exchange ideas. Lillith never made stupid suggestions or tried to talk her out of things. Lillith always kept a lid on things. At least, she did if you screwed it on tightly enough. You could confide in her.

'It's an adventure,' Edwina announced, and Lillith seemed to agree, as did the partially inflated Hettie II.

3

CLOUDS

However, when the residents of Sunset Hall peeled themselves out of the taxi the next morning, sleepy and rumpled, it didn't feel very much like an adventure yet. More like an imposition. Agnes, for whom even a trip on a cross-country bus presented a challenge, was completely drained by the long car journey. She had never seen so many grotty suburbs and sopping-wet sheep in one go. Was that really the world – her world? It looked different to what she remembered, full of green fields, sedate towns and beautiful scenery.

Where had all the scenery gone?

She pressed her walking stick into the taxi driver's hand and tried to steady herself on her bag. Charlie's chic feather hat looked a bit mangled; Bernadette's obligatory sunglasses were wonky; Marshall had a glazed, distant look on his face; and Winston, who wasn't getting on very well with his new, super-portable wheelchair, was sweating.

Edwina had got hold of an inflatable tortoise from somewhere and was jumping up and down with it like a monkey on a stick.

The wind tore and tugged at them, as if to stop them in their tracks.

Stop! Wait! Stay here! Don't go!

But the residents of Sunset Hall didn't listen.

The taxi driver finally drove off and they were left standing in front of the airport with their luggage.

'In there!' Charlie had got a trolley for all of their luggage and was pushing it confidently towards the revolving door of the squat, ugly building.

It turned out that an airport consisted mainly of three things, grey floors as far as the eye could see, booming announcements that Agnes couldn't even understand with her hearing aid in, and people. People everywhere. Agnes couldn't remember ever having seen so many people at once. Many of them were dressed inappropriately, in sandals and shorts and sun hats. Agnes was secretly annoyed to find that Edwina fitted in seamlessly, with her tracksuit, slippers and rubber tortoise.

Charlie pressed a piece of paper into each of their hands.

'Tickets! Over there!'

Agnes reluctantly trailed behind her housemates to the end of a queue and tried to make out that none of it was anything to do with her. Every now and then, something moved, and Edwina jumped a space forward on her tortoise. The others followed.

Agnes used the wait to discreetly inspect her fellow passengers.

They weren't the oldest there at any rate. Not by a long shot. Three ancient ladies in black were standing just across from her, and the chap in the wheelchair the three of them were manoeuvring along the queue as best they could looked as if he were already dead. If those doddery souls managed to battle their way on board, Agnes didn't have anything to worry about.

Eventually they had worked their way to the counter and had to produce their passports. It took a while because Edwina had rather unstrategically tucked hers into her bra. They got little coloured stickers stuck on their tickets, then they watched their luggage, complete with paper streamers, sail away from them on a conveyor belt. At that point, Agnes would have loved to send her suitcase off on the journey alone and quietly slip away.

She sighed.

Next, they had to squeeze their way through a kind of turnstile with lots of other hopeful passengers.

'All aboard the Skylark!' Edwina cheered, throwing the inflatable tortoise up into the air.

'To security,' Charlie corrected.

Agnes, who after many years in the police wasn't completely green, had expected as much. Presumably her hand luggage and clothes would be searched for weapons, maybe even drugs. Drugs! Agnes sighed. The chance would be a fine thing!

On the other side of the turnstile, they had to wait yet again. Like most of her fellow countrymen, Agnes didn't approach queuing lightly. She chose the queue that seemed the shortest to her and lined up with a sense of purpose.

Only after a while did she realise that her housemates had been corralled into another queue by an airport heavy. Instead of them, a chap in a Hawaiian shirt was standing behind her grinning. Agnes squinted desperately at a feather hat, a garish hippie blanket and an inflatable tortoise as they slowly, but inexorably drifted away from her like flotsam on the high sea.

She grappled with a pang of panic. All she had to do was somehow get through security. Then the others would wait for her, wouldn't they? Or, on the plane, at least! She would make it to the plane! After all, this wasn't her first time flying. But before, everything had been different. More . . . service. Fewer queues.

Agnes clutched her plane ticket.

This was just the time she should be looking forward to the journey. Anticipation is half the pleasure, after all, and if she didn't start straightaway, it would be too late. But Agnes felt her high spirits slump like a soufflé that had cooled too suddenly.

More quickly than expected, she had worked her way to the security area. She laid her handbag confidently in the little plastic tub and marched through the weird metal frame. It beeped. Agnes wanted to keep going but was stopped by a young woman in plastic gloves with some kind of hairdryer. She had to stand still and put her arms out while the woman with the hairdryer, which presumably wasn't a hairdryer, swept it over her body. It beeped again. It beeped a lot. Her brassiere beeped, and her support corset, her shoes and even the press stud on her skirt.

Agnes looked at the woman pityingly. Did she seriously think she was going to strangle the captain with her brassiere? According to everything she knew about modern aviation, the captain hardly did anything anymore anyway and was almost completely redundant when it came down to it.

The security measures seemed excessive to her.

Finally, the woman with the hairdryer was satisfied, and Agnes staggered past her in a bit of a daze. She'd had enough of this charade. Where on earth was the blasted plane?

She almost forgot her handbag, but her arm remembered even if the rest of her was in a bit of a tizz. Her arm felt empty.

Handbag! Right!

She had put it in one of those plastic tubs before, and now . . .

Agnes looked up and spotted her bag a few yards away, still in the tub. A security officer was fumbling around with it.

It was a magnificent handbag that had provided Agnes with many years of loyal service. She knew from experience that you could house a majestic picnic in it, a cat complete with kittens, or a small tent, and even today Agnes had taken full advantage of the bag's capacity. There was money and lipstick, a good book, her knitting, her reading glasses, all the equipment needed to keep false teeth in order, all the medicine she needed, and a whole load she hopefully wouldn't need.

And there was a pair of knickers. Just because. Spares. Her mother had long since drummed it into her that a lady should never go away without spare knickers, and although Agnes had never needed them, and had spent a lifetime pointlessly carrying around spare knickers, she had always kept to the rule. She could hardly wait to tell her mother, somewhere on the other side, where she could stick her spare pair of knickers rule.

The aforementioned knickers were currently being unfolded by the security officer and examined like some kind of archaeological find. That was a step too far! Agnes snatched her walking stick, which through some kind of miracle had made it through security unscathed, and scurried over to the chap with the gloves.

'Is this your bag?' the man asked, eyeing her critically over the waistband of her knickers.

Agnes swallowed. She would have liked to deny having anything at all to do with those knickers, appearing excessively big as they did, and a bit frivolous with their hint of white lace. But she had to get her bag back.

So, she nodded, with dignity, she hoped.

'Have you got any liquids in here?' The man laid the knickers to one side and carried on rummaging around in the bag.

Agnes stopped nodding. Liquids? She must have misheard! Of course she had liquids with her – the denture cleaning set, shampoo for extra fine hair and a bottle of orange juice. Surely that wasn't a crime!

She decided to ignore the man, and reached for her bag, but the security man was quicker. He held the handle with one hand, and used the other to dig deeper, and unearthed the orange juice, followed by the shampoo and denture set.

This could not be happening! Agnes took a deep breath. She could sacrifice the juice and the shampoo, if necessary, but she would give anything to keep the denture cleaner – well, apart from her eye teeth of course!

'Unfortunately, you're not permitted to carry more than

one hundred millilitres of liquids,' explained the madman in the gloves.

Agnes looked around for help. Someone would have to make him see reason! She spotted Marshall in another row, who was just being told that his trusty jackknife wasn't allowed to go with him, while Edwina was having to let the air out of her tortoise. It looked as if the garden shears had already been confiscated. It was a big palaver, and Agnes wasn't altogether unhappy about ending up in the other queue. So, no juice or shampoo. Fine. There wasn't much going on with her hair anyway, with or without shampoo, and she'd be able to find a bit of orange juice on board, surely.

But the denture cleaner! She gesticulated wildly at the relevant bottle, as the man packed it into a transparent plastic bag.

'I need that!'

'You'll get it back soon. I'm just going to put it through the scanner, okay?' With that, the man dragged the denture cleaner away, back to the start of the queue.

Agnes groaned. It wasn't okay, but what could she do? She wanted to finally get on the plane or just go somewhere where she could sit down. But not without her denture care!

She resolutely plopped herself down next to the plastic tub and waited. Her hip hurt. The air was bad. She felt a bit dizzy.

'Hey, Grandma! Anytime today'll do!'

Agnes gave a start and looked around. Grandma? Outrageous!

Somebody was standing next to her. He must have

come through security after her and was trying to push past her and her bag.

'Get back in your home,' he muttered.

Agnes really did wonder if she had misheard – it wouldn't have been the first time. Then she remembered her hearing aid. She hadn't misheard then. The snide grin also told her that she had understood correctly.

A home! Unbelievable! Who did the blighter think he was?

She looked up at him critically. Tall, but not really an adult. Thin. Pale. Male? Female? Male, Agnes presumed, but she couldn't say exactly how she'd reached that conclusion. The brat's shoulders were rather broad, his chin seemed square, but she also spied thin legs in black leggings, long black hair, eyes with dark eye shadow and long eyelashes and green-painted fingernails.

Young. That much was clear. Young and rude.

'What's the matter, Grandma?' the youth twanged condescendingly. 'Did someone confiscate your Valium?'

That was uncomfortably close to the truth, and Agnes would have gladly responded with something scathing and mean, but nothing came to her. She used to be sharp-tongued, but just recently . . . So, she made do with using her walking stick to make herself as wide as possible, so that the brat couldn't get past her.

'Don't get your knickers in a twist, Grandma!' the brat mocked, but she could do what she liked with her knickers, thank you very much, and how did he even know about that anyway? Agnes wondered.

Picking on her just because she was old and wasn't allowed her denture cleaner back was . . . She swallowed and tried not to get too upset. Getting upset was bad – for her, for karma and eventually for the blighter in black too. She was armed with a walking stick, after all.

'There you are!' Someone linked arms with her.

Charlie!

Agnes grinned with relief, but her housemate looked rather annoyed. 'Are you coming, Agnes? We could do with a bit of backup over there.' Charlie lowered her voice. 'Edwina brought Lillith, and now they're trying to confiscate her.'

Agnes groaned and looked two rows on, where a security official was quizzically sniffing a coffee tin, while Edwina had almost casually taken up warrior pose.

Not good at all.

The brat took advantage of her inattention and pushed past Charlie and Agnes, not without a hiss of contempt. Agnes hoped his flight was delayed, or at least experienced heavy turbulence, until his face was as green as his fingernails.

Then finally the security officer was back with her denture cleaner. He smiled innocently, as if he hadn't just subjected her to a completely unnecessary ordeal. Agnes snatched the plastic bag out of his hand, threw it in her handbag and grabbed the handle. She left the white knickers in the plastic tub. The nosy parker could do as he pleased with them!

Together with Charlie, she hurried over to Edwina, who was watching the man examining the coffee tin containing Lillith with a dangerous sense of calm.

'Is that soot?' The man took a second sniff.

Agnes planted herself squarely in front of him. 'Well,

it's not a liquid at any rate, is it?'

'No,' the man conceded.

'And it's not a weapon either,' Agnes added quickly. Once Edwina was in warrior pose, there was no time for dithering. 'The rest really doesn't concern you. So just pop the lid back on, and let us be on our way, yes? We're no spring chickens after all.'

The security officer looked up and saw Agnes leaning on her stick looking worryingly frail, and behind her were the other residents of Sunset Hall, all trying to look as senile as humanly possible.

He shrugged, hastily screwed the lid back on the tin and zipped up Edwina's colourful sports bag.

'Of course, Madam. Enjoy your flight.'

Agnes scoffed. Enjoyment really wasn't on the cards!

The rest of the time in the airport passed by Agnes like a particularly badly choreographed nightmare, complete with elbowing and jostling crowds, confusing announcements, departure boards with tiny writing that you had to decipher at record speed before it changed again, and a sense of rising panic because there really wasn't a single plane in sight. The whole thing was accentuated by a sharp pain in her hip and Edwina's constant whining. There were shops and restaurants. They were offered advocaat samples.

Bernadette wanted to get something to eat, Edwina had blown up her inflatable tortoise again and was in the way everywhere she went, and Charlie was pointing here, there and everywhere, insisting that everyone follow her lead. Agnes was terrified of missing the flight, and, at the same time, wanted nothing more than to be back at Sunset Hall, whether the boiler was out of action or not.

Eventually, through some kind of miracle, she did end up on a plane, pinned between a businessman and a strange woman in a faux fur coat staring intently at her phone.

Where were the others? Wandered off again? Was she even on the right plane? She craned her neck round as far as she could and spotted Marshall staring militarily out of the window a few rows back, and next to him was Bernadette, who was leading by example and was already asleep. Not a bad idea.

Agnes tried closing her eyes, but the businessman's elbow jabbed her unpleasantly in the ribs, and when she finally dozed off for a moment, she was awoken within seconds by an flight attendant wanting to know if she'd done her seatbelt up. Agnes didn't get on very well with the seatbelt, and in the end the woman in the faux fur took pity on her and helped her do it up.

It was far too hot. The flight attendant was now standing in the aisle messing around with a lifejacket. Agnes's head was sweating and simultaneously her feet were cold. It was hell.

Why had they chosen to fly? Why hadn't they just travelled to Cornwall by car?

Agnes knew full well why, according to the internet the car journey would have taken seven hours – but that only applied to normal people. For the residents of Sunset Hall, who were constantly hungry, or needed the loo, or wanted to stretch their legs, the journey would have taken a small eternity. Hell, it wasn't even guaranteed that they would ever have arrived at all. So, it was better to be on a plane jammed between faux fur lady and business bloke. At least it wouldn't stop every five minutes because someone needed the loo again. No, in an hour the torture would be over – a small miracle if you really thought about it.

And then, the luxury eco hotel. Agnes tried to imagine it, sitting atop the cliffs like a big, rather wrinkly carrot. Inside, good food, a soft bed and a functioning boiler. There her imagination failed her, but that was no bad thing. Soon she would see it with her own eyes.

It wasn't so bad at all, just floating into the unknown. She felt – *young* would have been too much, but like you feel when you finally discover something new again after a long time. It was one of the things that disturbed her most about getting old, that bit by bit new things ran out. Been there. Done that.

But not the luxury eco hotel!

Agnes realised she was grinning.

Then the plane shuddered beneath her, seemed to shake itself like Brexit when he was wet, and jerked into motion. The grin slipped from Agnes's face. Thin, diagonal strands of rain streaked the oval window to her right. Then the ground suddenly gave way, and Agnes was pressed into her seat. She grabbed for something to hold on to, unfortunately grabbed the businessman's hand and was rudely shaken off. The world on the other side of the window got smaller and smaller until it eventually transformed into the scenery Agnes had so sorely missed during the taxi ride, fields and woods, roads with ant cars and settlements that looked a bit like unsolved crossword puzzles. Interesting! They went higher and higher, until the landscape below had completely disappeared, and Agnes was looking down on a sunlit candyfloss wonder world. Clouds from above! Unbelievable! She leant farther and farther forward, until the businessman next to her, who had now flipped open his laptop and felt cornered, pulled a little grey screen down in front of the window.

Agnes leant back, disappointed. She tried to go to sleep again, but every five minutes, something happened. First, a flight attendant wanted to sell her drinks, then they tried to palm some perfume off on her, then the businessman had to go to the loo, then the rubbish was collected, then there were scratch cards, and after that the businessman came back from the loo. Agnes had to stand up to let him get back to his seat, and spotted Edwina's tortoise a few rows ahead and next to it, Charlie's shock of swan-white hair. Then she got a bit of a shock herself, the door to the front toilet opened, and a familiar figure with dishevelled black hair, a leather jacket and green fingernails stepped out.

The brat from before! He was on the plane. You couldn't make it up!

Agnes started plotting her revenge, but then she must have fallen asleep, because all of a sudden, she was speeding through long, winding corridors. The luxury eco hotel! She knew straightaway that it could only be the hotel. The walls were carrot-coloured, the air warm and pleasant like a summer evening long ago, and every now and then a little pink cloud floated mischievously past. It was exactly as she had imagined it! However, something obviously wasn't right, the pink clouds were getting thicker, and Agnes was having to shoo them away with her stick more and more frequently. Eventually, she was feeling her way through a thick cloud landscape, almost blind.

And there, not far away at all, hung something dark.

Agnes stepped closer and recognised the verger. He was just as dead as she remembered and was swinging back and forth. She stared at him angrily. What was the man doing at the hotel and in her dream? After all, it had been her plan to leave murder as far as humanly possible behind her!

She decided to get away, but at that very moment, the dead verger's hand shot forward and grabbed her arm.

Agnes's eyes shot open. Someone really had grabbed her arm. Luckily not the dead verger, but the woman in the faux fur! Agnes needed a moment to get her bearings.

Aeroplane. Right.

The plane jumped and shook violently.

Over the intercom, somebody said something about turbulence, flight attendants rushed down the aisle making sure that everybody was buckled in, and a queasy feeling spread in Agnes's stomach. She suddenly regretted having tried two tots of advocaat. It was her who had wished turbulence on the brat, and now she was getting her just deserts! First, Agnes concentrated on trying to shake off the faux fur lady's hand, but it was no good. The woman was holding on for dear life, as if she were drowning and Agnes were a particularly large inflatable tortoise.

The plane plummeted.

The woman next to Agnes groaned. 'We're all going to die!'

'Of course we are,' Agnes replied somewhat indignantly. 'But not today!'

She would have liked to sit next to someone sensible, maybe Marshall or at the very least Edwina – not much fazed her. Instead, she had ended up with the faux fur woman, who was sweaty and green in the face and had obviously confused Agnes with a rubber tortoise.

'If only I hadn't gone on the stupid aerophobia course!' the woman hissed. 'Then I wouldn't be here now! Then I would be at home with Caspar!'

Agnes was about to say that surely this Caspar had earned a few days of peace when the plane made a final temperamental leap and then bumped back down to earth with a thud. There you go!

The woman squealed a bit belatedly, and finally let go of Agnes's hand. Then she got her phone out again and started tapping away on it as if nothing had happened. Well, I never!

The businessman on the other side had slept through the turbulence but was now being woken and had to open the little screen again. Agnes could see damply glistening asphalt, trees being lashed by the wind and in the far distance a dark, stormy blue that was maybe, but only maybe, the sea.

Edwina and Hettie II got off the plane in high spirits. The wind blew cold, salty air in their faces, the laughable inspection at the airport before had only detected half of Edwina's arsenal of improvised weapons, and at the airport she had already spotted her first contact, a young man with a tousled mop of hair, and bad manners. Just like her, he had decided to camouflage himself by standing out; he was wearing green nail varnish and dramatic eye make-up, which Edwina was secretly a bit envious of.

She had observed the agent striding down the aisle – so hastily he almost knocked over a flight attendant – and then he had hung about near the loo, acting bored. And she had seen his dark eyes darting back and forth beneath his fabulously long lashes, urgently scanning the passengers. A man on a mission – no doubt about it!

Then her colleague disappeared into the loo for quite a while and had undoubtedly been engaged in some kind of secret spy business. Whatever it was, it had obviously been a success. When he strode down the aisle back to his seat again, he had a smile on his face, and Edwina had summarily decided to make contact.

Once the agent was right in front of her, she shoved Hettie II in his way.

He stopped, looking first at Hettie, then Edwina, and then he grinned.

'Careful with the sex toy, Grandma!' he said.

She had understood instantly. Communicating on the plane would have been far too risky. She winked conspiratorially at the young man and pulled Hettie II back onto her lap. Her colleague stomped farther along the aisle, and then, when Edwina had almost lost hope, he turned around towards her and winked back.

Edwina could hardly wait to unpack Lillith and discuss everything with her.

4

ROMANTIC PACKAGE

Agnes must have slept through the majority of the taxi ride. She vaguely remembered stepping off the plane into the drizzle, down some hazardously steep steps. Then it had been all about the luggage again, and then, taxi. Edwina, in a surprising show of cooperation, had let the air out of Hettie II for the second time that day. But it was still tight in the taxi. Minivan? More mini than van! Bernadette was bulging against Agnes to the left, Marshall's pointy elbow was poking her in the side from the right. Winston and his wheelchair also took up a lot of space. Charlie had snagged the seat at the front next to the taxi driver and was trying to engage him in conversation.

Outside, two overworked windscreen wipers were trying to fend off the rain.

It was slow-going.

'Everyone needs a break sometimes . . .' Charlie chattered. 'And the Eden seems to be really wonderful! Have you ever been?'

The driver mumbled something along the lines of, *only lettuce munchers go to the Eden*, and started moaning about the weather, but Charlie didn't allow herself to be put off.

'Something completely new, huh? A luxury eco hotel! I mean, *I'm* excited!'

Then Agnes had finally dozed off. She only came to when Bernadette shook her by the shoulder.

'Agnes! Wake up! I think we're nearly there!'

Agnes's eyes shot open and she peered out of the window. There it was, the sea, smooth as grey velvet, and there was their taxi struggling along a rather adventurous coastal road. There was a pretty sheer drop. Gulls hung masterfully in the air.

And up ahead . . .

She must have made an involuntary noise because Bernadette nudged her again.

'So? Can you see it?'

Agnes nodded until she realised that Bernadette obviously couldn't see.

'Yes. You could say that!'

'And?' Bernadette asked. 'Is it nice?'

'Yes,' Agnes said truthfully. 'Very nice!'

She secretly felt a certain sense of satisfaction because the hotel really was reminiscent of a carrot, a slim, tactile carrot, its point daringly jutting out over the cliffs. There could, however, be no talk of wrinkly. Agnes could see sun-bleached wood and a lot of glass. She craned her neck.

'Well?' Bernadette asked impatiently. 'What does it look like?'

Agnes was about to come out with the carrot metaphor, but Charlie beat her to it.

'Like a ship!' she cried. 'Like a ship out at sea!'

And obviously that was a much better comparison.

* * *

55

Then they stood in the lobby, a bit shy almost, and looked around. Agnes, whose last encounter with modern architecture had taken place in the seventies, was impressed.

The wall in front of her consisted entirely of glass, from floor to ceiling, and on the other side of the glass, the cliffs. Agnes looked far out to sea, where the gulls now seemed to be looking a bit envious. Clouds were gathering on the horizon. It felt like an adventure just looking out of the window.

Behind her was a reception area made of smoothly curved dark wood. The lady on duty there had just disappeared for a moment to take care of their luggage (finally, someone cared!), so Agnes had time to take a closer look at the hotel interior undisturbed.

The lobby was big but didn't feel big. It was – just right. Like a perfectly proportioned cave. Not too light. Not too dark. Not too colourful. Not too drab. Smooth and sleek. With a certain sense of melancholy, Agnes realised that the only wrinkly thing in the vicinity was them.

It smelt exceedingly good, of beeswax and hay. Even the temperature was perfect, it was warm and pleasant, but not *too* warm. The boiler was in excellent working order!

Everything around her was smooth, round and flowing, as if somehow the hotel hadn't been built but had been moulded into this tactile form by a current of water. Organically. But obviously in reality, it must have happened differently.

Obtrusive puffing noises ripped her from her thoughts, Edwina was blowing up the rubber monstrosity for the third time.

Agnes heard Charlie clear her throat behind her.

'Agnes? Maybe we should just briefly discuss the room allocations. What do you think?'

Agnes reluctantly tore herself away from the cliffs and the lobby and gazed uncomprehendingly at her housemate.

'We should discuss who's sharing with whom,' Charlie explained.

Sharing?

'One room is for Winston and Marshall, of course, but the rest? Do you have any preference, Agnes?'

Well, for a start, Charlie could go to hell. Share a room? Whatever next? She'd obviously had a vague suspicion that something like this was going to happen, but now she was at that point, the whole thing seemed most unappealing.

'I'm sharing with Lillith!' Edwina declared holding the freshly inflated Hettie II under Charlie's nose. 'And Hettie II, of course!'

Charlie sighed. 'That won't quite suffice, Edwina.'

Agnes made a spur-of-the-moment decision. The most important thing for her peace of mind was that she didn't have to share a room with Edwina. Everything else was by the by.

'I wanted to share with Bernadette.' she said quickly. 'We've already discussed it.'

Bernadette seemed surprised for a moment, but she quickly understood.

'All agreed!' she chimed.

'Ah, umm, yes, well.' Charlie picked at her worse for wear feather hat, visibly annoyed. 'Then it's only Edwina and me left, huh? And Lillith and Hettie II, of course,' she swiftly added before Edwina could protest.

'Very well. I think I might need a drink!'

She looked around for the bar, but before she could hit the jackpot, a woman appeared behind the reception desk again. Agnes wasn't sure if it was the woman from before, but she reminded her of someone.

The way she smiled. The way she raised her hand. It took a while, but then it came to her, the Queen. The woman on reception was obviously much younger, with brown hair and a smooth, determined face, but she exuded a similar gravitas. Maybe it was just the corgi sitting at her feet, managing as it did, to look simultaneously bored and disparaging. A born snob.

The regal reception woman raised her hand, and Agnes braced herself to have a knighthood bestowed upon her, or at the very least have her hand thoroughly shaken, but instead the lady graced each of them in turn with a sunny smile and distributed magic little cards, which could apparently unlock everything at the hotel.

'Welcome to the Eden!' She beamed, tucking a sleek brown wisp of hair behind her ear. 'I'm Helen and, together with my team, I'll be making sure that you have a pleasant and trouble-free stay!'

The dog at her feet didn't seem to belong to the team. He shot Agnes and her companions a look of contempt, sniffed disapprovingly at the rubber tortoise, trotted through the lobby on its short legs and disappeared amongst a labyrinth of comfy armchairs.

Agnes, however, stared sceptically at the woman. Trouble-free? With Edwina around?

'Hear! Hear!' cried Winston.

'Hurrah!' Edwina cheered, throwing Hettie II in the air.

Only Marshall stared a bit grumpily at his mobile phone, holding it here and there, seemingly dissatisfied.

'No signal!' he complained.

Agnes felt a wave of sympathy for Marshall, who wasn't so easily impressed by the regal Helen and the tasteful curves of the Eden.

The hotel lady carried on smiling, unfazed. 'Unfortunately, we don't get any signal here, and we decided to wholeheartedly embrace the digital detox. But there is Wi-Fi. For emergencies.'

'This is an emergency,' said Marshall curtly.

Helen passed him a little card. She already seemed accustomed to the fact that her idea of a digital detox wasn't very well received by guests.

'Regarding detoxing,' Charlie chimed in. 'What happens now? I read something about champagne somewhere.'

The hotel lady beamed at them all.

'Unfortunately, your rooms aren't quite ready, but you could relax here in the lounge or in our games room, in the library, or even in the spa. A rather lovely group meditation is starting in half an hour, which I can't recommend highly enough. And since you've all booked the romantic package, a luxury champagne afternoon tea awaits you. But maybe you'd like to freshen up first?'

'Champagne first!' Charlie said quickly. 'With the tea! That sounds good!'

Nobody objected. They'd abandoned freshening up years ago. No matter what you did at their age, fresh was never going to happen. Hot tea and something for them to get their false teeth into would definitely help them settle in at the Eden.

'Of course!' The reception lady beamed even more broadly, and the sleek brown wisp of hair jumped enthusiastically out from behind her ear. 'I'll arrange that for you right away. Please follow me into the garden room.'

Agnes was so mesmerised by all the good taste around her that something only occurred to her halfway to the garden room. Had she misheard maybe?

'The romantic package?' she hissed at Charlie. 'Why on earth?'

'Why the hell not?' Charlie whispered back. 'A bottle of champagne in the room and then this welcome tea, and there's something else as well. Champagne is never a bad thing, I thought to myself! Apart from that, it was already included in Edwina's package. Fair's fair!'

'But – *romantic*?' Agnes asked aghast. 'Me and *Bernadette*?'

It didn't bear thinking about!

'Courage!' Charlie grinned. 'Edwina isn't exactly my dream partner, but these days anything is possible, isn't it? You have to move with the times!'

She winked at Agnes. Then they stepped through a door and Charlie spread her arms wide.

'Fabulous!'

The afternoon tea with champagne really was fabulous, even if Agnes couldn't really focus to start with because she was worrying about the 'something else' that Charlie had booked with the romantic package.

But then, sandwich by sandwich, cake by cake, sip by sip, she did manage to relax after all. The food was rather complicated and had to be explained to them by a waiter first, foraged, organic or homegrown, but there was no denying that everything tasted quite superb. The tea was cultivated locally, here in England – and was good nevertheless. Sensational!

In general, it was about keeping some kind of footprint as small as possible. How that could be achieved with tea and cake remained a mystery to Agnes, but for once she had no desire to be pedantic.

Charlie's cheeks were red, Bernadette's sunglasses were sitting at a jaunty angle on her nose, Winston was beaming, Marshall was looking out into the world with champagne-sparkling eyes, and even Edwina was calm. It was a rare moment of harmony, and Agnes didn't want to ruin it with questions about footprints.

They toasted. To the trip, to their house share, to working boilers near and far, and above all to the future, which was looking decidedly rosy, temperate and champagne-soaked. For a moment it really was convivial, then the alcohol started to go to Agnes's head. She blinked. Her head felt like it was stuffed with something pleasant, but also useless. Candyfloss perhaps. Exactly, candyfloss! She blinked for a second time. Words running through her candyfloss head weren't making it to her lips anymore. So, she shut her mouth and just concentrated on not falling off her chair. Quite challenging, this sitting lark!

Edwina had got Lillith out of her sports bag and was blathering away into the tin through a small slit.

Bernadette was systematically hoovering up one canapé after another.

Winston, finally at one with his new wheelchair, was sitting there relaxed and dignified.

Charlie tried to flirt with the waiter and bring him round to the idea of a second bottle of champagne.

Marshall was gazing at Agnes with a weird look on his face.

Agnes leant back in her chair and first observed her housemates demolishing cakes in a rare show of harmony, then the beautiful garden room, flooded with light even on this grey day. More garden than room, actually. Palms and ferns crept sympathetically around tables. Water was gurgling somewhere. It smelt . . . green.

Agnes sighed contentedly.

So warm.

So looked after.

So safe.

That was it!

The Eden felt *safe*. No sharp edges. No pesky steps. No dark corners. You could see so far, yet felt protected, like being in a cave.

The Eden seemed to be a place where nothing bad could happen to you.

She must have nodded off a bit due to the champagne because when she opened her eyes, the first thing she set them on was a knife making its way towards her.

Agnes felt around frantically for her walking stick to defend herself, but only managed to get hold of the velvety armrest next to her.

Then, she realised her panic was completely unfounded. The knife turned its back on her and went about hacking one of the cakes on the stand in front of her into two bite-sized pieces. On the other end of the knife was a thin woman with tanned skin and ash-blondee dyed hair. A youngster, around forty maybe. When she noticed Agnes looking at her, she put her finger conspiratorially to her lips.

'Hey!' Agnes couldn't just let some random forty-year-old pilfer her cake like that. What was going on? Where were the others? Why was she sitting at the table on her own all of a sudden?

'Your friends have already gone to their rooms,' said the thief, as if she had read her mind, grabbing half a cake and shoving it in her mouth in one go, like a hamster.

As the woman chewed, Agnes spotted a note on her plate. She rummaged for her reading glasses.

We didn't want to wake you Agnes, was written in Marshall's jagged handwriting. *The rooms are ready. We didn't know if you'd finished.*

Agnes screwed up her eyes. The message was a bit muddled, but obviously her housemates hadn't been able to wake her and had decided to leave her behind – in the company of a madwoman with a knife!

The madwoman had now finished chewing and offered Agnes a somewhat sticky hand. 'I'm Trudy. Promised to keep an eye on you, until you were *compos mentis*.'

Compos mentis? Agnes was always *compos mentis*. The woman should try talking to Edwina!

She ignored the hand and looked reproachfully at the half cake.

Trudy went red and ran her hand through her hair. 'I . . . I mean, I really didn't mean to . . . But they looked so good.' She sat in the chair next to Agnes and hissed conspiratorially over to her, 'I booked the detox week! We run along the beach at the crack of dawn. Then yoga! And then cliff walking. And to top it off, nothing but fruit juice and rabbit food!'

'You should have booked the romantic package,' Agnes said pragmatically.

'It's too late for that now!' Trudy looked around, harried. 'If my trainer finds me here, she'll kill me!'

Murder? For half a cake? That hadn't even happened in Duck End yet, and the knives really were drawn there at the moment! Agnes realised that she really wasn't hungry anymore, and pushed the cake stand towards Trudy. 'Then at least help yourself to the other half!' Nobody should die for half a cake!

You didn't have to tell Trudy twice. She demolished the rest of the cake, a scone and a cucumber sandwich.

Then she closed her eyes and sighed with pleasure.

Agnes used the opportunity to look around a bit. They were the only ones in the room, if you didn't count the company of dozens of palms and ferns. But no, that wasn't quite true. In the Eden there weren't any corners, but in the dark curve at the end of the room, which was the closest thing to a corner, there sat the corgi again, and next to him, in a chair, a figure looking out at the sea. A figure in white. Had she been there before?

Agnes took off her reading glasses to get a better look.

A woman.

Younger than Agnes. Older than Trudy. Agnes wasn't very good at estimating the age of youngsters. Short hair, almost monastic. Loose, white clothes.

The woman sat there motionless, looking at the sea. But nothing about her countenance was relaxed. She reminded Agnes a bit of a cat in front of a mouse hole.

Expectant.

Ready to pounce.

But there was no mouse. Just the sea.

'The White Widow,' Trudy whispered. 'Now I really wouldn't want to be left alone with her!'

Agnes raised her eyebrows. 'Unusual name!'

Trudy took a deep breath. It was obvious that she knew a thing or two about the lady at the window and she wanted to get them off her chest. 'Three years ago, her husband, you know, while staying at the hotel . . .' Trudy ran her finger unambiguously across her throat. 'Ever since, she comes here every year at the same time . . . Weird, isn't it? If something like that happens, you'd think she'd never ever . . .' She lowered her voice. 'And apparently there was something fishy about his death.'

Gossip! Just like Duck End! And it was even along the same lines! Agnes leant forward. Not that she generally thought much of gossip, but there, in the unfamiliar world of the Eden, it felt like something familiar, a piece of home almost.

But before Agnes could find out more about the White Widow and her mysteriously deceased husband, Marshall appeared, a bit sheepishly, a harried expression on his face.

'Agnes, you're awake. How lovely! We didn't know if . . .' He broke off and looked even more sheepish. 'We're ready. I mean, our rooms are ready. They really are very nice. Would you perhaps like to . . . ?'

He held out his arm towards Agnes.

Agnes nodded and started the tedious process of extracting herself from the chair. 'Marshall, this is Trudy. She's on a diet.'

Trudy smiled wistfully.

'And over there is apparently the White Widow,' whispered Agnes, hoping to steer the conversation towards gossip again.

'How do you do?' Marshall didn't even look properly. Agnes sighed and let him pull her out of the chair. Unfortunately, Marshall had no palate for gossip, unless that was, it had to do with old weapons from the Second World War and was playing out on the internet.

But that didn't matter. Trudy was obviously talkative and easy to bribe with food. Agnes was intent on getting more out of her at the next available opportunity. The White Widow interested her. Something about her countenance, her eyes . . .

Unnatural.

Agnes had the feeling she had seen something frozen. Something standing still that shouldn't be standing still, like a pendulum, that against all logic suddenly stops and can hardly wait to swing away again, back and forth, from one extreme to the other.

Edwina was bored.

To her great disappointment, in her room she had found neither a conspiratorial box of chocolates nor anything else that would help her with her secret service ops. Charlie had just put her head down and was snoring in a surprisingly unladylike way. Hettie II and Lillith were falling short of what Edwina expected of companions.

But luckily, there was the mission to think about.

Edwina decided to leave Charlie snoring away and go on a bit of a reconnaissance mission. It was the exact opposite of what she had just solemnly promised her housemates not five minutes ago, but after all, Charlie had no idea that she was on active duty, and if she was careful, nobody would even notice she had left the room.

She briefly updated Lillith, while Hettie II looked at her inanely with her drawn-on eyes. Edwina was a bit disappointed in her.

She checked once more that Charlie really was asleep, then popped the hotel corkscrew into her trouser pocket just in case. Be it an ambush or an offer of a glass of wine, with a corkscrew, you were always well-equipped.

Then she stepped out into the corridor.

The light there was pleasantly muted. Edwina looked around. There were more hotel room doors. Marshall and Winston had disappeared behind one earlier, Bernadette behind another. As far as Edwina knew, only Agnes was currently on the move – although that maybe wasn't quite the right phrase for Agnes. She wasn't exactly good on her feet. It should be easy to keep out of her way.

She followed the corridor, first to the right, then the left, then straight on. There was a lift, but Edwina preferred to take the stairs. It was a few steps down, then a flat section and then a few more steps up. Rather confusing, but Edwina had an excellent sense of direction and knew exactly where she was, under the lobby.

The corridor got wider and brighter. To her right was a series of tall, narrow windows and beyond them, the sea! Edwina liked the sea a lot. It was full of animals and full of secrets, it smelt good and didn't interfere.

She would have liked to have stopped for a moment to watch the sea at its wave work, but there was the mission to think about, and it would not be completed by staring into space.

She spotted a sign with the word spa on it. It sounded conspiratorial. Edwina decided to follow the corresponding arrow. The arrow directed her around a corner, but she had other plans again. A glass door had appeared in front of her, and on the other side of the door, in a bright room with a wooden floor and windows with a sea view, lots of people were lying motionless on the floor. Only one person was sitting up, a woman who reminded Edwina rather pleasantly of a hedgehog.

She pressed her nose flat against the glass. Some kind of cult. She was in the right place!

Before she could draw her corkscrew, the hedgehog woman had already spotted her and was waving in welcome. Edwina let the corkscrew be and entered the room. The woman pointed to an empty mat in the back row.

'We've only just started!' she whispered breathily.

Edwina contentedly lowered herself down onto the mat and flattened herself out like the people around her. Not five minutes had passed, and she was already undercover. She'd like to see anyone else manage that!

She closed her eyes, felt the ground beneath her and just listened to the hedgehog woman for now.

'You can feel the ground beneath you,' said the hedgehog woman.

So far, so correct.

'But if you concentrate, you'll notice that the ground isn't still at all. You feel a rocking. A swaying. A gentle motion, like waves. You feel the warmth of the sun on your face, but there's also a gentle breeze, fresh and salty. If you were to open your eyes, you would see the sky above you, vast and blue and infinite. And if you were to sit up, the sea would be there.'

Edwina sighed blissfully. The sea! How lovely!

'Imagine, you're on a beautiful white ship. An ocean steamer. The ship is transporting you to an exotic island paradise, but now, in this moment, you're completely content to be on the journey. On the ship. Stand up and walk to the rail. Look at the blue sea from every angle. Then turn around and go from the deck, inside the ship. Inside, everything is lined with dark wood. It smells of flowers and tea and a hint of tobacco. Officers in white uniforms nod in greeting. You nod back happily. You are completely at home here, completely yourself.'

Edwina was completely herself.

As usual.

She opened her eyes and looked up at a whitewashed ceiling.

A ship! That explained *everything*! She wasn't in an ordinary hotel at all! She was on a ship – a bloody well-camouflaged one! That definitely made sense. Ships moved free as gulls outside of national territories, and were therefore ideal for shady deals, secret rendezvous and espionage of all kinds. She was in the right place!

She stood up, determined to take a closer look at the ship. It was cunningly disguised, that much was clear, but on closer inspection, it gave itself away, for one thing, there was the sea practically staring at you from every window, for another there was this wild wind blowing outside. If you stayed absolutely silent, you could even make out the quiet hum of the ship's engines. The only weird thing was that there were no rats. There were always rats on ships – no matter how glamorous they were!

Edwina had been on a cruise before, purely for pleasure – on her honeymoon, if she remembered correctly. She couldn't remember exactly who she had married, just that even then it had occurred to her just how good a ship like that would be for intelligence work. And now, here she was!

She started investigating a series of small rooms, all fitted out with just a lounger, sink and muted lighting. These rooms would be absolutely ideal for detaining someone for a while, if need be.

Next, she came across two or three little rooms that were unusually hot and steamy, just on the cusp of being bearable. Something like that might come in handy under certain circumstances.

She committed the location of the hot rooms to memory and carried on. Everywhere was like a morgue, maybe because the sun was setting, and everyone's thoughts were probably turning to dinner. Charlie would be up and about again by now – probably hopping mad. Maybe she should . . .

Just then, Edwina spotted the swimming pool.

She realised immediately that a few things weren't quite right.

For one, the temperature. It was far too cold for swimming, even for hardy people like her. That was because someone had left the terrace door wide open, and an icy wind was whipping through the room.

The wind rippled on the surface of the pool, and there the next anomaly was to be seen, someone was floating in the water, face down. That couldn't be healthy.

The third abnormality was that the person in the pool was dressed completely inappropriately. She was wearing a blood-red dress, which was billowing dramatically where air was caught beneath the fabric. Long, platinum-blondee hair was swirling in the water like seaweed.

Overboard, no doubt about it.

Edwina was just about to try to fish the blondee out of the pool to see if there was still anything to be done, when something made her stop.

During her many years in the Secret Service, she had developed an excellent intuition for certain things, and her intuition was telling her she was not alone.

Someone else was in the room.

Someone was watching her.

5

DEFLATED

Agnes was lying in the hotel bed trying to gather her thoughts. Bernadette had disappeared into the bathroom to 'make herself look pretty.' That was an ambitious undertaking; it might take a while. Agnes was absolutely determined to use the resulting celestial peace to come up with a plan. Everything ran more smoothly when there was a plan – a holiday should be no exception.

But she couldn't concentrate properly, which was largely down to the bed. The bed was distracting her. It was so soft and fresh, so smooth and fragrant and silky, as if it were made of candyfloss. Just much less sticky. The bed was perfect. Agnes closed her eyes. Even if she spent the whole time there in that bed – the trip was already a success.

Was that even a plan? Just staying in bed?

Not bad. Simple, but infallible.

Agnes closed her eyes and let herself fall.

But after a few minutes, she realised that she just wasn't falling. Rather, she was hanging in the air, her thoughts restless, her mind wide awake.

Maybe it was Bernadette's fault too, as she was in the shower, belting out a pop song from the sixties in her deep bass voice.

My ship is coming in . . .

I should be so lucky!

Agnes switched her hearing aid off and rolled onto her side, onto the better of her two dubious ears. But that didn't help much either. Usually, she nodded off in the most impossible of places, and now in this perfect bed, sleep was out of the question! That was the stupid thing about getting old – nothing went quite like you imagined it anymore, not even a simple thing like sleeping.

That put an end to the simple plan of spending the holiday in bed.

She thought about the room pleasantly snuggled around her, the harmoniously rounded lobby, and the muted lighting and hay fragrance in the corridor that had led her there, and felt like a foreign body inside the wholesome, relaxed hotel world.

A restless, wrinkly foreign body.

She sighed and rolled onto her back again.

It was time to face facts, harmony and relaxation were not her thing.

Agnes liked a certain degree of tension. She also liked to pick at her surroundings, but unfortunately, there wasn't much out of place at the Eden.

She struggled out of the bed, which put up gentle resistance, and decided to go looking for something that promised a bit of drama. The sea maybe. You could usually count on the sea for that!

She grabbed her walking stick, checked her hairstyle in the mirror (style virtually non-existent as usual) and made her way outside – just in time to witness her first murder of the holiday.

Agnes walked through the hotel for quite a while, but there was no sign of the sea. You would have thought it should be nothing to get to the sea from a seaside hotel like this. The sea was out there, really close, it flashed auspiciously through panoramic windows everywhere you went, but actually getting out there . . . it was enough to drive you mad!

There were signposts with little arrows promising all sorts of things, breakfast, relaxation room, sauna, restaurant, pool, massage, lecture room, and even chromotherapy. Only the sea was missing. Bit by bit, Agnes was losing any sense of time.

Then she saw the sign: Sea Lounge.

That sounded promising. Determined, Agnes followed the arrow. Several gentle curves later, a lounge really did appear in front of her with low, velvety furniture and a few comfortably lounging hotel guests. And behind them, glazed doors. The sea was waiting on the other side of the door!

Agnes almost cheered with joy, but she caught herself just in time and made a dignified expression as a bartender greeted her.

On arrival in the lounge, Agnes realised that it was even better than she had expected, the Sea Lounge's glass doors led out onto the curved terrace that formed the carrot nose of the hotel. Agnes got rid of the barman, who was immediately trying to foist organic nuts and local whisky on her, and hot-footed it away.

Outside.

The wind momentarily took her breath away. This was no civilised offshore wind. This was a wild, stirred-up, salty, icy air. Born of foam. Ocean-kissed.

There it was, so big and flat and open that you couldn't really comprehend it, the sea! Agnes took a deep breath and watched her neckerchief flapping.

Oh yes!

There!

That!

Now this was what she called a holiday.

A feeling.

Freedom. Space. Life!

She leant on the railing and looked down. Deep below her, the sea foamed against stoic cliffs – in surprising shades. Lead-grey, milk-white and a dirty shade of apricot struggled for supremacy on the high seas. Light was seeping away at the horizon. The dark sky was keeping out of it.

After a few breaths, Agnes, who had only put on a thin cardigan, was a bit cold. It was winter outside. Thanks to the fully functioning heating in the Eden, Agnes had almost forgotten about winter.

Just as she had decided to return to the warmth of the Sea Lounge after all, she registered two figures moving away from the hotel on a narrow footpath, right along the edge of the cliff. Unlike Agnes, they were both wrapped up in weather-proof jackets with hoods. One orange, one yellow.

Drunk, Agnes thought at first. The next minute, she wasn't so sure. But something wasn't quite right. The way they were leaning on each other. The rolling movements. Not a good idea to be roving about so unsteadily on the cliffs like that!

The two of them spun back and forth as if they were dancing. An arm flew into the air. An awkward embrace. This could take a while! Agnes decided to let the lovebirds – that's obviously what they were – be, and she turned back towards the warm lights of the Sea Lounge.

Just then she heard something. It could have been a wind-torn scream or a sound of surprise or even just a particularly adventurous gull, but the noise made Agnes turn around to look at the couple on the cliffs again.

Only there was no longer a couple there. The yellow jacket had disappeared, the orange one was standing there with drooping arms and suddenly looked very sober.

It was definitely strange.

Agnes craned her neck but couldn't catch a glimpse of the yellow jacket anywhere on the path. Her teeth were chattering with the cold. It wasn't good for her false teeth.

'Shit!' said someone next to her.

Agnes spun around and saw someone standing just where the light from the Sea Lounge didn't quite reach, leaning against the railing.

He turned his head towards her, and for a moment she could make out a thin face, pale as a ghost. Black hair blew in the wind. Shocked, darkly circled eyes looked erratically past Agnes.

The brat from the airport!

What was *he* doing here?

This was a step too far!

Agnes had no desire to allow herself to be insulted again, nor did she want to freeze her tail off. She turned away brusquely, rushed back into the Sea Lounge and allowed herself to be talked into a whisky after all.

And then another.

After a while, the warmth of the Sea Lounge found its way into Agnes's limbs. First, she regained feeling in her fingertips, then her toes, then her cheeks, burning red. It happened surprisingly quickly. She was warm again! The whisky helped too. She sipped contentedly and had to admit that the comfortable interior of the Eden had its benefits.

Outside, the sky was finally dark. The wind tore at the loungers, until one of them tipped over. Was the brat still out there? Agnes wanted to give him as little thought as possible.

But she was still curious about how the scene with the hood-wearers had played out, and kept her eye on the window to the terrace. From there you could see a good section of the path, and anyone who came back to the hotel would have to come this way. But until now, no hood-wearer had appeared. The two of them had been braving it out there for a really long time!

Agnes sipped her whisky and thought about how she could well and truly add a bit of drama to the little scene on the cliffs for the benefit of her housemates. While the others had been snoring away in their luxury beds, she'd already witnessed something interesting, and it was only the first day!

When she looked up again, someone was standing out on the coast path. An orange-red jacket reflected the light of the Sea Lounge like a glowing ember. The rest of the figure was shrouded in darkness, but by the way they were standing, Agnes could deduce that they were looking straight at her.

What initially roused Agnes's mistrust was the stillness of the hood-wearer. You didn't just stand around in the cold during a storm enjoying the architecture. Apart from that, there was something sly about the posture, something coldly calculating. Agnes fidgeted uneasily in her velvet chair, well aware that in the elegantly lit lounge, she must be clearly visible to whoever was out there. Although she couldn't make out a face, she sensed something, a feeling of eye contact. She lowered her gaze and looked down at her organic nuts with feigned fascination. When she took a surreptitious peek back outside, there was nothing there but a particularly inky night.

Agnes stayed sitting for a while, took a sip of whisky and thought about what she had just seen. Diddly-squat actually – or rather, lots of little facets of diddly-squat that couldn't be pieced together very easily. She didn't like it. She suddenly saw the dangling verger in her mind's eye and something like a hunch stirred inside her. A murder? Here at the Eden? Surely the whisky was to blame for such a hare-brained idea!

A gentleman in a bold salmon-pink blazer got up

from his seat three tables away and headed for the door.

Agnes realised that, apart from a plump woman who seemed to be engrossed in her book, she was the last guest in the Sea Lounge. It must be getting towards dinnertime.

The barman looked discreetly at his watch.

She hastily downed the rest of her drink and started to mentally prepare herself for the arduous and uncertain return journey to her room. Dinner had already been the subject of much speculation, and under no circumstances did she want to miss it. What would they serve? And how much would there be? At any rate, it could be counted on that the food would stand in stark contrast to the soups, stews, sausages and ready meals they usually had at home. She should probably get changed, spritz herself with some perfume, and remind her housemates to behave themselves again.

She waved the barman over and he stuck her hotel card in a machine.

'Crazy weather today, huh? There's going to be a proper storm tonight!' The barman smiled as if he were proud of the weather. It surprised Agnes how young he was. More surf teacher than hotel employee, with hair rebelliously sticking out in all directions and a healthy tan.

She nodded. 'Tell me, the footpath out there, where does it go?'

'That's our cliff-top path. It leads from the hotel to a viewing point, over there. It's a nice little walk, but . . .' He looked doubtfully at Agnes's walking stick.

Agnes ignored his look. 'And after that? Where does

it go after the viewing point?'

The barman furrowed his brow in concern. 'Nowhere. The path stops there, and I really would strongly discourage you from walking along the cliff. It's not very safe. Erosion. Accidents have already happened.'

'Really?' Agnes thought back to the White Widow's husband. 'Three years ago, you mean?'

The barman looked guilty somehow. 'I wasn't here three years ago.'

Agnes sensed he was lying.

The man gave her plastic card back to her.

'Enjoy your evening, Miss Sharp.'

She looked up in surprise. How did the youngster know her name? But before she could ask, he'd already turned away and was trying to get rid of the bookworm as well, by conspicuously lurking. Good luck! The woman was so engrossed in her book that it would presumably take a moderate earthquake to shake her out of her reverie. What on earth was she reading? Agnes couldn't make out the title of the book. But she did notice the woman's chunky necklace. A series of metal butterflies. How tacky!

Agnes enjoyed a rare moment of fashion superiority, then grabbed her stick and, more by luck than judgement, wound her way back to her room.

Bernadette was already there waiting for her, fresh as a daisy. And colourful as a . . . well, very colourful anyway. A bright red skirt made of shiny material was visually fighting against a hazel-brown blouse and green shoes. It was hard to stomach.

'Are you sure you want to wear that?' Agnes asked.

Bernadette grinned and demonstrated to Agnes how elastic the waistband was. 'Quite sure. How come? Is there something wrong?'

Agnes sighed. Bernadette only had a very vague idea of what colours were and absolutely no interest in being dictated to by any kind of fashion code. This was what they were up against.

Agnes took off her cardigan and rummaged aimlessly in her suitcase. She didn't have time to change completely, but maybe a pretty blouse? She found something in a lovely shade of green with a hint of lace on the collar that seemed appropriate for her first evening in this high-tech carrot of a hotel.

Then, right on schedule, she spritzed a little perfume on her wrists and tried to tame her wispy sticking-out hair with the help of a wet comb. Lipstick? But Bernadette was already pacing around in front of the door, just seconds away from a bad mood, so Agnes let the lipstick lie, grabbed her handbag and made her way out into the hallway. Outside they met Winston and Marshall, who obviously also had great expectations as far as dinner was concerned. Marshall was wearing an especially dashing full dress uniform, and Winston, who had swapped his usual woolly hat and hippie blanket for a tuxedo and bow tie, was barely recognisable.

They gathered in front of Charlie and Edwina's room and knocked.

On the first knock, nobody opened the door.

Nobody did on the second either, yet noises could clearly be heard coming from inside. Someone was running back and forth. Cupboard doors were being opened, furniture moved.

Bernadette hammered against the door with her cane – when it came to food, she did not mess about.

'Charlie? Edwina? Any time today?'

Finally, the door was flung open and Charlie stuck her head out into the corridor.

'I just need a bit longer.' She tried to close the door again, but Bernadette and her cane were quicker.

As soon as they got inside, they could tell something wasn't right. Cupboard doors were open, chairs were upturned, and even the heavy luxury bed seemed to be wonky.

'You're looking for something,' Agnes said mistrustingly. She looked around. 'You're looking for Edwina!'

'She's . . .' Charlie, red in the face as it was, went even redder. 'She was . . . Err, she was just . . .'

Agnes groaned.

'I just quickly put my head down, five minutes maybe, and she gave her word . . .' Charlie sounded on edge. 'She can't have gone far.'

In a certain sense that was true. The Eden was isolated, and even Edwina was too sensible to roam about on the cliffs after dark. Hopefully!

'In any case, she's not here,' Bernadette said pragmatically. 'We should search somewhere else. I suggest we start in the dining room.'

The suggestion was enthusiastically received. It really wasn't a bad idea, also because Edwina had an almost uncanny intuition for mealtimes, and normally always turned up at the very moment food was ready.

So, they persuaded Charlie to throw on one of her

glitzy evening dresses, then made their way to the dining room.

A white tablecloth and pointy candles awaited them there, but also an empty seat, Edwina's.

The empty seat ruined the mood.

Agnes, who had resolved to properly enjoy her first dinner, observe the other guests and keep a lookout for potential hood-wearers at the same time, couldn't really concentrate. She kept glancing over her shoulder towards the dining room door, until she got a crook in her neck.

No sign of Edwina.

Even the food itself was a challenge. Of all the things that were served, Agnes only recognised a few of them, and although everything was very tasty, much of it required a lot of chewing. It was hard work for false teeth.

When the dessert came and her friend still hadn't turned up, Agnes started to get seriously worried. Voluntarily missing a dessert – that didn't seem like Edwina at all!

She laid the spoon on the table and looked from one of them to the other.

'I don't like it one bit,' she murmured.

'I think the food's good,' said Marshall reassuringly.

'I don't mean the food,' hissed Agnes. 'I mean Edwina!'

'What could possibly go wrong?' cried Winston with false optimism. 'Worst case scenario, she's got lost.'

Nobody could really believe that. Edwina got up to a lot of mischief, but she did not get lost. Edwina always knew exactly where she was.

'Well.' Agnes fell silent for a moment, then she came out with her news. 'I think there's someone going around pushing people off cliffs.'

Charlie's dessert spoon clattered to the ground. Agnes realised that her housemates were staring at her in horror, all apart from Bernadette, who made a scoffing sound. She'd actually only said it to animate the others to a search, but suddenly the whole thing didn't seem so improbable anymore. In any case, it would have been a plausible explanation for the disappearance of the yellow hood.

She took her dessert in hand again, plums and cardamom and a kind of milky rice pudding. It was too good to leave, murder or no murder. As they ate, she explained what she had seen on the cliffs, or rather what she hadn't seen, a person returning to the hotel in a yellow jacket.

Bernadette let out a sceptical laugh.

'*One* person,' she said. '*Maybe*. Not exactly a serial killer, Agnes.'

'Not *yet*,' Agnes responded sharply.

'I can't imagine *anyone* managing to push Edwina off a cliff,' Marshall murmured reassuringly.

Nobody could really imagine it. Edwina might look like an owl in a tracksuit, but she was tough as old boots. If anyone with bad intentions got near her, they'd be in for a nasty surprise. And if anyone with good intentions got near her, it'd probably be the same. *That* was the real problem!

Charlie drained her wineglass and groaned. 'What a

nightmare! You just want five minutes of peace from Edwina, and then she's gone, and it's even *worse*! Do you know how long she does yoga for? Hours! It's just not normal! And her breathing exercises sound as if someone is trying to strangle her! I nearly had a heart attack!'

She showed how close she had been to having a heart attack – very close – but you could clearly make out that despite the moaning, she was worried. Having a meal without Edwina was strange. Nobody played with broccoli florets, nobody simulated conversation between cooked carrots, nobody asked stupid questions.

'It's not a proper holiday without Edwina,' Winston murmured.

They all fell silent for a moment. It was a somewhat surprising realisation.

'Nor with Edwina!' Charlie got up, sighing. 'Well, then. Let's look for her. Where should we start?'

They checked whether Edwina had perhaps turned up in her room in the meantime, then Agnes orchestrated the search.

Bernadette should stay in the dining room and wait in case Edwina turned up for dinner at some point. Agnes would inspect the fragrant hotel corridors. Marshall, who had the best knees, could look in the basement, Charlie upstairs, and Winston would stay in the room, just to be on the safe side.

It was a solid system.

'It shouldn't be all that difficult!' Marshall tried to exude optimism. 'Edwina drags that monstrosity of a tortoise around with her everywhere. How many of those can there be in the hotel? If we look for the tortoise, we'll find Edwina.'

A great idea. They immediately felt better.

But then Agnes tripped over something wrinkly. One of Charlie's liberally distributed items of clothing she thought at first, then she recognised the characteristic colours of Hettie II. The stay at the Eden hadn't done her much good, she lay there limp and airless, even more wrinkly than the other residents of Sunset Hall.

Icy silence descended over the room. Marshall bent over silently and picked up the empty shell of the tortoise from the floor. An unpleasant plastic smell filled the air.

'Impossible!' Charlie cried in shock. 'She even took the monstrosity in the shower with her. She would never just . . .'

But there was no denying it, they had found Hettie II, but there was no sign of Edwina.

The situation was more serious than they had initially thought.

6

HOOD

Agnes was resolutely battling her way up the stairs to the lounge when she suddenly heard heavy breathing behind her, as well as a padding and dragging sound. Someone was coming up the stairs, puffing loudly. Agnes's nerves were so fraught she immediately clutched her stick, ready to fight, but it was only the corgi, also wrestling with the steps on his short legs. He caught up and took a breather beside Agnes. They looked at each other with a sudden sense of sympathy, ill-matched allies against a common enemy, the stairs. Then the corgi pulled ahead of her, his tongue hanging out, and, with a sigh, Agnes turned her attention to the ascent again too.

Finally, she made it, crossed the lounge and padded along one of the beautifully curved corridors. Soft light dripped from the ceiling, the cork flooring dulled her footsteps, and every now and then a rounded stone sculpture attempted to create a relaxed ambience. But at the moment it would have taken more than just beautiful forms to achieve that. Edwina had disappeared, and somewhere around here, someone in a hood was up to no good. Agnes noticed she was a little unsteady on her feet – the whisky maybe, or the wine afterwards, then the stairs and on top of that, all of the excitement. She leant against the wall and breathed. In. Out.

There we go.

It's alright.

She was now oblivious to the wonderful hay fragrance that had been so pleasantly noticeable to her to start with. Funny how quickly you got used to the finer things in life – and how long it took to accept the not-quite-so-fine things. Such was life!

Until now, she had remained completely undisturbed on her journey, but now a group of guests in tracksuits turned the corner, led by a resolute lady with a bouncy ponytail. It must be the detox group! Agnes recognised Trudy and waved. Trudy waved back, red-faced and a bit sweaty.

Agnes waited until the coast was clear again, then she called out a restrained 'Edwina' along the corridor.

Nothing. Had she already looked there? She wasn't sure, but padded painstakingly on. It was weird, the longer she searched, the less worried she was. Finally, the holiday was going the way she secretly imagined it would. She got to the end of the corridor. Doors everywhere, presumably to hotel rooms, but no Edwina in sight.

But the door in front of Agnes looked different to the others, no number, but furnished with a sign. Agnes took a step back in order to be able to better read it, and squinted.

HOUSEKEEPING

STAFF ONLY

Aha!

Now this was more like the kind of door you might

imagine Edwina to be behind. Agnes cast a surreptitious glance first to the left, then to the right. Nobody. She tried the handle. The door opened.

'Edwina?'

Silence.

Agnes looked around, a small room packed full of all the things that make a hotel room so pleasant, soft white bedsheets, fluffy towels, fragrant handmade organic soaps, and even the paper-wrapped chocolates Agnes and Bernadette had found on their pillows earlier on. All arranged neatly and systematically on shelves.

Agnes nibbled a chocolate, not because she was hungry, but out of principle, screwed up the paper and threw it in a spare toothbrush cup. Strangely satisfied to have created a bit of chaos in there, she remembered her mission.

Edwina wasn't in there anyway. That would have been too easy.

Despite that, Agnes found the little room interesting. All the creature comforts they didn't have at home were there, readily available, forming a guard of honour. If something disappeared, was used or eaten, it could be replaced without any fuss.

She grabbed herself a second chocolate, turned to leave – and froze. Because there, behind the door, a familiar face was staring back at her.

Marshall was a bit annoyed about having been given the lower ground floor to search. This is where all of the things were that he had absolutely no interest in, pool, sauna, chromotherapy, and to cap it all, the spa area. Truth be told, he had imagined the whole trip differently, more military somehow, with little gallant skirmishes and adventures he could potentially impress Agnes with – or someone, at least.

Instead, he was spending his time there exactly as he often spent it at home, looking for Edwina.

Apart from that, he was starting to get really hot. Like in the tropics! It had been a mistake to move out in full dress uniform this evening!

Nevertheless, Edwina had to be found, and that wasn't going to be achieved by just standing around. So, he gallantly opened a door. He was confronted by hot steam, and he slammed the door shut again. She wasn't there! Thank goodness! Onward!

He was sweating. She had to be somewhere . . .

'Excuse me!' shouted a voice behind him, in a tone that did not bode well.

Marshall didn't even turn around, instead on the spur of the moment, to escape the voice, he stepped through the next doorway. Luckily, he didn't end up in another steam pit, but in a big room with loungers and panoramic windows, behind which only an inky night was currently to be admired.

And there, right by the window, in a pool of light created by a gently glowing mood lamp, he spotted the unmistakable sky-blue tracksuit.

He almost wouldn't have noticed her. Edwina was sitting in a lounger, unaccustomedly still, her gaze not focussed outside into the night, but on her lap. Was she asleep, maybe? Thinking about it, he had never seen Edwina sleep. This wasn't normal!

'No shoes!' hissed someone behind him, but Marshall

ignored the voice and rushed towards his housemate.

Something was wrong with Edwina!

'Edwina!'

She didn't even look up.

Now Marshall really was worried. He was just about to rush off to shake Edwina out of her torpor when a hand landed gently but firmly on his shoulder.

'Excuse me! You can't just . . .'

The hand did not let up. This time Marshall had to turn around and was faced with a young woman with an ample bosom wearing a tailored blouse.

'Hmm,' said Marshall attempting to stand to attention. It wasn't easy in this heat. 'But I . . .'

'This is the relaxation room!' hiss-whispered the woman, the loudest whisper Marshall had ever heard, a real sergeant's whisper.

Heads turned to look at them.

'I've got to . . .'

'You've got to take your shoes off!' explained the woman. Her bosom quivered with outrage.

Marshall looked around. Two women in white dressing gowns were giving him the evil eye from their loungers. Only Edwina still hadn't looked up yet.

'Just my shoes?' he asked incredulously.

'Well, if you want to sit around here in uniform, I can't do anything to stop you. But shoes are not allowed!'

Marshall started to struggle out of his shoes. He was willing to make any sacrifice to get rid of the blouse woman. And genuinely, as soon as he had cast off his shoes and socks, and was staring rather sheepishly at his pale, bony toes, she released her hand from his shoulder.

'Welcome to the relaxation room!' she said, beaming as she passed him a towel and finally retreated.

Marshall gathered his shoes up from the floor. Now, what was it he was just about . . . ? That's right, Edwina! He padded over to her, barefoot, and sat down on the lounger next to hers.

'Hello, Edwina,' he said softly.

'Hello, Marshall.' She didn't look up.

'Edwina, what's . . .'

She put her finger to her lips. 'Sshhh! He's asleep!'

He?

'His name's Oberon,' explained Edwina. 'Isn't he gorgeous?'

Marshall looked at Edwina's lap for the first time, where, happily rolled up in a towel, lay a big white snake. As if he had noticed Marshall's flabbergasted expression, Oberon suddenly opened two absolutely beautiful lemon-yellow eyes and flicked his neat pink tongue at Marshall.

Agnes stared at Edwina's face as it grinned back at her from the back of the door, flabbergasted, then at Marshall's, and Winston's dignified expression. On the second row there was Bernadette and Charlie to admire, and – was the person with the weirdly wispy hair and the somewhat pinched smile her? Must well be! There was also an unfamiliar couple with hyena-like facial expressions (you could tell straightaway that the two of them were married and had spent decades perfecting the hyena faces together.)

What was it supposed to be? A kind of hit list? It brought back unpleasant memories of mugshots from her time in the police. She had the feeling she should do something but didn't know what.

Then she heard a noise out in the corridor, a rasp, as if it were made by a gigantic cockroach.

It was time to get out of there!

She put the second chocolate back in its place and was just about to leave when the door handle went down, as if of its own accord. Someone was coming! Strictly speaking they were already there.

Agnes looked around for a place to hide, but there wasn't anywhere, and amongst all the white sheets, she stuck out like a sore thumb in her jade-green blouse. Not to worry, she would just have to roll out her confused-old-lady routine, a strategy she had honed to perfection over the years.

The door swung open and Agnes recognised the barman from before. She hastily peeked at his name badge.

So, Max was his name.

When he noticed her, he visibly flinched.

They stared at each other in silence for a moment.

'I . . .' Agnes began.

She waited for the barman to say something, but he was still staring at her, flabbergasted. She looked at the ground. 'This isn't my room, is it?' she mumbled vaguely.

Eventually, it seemed to occur to the barman that although she was in the wrong place, she was still a guest when it came down to it, so he should treat her as such.

'Are you lost, Miss Sharp? Should I maybe take you to your room?'

'Yes,' Agnes squeaked, although her hotel room really was the last place she wanted to go at the moment. She had to find Edwina, and she had to find out what the photos on the door were all about!

Max noticed her looking. 'That's a nice photo of you, isn't it, Miss Sharp?'

Agnes seized the opportunity. 'Yeah. Maybe. But why is it up there? And' – she waved her hand vaguely – 'the others?'

'So that we can call you all by name from the word go.' Max beamed at her and in doing so exposed an unsettling number of white teeth.

Agnes needed a moment to digest the information. She faintly remembered Charlie insisting on taking pictures of them all on her phone during the holiday preparations. She hadn't questioned it. A mistake, as it now turned out.

'All of that so that you can say "Good morning, Miss Sharp" when you bump into me in the corridor?'

'I guess so.' Max was still beaming, if a bit fixedly as it seemed to Agnes.

'Isn't that . . .' Agnes searched for words. The whole thing was more harmless than she had feared, but despite that, it all still seemed a bit intrusive to her.

It seemed to suddenly occur to Max that he had bumped into her not in the hallway, but in an out-of-bounds housekeeping store, and firmly held his arm out towards her. 'Come on, Miss Sharp, I'll take you back to your room!'

Agnes grabbed hold of his arm, determined to go back there at the next available opportunity to swap one or two of the pictures around and spice things up a bit at the Eden.

Then she gasped, on a hook in the corner behind the door, hung an orange hooded jacket.

* * *

94

Marshall was sweating, even though he had already taken off his uniform jacket and was going around, unusually for him, in shirtsleeves. Oberon the snake was now occupying his jacket, and for inexplicable reasons, Marshall had let himself get roped into smuggling the reptile out of the spa area with Edwina's help.

To what end and to where, was unclear, but by then anything was fine by him, as long as it got him somewhere that was a more reasonable temperature.

'We can't just leave him behind,' Edwina had explained over and over, and Marshall, who wouldn't even have left his worst enemy in the spa area, had finally caved.

The whole thing didn't prove to be all that easy, since it turned out that the white towels that had been camouflaging Oberon up to that point had to be returned at the entrance, and Edwina, not without good reason, imagined that a big white snake would stir emotions amongst the dressing-gown-clad ladies.

Jealousy, thought Edwina.

Blind panic, suspected Marshall.

So, he had draped the dozing snake over his arm, and then thrown his jacket over him. Oberon was pretty heavy and was unpleasantly flicking his tongue in and out of the crook of his arm. Marshall could hardly wait to pass the snake and the responsibility back to Edwina again.

But first they had to get past the blouse-woman on the spa reception, and Edwina had promised to create a distraction. Under normal circumstances a distraction being taken care of by Edwina would have put Marshall on high alert, but in this heat, nothing mattered. He stood patiently in an alcove as Oberon, who had been incredibly lethargic, started to inspect his arm. First his lower arm, then his upper arm. Marshall observed his wriggly, excitable jacket with a certain apprehension.

He heard frenzied squeals coming from behind him, then a large-bosomed woman rushed towards him and then past him, without so much as looking at him. The next thing he knew, Edwina was suddenly back, dripping wet and pulling at his sleeve.

'Come on, Marshall! We should go!'

He followed her obediently. A glass door opened silently, then it suddenly got cooler. Marshall could finally think clearly again. He and Edwina were in the process of smuggling a surprisingly heavy reptile through a luxury eco hotel, God knows where to. Not an everyday occurrence, not even for the unconventional residents of Sunset Hall.

'Where now?' he asked.

Edwina rolled her eyes. 'To the room, of course. Oberon needs to relax. He's been through a lot. He's a stowaway, you know?'

'Hmm.' Marshall didn't have any better ideas, so he resigned himself to following Edwina through the corridors, past the reception and towards the stairs. She knew her way around alarmingly well.

'Oberon comes from South America,' she happily babbled as she wrang out her wet tracksuit top. 'But he heard so much about England he had to see it with his own eyes. So, he smuggled himself onto the ship.'

Marshall, who closely followed political goings-on,

couldn't imagine that someone who had heard a lot about England would ever want to visit, and a whole lot else about Edwina's story didn't add up either. And what was all this nonsense about a ship?

He sighed and decided to keep his mouth shut. Once Edwina had imagined something, the ship had already sailed anyway, almost literally in this case.

Instead, he concentrated on the stairs and took some deep breaths. He'd get rid of the snake, then take it from there. At least it wasn't poisonous. A boa constrictor, if he wasn't mistaken. A youngster who wanted to get to know England. The snake should brace himself for disappointment . . .

Back in Edwina's room, Marshall flopped into an armchair, exhausted. What now? It seemed like a hopeless situation. Sometimes he longed to have his life in active service back, where at least you were allowed to shoot if you reached a deadlock. He even longed for the empty, glazed state that overcame him from time to time. No worries, no thoughts, just a gentle, almost pleasant absence. Whereas now he was all too well aware of his precarious, morally questionable role as snake-bearer. The others would . . . At least Charlie wasn't there yet, and he had a moment to . . .

Just then, the door flew open, and Charlie was standing in front of him with her dress slightly askew, but looking terrific as ever.

'Marshall, how's it going? I've looked everywhere for . . .' She broke off when she spotted Edwina, who had covered Oberon with a scarf and was now making a wet patch on the bed.

'There's good news and there's bad news,' Marshall said gingerly. He looked over at Edwina sheepishly. 'Actually, just two lots of bad news!'

Her room had been ridiculously close, just around the corner, so to speak, and Agnes had had no idea! How embarrassing! Max had delivered her to her door in a matter of steps, tentatively smiled and disappeared, visibly relieved to have removed her from the housekeeping store.

The whole thing made Agnes think. What was he, a barman, even looking for in the housekeeping store? Did he maybe have something to do with the orange hood? On the other hand, Max was one of the few people who couldn't have been in that hood, after all, he had been pouring Agnes a whisky while the hood was wandering around in front of the Sea Lounge's panoramic windows. But maybe he knew something? Or he had an accomplice? Should Agnes have questioned him about the case?

And *was* it even a case?

Case or no case? That was the question!

Strange, the dead verger had so clearly been a case, but she had decided to do nothing. This was revenge. Her conscience, which had been distracted for a while by boilers, prize draws and holidays, was beginning to rear its head again. She shouldn't have ignored it. Murder was more than an inconvenience – murder was a crack in the fabric of the world, a crack that lets darkness into life. Murder concerned everyone. You had to care, no matter how old and frail you might be.

So, it looked like fate was offering her another chance to do something about the darkness in the world. Something wasn't right at the Eden, and Agnes would get to the bottom of what it was. She was hell-bent on sending Marshall up the cliff-top path the next morning, so he could get an idea of the lie of the land. Until then, she would have to practise patience.

Or maybe not?

Agnes thought for a moment. The guest photos in the housekeeping store had given her an idea. She fished a hotel brochure off the coffee table and began to study the layout of the hotel. The hotel may have looked like a carrot from a distance, but from above it looked more like it was modelled on an octopus, stretched out flat, arms in all directions.

One arm was the restaurant.

One arm was the library, garden room and the mysterious games room.

One arm for the terrace and Sea Lounge.

Four arms of hotel rooms. Four short arms – the Eden was too ecological and exclusive to be really big – and so presumably also four corridors with housekeeping stores!

Here was the thing, if someone really had gone flying off the cliff, it was either a guest, or a member of staff. Anything else was practically impossible thanks to the hotel's isolated location.

A missing member of staff would quickly become apparent, and Agnes had already resolved to make a few enquiries at reception later on, but first she wanted to explore the other eventuality, if the victim had been a guest, there must be a photo of him in one of the housekeeping stores. Or her. And if Agnes saw the photo . . .

Sure, it had been murky and stormy, but maybe

something had lodged in her memory? Memory was a funny thing after all. All sorts of things slipped through like a sieve, while every now and then, the most banal things stuck, unwieldy, useless, unforgettable. And sometimes a little nudge was all that was needed to jog the memory. A wisp of hair, a silhouette, a gesture . . .

It was worth a try, anyway!

Agnes checked that Max had disappeared from the corridor and off she went again, actually did get lost and a bit confused, but finally found the next housekeeping store and peeked inside.

Well-fed guest faces stared at her mutely. A piggish man. A woman with thick horn-rimmed spectacles. A man, who looked a bit like a penguin. A particularly good-looking couple stood out to Agnes, the man had high cheekbones, interesting lines on his forehead and a lustrous silver-fox hairstyle, the woman was unusually blonde and pale and young.

Agnes waited for her memory to speak up, but it remained silent.

Suddenly she was annoyed again. Stupid photos behind the door, stupid unfamiliar faces! Stupid plan, stupid Eden! She remembered her decision to swap some photos around and spice up proceedings in the hotel a bit. Without giving it much thought, she pulled a few pictures from their frames.

Then it was time to redistribute them. The pretty blondeie got matched with a piggish husband, the silver fox drifted next to the woman with the horn-rimmed glasses. New partner, new luck! It was a romantic hotel after all! Agnes looked at her handiwork with a certain sense of satisfaction and no idea that she had just made a small but pivotal contribution to the local murder rate.

The faces behind the next housekeeping door were a bit less well-nourished. Steely and also a bit hungry, the members of the detox group stared back at Agnes. A pack of upmarket wolves with shiny hair, bony shoulders and strategically placed tans. Agnes spotted Trudy on the bottom row. She looked less determined than the rest of the troop and even hungrier, if that was possible. In fact, she looked like someone who would rather be anywhere but there.

Agnes granted Trudy's wish and swapped her picture with a non-detoxer, a woman with a longing look and racy cleavage. There! Hopefully Trudy would appreciate that!

Then she looked from one face to another and rummaged in her memory as she normally only did in her enormous handbag. Shame you couldn't just tip out your memory and neatly arrange the contents on the table. This, however, was tedious. Nothing sensible came to light, and Agnes carried on with a now painful hip and ever-worsening temper.

On the third attempt she finally came across a few familiar faces. The White Widow was there, for example. Marie de Gurney was her name – a proper white-widow name! And there was the brat, complete with eyeliner and floppy black hair. Monsieur Fleck. She'd have to question him too; he was almost a kind of witness after all, but Agnes had no desire to be insulted again, and was intent on only taking the brat to task once she had exhausted all other lines of enquiry.

Then she noticed the chap with the floral cravat and pastel jacket. Walter Ross. A memory stirred. Rough sea, apricot-coloured waves, piano tinkling and candlelight. That's right, he had something to do with her experience in the Sea Lounge. But what? Then she realised he had been one of the guests – the chap in the salmon-pink blazer! That meant that he was out of the question as a possible suspect and victim. Agnes, who had briefly felt something like the thrill of the chase, sighed disappointedly.

The door to the housekeeping store opened so quickly that Agnes let out a little scream in shock. But the other person's scream was louder. Max! Again! Didn't he have anything better to do than stalk her?

She could tell by the barman's uncontrollable blinking that he was asking himself a similar question. Quick as a flash, she reached out her arm and grabbed a handful of chocolates.

'I'm hungry!' she cried, before Max could say anything. It was a spurious excuse because the routine at the hotel was structured in such a way that nobody could ever get hungry (except, of course, if you were in the detox group; then hunger was practically par for the course).

Max quickly pulled himself together and sighed. 'You don't have to come and get the chocolates yourself, Miss Sharp. You only need to ring and someone will bring you some. As many as you want. Apart from that, there's room service. Round the clock. Have you seen our menu?'

Max opened a cupboard and pulled out an orange

hooded jacket. Agnes was suddenly wide awake.

'Nice jacket,' she said. 'Is it yours?'

Max shrugged. 'Not really. We put them on when we have to do something outside. Staff jackets, so to speak. I really have to . . .'

Them?

'Are there several of them?'

'There should really be at least one of them in each housekeeping store.' He gave Agnes a stern look. 'You can't just take a jacket from the housekeeping store, Miss Sharp. They're for staff use!'

'Of course not!' Agnes looked at him indignantly.

Cogs were whirring in her mind. So, someone had just grabbed a jacket from one of the housekeeping stores, hadn't they? Child's play! Any guest with enough of a criminal instinct to ignore a staff only sign could get hold of a hooded jacket like that any time, commit a murder in it and then dump the jacket here again. The orange jacket was absolutely perfect for committing a crime in.

7

CORKSCREW

After Max had deposited Agnes in her room for the second time that evening, she sat on her bed, frustrated. She was tired. She had spread herself too thin. And Edwina still hadn't been found.

Agnes sank into the pillows. Soft and warm. Just stay in bed – hadn't that been her plan? It was actually very nice there in her room. Relaxing – if it hadn't been for the noise coming from next door. Someone was shrieking. Agitated voices. A door being slammed shut.

Then it dawned on Agnes that the neighbouring room was Charlie and Edwina's. She reluctantly heaved herself out of bed, grabbed her stick and went to make sure everything was alright.

A stressed-looking Marshall opened the door to her.

'I . . .' he began, then gave up and waved Agnes inside without saying another word.

Inside was Charlie, dressed in an evening gown, was somewhat manically blowing up Hettie II, and Edwina was drying her wet hair with a duvet. Edwina! She was back! Thank God! Why was she so wet? And why was Charlie so agitated?

'There!' cried Charlie. 'Done! Hettie II! What do you say to that?'

Edwina had a look of scorn on her face. 'Hettie II is puffed up.'

'That didn't bother you before!' Charlie hissed.

'Before is before,' Edwina explained calmly. 'Now is now.'

Charlie changed tack. 'I think I have a right to have a say in who gets to stay in my room!'

Edwina nodded earnestly. 'You do. But it's democratic. The people decide! I'm in favour. Oberon is in favour. And Lillith is in favour too!'

Who the hell was Oberon?

'Oberon is not the people! And Lillith is in favour because she happens to already be dead!' Charlie ruffled her beautiful hair. 'I, on the other hand, would like to stay a teeny-tiny bit alive, if that's okay with you, and not be poisoned by a snake while on holiday!' She put her hands on her hips. White hair sticking out all over the place, completely outraged.

'Oberon is not a venomous snake,' Marshall said, trying to appease her. 'He's a constrictor. From South America. I've checked online.'

'Oh, a constrictor,' Charlie said coldly. 'That's alright then.'

Edwina, who didn't really get sarcasm, smiled happily.

It took a while for Marshall to bring Agnes up to date. The situation was a mess, Edwina had somehow managed to adopt a boa constrictor there in the hotel, but Charlie didn't want to share a room with the reptile. The lines

105

were already drawn. Agnes secretly congratulated herself for having chosen Bernadette as a roommate.

'He doesn't have to sleep in a bed,' Edwina said, willing to compromise. 'We can house him in the bathroom and only let him out under supervision. What do you think?' By Edwina's standards that was an unusually rational suggestion, but it met with staunch resistance from Charlie.

'So I'm scared to death every time I need the loo in the night? No way!'

Edwina had a new idea and peeled back a scarf to show them how loveable Oberon was. Agnes cast a fleeting glance at a knot of smooth, pale snake skin, not dissimilar to unbaked Chelsea buns.

Just then, there was a knock at the door. Probably someone wanting to complain about the noise, Agnes presumed, but it was only Winston, red in the face, reporting that Edwina was nowhere to be seen.

Had they really all been looking for Edwina as recently as an hour ago? Had they really thought that her *absence* was a problem?

'Edwina is back,' Marshall declared gloomily.

Then Edwina grabbed the snake and introduced them to it, a twinkle in her eye.

After a lot of hoo-ha, Charlie finally did go to bed after all, but not without checking that the door to the bathroom was shut properly. Oberon was now residing in the bathtub, flicking his tongue and looking beautiful, Edwina's heat lamp shining down on him.

So far, so good. But Edwina was too pumped up to just fall asleep. The holiday was going even better than she could ever have dared dream possible, and the mission . . . well, it was now obvious what it was about, her assignment was to keep Oberon out of danger. A mission made for her!

She listened to Charlie's regular breaths and made plans for the following day. From now on, she must always be armed, that much was clear, and she must let Oberon out of her sight as little as possible. Was the bathroom really secure? Maybe he would be in better hands in bed with her. But she had given Charlie her word . . . Yeah, and? It looked like Charlie was dead to the world, although she'd declared over and over again that she wouldn't sleep a wink with a snake in her room. Both her eyes were firmly shut, her mouth slightly open, and Charlie was gently snoring away.

Edwina clambered out of bed. A crescent moon shone outside, brightly enough to light the way to the bathroom. The sea raged beneath the moon. A storm, and not a small one at that! Fascinated, Edwina stepped closer to the balcony door.

And suddenly someone fell from the sky, or at least from above, landed awkwardly on the balcony and frantically looked around in all directions.

A figure in black.

The Eden's big panoramic windows were exceptionally well soundproofed, so Edwina couldn't hear the wind that was presumably howling out there as it tore at the figure's hoodie, or their footsteps.

He rushed left and right and peered out to sea. Then he made to climb over the railing but thought better of it.

A killer, Edwina instantly thought. Someone with their sights on Oberon!

She couldn't just let him sit out there on the balcony.

She opened her wardrobe looking for a weapon. The corkscrew? Edwina wasn't sure if it would suffice against a trained killer. Charlie's nail file, maybe? She got cross again that they had confiscated the garden shears from her at the airport, then she grabbed the corkscrew and stepped towards the balcony door.

The guy was standing right against the window, his hands on the glass peering inside.

Edwina put a hand on the pane too and peered back. The other hand was holding the corkscrew.

They stood nose to nose for a while, at least almost, because the killer was a damn sight taller than her, tall and thin, but that didn't worry Edwina. It didn't always come down to size.

Then the intruder suddenly spotted her behind the glass, got a huge shock and jerked backwards. Was he even an intruder, since he hadn't actually intruded anywhere? But that was quite clearly his intention!

The guy looked up again, a bit harried it seemed to Edwina, then he started to frantically bang on the window. A dull, piercing sound, hesitant at first, then more and more frantic.

Edwina was getting angry.

Intruding was one thing, but waking Charlie up was quite another! She knew how things were wont to go in their house share, even if she couldn't do anything about the guy on the balcony, Charlie, Agnes and the others would find a way to lay the blame at her door. Any excuse, if it was a chance to nag at Edwina again. And then she might lose the Oberon dispute. Her mission was at risk, just because that clown out there couldn't act professionally!

She signalled to the killer that he should stop banging, and put an admonishing finger to her lips. The guy stopped, seemed to understand and pointed at the side of the window, gesticulating wildly, where inside there were two buttons at eye-level.

Open.

And shut.

Charlie rolled over onto her side and stopped snoring.

Edwina thought for a moment. The guy wanted to come in, no doubt about it. She had resigned herself to the idea that she would have to take on the figure on the balcony, unmask them and ideally neutralise them. The only question was how to achieve that without waking Charlie up.

She put her finger emphatically to her lips once more. The killer nodded. He lowered his hand and wrapped both arms around his body, freezing.

Just then, the storm finally managed to tear the black hood from his head.

Edwina lowered the corkscrew.

It wasn't a killer! It was her contact with the dark eye make-up! But his eyeshadow was now tear-smudged, and he didn't look very good at all.

Edwina gave the thumbs up and pushed the button.

Even Agnes felt drawn to the moonlight-drenched natural spectacle on the other side of the window. After all of the excitement with Charlie, Edwina and Oberon, sleep was out of the question. She pressed her nose against the cool glass and stared out into the night. The storm had successfully swept all the clouds from the sky. It was now tackling the gorse bushes on the cliffs, the little stunted pines and the tall grass. She couldn't hear it howling through the glass, but she could imagine it, wild and free and soulless.

Agnes felt a bit dizzy.

She might well have been walking this earth for a while now, but in that moment, she felt new, freshly hatched, clueless. These ancient, secret powers resolving their feuds for eons . . . what was she even doing there? Did it actually make a difference if she kept her housemates in check, took her blood pressure tablets and caught a murderer or two?

And if it didn't . . .

It was a surprisingly freeing thought.

While Bernadette snored away like a freight train, thereby undoubtedly destroying the intended calm ambience at the hotel, Agnes sank into a chair and tried to imagine what it would be like to just surrender herself to the elements outside, wildly dancing and reeling, bending like grass, floating like a leaf, falling like a stone . . .

She couldn't possibly know that inside the hotel, a whole host of secret activity was happening on this storm-tossed night. Edwina had just taken the quivering brat by the hand and led him to the wardrobe, where he could hide with Lillith and Hettie II.

On the floor above them, stood someone in an orange jacket, a knife in their hand and blind rage in their soul.

And a killer had been keeping watch at their door for quite some time already. He had followed Bernadette out of the dining room to their hotel room, very quietly and with the utmost professionalism, and was standing out in the corridor, deep in thought and still as a mountain.

'Isn't he lovely?' Edwina asked, masterfully decapitating an organic soft-boiled egg.

'He's rather big,' Agnes replied neutrally. 'Is he still growing?'

'Boas carry on growing their whole lives,' Marshall schooled her, he had clearly already researched the topic on the internet.

'Splendid!' Agnes sighed. She had woken up in an armchair this morning, stiff and cold, and, with the best will in the world, couldn't remember what had possessed her to leave that wonderful bed in the middle of the night.

Now she was sitting at breakfast disgruntled and dog-tired with a nagging headache and was talking about the snake again, although she would have much preferred to discuss more wholesome topics – the murder for example, or the possibility of a murder, or at least the White Widow, who was clearly visible sitting at a table for one at the other end of the breakfast room, feeding the corgi little pieces of cheese, drinking orange juice and looking especially shady.

Instead, it was obviously all about Oberon, the problem snake. Edwina had shoved him into her big sports bag, covered him with a scarf and deposited him next to her chair. Every now and then she pushed the scarf aside and smiled lovingly into the bag.

Agnes rolled her eyes.

Yesterday they had adjourned the discussions due to general exhaustion, but now it was time for the next round, strengthened by toast, organic eggs and fruit salad.

'I didn't get a wink of sleep,' Charlie groaned, and belligerently grabbed a bowl of Bircher muesli. 'The snake has got to go!'

Edwina stabbed her spoon threateningly into her egg yolk.

The rest of the housemates were staying out of it. Winston was cutting a croissant in half with an excessive level of precision, while Marshall was fascinated by the cloud formations floating around rather buoyantly in the bright blue sky. Bernadette demolished some scrambled eggs with abandon, and everyone expected Agnes to solve their problems and bring about peace.

Agnes thought for a moment. Oberon really was an attractive snake with lemon-yellow eyes and a gleaming pale snake body. Ornamental. And he let Edwina carry him around without complaint – you could by no means say that about many creatures. The snake was obviously used to lunatics.

Agnes fundamentally did not want to interfere. The matter was clearly Charlie's problem. She had insisted on coming on this holiday, and there were certain risks attached. Now she had a snake on her hands. That was life in old age! Nearly everything turned out differently to what you imagined!

But Charlie had finished her muesli and was still railing against her fate. 'You don't even know what he eats!' she said confrontationally.

'Rats!' Edwina beamed. 'He eats rats. But not very often. A rat every few weeks will suffice!'

Agnes sighed. A spartan rat diet wouldn't ingratiate Oberon to Charlie either. She hoovered up the last crumbs of her excellent and false-teeth-friendly wholewheat croissant and made a heroic decision.

'Let's swap!' she announced. 'Charlie can share with Bernadette, and I'll move to Edwina and Oberon's room.'

'And Lillith's!' Edwina added.

'And Lillith's!' Agnes confirmed. Lillith was the only one of her future roommates from whom she didn't expect any issues. Agnes gazed at her housemates, her eyes gleaming, until the information had filtered through.

Marshall understood instantly and looked admiringly at Agnes.

Winston seemed almost excessively relieved, but Bernadette seemed a bit miffed. Given that Agnes had chosen a snake over her as a roommate.

Edwina was busy with a waffle and had apparently already partially forgotten the argument about Oberon.

And Charlie had tears in her eyes. She leant over to Agnes and pressed her hand. 'Thank you, Agnes! You're a wonderful friend. I'm not very good with snakes. My second husband . . .' She broke off, obviously determined to waste as few words as possible on husband number two, the snake.

Agnes blushed slightly. Sure, she'd solved the snake problem, but Charlie really didn't have any idea how pervasive Bernadette's snoring was. On the other hand, Agnes couldn't be responsible for everything on this earth.

She savoured a berry compote and basked in the unusual admiration of her housemates for a few minutes, then she wanted to inconspicuously but decisively turn the discussion towards the murder.

Potential murder.

Agnes had a feeling about it . . .

But just as the appreciation at the table had passed its zenith and Agnes was about to bring up the mysterious orange hood again, something in the breakfast room caught her eye.

She probably wouldn't have noticed as quickly if her coffee cup hadn't been empty. She was looking around for a refill. Normally a helpful young person would instantly appear and give her a top up – she'd already tried it three times that day, and it had worked quite splendidly.

But this time she looked around to no avail.

And established that guests at other tables were also uncertainly on the lookout for a drink refill or some fresh scrambled egg. There was nobody there anymore who seemed to be taking responsibility for it.

It was as if the ground had swallowed up the little army of whippersnappers.

Agnes let her eyes wander and finally spotted them on the other side of the glass door that constituted the entrance to the breakfast room.

They formed a shapeless cluster and were speaking urgently to one another. Brows were furrowed, arms gesticulating wildly, a young woman put her hands to her temples in horror.

Agnes could sense that emotions were running high, even from a distance.

But what sort of emotions?

The emotions of people who had just learnt that one of their guests had been found squished at the bottom of the cliffs?

Or maybe the emotions that stir when a boa constrictor

weighing several pounds is, well, on the run?

Or was it about something completely different? Agnes craned her neck out of curiosity. The tumult out there seemed a bit excessive for a snake alert – and even for a fallen guest, actually. Obviously, it wasn't nice if someone fell from the cliffs – presumably it wasn't good for business either – but the faces didn't just look upset, they looked downright shocked.

Something had happened. Something important.

Unsteady and weighted down by too many wholewheat croissants, Agnes got up and moved as quickly as she could towards the entrance door. At any moment the hotel employees out there would drift apart and put on their friendly professional faces again, but if she hurried, she might still catch a word or two. She flung the door open with so much force she almost fell over and stuck her head outside.

There was a muffled babel of voices, and thanks to the overly efficient hearing aid, Agnes struggled to make out individual words. Everything was buzzing. She tried to concentrate.

'Police' was to be heard every now and then, 'for days' and – had she misheard? – 'helicopter.'

And over and over again, 'cut off.'

This was clearly not about a snake.

The agitated chatter slowly ebbed, a single voice raised above the general hubbub. Helen, the woman from reception. She sounded calm and professional.

Agnes couldn't understand everything, but apparently it was about 'maintaining calm' and 'professionalism.' Most of the employees did their best to pull themselves together.

Helen nodded appreciatively. 'We carry on as normal. Service is our priority. Most of them probably won't notice a thing.'

Then she spotted Agnes next to the door and her feisty smile slipped a little.

'Good morning, Miss Sharp. Did you enjoy your breakfast? Can we get you anything . . . ?'

'I'm looking for . . .' Above all, Agnes was looking for a good excuse. Where were all the good excuses when you needed them? '. . . the loos,' she finally stammered.

Helen pointed mutely at a door marked WC that was clearly visible just a few steps away from Agnes.

Agnes was annoyed.

Now she actually had to disappear into the toilet under the watchful gaze of the waiters, instead of being able to discuss the latest developments with her housemates straightaway. She had been right. Someone was dead! Maybe the body had to be recovered by helicopter? And 'cut off' clearly sounded like murder! Agnes wondered what had been cut off. A finger? An arm? Maybe even the head? There was no limit to her imagination. Had the murderer kept a trophy, or was it about hiding the victim's identity? It didn't quite fit with what she had seen yesterday on the cliffs, but everything didn't always have to match up right away, after all – that was the interesting thing about murder cases. They were on the right track, anyway!

Even the Eden's toilets had a certain charm. Gently curved natural stone formed almost incidental basins, white towels were stacked in neat little towers, and it smelt good. Not of toilet, but very convincingly of grass and greenery. Loudspeakers sent subtle sounds of the sea and rain through the room, accompanied by soft music.

Agnes eyed herself in one of the many mirrors. She didn't look rested in the slightest. Her cardigan was buttoned up wrong and her lipstick was applied lopsidedly, as if someone had retrospectively stuck a mouth on her face and miscalculated slightly.

Relaxed? Yeah, right!

A little later she was standing on the terrace with Marshall, right at the end, on the point of the carrot's nose, looking down at the cliff-top path below. It snaked merrily along the cliffs, wide and bright, and in the sunshine looked downright unashamedly harmless.

'Along there,' said Agnes. 'Follow the path until you get to the viewing point over there. Do you see, where the flag is? I'd like to know if there's any possibility of leaving the path or carrying on somewhere else. Or if you could hide something there – or someone. Absolutely anything that's in any way conspicuous!'

She looked at Marshall hopefully.

Apart from him none of her housemates had been willing to even slightly change their holiday plans to catch the murderer. Edwina and Oberon had disappeared remarkably quickly, Charlie had booked a beauty treatment, Bernadette was preparing for lunch by taking a nap, and Winston was listening to a talk about the coastal cliff ecosystem.

Only Agnes and Marshall were still on the ball.

Agnes eagerly watched as Marshall resolutely followed the cliff-top path in his camo anorak. The sea glittered.

Everything looked so bright, so fresh and colourful and clean – it suddenly seemed very unlikely to Agnes that something sinister might have happened there yesterday evening. Maybe the thing with the verger had set her on the wrong path! Maybe the whole murder case was just in her head! Edwina dreamt up a journey on a ship to relax, and Agnes a murder. That really spoke volumes!

She sighed. If Marshall didn't uncover anything suspicious on his walk, she would let the matter rest and finally relax properly, she decided. But until then . . .

She was so deep in thought that it took a while for her to realise that someone next to her was persistently clearing their throat. She looked around and saw a man leaning on the railing, not too close, but also not that far away. He had a generous head of white hair and a pair of round red glasses on his nose, which gave him a vaguely academic air. Behind the glasses, two grey eyes glinted conspiratorially at Agnes.

'Your husband likes walking, I see,' said the glasses-wearer. 'I don't get it personally – just leaving such an attractive woman on her own on holiday . . .' He shook his head in astonishment and slightly sadly, while Agnes looked around for the attractive, abandoned woman, until she realised that the man with the hair must mean her.

Well, that was . . . Agnes noticed herself going red, redder than the chap's glasses. At the same time, she got a fit of the hiccups. Not a particularly attractive combination, but nevertheless, the man offered her his arm.

'It's a bit cool out here, don't you think? Come on. Why don't we have a lovely coffee, until your darling husband gets back from his jaunt?'

Agnes actually felt rather hot just then, all the same she grabbed the arm, mainly so as not to lose balance in this confusing situation. She couldn't remember the last time someone had called her 'attractive,' and she had no idea how she should react. Outraged? Flattered? Embarrassed? Apart from that, in the space of ninety seconds she had gained not only an admirer, but a husband too. It took time to digest something like that.

Before she could come up with a plan, she was sitting in the lounge drinking another coffee.

Not good for her nerves.

The chap was sitting opposite her, his white hair billowing confidently from behind his ears.

He was called Howard.

Howard Hope.

He came to the hotel every year. So wonderfully remote, the back of beyond, and yet so beautiful and comfortable at the same time. And environmentally conscious. It was so important to think of the environment, especially these days.

Agnes nodded. On that they could agree. Before she knew what was happening, she had a few more compliments thrown at her, one for her elegant cardigan (buttoned up wrongly), one for her lipstick (lopsidedly applied) and one for her beautiful blue eyes. Well, maybe there was something in that one.

She sheepishly stirred her coffee. Her head was buzzing from the amount of caffeine, and she had no idea what she should say. Luckily Howard had the conversation firmly in his grasp and steered masterfully back and forth between the hotel cuisine, the courses on offer and the great service.

Agnes only needed to throw in a nod or a smile every now and then.

'No wonder this hotel is so popular with couples,' Howard declared. 'But do you know what's occurred to me?' He leant confidentially towards her, and Agnes instinctively leant forward a little too. A woody smell wheeled its way into her nose, like expensive aftershave.

'A lot of the guests here aren't exactly on honeymoon, if you catch my drift.' He sighed, and Agnes, who didn't really understand, quizzically raised her sparse eyebrows.

'I get the feeling that lots of the couples who come here – now, how shall I put it – are in crisis,' explained Howard. 'They're looking for something. Healing perhaps.'

He looked at Agnes expectantly.

It was an interesting thought. It obviously hadn't escaped Agnes's attention that most of the guests were visiting in couples, and many of them didn't exactly seem to be spring chickens anymore. Maybe the Eden was just a good place to hash out relationship issues. After all, the hotel was beautifully remote, in moments of crisis you could order a warm soup any time of the day or night, and if you got too agitated, the yoga studio and group meditation were at your disposal.

Agnes wondered whether the thing she had witnessed on the cliffs had arisen as a result of such a relationship crisis. Maybe yoga wasn't enough for some people. Maybe some people had to *cut* something *off* in order to feel better.

She had forgotten Howard for a moment – a mistake, as it turned out. When she found her way back to the present moment, he was holding her hand and looking deeply into her eyes. Agnes looked around in desperation.

'I see I've hit a raw nerve there. Sorry, I really didn't mean to . . . Only, it's sometimes difficult to just watch – especially with such a wonderful woman, like you, Agnes! I can call you Agnes, can't I? I *must* call you Agnes!'

Agnes managed to release her hand, and Howard jumped nimbly up. He had to be several years younger than her.

'Now I've made you sad!' he huffed, much too loud for Agnes's liking. The people at the neighbouring table looked over curiously. 'I only meant to . . . Forgive me, Agnes!'

Howard flounced out of the lounge, his hair wafting, leaving Agnes thoroughly confused. What had that all been about? She felt as if she had spent the last few minutes in a somewhat peculiar novel. *Pride and Prejudice and False Teeth* perhaps! Ridiculous! Howard would probably get on like a house on fire with Charlie! But Agnes had to admit that she didn't want Howard to meet Charlie, look deep into *her* eyes and take *her* for coffee.

No, that was the last thing she wanted!

She spotted Marshall, who had returned from the viewing point, breathless, and looked a bit out of place in his anorak in the lounge.

He hadn't seen her yet, and she imagined what he would say about Howard mistaking him for her husband and attributing not just a marriage, but also a marriage crisis to them as well. They would both have a good chuckle and that would be that.

But when Marshall finally spotted her and headed

towards her, his eyes gleaming, she realised that she had no desire to tell him anything about Howard, and if she was quite honest, she doubted Marshall would have found the whole thing very funny anyway.

She pushed Howard's empty coffee cup a bit farther away from her, slapped on a smile and waved at Marshall.

'So? Did you find anything?' she asked, patting the space next to her, where Howard had just been sitting. The seat was still warm.

'I'll say!' Marshall said, taking off his camo anorak. A camo shirt in the same pattern emerged from beneath.

Agnes was curious. 'A yellow jacket, maybe?' she asked hopefully. 'Scuff marks? Blood?'

Marshall shook his head.

'Nothing like that. So, first off, you were right, it's practically impossible to leave the cliff-top path. It leads to the viewing point and that's it. There's only cliffs and gorse either side. Nobody could just cut across country – especially not at night!'

Agnes nodded contentedly. 'So, if someone didn't come back and isn't there anymore . . .'

Marshall signalled falling with his hand.

'And are there police . . . down there . . . are they carrying out a search?'

Marshall shook his head. 'There's absolutely nothing down there. Nobody. Sea. A bit of beach, a few gulls. That's it.'

'But I thought . . .' Agnes had expected a discovery. Some kind of severed body part that was bad enough to send the hotel employees into a spin.

She was distracted by a moody couple storming into

the lounge with packed suitcases.

'But we can't just stay here . . .' cried the man, terribly red in the face.

The woman looked as if she wanted to hide behind her oversized suitcase.

'Look at her!' The man pointed accusatorily at the woman, who shrunk in response. 'My wife's having a breakdown! We've got to get back to London!'

Agnes thought about what Howard had said about the couples at the Eden. Maybe there was something in it. These two, at least, seemed miles away from marital harmony.

Suddenly the hotel manager appeared, armed with her dutiful smile again. She stepped towards the pair, so close it almost seemed threatening. After some whispering and lots of unpleasant hissing on the part of the man, the couple left the lounge and Helen made sure their suitcases were taken away too. *She really is very good at making people do what she wants*, thought Agnes.

'What on earth was that all about?' she whispered to Marshall.

Marshall looked at her triumphantly.

'That's the second thing I found out.'

He scooted a bit closer to her and told her what he had discovered on his jaunt to the cliffs. Agnes listened until her hearing aid buzzed. And suddenly the words 'cut off,' 'for days' and 'helicopter' all made perfect sense.

8

WARNING SIGN

'Gone?' Winston asked in disbelief.

'Gone,' Marshall confirmed.

'But it can't just be gone!' cried Charlie, still rosy and radiant from her beauty treatment. Her rosy mood, however, was a distant memory.

'Ding dong! The road is gone, the road is gone,' sang Edwina, swinging Oberon back and forth in time with the song. Oberon flicked his tongue stoically.

The others seemed to be taking the news less well.

Staying at a secluded romantic hotel to get a bit of sea air was one thing, but being in a hotel that really was isolated seemed a significantly less attractive proposition. That was what Marshall had discovered from the viewing point, a big piece of cliff had broken off overnight and plunged into the sea, taking the attached coastal road with it.

Now they were *cut off*, only accessible by *helicopter*, probably *for days*, and the *police* couldn't help them either, at least not straightaway.

The Eden, which didn't even have a footpath leading to it anymore, was no longer in Cornwall, but at the end of the earth.

After Marshall's report, Agnes had insisted on discussing the radical new development with the other housemates immediately. That was the great strength of their household, discussing things, until there was barely anything left of them. Mostly, it was about trivialities, but this was a real crisis, and they couldn't just let it pass them by.

Agnes had got Bernadette out of bed and Charlie out of the spa, ordered tea and gathered them all in the library, which was deserted at this early hour. The sun was shining, the tea was steaming, it smelt of old books, and apart from the pleasant feeling of warmth and the quality of the biscuits, they could almost have been back at home in Sunset Hall.

Agnes sighed wistfully.

Cut off.

She suddenly felt homesick.

'What now?' Charlie asked. 'How are we going to get out of here?'

'Well, for now, we aren't,' Marshall responded. 'I mean, I'm sure they'll come up with something, but it'll probably take a while.'

'Ha!' Charlie puffed up her cheeks, stressed. 'What are we going to do?'

'Have a holiday,' Agnes suggested, grabbing one of the nut balls that had been served with the tea. Delicious, but not exactly ideal for her dentures. The little pieces of nut got stuck everywhere. Agnes chewed.

Then she looked through the panoramic window and got a huge fright. The orange hood! It was back! Agnes choked on the blasted nut ball and coughed. Marshall leapt up and patted her helpfully, if a little too vigorously on the back. Despite the tears streaming down her face, Agnes could see that the hood-wearer must be a hotel employee. They weren't staring rather threateningly in her direction, but trudging away from the building armed with a chain and a sign, heading to cordon off access to the coast path. Agnes motioned for Marshall to finally stop with the patting, and tried to concentrate. Was that the mysterious hood-wearer from the day before? Unlikely. The jacket did, however, look exactly the same. A staff jacket from the housekeeping store.

She took a big gulp of tea, to finally get rid of the little piece of nut.

'Things aren't quite that bad, Agnes!' Winston patted her hand to comfort her, and even Charlie pulled herself together and poked her in the side to cheer her up.

'So, if you really think about it, we're always a bit cut off, Agnes. Think about it! We sit in Sunset Hall for weeks on end and don't step foot in the village, never mind anywhere else. At first, I thought I was going to go stir-crazy! But I didn't!' Charlie looked at them all triumphantly.

'And they cook for us here,' Bernadette added. 'There's a bar. And a functioning heating system.'

'And treatments!' Charlie cried.

'And as much warm water as you like!' Marshall added, who liked taking long showers, regularly used up all their warm water and in doing so rocked the boat a bit at Sunset Hall.

'And company!' said Winston.

'People to refill your tea!' cried Bernadette.

'The sea!' said Marshall.

'And Oberon,' cried Edwina, holding the snake up to Agnes's face to cheer her up.

Agnes was touched, and stroked Oberon's smooth tummy. Or side. Or was that his tail? Her housemates were right. It wasn't really a problem. Not yet. They would spend the coming days as planned, having beauty treatments, eating and bickering. Apart from that, it might be interesting to see how the other hotel guests reacted to the collapse of the coastal road – because no matter how hard the hotel tried to keep it quiet, it was surely only a matter of time before the news spread.

Then Agnes's thoughts returned to the orange hood. It had been standing roughly where the equally orange sign was now displayed warning against walking on the cliff-top path.

Her optimism turned to unease.

If a murderer really had been beneath the orange hood yesterday, he was now trapped in the hotel with them.

And there was nothing more dangerous than a murderer who felt trapped!

Edwina didn't really understand why the others thought the loss of the road was so noteworthy. They were on a ship. There were no roads on a ship, that should have been obvious, even to a rather unworldly person like Agnes.

The Eden was at sea, on a grand adventure, and Edwina had no time for petty-minded discussions. Apart from that, she had to take care of her contact. She stood up from the table and put Oberon back into the sports bag. Her contact was currently in a bad way, and Edwina was hoping that together she, Oberon and Lillith would manage to pep him up a bit.

The panoramic room next to the lobby had instantly become one of Bernadette's favourite places, although she gained very little from the main attraction – the alleged panorama.

She could, however, lower herself into one of the loungers, lean back and eavesdrop on some entertaining and not-so-entertaining conversations. And she was left in peace. The temperature was pleasant, it smelt of fresh sea air, and – the best thing of all – she didn't stand out in there at all. As soon as she had tucked her cane under the seat, she was just another hotel guest in sunglasses, not a blindworm to be pitied and patronised.

She stretched contentedly and let the trivial conversations babble over her like water. *That's the difference between Agnes and me*, she thought. Agnes was constantly wanting to find things out; she on the other hand was mainly trying to make sure that people found out as little as possible about her. That would suffice.

Just as she had successfully seen that thought through to its conclusion and was mentally preparing for another nap, a big, heavy hand landed on her shoulder from behind. Bernadette was instantly wide awake again and felt around fruitlessly for her cane.

'Sam! Samantha! I can't . . .' chimed a voice behind her.

A voice from the past. If the perfectly balanced lounger had allowed it, she would have fallen off her chair. Instead, she lay motionless and flat as a flounder, and listened. The hand let go of her shoulder, steps circled the deck chair. A second lounger was pulled up and then creaked under a not altogether insignificant weight. Bernadette quickly and unsentimentally made her peace with the world. The only regret she had in life was not having also tried the porridge with cinnamon, plums and butter at breakfast. That really was annoying. *Tomorrow is another day*, she'd thought to herself. Wrong!

'My God, it's really you!' said the voice, now right next to her, so quietly that Bernadette could only just hear it. Quiet, but unmistakable. Jack! 'I wasn't quite sure, but now . . . Do you need your cane? The one with the knife? Do you really want to stick me, in public, without having a coffee with me first?'

'I think I need something stronger!' Bernadette groaned.

Here was the thing, while every single person obviously has some kind of past, Bernadette had a PAST, big, loud and blazing. It was the sort of past you didn't share with relatives, or neighbours, or even your closest friends. The sort that, every now and then, when you were sitting cosily at home nibbling on fondant creams, suddenly made you freeze and listen, for quiet footsteps and restrained breaths and the swoosh of a knife in the air.

Now, decades on, her past had caught up with her, was sitting at the bar with her and ordering two more coffees laced with whisky.

Bernadette clung to the bar – warm, comforting, tactile wood – and was trying to think – unsuccessfully up to now. Why here? Why now? What to do?

'You've definitely got fat!' said the voice next to her. 'I know I'm one to talk, but you . . . Who would have thought?'

Bernadette supressed another groan. She had just been thinking that the situation couldn't get any worse, and now . . . That he had found her after all these years was catastrophe enough, but that he thought she was *fat* – unbearable! Bernadette wished the ground there on the cliffs would just open then and there and swallow her up.

She obviously knew that she'd put on a lot of weight – the legions of fondant creams, and the fact that it was difficult to jog with her cane, but up to now it had never bothered her. Quite the opposite, the weight made her more solid, gave her a feeling of security. Nothing could knock her off balance. She couldn't see herself anyway. Apart from that, she didn't give a jot about her health. It seemed nothing short of a miracle that she was still alive, and if the miracle ran out at some point, well, that was to be expected. No reason to deny yourself a good meal or a cake in the meantime. And now it was looking like a heart attack and the like as potential causes of death were receding into the distance anyway!

A knife between the ribs, at just the right spot, soundless as a thought, was far more likely. She wouldn't even notice it straightaway. Had it already happened?

She felt for her ribs, discreetly she hoped.

'Please don't get me wrong,' said the voice next to her. 'It suits you!'

'Are you looking for something, Miss Sharp? Can I help you with anything, perhaps?'

Agnes, who had tried to approach the reception as inconspicuously as possible, flinched. She looked left and right, caught red-handed, and finally spotted a bowl of apples.

'I actually just wanted an apple.' She grabbed one and then stood there a bit idiotically, apple in hand. With her false teeth, it was as good as impossible to just bite into an apple like that. She needed a plate, a sharp knife and a generous dose of patience and determination.

She spirited the apple away into her cardigan pocket and padded closer to the reception desk. Helen was standing there, the woman who had welcomed them yesterday. Today she seemed markedly less relaxed and was leafing through her bookings diary a bit desperately. The bored-looking corgi was sitting at her feet again eyeing Agnes with contempt. Agnes, who otherwise usually had a little soft spot for dogs, ogled him back.

'I was wondering . . .' she began gingerly. She wanted to find out if a member of staff was missing maybe. But she had to be clever about it.

Helen reluctantly looked up and looked at her warily.

'Yes, Miss Sharp?'

'If anybody is missing?' Agnes blurted out. 'Here at the hotel, I mean. Is anybody missing?' It wasn't exactly the diplomatic approach she'd had in mind. Agnes bit her tongue, but it was too late.

She watched as red stress blotches formed on Helen's flawless skin.

'Nobody's missing!' the reception lady shouted, almost angrily. 'Absolutely nobody!' Then she looked back at the desk as if there were something terribly important on it.

The corgi looked at Agnes with its amber eyes and sighed deeply.

'Hm,' said Agnes at a bit of a loss. 'That's alright then.'

Off she went, apple in pocket. Her question had obviously hit a nerve. Was that just the stress of suddenly being trapped in the hotel with your guests, or was somebody really missing? It was hard to say.

In any case, Agnes had done her duty for now and had earned a bit of R&R. Maybe it was about time she left all her cares behind. Uninvited and admonishingly, the image of the swinging verger flashed into her mind's eye and reminded her that now was not the time for relaxation. Murderers didn't just hand themselves in of their own accord.

But she had at least earned a snack! Was it already lunch-time? Agnes made her way to the dining room just in case.

Edwina, Charlie, Winston and Marshall were already waiting at the table, peacefully immersed in their spelt soup with beetroot crisps.

Charlie spotted Agnes and waved at her with a rather indecent-looking wholegrain stick. 'Yoo-hoo! Agnes! Over here!'

Agnes joined her housemates, hell-bent on finally enjoying herself a little.

The soup smelt promising, Marshall poured her a glass of white wine, and the pianist at the other end of the room switched to a rather snappy version of 'Dust in the Wind.' There we go!

'We obviously would have waited for you both,' said Marshall apologetically. 'But you were nowhere to be found. We thought we'd meet you both here anyway.'

Both.

Oh.

Where was Bernadette?

Agnes looked frantically every which way, on the lookout for a fat person wearing sunglasses and a random selection of clothing. Nothing.

That was out of character, at the very least. Where food was concerned, Bernadette was regular as clockwork, perhaps even more so. Agnes realised she was starting to worry again. That was why she couldn't just relax! Every time she lost sight of one of her housemates for five minutes, she feared foul play.

Winston noticed the look on her face and patted her hand soothingly. 'Don't worry, Agnes. Nobody's pushed Bernadette off the cliff! How would they even manage it?'

He was obviously right. It would have taken a champion wrestler to heave Bernadette off the terrace.

She felt so light. And woozy. And giddy.

Bernadette leant on the wall – a show of weakness she would never have allowed herself under normal circumstances. But at that moment, she needed all the support she could get. Too hot. She was freezing. Had he perhaps slipped something in her coffee? It wasn't really his style, on the other hand, the decades could well change a man and his *modus operandi*.

She gasped for air. The ground didn't seem stable anymore, but was swaying beneath her feet, as if she were on a ship. Her cane slipped from her hand and clattered to the floor.

Bad. Very bad.

Especially now, since she had so many questions, How had Jack found her? Was he still angry with her? And how had he been since that fateful Sunday morning all those years ago, when he'd waited on a bench in vain, full of hope, while the police were arresting the boss and his gang in the stinking warehouse at the harbour?

She might not look it, but inside, Bernadette was kind of like a bat, always all ears. Nothing got past her, not the slightest sound. That's why her world was never completely silent. Something was always stirring.

Except now that is.

She sank to the ground, and a great silence spread within her, like a flood.

9

ICE CREAM

Oberon the snake was lying in the bathtub missing Paradise. In Paradise there was sand, and stones offering hiding places, branches you could rub yourself against, and there was a deep, cool basin filled with refreshing water.

Above all, there was her. Her skin was even paler than his own, her hair was a fair forest you could sink your head into, her voice like the wind. She liked to dance with him on her shoulders. Sometimes they danced together.

But then something in Paradise had gone awry, hadn't it?

He had turned up, rude and rough and insensitive, without any understanding of the delicate balance of the world at all. He had claimed her skin, her hands and thoughts, and her hair.

The shoulders had eluded Oberon. The forest of fair hair had been tied up. Hands had packed him into an uncomfortable crate more and more often.

Then a journey, a journey through the darkness.

Suddenly there was salt in the air, and salt dripped from her eyes in big tears onto his head, burning his skin.

It went steadily downhill from there, quite literally.

Oberon found himself in the dust again, on the ground, or in this case, the carpet. His usual vantage point on the shoulders was routinely denied him. She was spending too much time in bed, flat and useless, and her hands, whose job it was to stroke his skin, mostly just lay there lifeless and dumb, or they wasted their time wrestling, one hand against another. Sometimes inner tempests shook her delicate body, sometimes she swallowed little round things and lay in a stupor.

Oberon the snake was ignored.

Then the day had come that would bring with it an even more drastic change. And yet it had begun quite well, that's to say, she finally pulled herself together and let Oberon occupy his traditional position on her shoulders. But catastrophe was already in the air, a storm brewing and gathering strength, barely more than a whisper.

Somebody had whispered something to her.

Oberon had sensed the muscles beneath her fair skin contract and become hard and fragile, like glass. Then she had got up abruptly and strode off with him, but instead of feeling a sense of triumph up on her shoulders, he had been worried.

Something hadn't been right with her.

She'd gone off without giving him so much as a second thought.

As if she'd already forgotten him, but not just him – the world and maybe even herself too.

And now she was nothing but a memory, and he was sitting there in the bathtub in a pool of warm light. It was better than the crate, but it was no Paradise.

Sooner or later, he would take a shot at returning to Paradise, that much was clear.

Probably later.

He'd consumed a juicy rabbit just a week ago, complete with skin and fur, so he felt rather full and sluggish.

Digest a bit first, for a week or two, then see.

Later was soon enough.

Paradise could wait.

Edwina only opened the door a crack at first, to make sure the coast was clear. Literally speaking, of course, the coast at the Eden was definitely clear after the storm, but what about in the figurative sense? Edwina stuck her head out into the hallway. In the distance, two women wearing blue aprons busied themselves at a trolley of pillows and towels, but neither her former roommate Charlie, nor Agnes, were anywhere to be seen. Edwina closed the door. She wasn't sure what to make of the room swap. Charlie was nervy, she got worked up about the slightest little thing and even found fault with Oberon, the most perfect snake in the world. Agnes, on the other hand, was less nervy, but she was nobody's fool, and it wouldn't be easy to hide the fact that one of the wardrobes was now housing not just Lillith and Hettie II, but also a pale and somewhat hysterical young man.

Edwina opened the wardrobe door and the whippersnapper gave a start.

'Hello, young man!' she said cheerily. 'Hello, Lillith!'

Her friend in the tin was as stoic as ever, but the whippersnapper actually looked even worse than Edwina had remembered. His eyes were small and puffy, a blue five o'clock shadow blemished his chin, and his hair was standing up in the most unlikely of directions. Apart from that, he stank. Was this really her contact? Where on earth did the Secret Service get their staff from nowadays?

Edwina sighed.

'We need to talk, young man!'

'Mojo,' the whippersnapper mumbled. 'I'm called Mojo. And I'm pretty desperate for the loo.'

Edwina nodded. 'The bathroom's over there. I'll keep watch. And I suggest you wash your face afterwards too.' Even Edwina expected certain standards of the people she was working with.

Mojo the whippersnapper awkwardly peeled himself out of the wardrobe and staggered over to the bathroom.

'And if you scare Oberon, you'll have me to deal with!' Edwina threatened.

A yowling sound suggested that it was more likely the other way round, and the whippersnapper returned surprisingly quickly from the bathroom. The eye make-up residue had disappeared and he looked younger and paler than ever before.

'Well, don't just stand there,' Edwina urged him. 'What if Agnes turns up? Agnes has lots of opinions, on tortoises and snakes and remote controls and desserts – and on you too, I shouldn't wonder. It's best if she's none the wiser.'

To her surprise, Mojo didn't toddle off out of the room as she had expected, but climbed awkwardly back into the wardrobe. It puzzled her a bit. Most of the people Edwina knew preferred to spend their time outside of wardrobes, but luckily this one was spacious, and apart from Edwina's sports bag, airless Hettie II and Lillith, it was completely empty.

'You chill?' the whippersnapper asked once he had made himself comfortable again.

Edwina nodded hesitantly. He could just sit there if he didn't have anything better to do with his holiday. She remembered her manners and tapped on Lillith's coffee tin.

'This is Mojo,' she declared to her former housemate. 'He'll be sharing the wardrobe with you, until the coast is clear. And that's Lillith,' she seamlessly continued. 'Unfortunately, she's dead, but she's still a very good friend. I think you'll get on well.'

Edwina was content. The formalities had been observed, now they could finally have a good chat, agent to agent.

After lunch, Agnes tried to get her housemates interested in looking for Bernadette, but she was banging her head against a brick wall. The pensioners of Sunset Hall had no desire to spend their whole holiday looking for something, first Edwina, then a murderer and now to top it all, Bernadette as well. It wasn't Easter after all. And apart from that, the Eden had enough other entertainment on offer. Charlie had signed herself up for organic wine tasting, Marshall and Winston wanted to go on a behind-the-scenes guided tour and get a closer look at the hotel's state-of-the-art heating system; Edwina and Oberon had already disappeared.

It was only Agnes who just couldn't relax.

'Why don't you come behind the scenes with us?' Marshall asked soothingly. 'Bernadette can look after herself!'

Agnes looked at him, aggrieved. 'But she didn't come to lunch! Bernadette *always* comes to lunch!'

'It's maybe a bit out of character,' Charlie conceded, 'but then again, it's not that unusual. We normally hang around together all of the time, perhaps Bernadette just needs a bit of space. Distance. You know, Agnes, holidays are meant to be for letting go and trying something new. Just look at the detox group!'

Agnes looked doubtfully over at the detox crew, who were sitting at one of the neighbouring tables hungrily nibbling on crudités. She tried to imagine Bernadette amongst them, big and colourful and cynical. She did not manage it. No, Bernadette was not the type to try things out. Something had to be wrong.

Agnes got up, determined. 'I'll take a look around!' She had ignored the dead verger; she wouldn't make a mistake like that again in a hurry. Apathy – it was one of the worst things about old age! Apathy!

The rest of the household looked at her pityingly.

Only once she was out in the corridor did it dawn on Agnes that she had absolutely no desire to trudge fruitlessly through the hotel again like a lame hen. It would be much nicer to just sit somewhere, preferably in a soft armchair, and look out at the sea. And if she bumped into Bernadette in the process, all the better!

The Eden was full of cosy nooks, soft armchairs and grandiose panoramic windows, and Agnes found it hard to decide. Finally, she chose somewhere between the lobby and the Sea Lounge, partially hidden behind some artistically arranged dried branches. From there she could not only keep an eye on the cliffs, but also the goings-on in the hotel.

140

There!

She was sitting down.

Her hip was glad.

It was quiet in the hotel, the reception was abandoned – logical really, after all, currently nobody could either arrive or depart. For a while, Agnes dutifully kept a lookout for Bernadette, but when nothing happened, her eyes lingered more and more often on the natural spectacle out there. Not even three o'clock, but the light was already slipping away. The sky shimmered with colour, red and yellow, orange, purple and, well, sky-blue. The dark sea threw itself at the black cliffs.

It was a long way down.

Suddenly, Agnes felt like she really was on holiday.

A holiday was more than a change of location.

A holiday was motion, inside and out.

A holiday meant everything changed.

She looked down at the sea and was almost a little scared of the motion that had seized her and all of the other guests there. Edwina hadn't been so wrong at all, the Eden was a kind of ship! Just as ocean liners split the sea, the Eden splits time, the glassy carrot nose always out in front.

Unrelenting, unstoppable, towards an uncertain end.

'Apparently there's going to be an ice-cream buffet here in an hour!' someone suddenly ranted next to Agnes. 'Ice-cream buffet! That's never happened before!'

Agnes spun around and discovered the White Widow, perfectly camouflaged in a white armchair that was even better hidden than her own. The corgi on her lap was snootier than ever before, as if he and Agnes had never struggled up a staircase together in solidarity.

'Yikes!' she said in surprise. Then she was annoyed. Not exactly eloquent, since she wanted to make a competent impression, especially on the White Widow.

'Maybe it's organic ice cream?' she said hesitantly. Not exactly ingenious either.

'Of course it's organic ice cream. That's not the point!' hissed the White Widow as she stroked the corgi slightly aggressively behind the ears. With the furry animal on her lap, she suddenly looked like a Bond villain.

'And what is the point?' Agnes turned in her chair, as far as her hip and neck would allow, and looked into the Widow's eyes.

Blue.

Blue, blue eyes, alert and piercing somehow.

'The point is, it's new,' said the White Widow. 'And it's wrong. People come here to re-energise, for some healthy living. Not to stuff themselves full of ice cream. Nothing like this has ever happened here before!'

A new theory for why people came to the Eden. To patch up relationships, according to Howard. To re-energise, said the White Widow. Agnes wondered why on earth the murderer had come. Just to murder? Or had another purpose brought him here?

'And why are you here?' she said out of curiosity.

'To remember,' responded the White Widow and looked wistfully out at the sea. 'And you?'

For a moment, Agnes was tempted to say something deep and meaningful, but then she decided to tell the truth.

'Because our boiler broke,' she admitted.

The White Widow seemed to like that. She chuckled softly and offered Agnes an unusually big and strong hand. 'I'm Marie,' she said.

Agnes looked startled. 'Agnes,' she said finally and took her hand. 'Agnes Sharp.'

The handshake lasted far too long for Agnes's liking.

The Widow gently pushed the corgi off her lap and got up. Agnes looked her up and down. White sweatshirt. White jogging bottoms. White trainers. She was tall, and somehow all the white made her appear even taller, especially when a short-legged corgi was standing next to her.

'I'll be off then, so this stupid ice-cream buffet doesn't ruin my mood. And I'd be careful if I were you!'

'Careful?' Agnes's heart was suddenly in her mouth.

The Widow grinned. 'Well, you know, with all the ice cream. It's not exactly healthy!' With that, she strode off, one white trainer in front of the other. When she moved, she looked younger – and like a panther, despite the colour.

Agnes watched after her, her heart pounding. Had the woman just threatened her? She didn't like it. She suddenly felt anything but safe in her hidden armchair in the lonely lobby. She struggled up to get out of there. Maybe Bernadette was back in their room – and if not, an ice-cream buffet was the ideal place to look for her.

It turned out that Bernadette had long since been found. She was lying in bed, a bit pale, Agnes thought, surrounded by Charlie, Edwina and Oberon, who were all trying to convince her to go to the ice-cream buffet.

Very out of character.

'Are you ill?' Agnes asked in concern.

Bernadette shook her head. 'I just felt a bit dizzy back then. It'll be alright.'

'That's because you missed lunch,' Edwina said, and waggled her finger admonishingly, although Bernadette couldn't see any of it. 'But you're bound to feel better after the ice-cream buffet. *Everyone* is going. They even postponed my meditation.'

'And my wine tasting,' huffed Charlie.

Bernadette sat up jerkily. 'Everyone, you say?'

'Definitely,' Charlie confirmed. 'They've really been touting it.'

Oberon flicked his tongue angrily, as if the ice-cream buffet had messed up an important appointment for him too.

'Then I'm going too!' Bernadette was already out of bed. She swayed a bit, grabbed her cane and headed for the door, as if she were afraid that the whole ice-cream buffet would melt away.

She suddenly stopped partway.

'How do I look?'

Agnes, Charlie and Edwina stared at her wide-eyed and speechless. Bernadette worried about her appearance. Unheard of!

Edwina was the first to recover from the shock. 'Like you!' she reported.

That analysis didn't seem to satisfy Bernadette. 'And, err, what about what I'm wearing?' She pointed vaguely down at herself.

'It's a nice skirt,' Agnes said neutrally. The fact that it gave Bernadette the air of a circus elephant was better left unsaid.

'Describe it to me!' Bernadette pressed.

'It . . . It's blue,' Agnes said, at a loss for words. 'Ankle-length. Just a skirt. The fabric shimmers a bit . . .' She broke off. What sense did it make to describe something when Bernadette didn't know what 'blue' meant – and 'shimmer'? What on earth did she want from them?

'It's like the sea,' Edwina said helpfully. 'Just like the sea.'

'Like the sea!' Bernadette sighed with relief. 'That's good, isn't it?'

'Very good!' Agnes confirmed.

Bernadette clutched her cane more tightly and was already halfway out of the room when something else dawned on her. 'And . . . does it make me look fat?'

Charlie choked and started to cough heavily.

It was the last straw for Agnes. For years, Bernadette had tormented everyone in the household with outrageous ragged jumpers and perverse colour combinations, and now she wanted to know how she *looked*. And *not fat* into the bargain – after all the fondant creams she had demolished, practically single-handedly.

'It doesn't *make* you look fat,' she said acerbically. 'You *are* fat!'

'Ah. Hmm. Yeah.' Bernadette pulled a disappointed face. 'Well, nothing can be done about that, can it?' She sighed deeply and then she was out of the door.

Charlie, Edwina, Agnes and Oberon looked at one another.

'Make her look fat!' Agnes ranted to herself. 'It's just . . . What on earth is the matter with Bernadette?'

Edwina shrugged. 'She's in love!'

145

Here was the thing, if Edwina ever happened to see something clearly, it was clear as day. In love! Of course. There was no other possible explanation for the sudden obsession with her appearance and being fat!

'In love!' Agnes had to sit down. 'But who with?'

Just then, something tightened in her stomach. With Howard? There was no specific reason for it to be Howard of all people, but once the idea had established itself, it was hard to shake off.

Edwina stroked Oberon's triangular snakehead with her index finger. 'Probably with a man.' She thought for a moment. 'Or maybe with a woman.'

Then she fell silent, pleased to have described the situation so accurately.

Agnes heaved herself out of the chair, sighing, and tugged at her hair in the mirror. It was beyond help. But at least her cardigan was buttoned up correctly this time. She considered putting on lipstick, but decided against it due to time constraints, and rushed to the door.

'Where are you going?' Edwina asked.

'To the weird ice-cream buffet!' Agnes declared. The hunt for the Eden murderer had faded into the background for the time being. There was a much bigger mystery to solve.

'I've got to find out who it is!'

There really was a lot going on. Agnes had never seen so many hotel guests in one go. Staff, however, were rather thin on the ground, and so it was every man for himself at the buffet, armed with ice-cream bowl and spoon. The atmosphere was tense, feverish almost.

Was that normal when a crowd of people who had been fed healthily for days were suddenly let loose on calorific foods, or was there something else behind it? Most of the hotel guests must have found out by now that there was no escape from the Eden right now. How had they taken the news? Were they worried? Were they angry? What was going on in all of the well-coiffed and not-so-well-coiffed heads crowding round the ice-cream buffet?

Agnes, who was vaguely interested in the chocolate ice cream and the plum sorbet, made two half-hearted attempts to push to the front row, and got an elbow in the ribs for starters, then a shove from behind, then someone stood on her foot with a pointed heel. She gave up in the end. She was too old to tussle with strangers over a dessert, and if she was honest, too full as well.

Instead, she sat at a free table and kept a lookout for familiar faces. There was the chap with the pastel suits again, happily shovelling colour-matched ice cream. The whole detox group was in the front row, their eyes gleaming feverishly. Sugar rush.

And there was Bernadette, unmistakable in her puffy mermaid skirt. She hadn't dared to venture to the buffet either, but was sitting expectantly at a table seemingly listening for something.

Then, suddenly a man was standing next to her. Agnes hadn't seen him coming, and even Bernadette seemed surprised for a moment. The man was holding a bowl of ice cream in each hand and looked like an overweight penguin, plump, but kind, his grey hair dashingly combed back with pomade.

Agnes craned her neck.

The man put one of the bowls of ice cream on the table in front of Bernadette, then he leant forward and whispered something into her ear. Agnes almost fell off her chair – Bernadette didn't let anybody get that close to her ear, especially not a stranger, especially not from the side.

She waited for the penguin to get what was coming to him, probably a well-aimed blow from the cane. But no, the cane leant neglected against the wall, and Bernadette blushed. All of a sudden, she really didn't look like a circus elephant, but pretty, in a well-fed kind of a way.

The penguin was her admirer, no doubt about it! How on earth had he managed to sidle up to Bernadette so quickly? And how . . .

Just then, something strange happened. The man had sat down next to her friend and started eating his ice cream. Bernadette said something. The penguin laughed softly, but his dark eyes weren't focused on Bernadette, they wandered seemingly casually through the room.

And then he saw Agnes, or rather, he saw that Agnes was watching him. All the friendliness drained from his eyes, until they were as hard as black glass. Suddenly he didn't look like a penguin at all, but a lone shark, smooth and dangerous. Then the moment passed and the man turned back to Bernadette and laughed a really very congenial laugh.

Agnes blinked. Had she just imagined the whole thing?

'Like Christmas, huh?'

Agnes gave a start. Trudy from the detox group, armed with a generous bowl of ice cream, plonked herself merrily down in the chair next to her and shovelled away. Her cheeks were glowing.

'Bon appetit,' Agnes said politely.

Trudy grinned. 'You can say that again! Nothing but rabbit food for days, and now this. To be honest with you, I don't think I would have kept it up much longer.' She leant over to Agnes and whispered, 'I started seeing things.'

'What sort of things?' Agnes asked out of interest.

'Oh, mostly food. I think there's a bar of chocolate on my bedside table, and when I go to bite into it, it's only the remote control. Or I see doughnuts, where there aren't any doughnuts.' She sighed. 'But the thing yesterday was a real warning sign!'

'A Bundt cake?' Agnes asked sympathetically.

Trudy shook her head. 'A man! It was late and I was in the gym, to . . . well, I wanted to see if someone had maybe left an energy bar behind. I know, I know . . . I'm not proud of it either, but I felt so lacklustre . . . and then . . .'

She broke off and ate a few spoonfuls of ice cream to keep her going. Agnes nodded encouragingly.

'So, the light was off in the gym because I didn't want anybody to see me, especially not our trainer . . .' Trudy shuddered. 'And there's a window that looks out onto the hallway so that everyone can see how hard we're all training. And suddenly this man drifted past outside. It was like on the television. That's why I wasn't scared, I think. It was exactly like it is on the television.'

'Was he wearing a jacket?' Agnes asked.

Trudy gave her a funny look. That wasn't the reaction she had been expecting.

'He was carrying a woman,' she said. 'A dripping-wet woman. Bare shoulders and really fair hair, like melting snow, and then this sopping-wet, blood-red dress . . . He

149

was carrying her very carefully, as if he didn't want to wake her.'

Trudy broke off and demolished the waffle crowning her bowl of ice cream. 'Her head was resting on his shoulder and making a wet patch on his jumper. It made me feel a bit uneasy. I don't usually imagine things in such detail. And then when he was almost past the window, a wisp of hair slipped from her face, and I saw her eyes. They were open. And fixed. Like . . . ice.'

Trudy paused and picked up the spoon again. 'Not a nice vision. In future, I'd rather imagine doughnuts.' She laughed drily.

'You must have got quite a shock,' said Agnes sympathetically.

Trudy shook her head. 'I knew straightaway that it wasn't real. I mean, as if, here in the hotel! I was only shocked later, when I came out of the gym. There was . . . water. Little puddles. As if someone had carried a dripping-wet woman past. But they'd probably just mopped the corridor.'

'Probably,' said Agnes.

Trudy looked a bit fresher now and polished off the rest of her ice cream with gusto. 'But now I've finally got something in my belly,' she said. 'Nothing like that's going to happen to me again in a hurry!'

She winked at Agnes and rushed back to the buffet, presumably to get seconds and to banish visions of doughnuts and sopping-wet women from her mind forever more. Agnes stayed where she was, deep in thought.

Obviously, Trudy hadn't just imagined the whole thing. Nobody conjured up men out of thin air, men carrying sopping-wet corpses through the spa area. No, that had really happened, and it didn't quite fit with what she had witnessed on the cliffs at all. Was it possible that the orange hood hadn't pushed a living person into the sea? Had it been about disposing of a body from the get-go?

She tried to call the cliff dance of the two hoods to mind. Maybe it hadn't been an embrace at all? Had the orange hood been carrying the yellow one? It would have required quite some physical strength, but it wasn't impossible!

'Don't you want any ice cream, Agnes?'

Agnes was shocked out of her thoughts. Howard was standing right behind her, looking at her with the innocent eyes of a scholar. How long had he been standing there? And what did her hair look like from that angle? Pretty flat probably.

'Howard!' Agnes felt herself blush and was annoyed. Why?

'How wonderful to see you!' Howard beamed at her. 'I thought I'd bring you an ice cream. It's a bit of a scrum over there!'

He did indeed have a bowl of ice cream, not plum and chocolate as she had wanted, but chocolate and vanilla at least. A classic combination! Agnes gratefully reached out her hand, and Howard passed her the bowl. Their fingers touched, Agnes's warm and dry, Howard's cool and somewhat sticky, presumably from the ice cream.

Just then, Marshall entered the room and looked around frantically. When he caught sight of Agnes and Howard, both their hands on the same bowl of ice-cream, he stopped dead, thunderstruck.

Agnes hastily put the bowl down and folded her hands

in her lap. She felt like she'd been caught red-handed and didn't really know why. After all, she had the right to eat as much ice cream as she liked!

Howard bent down towards her and whispered a 'See you later!' as Marshall homed in on her like a battleship. Then Howard had suddenly disappeared and Marshall stopped in front of her, a bit breathless.

'Hello, Agnes!' he said.

'Hello, Marshall,' Agnes responded, slightly miffed. Why did Marshall have to stick his oar in every time she spoke to Howard? And why the rush? She was on holiday after all!

'Err, yeah,' Marshall mumbled looking around frantically again. 'Could you perhaps quickly . . . ?'

'No!' Agnes interrupted him. 'I'm quite happy here eating my ice cream.' She looked surreptitiously at the bowl. It was too warm in there. Howard's ice cream had started to morph into an unattractive brown soup, and a chocolatey drip had already landed on the white tablecloth.

Then she saw that Marshall must have got ice cream on himself as well, on his cuff and sleeve. But she realised straightaway that no ice cream was that red, not even plum.

Her heart stopped for a moment, then it started pounding away again, in big frantic leaps.

Marshall had blood on his sleeve! And he was looking at her pleadingly!

10

WARDROBE

Agnes was back in her room digesting something even colder than ice cream, murder!

There was good news and there was bad news.

The good news was that the blood on Marshall's sleeve wasn't his own.

The bad news was that there was a lot more where that blood came from.

A whole pool of it.

A little dark-red, gradually curdling lake.

And in it . . .

To think it had all started with Marshall and Winston wanting to relax.

They had made their way to the lobby at the agreed time to take part in the behind-the-scenes tour. Apart from the two of them, nobody else seemed to be interested in the goings-on behind the scenes, so Marshall and Winston were the only ones guided through a grey and somewhat unspectacular door by a spotty youngster.

The youngster had unlocked the door for them and smiled broadly. 'Welcome to the heart of the Eden,' he had said.

Similar to a real heart, the Eden's heart consisted of a series of chambers too, all fulfilling important functions. There were heat pumps that somehow magically kept the hotel warm, there were cold stores, drying and storage rooms, an in-house smokery and a huge kitchen.

They had already been on the go for a little while, and the enthusiastic youngster was just about to unlock the door to the pool pump room to show them the sophisticated filtration system that cleaned the water in the swimming pool without chlorine, but then he had stopped, because the walkie-talkie on his belt had squeaked. He had listened in to the device and then squeaked too. Winston and Marshall had watched all the enthusiasm drain from his face, as he had gone pale and said 'Jesus!' twice and 'right away' three times.

After that, the behind-the-scenes smile was a bit wonky.

'The tour ends here today!' the youngster had declared breathlessly. 'Unfortunately, I've got to . . . Please wait here. I'll send someone to take you back to the lobby.'

Then he had turned around and rushed away along the corridor, in such a haste that he almost lost a shoe.

Marshall and Winston had exchanged conspiratorial glances. The youngster had forgotten to lock the door again, and they were still curious about the filtration system in the pool pump room . . .

'And there he was,' declared Marshall.

'On the ground,' Winston added.

'Blood everywhere!' Marshall sighed and looked angrily at the brown stains tarnishing his cuffs.

'Dead?' Agnes asked.

'As a dodo,' said Winston.

'Stone-dead,' Marshall confirmed.

'You can't get much deader than that,' Winston added for good measure.

'A fall?' Charlie asked.

'Beaten to death,' Marshall explained with utter conviction.

'With this,' Winston said, conjuring a transparent plastic bag from the depths of his wheelchair bag. There was a red mess in the plastic bag. It took a while for Agnes to make out the outline of a metal dumbbell.

'You took the murder weapon?' Just a few hours ago she had been having difficulties getting her housemates interested in the investigation at all! Agnes couldn't believe it. 'What on earth were you . . .'

'We didn't want the murderer to spirit it away,' Marshall explained.

'He must have a key after all,' Winston mumbled.

'But how does that look?' Charlie groaned and wrung her hands. 'When the police get here . . .'

'That's the other thing.' Winston sighed. 'We don't think the police are coming. Or not very quickly at least.'

Marshall reported how they had examined the crime scene and taken photos. Afterwards they made their way back to the other side of the pool pump room door and waited to be picked up as promised. When nobody came, they had gone off on their own, had got thoroughly lost and finally managed to get back to the hotel's guest areas next to reception. There, they had come across Helen, surrounded by a small but bewildered troop of hotel employees straining to hear on the telephone and shouting 'Dead! Dead! Dead!'

She didn't mean the murder victim.

She meant the phone.

It looked like either the storm, or something else, had cut the hotel's phone line.

Edwina did not approve of all the excitement. She had been able to spirit Mojo away into the wardrobe just in the nick of time before Agnes, Charlie, Marshall and Winston had descended. Now her contact was trapped, probably pressing his big, deer-in-headlights eyes to the thin crack in the wardrobe door, and getting paler and paler as the conversation developed, a bit like the moon. All this talk of murder and telephone cables being down would be the final straw for his already frayed nerves.

She had to admit that something wasn't quite right with Mojo. The way he sometimes spoke and laughed and swallowed and trembled, all at the same time. Like someone . . . Now, she'd heard of people who were a sandwich short, who weren't quite right in the head, and the more she talked to Mojo, the surer she was that he was, well, addled. In any case, he got unnecessarily agitated about a lot of things and was still refusing to leave the wardrobe.

During their conversations up to now, Edwina had managed to identify three problem areas,

First off, he didn't have any gear, and that was his grandmother's fault, the old witch. Edwina had first offered him a hotel blanket, and then her favourite knitted jumper, to no avail. Neither of them seemed to be the right kind of gear. The right kind of gear was nowhere to be found, either there in the room or anywhere in this dump of a hotel.

The second problem was the disappearance of the

internet. It had taken its leave of Mojo's little mobile phone this morning, and he missed it painfully. Edwina had nothing against the internet, it was useful when you wanted to watch tortoise videos, order things or win prize draws, but she didn't understand why Mojo was taking it to heart like he was. Apparently, he had followers who would *flip out* if they didn't hear anything from him for just a few hours. As it had turned out, Mojo's followers weren't at the hotel, but somewhere a long way away. Edwina wondered what the point in followers was if they didn't even follow you.

The third and most pressing problem had led Mojo first onto her balcony, and then into the wardrobe. He was absolutely convinced that something terrible had happened to him last night, or had almost happened, or was still happening. Now he had to hide. Delusional, no doubt, but the tales of murder that Winston and Marshall were harping on about would just give even more wings to his existing flight of fancy.

Edwina sighed. How was she supposed to concentrate on her mission with all of this excitement?

'Still, at least we now know that there really is a murderer on the loose!' Agnes couldn't suppress a certain sense of satisfaction.

'Hurrah!' Charlie said drily.

'And a victim,' Winston reminded them. 'Probably more than one even. What do we know about the victim?'

Agnes put on her reading glasses as Marshall showed her the photos of the crime scene on his phone. Not exactly tidy. Someone really had gone for it, and the victim's face was, well, Agnes was no great art connoisseur, but *abstract* seemed like the right word for it. The body, however, was completely unscathed and strikingly pale. A man, rather athletic and not that old. He was wearing a vest and jogging bottoms. His flip-flops had made a bid for freedom and were lying quite a way from the victim, as if they were trying to make a run for it under their own steam. Agnes couldn't blame them.

'It could be anyone,' she said. 'A hotel guest on their way to the fitness area or an off-duty employee. Maybe someone who had just got changed? You can't really tell.'

Charlie had now found her reading glasses, she took a quick look at the image and groaned. 'Oh God. That's really . . . The poor mite! I mean, Why? Who would do such a thing?' She looked around imploringly, presumably for the minibar.

Agnes nodded. Valid questions. In principle, there were two types of murder. One was designed to solve a problem, the other was, well, just for fun.

To pass the time.

For entertainment.

So, either the murderer was particularly stressed and beset with problems, or he was in the process of really unwinding. Or was he maybe mixing business with pleasure, killing two birds with one stone, as it were?

Up to now she had assumed that the killer was a practically minded murderer. After all, pushing someone off a cliff was a discreet, tidy and not particularly risky affair. How would the people at the hotel put it? A small footprint? Exactly.

What happened in the pool pump room, however, had left behind a considerable, and, moreover, bloody footprint. Discreet it was not. Someone had let loose, got carried away, with little regard for the consequences. Were there maybe

158

two killers at work – one more practically minded and a bloodthirsty nutcase? Unlikely in such a small, exclusive hotel. But it wasn't impossible.

'When did it happen?' Agnes, Winston and Marshall leant over Marshall's phone. Charlie, however, had started flinging cupboard doors open, and Edwina had taken up warrior pose again.

'Difficult to say,' Marshall mumbled. 'Seemed pretty fresh to me.'

'Today, an hour or two ago,' Winston guessed. 'Or three at most.'

He shrugged. None of them were experts.

'Ha!' Charlie let out a shrill, triumphant scream. Agnes spun around, but her housemate had just located the minibar. With a practised hand, she poured herself a gin and tonic, and sank into one of the comfortable hotel armchairs with a sigh. 'There. That's better. Anyone else for a drink?'

Agnes felt a bit queasy after the horrid picture and let Marshall pour her a whisky.

They toasted; nobody could say exactly what to – maybe just to the fact that it hadn't been them instead of the guy in the vest.

And come to think of it, that was definitely a cause for celebration.

'If you could undress, please. And get yourself nice and comfortable.' The young woman smiled and pointed enthusiastically at a medical-looking bed.

Agnes stared at her aghast.

'I am undressed!'

'But not down below!' The masseuse wasn't letting up.

'Don't worry, it's all very discreet. I'll leave you alone for a moment. And when you're ready, cover yourself with the towel, and I'll be right back.'

Agnes could tell she meant business.

As soon as the masseuse had left the room, she ripped her clothes from her body in record time and rushed over to the bed. Without her support stockings and slip she felt like a tortoise without its shell. Vulnerable. Exposed.

For a panic-filled moment, it looked like she wouldn't make it onto the bed under her own steam, but then she managed to get her bottom on, and not a second too soon.

Agnes had barely wrapped the towel around her body, and the masseuse was back.

'So, are you nice and relaxed, Miss Sharp?' she chirped.

Agnes could hear her heart beating. What had she let herself in for?

The whole thing had obviously been Charlie's idea.

'We're on holiday,' she'd said. 'Murder or no murder. It's more important than ever that we spoil ourselves. I'm guessing the guy in the vest would be jolly glad right now if he had treated himself to a massage last night!'

You couldn't really argue with that, so Agnes had let Charlie drag her into the spa area, slightly tipsy and, against her better judgement, curious about the first massage of her life.

Now she was stuck, naked and wrapped in a towel like a newborn. And as usual she only had herself to blame.

'Have a little sniff!' Even now, after Agnes had obediently turned onto her tummy, the masseuse wasn't going to leave her in peace. 'I'm just going to hold some of our foraged scented oils for you to smell, just let me know which one you like.'

The bed had an oval opening through which Agnes could see the treatment room's marble floor, a bit like a toilet seat, but for your face. Not a very appealing thought!

A little bottle appeared under Agnes's nose.

She sniffed. What else could she do?

'The first oil is a lovely mix of rose and rosemary,' the masseuse gushed. 'Fresh and zesty. A bit like the sea!'

Agnes could only smell rose at first, but then the sea really did materialise, wild and foaming, and before she knew what was happening the orange hood was there again too, staring at her threateningly.

'Not that one!' she said quickly.

'As you wish,' responded the masseuse. She sounded a bit offended. What was she called again? Violet or Scarlet, some kind of colour name. Lilac? Agnes was almost certain she was called Lilac.

The little bottle was taken away and a new one appeared.

'This is our woodiest fragrance,' Lilac explained. 'Wonderful for meditating and inner peace!'

The forest fragrance really wasn't bad, and Agnes was up for a bit of inner peace. But before she could say anything, Lilac whipped out a third little bottle. Agnes took a sniff. If this carried on, Agnes would soon be a master sniffer like Brexit the wolfhound.

There were warm notes of pine and leather that reminded Agnes of something pleasant.

'Yes! That one!' she said into the hole.

From now on, all Agnes needed to do was breathe deeply and think 'nice thoughts,' while Lilac got to work on her feet. How hard could it be?

Initially, Agnes thought about the fact that she had been right – being right was always a nice thought, especially when you had to deal with Charlie, Edwina, and Marshall day in and day out! Nobody had taken what she had seen seriously, but she hadn't just imagined the thing on the cliffs – there really was a murderer on the loose in the hotel! Now he had struck again – quite literally! And the pensioners of Sunset Hall had work to do.

First and foremost, it was obviously about not falling victim to the murderer themselves. Were the attacks random, or was there a plan? Agnes guessed there was a plan, and he would probably adapt his plan as soon as he realised that she and her companions were hot on his heels. They had to be careful!

Secondly, it was obviously desirable to prevent any further murders. Normally the police were responsible for things like that, but with no road or phone, that would presumably fall to them too.

With a bit of a fright, it dawned on Agnes that despite all their shortcomings, she and her housemates were probably the most criminologically qualified people at the hotel. An unsettling thought.

A hand slapped her backside. Agnes flinched, but it was only Lilac, who had now worked her way towards the centre of her body.

'Miss Sharp,' she chided, 'I can feel a lot of tension. Let yourself fall, like a . . . like a . . .'

Murder victim, thought Agnes, but Lilac was out of ideas, and just carried on mutely with the massage.

Agnes didn't allow herself to be rattled. Thirdly, she had to make sure, despite all the odd questions she would presumably have to ask in the course of her investigation, that she didn't rouse suspicions amongst the other guests or the hotel management. The possession of a bloody murder weapon would not look good, for instance.

'Miss Sharp!' Lilac admonished. 'You're not relaxing! Give your thoughts free reign!'

Agnes would have gladly spun round and explained to the masseuse that it was precisely those thoughts with free reign that were the problem, but she remembered just in time that she didn't have a scrap of clothing on, and stayed where she was.

Finally, there was also a fourth thing to consider, the more she thought about it, the surer she was that she wanted to enjoy her holiday despite all the complications. Life was short, that had just been dramatically demonstrated to them, and Agnes was suddenly hell-bent on making the most of her holiday.

There! She felt more relaxed already!

Lilac was now pummelling her back. It was a bit disconcerting being touched like that – Agnes couldn't remember when last someone had touched her bare back, but it wasn't unpleasant. Ethereal clouds of oil wafted around her, and suddenly she remembered what the fragrance reminded her of, Howard!

From then on, it was very easy to relax. Agnes obediently let her thoughts wander and made up pleasant little scenarios where, sooner or later, Howard would appear.

First, he brought her a glass of orange juice from the buffet, and they had breakfast together. Agnes's cardigan was buttoned correctly for once, and she looked fabulous!

Next, she and Howard bumped into each other in the

library and were soon embroiled in a profound literary debate. Howard was intelligent and knowledgeable, but he finally bowed to Agnes's superior analysis.

Then they played a game of chess, and Howard was impressed by her brilliant strategy. That was a bit ridiculous because she didn't play chess, and definitely not brilliantly, but the thought appealed to her.

'Wonderfully relaxed!' Lilac praised her and tackled Agnes's bony shoulders, while Howard suggested a little walk to the cliffs.

Why not? thought Agnes. She was good on her feet. She felt magnificent. She was wearing a brightly coloured silk scarf, which wafted elegantly in the wind and had already been on the receiving end of some of Howard's compliments.

They moved briskly towards the cliff edge. Howard gallantly helping her over little obstacles (very small obstacles, because even in her dreams, Agnes knew that she mustn't bite off more than she could chew), the sun was shining like mad, and Agnes felt so carefree that she could almost have burst into song, any old stupid pop song from her youth. And so what? She was sure that even that would have pleased Howard!

Instead, she looked back at the hotel. Was there someone watching them from the terrace? Probably Marshall again! Did the man have nothing better to do than spy on her?

All of a sudden, Agnes noticed that the coast path they were walking along had vanished into thin air. Instead, an abyss opened up, deeper than the sea, so deep it was as if it led straight to hell.

Agnes went to grab Howard's arm in fright, but as she turned around, she saw that all of a sudden he was wearing an orange hooded jacket.

11

LILLITH

'So? What did you think?' Charlie asked. She had fished two slices of cucumber out of her glass of water and put them over her eyes; she now looked exactly like Agnes had always imagined a spa victim to look.

'Oof,' said Agnes, 'not bad.' She didn't want to admit that in fact, she had actually really enjoyed the massage. Now she felt warm and limp, as if someone had just rolled her out with a rolling pin, but in a good way. Soft. Yielding. Practically boneless. For someone whose bones otherwise usually caused her constant pain, that was no bad thing.

Charlie grinned beneath her cucumber eyes. 'Thought so!'

After their massages, they had both been deposited into a relaxation room. There they lay, wrapped up like mummies, and were supposed to drink water and herbal tea to restore their fluid balance. Classical music was playing, accompanied by raindrops hurling themselves against the window with gay abandon.

Agnes felt surprisingly young and fresh, and boldly bit into one of the slices of cucumber. Her false teeth played ball! Wonders never ceased!

'I wonder if they've found him yet?' she asked happily.

'Who?' Charlie was an expert at suppressing unpleasant truths. That was why she had fallen for husband number two back then.

'The body!' Agnes responded impatiently.

One of the slices of cucumber fell off Charlie's face. The eye that appeared underneath looked angrily over at Agnes.

'Really, Agnes, do you have to harp on about it right now? I've just had a lovely massage. I'm looking forward to dinner. That body is just about the last thing I want to be thinking about at the moment.'

'When then?' Agnes asked in annoyance. 'At dinner perhaps? Or after dinner, with a full stomach? Or maybe at night when the lights are out?'

Charlie made a noise that was difficult to interpret and lost the second slice of cucumber as well.

Agnes didn't let up. 'The truth is, there is no right time to think about dead bodies. Not when you're feeling good, and definitely not when you're feeling bad. But it has to be done. Like' – she searched for a comparison – 'like cleaning your teeth!'

'Cleaning your teeth!' Charlie snorted in disbelief.

'Think about it.' Agnes was adamant. 'Most of the people here are like you. They don't want to deal with dead bodies. Understandable, especially on holiday. But someone does want to deal with dead bodies, the murderer. And sooner or later, the time will come when you can't ignore him any longer. Can you imagine what'll it be like then? Carnage! Everyone will suspect everyone else; everyone will be trying to somehow stay safe. But obviously, nowhere is really safe, not for as long as we are cut off from the rest of the world. If panic breaks out, we can't afford to be on the back foot. Especially since most of the people here are already quicker on their feet than us. We've got to . . .' Agnes hesitated. She had gone off on a bit of a tangent. 'Be on the front foot. Know what's going on! Do you see what I mean?'

'Yeah,' Charlie mumbled. 'When you put it like that.'

She slurped some healthy cucumber water through her straw.

Agnes did the same. Both of them sucked until their glasses were empty and the straws were making wet bubbling noises between the remaining slices of cucumber.

'So, you don't think it's over yet?' Charlie finally asked.

'It's not over,' said Agnes. 'You can bet your life on it!'

Oberon the snake had had enough of the bathtub. He had soaked himself full of warmth under the heat lamp and felt like he'd swallowed the sun like an egg. Full of energy. From the inside out. Time to take a little look around!

Leaving the bathtub wasn't a problem when you had a body that consisted almost entirely of muscle. Oberon raised himself up and swayed back and forth a little until he got hold of the tap and managed to pull himself up onto it.

Aha! The other side of the edge of the bathtub didn't look very promising either. A little piece of fabric. Stupid, dead straight tiles. No sand or branches, or anywhere you might be able to find some prey. Prey! Oberon realised he had started to have a vague interest in finding prey again. His last meal wasn't that long ago, but it didn't hurt to have a look around with that in mind.

He slid from the edge of the bath, then through a crack and into a bigger room. There he paused and tasted the air with his tongue. Still no branches, but Oberon could feel vibrations, gentle movements, and he could taste breath in the air. Something was moving! Something alive!

He slid resolutely across the carpeted floor, into one of the dark places under the bed and carried on towards where he had sensed movement.

The disappointment was immense, as it turned out that the potential prey was actually two legs busying themselves on the other side of the bed.

Legs!

Oberon didn't care for legs. In fact, he despised them. Even if in principle he didn't have anything against humankind, it was regrettable that as a rule they moved around on little more than just two unrefined legs. The truth was, there wasn't much going on with humans down below. It only got interesting in the upper echelons. There were arms that could have something elegantly snake-like about them, shoulders that carried you around, a head as a lookout point, padded with soft hair if you were lucky.

Legs on the other hand spent their entire existence trudging around in the dirt, they had no idea about higher things, and they were pretty difficult to swallow too.

Indigestible. Cumbersome. Awkward.

Oberon shot his tongue out angrily. Legs were without a doubt the most charmless way to get around. Thanks to them, humans were constantly stumbling from one step to the next, without any feel for nuance and transitions. No wonder what went on in most of their heads was so small-minded.

In that respect *she* had represented a certain exception, but even she had fallen victim to her naïve leggedness in the end.

No, he didn't want anything to do with legs, but the two specimens in front of the bed were making their way towards him oblivious to that fact. Oberon the snake rolled himself into a muscular bundle and hissed at the unwelcome legs.

The next moment, a face bent down towards him. That was better! Soon he would be picked up, out of the dirt, up to the lofty heights. Oberon uncurled himself expectantly, but the face was already in the process of moving away. Even the legs retreated – good job too! – and the next minute the whole human sank to the floor like a sack. Disappointed, Oberon slid closer. He could forget lofty heights now. But the fallen human exuded a pleasant warmth. A he! Oberon didn't much care for males of the species, they mostly had too little head hair, a rough chin and smelt funny, but a soft, warm resting spot near the centre of the body was not to be hissed at.

He scaled the human, elegantly furled up his beautiful snake body and philosophically flicked his tongue.

* * *

'There!' Agnes held the Do Not Disturb sign up to Edwina's face. 'From now on, this sign is your best friend!'

'Oberon's my best friend!' Edwina moaned, crossing her arms.

'Exactly.' Agnes nodded. 'And this sign will mean he stays your best friend.'

She had returned from her massage with a spring in her step, warm and fuzzy, rosy and well-hydrated, only to discover an unconscious housekeeping person with a melted chocolate in his hand and a snake on his chest. Luckily just after, Edwina had turned up too, taken Oberon back into the bathroom after a few stern words, and then thrown a toothbrush cup full of water in the hotel employee's face.

Then they had convinced him that he had just imagined the white snake – with moderate success, but it was enough to confuse the man and shut him up. Now he had finally toddled off out of the room, and Agnes's deep relaxation had gone to hell.

'We've been over this a hundred times,' she ranted. 'As long as Oberon is here, the bathroom door stays shut!'

'The bathroom door was shut,' Edwina said defiantly.

'So how did the snake get into the room then?' Agnes asked, although she knew that logic alone wouldn't get through to Edwina. 'This is exactly what should never have happened!'

'He shouldn't have just walked in here like that,' Edwina muttered. 'It's his own fault!'

'He was putting chocolates on our pillows,' Agnes explained in exasperation. 'That's what they do in luxury hotels. Unless . . .' She held up the Do Not Disturb sign again.

Edwina looked at Agnes pityingly. That just went to show that her friend didn't have a clue when it came to espionage. It would take more than a cardboard sign to deal with the dark forces that were after Oberon's blood. On the other hand, the man hadn't really been after anything. He had fainted on the spot, and kindly served as a cushion for Oberon.

'And what is that supposed to be for?' she asked warily.

'It means that you don't want any maid service,' Agnes explained. 'No maid service, no chocolates, no encounters with snakes, no fainting. What do you imagine is going to happen if something like that happens again?'

Edwina went pale.

'They'll be jealous! They'll take him away from me!'

That seemed like an overly optimistic scenario to Agnes, but it was along the right lines. She nodded. 'Exactly. If someone from the hotel comes in here and discovers Oberon, he's a goner. This sign will mean that nobody comes in. Simple.'

'Okay!' said Edwina.

Agnes was taken aback. Okay? Negotiations with Edwina didn't usually run that smoothly. But all the better. She had enough on her plate, what with the murders, the White Widow, Bernadette's admirer and, well, Howard; she couldn't take care of Edwina's skirmishes with the staff as well.

Edwina rushed to the door to put the sign in position, and Agnes went to pick out a particularly chic blouse for dinner. Charlie was right, life was short and, well, possibly even shorter thanks to the presence of a murderer. You had to make the most of every second, and to be on the safe side, Agnes had decided that today she would have an aperitif in the Sea Lounge and look fabulous doing so.

Edwina waited until Agnes, lipstick round her mouth and enveloped in a cloud of perfume, was out of the room. Then she flung the wardrobe door open and stared angrily down at Mojo.

Mojo shrugged. 'I needed the loo.'

'But it was against the agreement!' Edwina hissed. 'And you could at least have shut the door. Anything could have happened . . .' Words failed her.

'It was funny though.' Mojo stretched his legs out of the wardrobe and grinned. 'You should have seen the guy's face when he realised there was a snake in here.' He grimaced and put his hands to his cheeks. Edwina had once seen a painting of a long, shocked face like that, but she hadn't liked it very much.

'I can hardly wait to post about it!' Mojo declared. 'Wardrobe diary, day one. Cool!'

'It was against the agreement,' Edwina insisted. Mojo hadn't known her for long enough yet to find her quiet, reasonable tone alarming.

'At least there was something going on,' he carried on regardless. 'The internet still isn't working and your friend in the tin doesn't make for very good company.'

He waggled his pale toes. Edwina noticed he had taken off his socks, and turned up her nose.

Right.

That was it!

She'd tried to be understanding of his mood swings and shocking lack of professionalism, but enough was enough.

She opened the door to the hallway. The Do Not Disturb sign jiggled.

Then she grabbed Mojo by the ankles and dragged him towards the door. Mojo was too surprised to find her off but managed to grab hold of a bedpost partway and hung on for dear life.

Edwina pulled harder.

'Let go of me!' Mojo screeched.

'We had an agreement,' Edwina explained. 'You can live here in the wardrobe, as long as you take care of Oberon. But did you take care of Oberon?'

It was a rhetorical question. Edwina pulled harder.

Mojo tried to kick but couldn't against Edwina's grip. Tears suddenly streamed down his cheeks.

'I'm sorry,' he whimpered. 'I won't let it happen again. Please! I can't go out there. Something awful will happen to me. Something awful!'

'Something awful might happen in here too!' Edwina threatened. 'Especially if you don't keep to agreements.'

'It won't happen again!' Mojo promised.

'No,' Edwina agreed. 'Too right it won't!'

She waited for Mojo to loosen his grip slightly, then she pulled again.

Just then, a gaunt married couple walked past, both with hyena-like expressions on their faces. They spotted Edwina pulling on a pair of scrawny legs and stared at her aghast.

'Do not disturb!' Edwina hissed, letting go of the legs

and slamming the door in the hyenas' faces.

Mojo used the opportunity to roll up like a woodlouse, without, however, letting go of the bedpost.

Edwina crossed her arms.

'Last chance!' she said.

'Last chance!' Mojo promised.

It took a while for him to dare to let go of the bedpost, then he staggered back into the wardrobe.

'What on earth do you imagine is going to happen to you out there?' Edwina asked, but Mojo didn't seem to hear her at all.

He was clicking and jabbing away at his phone, then he threw his head back and groaned.

'No internet. No signal. Nothing! What sort of dump is this anyway?'

'A luxury eco one,' Edwina explained. 'And apart from that, we're on the high seas, so the internet thing isn't quite that simple. At least we don't have to worry about rats,' she added comfortingly.

Mojo eyed her with sudden interest. His eyes, usually wide, vague and a bit doe-like, narrowed to slits, and he looked older all of a sudden. Older and more jaded. Maybe they'd make an agent out of him yet!

'You're high,' he said excitedly. 'You've got some gear! Come on, where d'you get the gear?'

Edwina rolled her eyes. They'd ended up back at the wretched 'gear' again.

'Gear could be anything,' she said philosophically.

'I want some!' Mojo screeched. 'Where is it? Give it to me, you old bat!'

He leapt up, grabbed her by the shoulders and started

shaking her. Edwina relaxed into the movement and waited for the whippersnapper to make a mistake. It wouldn't take long.

But before she could launch a counter-attack Mojo had already let go of her and was peering under the bedcovers, then in Agnes's suitcase, then in the bedside drawer.

Finally, he clapped eyes on Lillith's tin.

'It's in there, isn't it? I should have known, after your stupid story. Ashes. My arse!'

He grabbed Lillith and went to unscrew the lid.

'No!' Edwina squealed. 'That's private! Leave Lillith in peace!'

But Mojo ignored her.

Edwina leapt. At the same moment, Mojo undid the lid and sniffed expectantly at the tin. Edwina's elbow landed in his stomach. He made a gagging sound and fell backwards. Edwina was pulled along by her own momentum and toppled after him.

Then they both lay on the floor, and Lillith spread over them like a fine black mist.

Increasingly impatient, Agnes sat in the Sea Lounge waiting for some romance.

She was now on her third whisky of the day, and up to now, no romantic liaisons had occurred, not for her, or it seemed for anybody else. The lounge was fuller than last time – on the evening of the first murder – but the general mood didn't feel very romantic to her, more tense and a bit hyper. That could be down to the amount of sugar the guests had consumed at the ice-cream buffet, or to the fact that the Eden was so utterly cut off from the outside world – now it wasn't just the road that had slipped away, the telephone and internet had disappeared too. That was bound to fray nerves. Marshall was very dependent on the internet and soon got grumpy if he couldn't converse with other firearms enthusiasts. Agnes assumed that other people were similar. She noticed that lots of mobile phones had been placed on tables ready for action, and were being optimistically checked every now and then, only to be put down again in disappointment.

Was it a coincidence that the telephone line had given up the ghost?

And if it wasn't a coincidence – what was it? Did it mean the murderer planned to strike again?

Agnes gave up wishing for Howard to come by – him and his bushy hair could go to hell – and turned her thoughts to the case again. Because it was a case.

At least one.

Invigorated by the whisky, Agnes ran the crime scene photos past her mind's eye again. Loss of control. That was what she found unsettling. Someone was in the process of completely losing it. Did it bother the killer that he had left behind such unambiguous proof of his murderous existence? What had happened in the pool pump room couldn't be interpreted as an accident, not even by a naïve observer.

Had the body even been found yet, officially found, not secretly like by Winston and Marshall? How often did people have to go into that pool pump room? Did the hotel management now know that they had a murderer on their hands? Were they doing something about it? Or would they just try to cover it all up? Agnes could understand that as luxury eco hotel management, you wouldn't want to set off alarm bells, but simply doing nothing definitely wasn't a solution either.

She was reminded of the verger back home in Duck End again. He had set off alarm bells alright. Did that mean something? Was it a clue? And if it was, what did it mean?

Was she homesick maybe?

The pianist, who had been tinkling the ivories up to now, gave up and strolled over to the bar to get a drink. For a moment it was conspicuously silent, then the conversations got louder, a little aggressive, it seemed to Agnes. Not a buzz, more of a hiss.

She tried to concentrate. She could deal with the verger later, for now it was about solving the on-site murders as quickly as possible so that there were still a few days of holiday left.

She suddenly had an idea. Several ideas, actually. Too many! She needed a notebook! If only she'd brought her handbag . . . but unfortunately, she'd left it in the room because the little monstrosity hadn't seemed elegant enough. To hell with elegance! What she needed right now was paper and pen!

Agnes turned to the bar and waved until a bartender made his way towards her. It wasn't Max, but an unfamiliar face. Max was nowhere to be seen – presumably lurking in one of the housekeeping stores in hope of putting the fear of God into her.

Agnes asked the current bartender for a pen and then started to scribble questions on a napkin.

Who had taken part in a behind-the-scenes tour in the last few days?

Who had a Do Not Disturb sign hanging on their door?

Who was the body in the pool pump room?

Was anyone missing him?

Apart from that, it was about gaining an overview of developments over the last few days, and Winston was responsible for overviews, chronological and otherwise.

Agnes got up, abandoning her half-drunk whisky, and went to look for Winston.

12

BUTTERFLIES

Bernadette was making her way through the hallways of the Eden as if she were in a dream. She felt as light as a balloon, albeit a pretty enormous one. Effortless.

Floating.

And something else had happened, something completely unheard of, she wasn't hungry anymore, no appetite at all really. She felt full, not of ice cream, but something fluttery, fleeting.

Butterflies maybe.

The jitters had her stomach firmly in their grasp and were in the process of spreading towards her head and heart. Bernadette wasn't quite sure what to make of it.

On the one hand, it was a nice feeling.

The best ever.

On the other, she felt a bit silly, and she found the ease with which she was about to transform back into Samantha unsettling. Samantha was someone she hardly knew anymore and maybe didn't even want to know either.

He, however, knew Samantha by heart.

They had sat together, eating ice cream and playing old games, as if fifty years hadn't passed. He whispered into her ear what he could see. Ridiculous hairstyles and long faces and little squabbles at the buffet. Evil looks and longing looks. The sea outside, so wide and empty, as if swept clean with a broom, and gulls shooting through the air like arrows.

Bernadette listened and felt a world taking shape around her, a world that was normally off-limits to her.

Then she leant towards him and whispered about the things that couldn't be seen. Barbed remarks, murmured secrets. Clouds of perfume. Suppressed, nervous giggling. Hasty footsteps out in the hall somewhere. Someone was running. Muffled, agitated voices, maybe even a sob.

It had always been like this.

Together, they redoubled the world.

It was a wonderful game, but the question preoccupying Bernadette was: Was he with her or against her? She was under no illusions; what she had done to the boss and his gang back then was unforgiveable. That's why the police had given her a new identity, wasn't it? That's why she had become Bernadette and started a desk job in a government department, somewhere in the anonymity of London.

But she'd saved him, hadn't she?

That much was hopefully obvious to him!

Saved him and dumped him.

The thought of it still hurt her, even after all this time.

But maybe there was such a thing as a second chance? The air around her was full of possibilities. Bernadette could sense them, close enough to touch, crackling and enticing, and maybe deceptive.

Had their meeting there really been a coincidence? A twist of fate? Or was it a trap? And if it was a trap, Was she really crazy enough to walk blindly into it?

Agnes must have taken a wrong turn on her way back from the Sea Lounge, because after a moment of confusion, instead of ending up back in her room, she suddenly found herself in the library again. Earlier, in the sun, the room had been cosy, a little homely almost, but now, deserted and lit only by the islands of light created by the reading lamps, she found it creepy. If she had been in a film right now, or a novel even, this is exactly where she would have found the next body. She could just imagine it, two outstretched legs in the beam of a lamp and then, on closer inspection, blood, seeping into the exquisite Persian rug.

Murder in the library. These days, something like that was almost par for the course.

Instead, Winston and Marshall had found the most recent body behind the scenes, and there was nothing scenic about it. The murderer obviously couldn't care less about the backdrop.

A cackle from the neighbouring room made Agnes jump. The games room was next door, a room they had avoided up to now. She wasn't sure exactly what a games room was supposed to be like, but vaguely imagined something involving lots of brightly coloured balls, mature gentlemen in their fifties and well-coiffed ladies frolicking amongst them. But that was nonsense, surely. In a hotel like the Eden, even the games room would be a tasteful and elegant affair.

Agnes plucked up the courage and went in.

Fortunately, there were no balls, just a group of well-nourished ladies loudly and a bit argumentatively playing a game of cards at one of the tables. And to her great joy, Agnes spotted Winston and Charlie.

The two of them were playing Monopoly and, unsurprisingly, seemed annoyed. Agnes could tell emotions were running high straightaway. At home in Sunset Hall, they almost never played board games because getting annoyed was always on the cards, even if strictly speaking there weren't even any cards involved. On this occasion, Charlie was annoyed because she was just about to lose, and Winston, mildly so, because Charlie was such a sore loser.

Agnes, who was well-versed in such matters, quietly plopped herself down at their table and swept a few pieces off the board, without giving it a second thought. With that, harmony was abruptly restored because now they were both annoyed with her.

'Mind what you're doing, Agnes!' Charlie groaned. She seemed to already have forgotten how badly Monopoly had been going for her.

Agnes ignored her and pushed a fresh napkin and the pen she'd stolen from the Sea Lounge towards Winston.

'We need to get organised,' she said, leaning in. 'We need a timeline. To get a better overview of the murders!'

Charlie rolled her eyes, but Winston seemed delighted to have put the blasted board game behind him and grabbed the pen.

'So far, we have three possible victims,' Agnes declared.

'Three already?' Charlie looked horrified. 'Who else, then?'

'First the yellow hood,' Agnes explained. 'Then the

man behind the scenes. And finally . . .'

She paused for dramatic effect. 'I'm not quite sure how it fits together, but I think we should also put *the wet woman* on the list too.' She explained to the others what Trudy had told her about her vision in the gym.

Then they all stared at Winston's list together.

The Yellow Hood.

The Man Behind the Scenes.

The Wet Woman.

They would all have made respectable titles for a novel, and Agnes couldn't help but wonder what sort of poetic turn of phrase would suit the next victim.

They wouldn't have to wait long to find out.

Then, while Winston and Charlie subsequently hot-footed it to dinner, Agnes had decided to stop by reception to find out exactly what the behind-the-scenes tour entailed. If the murderer was a guest, he had maybe learnt of the existence of the pool pump room and its potential as a murder venue during one of those tours. And if he was a member of staff – well, Agnes wanted to finally find out if anybody was acting strangely or if anything else of note had happened in the staff areas.

But as she entered the lobby, she realised the room was empty. Unmanned like that, the reception desk looked more than ever like artfully draped driftwood, smoothed by time. Agnes felt a bit like jetsam too. Washed up. Forgotten. Out on a limb.

She waited a while and was just about to make her way to dinner when, thanks to her new hearing aid, she noticed a quiet sound.

Someone was crying.

More than that, someone was sobbing.

The sound was so at odds with the serene sounds of the Eden that Agnes didn't trust her ears to begin with. But then she spotted a crack in the smooth wall behind the reception desk that she hadn't noticed before.

A hidden door.

And on the other side of it, someone was crying their eyes out.

Agnes stepped closer. She only really wanted to listen and perhaps carefully peek through the crack but lost her balance at a decisive moment and had to lean on the door. The door slid open like butter, and suddenly she was standing in a small, well-organised room full of folders, files and technical equipment. She was no expert but thought she could identify a printer or maybe a fax machine.

In the middle of the room stood a big desk, and there, with her head in her hands was the origin of the sobbing.

She must have sensed Agnes or spotted her through the gaps between her fingers, because she suddenly lowered her hands, looked flabbergasted and tried to pull herself together. She didn't really succeed.

'I . . . I . . .' Her voice broke, and a hiccup joined the sobbing. Agnes had to look twice. Was that Helen the hotel manager? Almost unrecognisable with puffy eyes, frantic red blotches on her cheeks and messy hair?

Fortunately, her name tag cleared Agnes's doubts.

'Sorry,' she said. 'I didn't mean to just barge in. I'm just a bit unsteady on my feet sometimes.' She rummaged in the depths of her skirt pocket, brought a tissue to light and passed it to the hotel manager.

Helen blew her nose loudly.

'Oh God.' She groaned. 'This is so unprofessional. You're a guest. I should be providing you with tissues, not the other way around. What can I do for you?'

Agnes spotted a second chair and pulled it up to the desk.

'It looks like I should be asking you that,' she said. 'I mean, it can't be that bad, can it?'

'No,' Helen groaned, reaching for the tissue. 'It's even worse!'

As a rule, Agnes kept a generous supply of tissues on her at all times. They were practical if your eyes streamed in the cold wind, or Edwina made a mess somewhere, or Brexit left his damp nose prints all over the place.

Now, one tissue after another made its way across the desk, to be snivelled full and finally land on the desk in a crumpled heap. And with each tissue, Agnes managed to wheedle a few more pieces of information out of the manager.

In principle, the matter was quite straightforward, a hotel employee had discovered the body.

Agnes nodded. That was obviously to be expected, but now the staff were in a blind panic.

'Normally I would call the police straightaway.' Helen gulped. 'But the phones are dead, and the road's impassable. Nobody's coming and my team expect me to do something, and I just don't know what . . .'

'Has this happened to the phones before?' Agnes asked.

Helen shook her head and went even paler beneath her red blotches.

'Never! You don't think . . . Do you?'

Agnes shrugged. 'It's quite a coincidence at any rate. It'd be good to find out exactly what's happened.'

'Interesting. Exactly!' Helen nodded frantically. 'I should be taking care of things like that, making enquiries, and I don't even know . . . What shall I say to the guests? That's the question! It's not right to keep something like this from them, but on the other hand . . . Our guests should feel at ease. And be able to relax. If they get wind of the fact that they're cooped up in here with a murderer, you can kiss goodbye to relaxation! They'll never come back! If word gets out, we're finished! Apart from that, I'm worried about them. Not just because of the murderer, but also because – well, if they find out about it all, some of them are sure to try to get out of here under their own steam, on foot, along the cliffs, and it's really dangerous. I can't be responsible for that. But just lying to them . . .'

She paused, blew her nose into another tissue and looked pleadingly at Agnes.

'It's not a lie,' Agnes reassured her. 'More an omission. I don't think it would be helpful if all the guests knew exactly what was going on.'

'Really?' Helen dropped the tissue on the desk and seemed grateful. Then a horrified look crossed her face.

'But you're a guest! And I've just told you everything! How could I . . .'

'Oh, mum's the word!' Agnes said and tried to look like a sedate and trustworthy granny rather than a volatile old woman.

It seemed to work. Helen swept the soggy tissues from the desk into the bin and took a deep breath. 'I sent Max down to the village on foot. Not an easy hike, but it should be possible in three, maybe four hours. And then the police will hopefully come in a bloody helicopter and arrest the culprit! I've just got to keep it together until then!'

Agnes nodded encouragingly, although she knew that as a rule you couldn't expect much from the police, helicopter or no helicopter.

'The Eden should be an exceptional experience.' Helen sighed. 'But not quite as exceptional as this. I've got to somehow convince them that everything's okay. And then every time I have anything to do with a guest, I wonder if they're a murderer, and my smile gets stuck in my throat. I should be making them feel at home here. Instead I'd rather just chuck them all out. Every last one! I don't want to see anyone, at least until the police have cleared everything up. It could be anyone! Absolutely anyone!'

She eyed Agnes, her eyes glistening with tears.

'It wasn't me,' said Agnes.

Helen let out a high-pitched, hysterical laugh. 'Of course not, I didn't mean you . . . On the other hand, that's exactly what a murderer would say!'

'I'm what you could call the opposite of a murderer!' Agnes declared confidently. She had an idea. A desperate woman like Helen would clutch at any straw, and if she managed to pull it off, maybe she, Agnes, could be a straw of sorts!

Agnes explained to Helen that she was a kind of policewoman, albeit a retired one. (She kept precisely how long she'd been retired to herself, to be on the safe side.) And as luck would have it, she was there with a few friends,

187

who all used to be in public service roles. An experienced team of investigators, a bit rusty maybe, but capable. As long as Helen was in agreement and she provided a bit of support, it should be more than possible to make a few enquiries and, with a bit of luck, identify the murderer before he could wreak any more havoc.

'But I need information,' Agnes concluded. 'Guest lists. Rotas. That kind of thing.'

Helen nodded eagerly. The fact that she accepted Agnes as an ersatz Sherlock Holmes just like that showed just how desperate she was.

'Shall we start with the victim?' Agnes said quickly, before the manager could start doubting her ability. 'Have you already established who it is?'

Helen nodded sadly. 'One of our most loyal guests. Unfortunately. Would you perhaps like to take a look yourself? We . . . we put her in the freezer.'

Agnes went cold and felt dizzy. She was relieved she was already sitting down.

Her?

Whoever the hotel employee had found, it wasn't the man in the pool pump room.

It was only their second dinner at the Eden, but the Sunset Hall residents' discipline was already slipping dramatically.

Marshall was wearing his waistcoat inside out, but nobody had said a word.

Winston had already jumbled up his neatly arranged cutlery and was getting stuck into the starter with his dessert spoon.

Bernadette was absent-mindedly poking around in a

fantastic nut and goat cheese salad, which really deserved her full attention.

Edwina arrived late and in her tracksuit. She had her sports bag over her shoulder and had suspicious black patches on her neck and behind her ears. She had obviously tried to wash her face but missed a few spots in the process.

'What on earth happened to you?' Charlie asked chidingly, although she probably really didn't want to know the details.

'Chromotherapy!' Edwina hissed.

'Chromotherapy? With the colour black?' Charlie was horrified and decided not to partake in the hotel's chromotherapy offering.

Edwina looked so angry that the others kept their comments to themselves.

'I'm so full,' groaned Bernadette pushing the half-eaten salad aside.

All most out of character.

Agnes would definitely have delved deeper.

But Agnes wasn't there.

'There!' Said Helen, her breath forming white clouds. 'Terrible, huh?'

The hotel's freezer was bigger than the utility room at Sunset Hall, and even colder, if that was possible.

All the shelves had been cleared – she was starting to see the ice-cream buffet in a different light – and the body was lying on the ground like a beached whale, taking up an awful lot of space. Agnes had expected the latest discovery of a corpse to be the mysterious wet woman, but she could

189

see straightaway that that wasn't the case.

For one thing, the woman wasn't wearing an evening gown.

For another, it was immediately clear that nobody had carried this woman through the hotel. Too heavy. Helen reported that it had taken five members of staff to move the body from the library to the freezer during the ice-cream buffet.

From the library! So the murderer had used the scenic backdrop in there for his purposes after all! It was just a shame that the employees had found the body so quickly, sealed off the library and organised the ice-cream buffet.

Had the murderer been disappointed? There was something theatrical about a body in the library, and Agnes wondered if the killer had expected an audience. Was he starting to stage his murders – or had the victim just been in the right place at the right time?

What had happened seemed obvious, while the fat woman had been absorbed in her book, the murderer had crept up from behind and strangled her with her own chunky necklace made of metal butterflies.

'Poor Mrs Meyer-Brinks!' Helen lamented. 'She was such a gentle soul. Never a complaint. Never any kind of problem. All she wanted was a nice view and a quiet spot to read her book!'

Agnes shuddered, not so much because of the crime, but because it really was freezing in there. Was Mrs Meyer-Brinks a random victim, or had the murderer sought her out? And if he had – why?

She noticed the book, that someone – presumably out of respect – had laid on the dead woman's chest. The last book she would ever read. Agnes leant forward out of curiosity. A murder mystery, obviously! *A Caribbean Mystery* by Agatha Christie. While reading, Mrs Meyer-Brinks probably hadn't reckoned on soon playing such an active role in a real murder case.

'Did she have any relatives here?' Agnes asked, her false teeth chattering. It was time to get out of the walk-in freezer.

'No.' Helen sighed. 'Fortunately, not. Fortunately for us I mean, it probably wasn't that nice for Mrs Meyer-Brinks. She was a regular guest. And she always came on her own.'

Agnes nodded and eyed the door. 'I think I've seen enough. But I'd like to know exactly when she was found and when she was last seen alive. And I would also like to speak to whoever found her.'

Helen nodded and respectfully held the door open for her.

Agnes had a dull, flat feeling in her stomach. Part of it was the excitement that she was suddenly on an investigation again, almost officially, after all these years. But there was something else, and it took a moment for her to correctly identify the second feeling, hunger! It was high time for dinner! She was late! Now, where was the dining room?

She cast a final glance into the freezer, Mrs Meyer-Brinks's temporary resting place, and wondered how many more bodies it could accommodate if need be.

She probably should have told Helen about the *man behind the scenes*. But she was still wavering. Mrs Meyer-Brinks with her fixed, bloodshot eyes might not be a particularly nice corpse, but she didn't come close to the faceless man Winston and Marshall had discovered. If Helen was already teetering on the edge of a nervous breakdown, what would she say about the victim in the pool pump room? It didn't bear thinking about! In order to gently break the news to her, Agnes would need a fresh supply of tissues, at the very least, and a little time.

At least it was now clear where the bodies should go.

Because, despite Mrs Meyer-Brinks's full figure, the freezer was by no means at full capacity.

13

ON THE HOUSE

The Sunset Hall crew had already made their way through the starter, the first *amuse-bouche*, and the soup, when Agnes suddenly appeared at the table in strangely high spirits.

They tucked into the main course in an unusually calm display of harmony – a braised mushroom ragout with parsnip purée and wonderfully fresh young greens. Apart from Edwina, who was secretly whispering to Oberon in the sports bag, each of them seemed to be lost in their own thoughts.

After a waiter had cleared their plates, Agnes asked Winston for the strategy napkin and added the latest victim.

Now the list looked like this,
The Yellow Hood
The Man Behind the Scenes
The Wet Woman
The Bookworm
But was that the right order?

Agnes knew the precise moment the incident with the yellow hood had happened – after all, she had been there, in a manner of speaking. And as far as the library victim was concerned, at least she had learnt when the body had been found. The rest was more difficult to narrow down. But maybe . . .

'How long is the gym open for?' she asked abruptly.

'I didn't know you were interested in fitness,' said Marshall warily. 'You've still got a really lovely figure . . .'

Agnes sighed. 'I'm not interested in fitness. I'm interested in the opening times!'

She waved over one of the now rather strung-out youngsters and asked.

'Daily until five,' the youth said apathetically.

Agnes said thank you, turned the napkin over and wrote a new list.

The Wet Woman
The Yellow Hood
The Man Behind the Scenes
The Bookworm

Yes, that could be right, even if the times of death for the bookworm and the man behind the scenes were still in doubt.

Agnes had been in the lounge yesterday evening at around six o'clock and had watched the drama on the cliffs unfold. At that time the gym would already have been closed, so Trudy must have seen the wet woman beforehand. That threw Agnes a bit. For some reason she had always assumed that it had all started with the yellow hood. It had been the most discreet of all the murders committed at the Eden. No violence, no drama, just a little shove in the right direction. An entry-level murder for beginners, you could say. But as it looked now, the murderer had already been in full flow. And that meant . . .

Before Agnes could think about exactly what that could mean, dessert was served. Not ice cream – thank God! Mrs Meyer-Brinks had completely ruined her appetite for anything frozen. Instead, there was a colourful fruit salad on a buttery, sugar-crisp pastry base. Delicious! Agnes quickly spirited the napkin into her skirt pocket, successfully identified the dessert fork and tabled the thinking for later. Her latest sleuthing successes had given her a huge appetite, so much so that it took a while for her to notice that her table companions had stopped eating and were eyeing her with interest.

Someone tapped their glass and one after another, the voices in the dining room fell silent.

Someone smart had stepped into the middle of the room and was smiling and clearing her throat. The corgi was sitting at her feet, with a snobby doggy smile.

'Valued guests. I know that some of you have noticed some irregularities at the hotel today, and for that the hotel management would like to offer their sincerest apologies. I'm here to bring you up to date, explain what the issues are and what we are doing to restore normal service as quickly as possible!'

Agnes squinted. Was that really the same Helen that had just been standing next to her in the freezer, blotchy faced and jittery, tripping over her own tongue, lamenting the death of Mrs Meyer-Brinks?

Now she seemed calm and collected. Her hair was smoothed down, her voice steady, her lips red, and her eyes dry. Her complexion looked even again. Agnes presumed make-up was at play, but not only that.

Something else had happened. Someone – presumably her with her flimsy promise to help with the investigation – had caused a drastic change of mood. Either that – or she was just a quite exceptional actress.

Helen smiled apologetically. 'It will not have escaped your attention that we currently have no Wi-Fi or phone service. The phone line has been cut off, and I fear it will take a little while for us to be reconnected. The whole situation is made more difficult by the fact that, unfortunately, yesterday's storm has temporarily rendered the coast road impassable.'

People muttered uneasily. It was obvious that the lack of road and Wi-Fi wasn't going down well, but Helen didn't allow herself to be rattled.

'These are unusual circumstances, but I can assure you that you will be as well taken care of here in the safe haven of the Eden as ever. We will make every effort to ensure your stay is as pleasant as possible and are working tirelessly to ensure that normal service is resumed.'

Not for Mrs Meyer-Brinks though, thought Agnes. Not for the wet woman, the man behind the scenes and the yellow hood. Helen really was sticking her neck out with her promises, but it was clear to see that the little speech had hit a nerve with the hotel guests.

Calm reigned over the room, a collective sigh, as if everyone there had finally taken a deep breath after holding it for a long time. Relieved whispers filled the room.

And then, at Agnes's feet, snarling. The corgi had left his post and was warily sniffing Edwina's sports bag. Hissing was coming from the bag.

'Go away!' Edwina whispered, but the dog didn't even consider leaving the suspicious bag in peace. Little wonder, really. Agnes didn't know much about corgis, apart from the fact that they looked deceptively sweet and cuddly, but she knew they were outstanding ratters. In Oberon, the dog had presumably recognised a competitor, and if they didn't do something about it, he would blow the snake's cover. Agnes had no desire to lose Helen's hard-won trust again due to illegal snake possession. She tried to push the dog aside with her foot. The corgi snarled even more loudly.

With a heavy heart, Agnes broke off a big piece of pastry and shoved it in the dog's mouth. Hush money. It seemed to work. The corgi stopped snarling and chomped up the pastry in record time. Then he turned his button eyes demandingly towards Agnes again.

Agnes reluctantly sacrificed the rest of her dessert.

What now?

Luckily, nobody else had noticed anything.

Helen seemed to sense the mood in the room turn in her favour, and carried on, encouraged. 'Please speak to a member of staff if you have any queries or requests. Needless to say, we will do everything humanly possible to continue to help you as best we can. And as a small gesture of goodwill for the inconvenience, all drinks at the bar are on the house this evening!'

Somebody started to clap, others joined in. Luckily, the sudden noise drowned out the corgi's renewed snarls. Someone whistled, and someone shouted loudly, 'Fabulous!' Was it Charlie? Of course it was! Agnes looked around and only belatedly realised that the manager's gaze was suddenly fixed on her. Helen was even winking conspiratorially at her. Agnes stared back at her blankly. Had the woman lost her mind?

Of course, it was in the best interest of hotel management if the guests caught wind of as little as possible from now on, but was alcohol really the answer? Would it not be child's play for the murderer to attack clueless, inebriated guests? On the other hand, he'd had no trouble subduing his victims so far. Come to think of it, it was quite remarkable, neither the hood on the cliffs, nor the bookworm, nor the man behind the scenes seemed to have defended themselves. The murderer had to be someone that people let near them without giving it a second thought. Someone that could be trusted . . .

Charlie leapt up. 'Well, come on, kids. In a situation like this, the last won't be the first! Quite the opposite! Quick sticks!'

'Where to?' Edwina asked warily.

'To the Sea Lounge, of course!' Charlie grinned. 'If we don't head off soon, we won't get a seat!'

She was right. The first guests had already left their tables and were striding out of the room with hopeful expressions on their faces.

Edwina pulled a face. 'I've got stuff to do!' she declared, grabbing the sports bag and rushing off. The corgi stayed behind with a disappointed look on his face. Agnes exhaled. At least the dog problem was solved for now.

'What on earth has she got to do?' asked Charlie.

Under normal circumstances, Agnes would have asked the same, but there were more important things to be thinking about. First, she had to keep her team of 'investigators' out of the general booze-up, then they had to immediately start at least sifting the information they now had access to, thanks to Helen.

'The bar? Out of the question!' she said loudly. 'We've got a lot to do. We can't just get drunk when there's a murderer on the loose!'

'You cannot be serious!' Charlie looked at her in horror.

'Think about it!' Agnes crossed her arms combatively. 'It's too dangerous! Do you remember how the guy in the pool pump room had been battered? And believe me, Mrs Meyer-Brinks wasn't exactly a pleasant sight.'

'Precisely!' cried Charlie. 'That's exactly why I could do with a tipple or two.'

'And then?' Agnes asked. 'Would you like to maybe end up in the chiller too? There's plenty of space left!'

Charlie stuck out her bottom lip sulkily, and Agnes had to admit that irritatingly, even that looked girlish and attractive on her. She decided to change tack.

'Helen is depending on us. And she's the manager. Can you imagine what we'll get once we've found the murderer? But not before!'

'Hear! Hear!' cried Winston. You could tell that he was happier about analysing some kind of data than the booze-up afterwards.

Charlie relented. 'Okay then,' she said hesitantly. 'But you're coming to aqua aerobics with me tomorrow morning, yes? No excuses!'

Agnes sighed. Charlie had bought herself a chic red swimsuit before the trip and was hell-bent on trying it out as soon as possible. Agnes's swimming costume, on the other hand, looked as if it had come out of a period drama, black and misshapen, and that was even before it came into contact with water. Afterwards . . . She shuddered but didn't really have a good argument against aqua aerobics.

Alcohol or swimming costume. Those were the only options for Charlie at the moment.

'Okay,' Agnes said finally. She had little desire to make a fool of herself in front of some kind of gym bunny, but it was better than a premature drunken stupor every time.

They shook on it, and with that the matter was decided.

Bernadette had taken the news that Mrs Meyer-Brinks had been strangled very badly and was no longer on cloud nine, but cloud two at best. And there was a really good view of the underworld, the murky and elaborate regions of Hades that, by some kind of miracle, she had escaped long ago.

She hadn't so much forgotten what Jack used to do for the boss, no, she had actively, and with great difficulty, suppressed it. But thanks to Mrs Meyer-Brinks, it was becoming more and more difficult to ignore. It was gnawing away at her. Jack hadn't just been a casual criminal back then, no, he had been a professional. A specialist. Someone who did away with undesirables promptly, politely and discreetly. Back then she had accepted it without any qualms. After all, Jack had always acted respectfully and sometimes even kindly, at least in comparison to some of the other things that happened in that line of work. Her many years in public service had changed her attitude a bit though, and it was preying on her mind.

She obviously couldn't change what had already happened.

But what about now?

Was he still working?

She didn't have to think about that for very long. Probably. Someone like Jack didn't just retire at sixty-five, or whatever the retirement age was these days.

And this brought her swiftly to her next question, Was he working here at the hotel?

And more specifically: Did he have Mrs Meyer-Brinks on his conscience?

Agnes was briskly striding through the Eden's corridors again, with such determination this time that her overworked hip didn't even raise its head.

She had sent her housemates to Marshall's room. It was the most spacious of the three rooms, wasn't inhabited by a controversial snake and would now serve as Murder Hunt HQ. She had popped by Helen's office again to collect some important paperwork herself, rotas, guest lists, seating plans. She would feed all of this information into Winston and then hope that he would be able to draw some interesting conclusions from it.

The folders were heavier than she'd expected, and the journey back was protracted. Her heart was beating unusually loudly. Was it the thrill of the chase or something else? The hallways seemed alien to her; long, complicated and serpentine like the innards of an enormous sea creature that the storm had washed ashore.

Marshall had been dead set on accompanying her, but

Agnes wouldn't hear of it. The murderer had committed four energy-sapping murders in the past twenty-four hours, so she found it unlikely that he would strike again straightaway. And the less Helen found out about Agnes's 'team,' the better, Agnes had decided. Apart from that, Marshall had got his waistcoat on inside out. Things like that didn't make a very good impression.

Now she was wondering if she had maybe been too nit-picky.

It was surprisingly lonely in the Eden this evening – lonely and still. Muffled high-spirited singing carried over from afar, presumably from the bar.

Agnes felt sluggish, weighed down and vulnerable. A snail with no shell, but a stack of files in her arms instead.

She stood still and listened. Was there something there? Footsteps? Something like instinct told her to press herself against the wall next to a houseplant and to cautiously peer down the corridor.

There was definitely someone there!

A man!

Her heart was pounding, much too loudly for her liking.

But the next moment, she felt something inside her relax – deeply relax. She felt soft and warm and boneless again, like rolled pastry.

Howard!

Now the romantic liaison she had previously imagined in vivid technicolour detail could actually happen, albeit somewhat uncomfortably there in the corridor, but never mind! But instead of calling out, waving or otherwise making herself known, Agnes stayed behind the houseplant, rooted to the spot.

Something wasn't right. Howard had stopped too. He was looking at a door, hands in his pockets, doing nothing.

There's really only one good reason to stand idly in front of a door, if you've knocked and are waiting for someone to open it. Only, Agnes was fairly sure Howard hadn't knocked.

Could he be . . . ? Was it possible that . . . ? Was Howard *lurking*?

The suspicion seemed ludicrous. Howard wasn't the lurking type, was he? He was sophisticated. Scatter-brained. *Harmless.* She was too preoccupied with the spate of murders and not enough with the more enjoyable aspects of hotel life . . .

Howard cast a covert glance to the left, then to the right, but failed to notice Agnes, who was now stuck to the wall like a flounder. Then he was on his knees and stood up again straightaway, put his hands back in his trouser pockets and walked off, fortunately not in Agnes's direction.

Agnes remained glued to the wall for a while listening to her own heartbeat.

What had that all been about?

She had seen something that she shouldn't have, that much was clear.

But what exactly?

She had the impression that Howard had pushed something underneath the door. Something small, flat. A folded piece of paper, maybe?

Agnes didn't like what he had done or how he had

done it either. Casually. *Practised*. As if he had done it a thousand times before.

Undoubtedly there were lots of innocent explanations for what had just happened, but right now Agnes couldn't think of a single one. She had a heavy, paralysing feeling in the pit of her stomach, as if she had unknowingly swallowed a stone.

Tortoises sometimes swallowed stones, and it was good for their digestion, but it had a disagreeable effect on Agnes.

Dammit! She was disappointed, not so much in Howard, but more in herself. All she had hoped for was a few day-dreams, an ounce of admiration and maybe a nice chat or two, but Howard had even bungled that. Now she felt betrayed. She had fallen for something and didn't even know quite what. That was quite enough of that!

The only thing about Howard that would interest her from now on would be what he had pushed under that door. Agnes considered trying to peer under the door, but if she even made it onto her knees, it was unlikely she would ever get up on her feet again. Aside from that, there were files under her arm and a murderer on the loose; sometimes you had to put your private interests to one side.

She noted the relevant room number – just in case – clutched her files and carried on, sluggish and disillusioned, the stone still in the pit of her stomach.

'That's as good as it's going to get,' groaned Mojo.

Edwina nodded regretfully.

They had both tried hard to get as much of Lillith back in the tin as possible. It was a considerable amount, but just not all of Lillith. Edwina wondered what was missing. An eye? An ear? A foot? Hopefully not her fingers. Lillith had always been so proud of her green fingers!

For the hundredth time, Edwina leant over the tin and murmured apologies. Lillith remained silent as usual, but this time it seemed to Edwina, she was offended and hurt.

Now, she and Mojo were in the process of cleaning up the final bits of ash from the floor with the help of damp towels.

'All because of the stupid gear,' Edwina muttered. It was now obvious even to her that Mojo wasn't talking about his stuff but, well, drugs. He had fallen out of favour with her as an agent, but he was still occupying her wardrobe, so Edwina felt a certain sense of responsibility.

'I'm sorry,' Mojo whined. 'I'm trying to get off the stuff. Really, I am. It causes nothing but trouble. That's why I'm here in the wardrobe! But sometimes I just need . . . I thought you had something in the tin! I thought you were lying to me! I only wanted . . .'

Edwina waved dismissively. Mojo's private problems didn't interest her in the slightest. How on earth was she going to explain the stains on the carpet to Agnes?

Best not at all!

Edwina grabbed the rug beside her bed and dragged it to the spot where a piece of Lillith and a piece of sheep's wool were now forever one. There! Good as new!

'Done!' she said proudly. 'I've got to go over there now. Agnes is investigating.'

'Cool,' said Mojo. 'What's she investigating?'

'Some murders.' Edwina shrugged. Agnes didn't have many other hobbies. If she really got interested in something, it was mostly the boiler or a murder. It could get a bit monotonous at times!

'Cool,' said Mojo again, if a little less enthusiastically. 'And, err, what murders would that be?'

'Of a man,' Edwina explained. 'And a woman. And maybe another woman. And of a hood.'

'Cool.' With the word *hood*, the last shred of enthusiasm had disappeared from Mojo's face, and he went really pale again.

Edwina passed him a wholegrain stick that she'd smuggled out of dinner, but even that couldn't elicit a positive reaction from him.

'Not hungry?' she asked sympathetically.

Mojo shook his head. 'He's after me,' he whispered. 'He's not going to give up just like that . . . I think I want to go back in the wardrobe. And I think . . . I'd like you to . . . lock it?'

'The wardrobe?'

Mojo nodded.

'With you inside?' Edwina wanted to be sure. 'It's not very practical.'

The whippersnapper shrugged. 'It would be easier, I think. If I want to go looking for gear again, or . . . if I get any ideas . . . it's better this way. Safer. Sometimes being locked up isn't so bad, d'you know what I mean?'

Edwina did not know what he meant. She didn't usually get many ideas and hated being locked up. Hettie hated it, so did Oberon, and he had now already absconded from the bathroom twice in his quest for freedom.

What in all the world could be worse than being locked in a wardrobe?

'Are you sure?' she asked.

'I'm sure!' Mojo said, folding himself back into the wardrobe. He had blown up Hettie II and was using her as a pillow. It actually looked quite comfy.

Edwina sighed. If that made him happy, she could lock him in the wardrobe for a bit.

She closed the wardrobe door and listened.

'Now?' she asked.

'Quickly!' Mojo urged her.

Edwina locked the wardrobe door, put the key on the chest of drawers and headed off with Oberon to help Agnes with the investigation.

14

LEGLESS

'It's clear as mud,' Winston muttered.

Nobody could really argue with that. Marshall's bed looked like a wasteland. There were lists, rotas and statements lying around all over the place, higgledy-piggledy, printed in sadistically small print and on special environmentally friendly recycled paper, which at any rate, wasn't especially easy to read.

Everything had actually started quite promisingly. As soon as Agnes had turned up with the folders, Winston had started placing the papers onto the bed, piece by piece, peering through his reading glasses every now and then, saying 'aha' and 'oho.'

But now he seemed to have run out of steam. He was sitting there exhausted, while Marshall glumly surveyed his bed, messed up beyond recognition.

Charlie was still sulking in the corner because she wasn't allowed to go to the bar, Bernadette was in cloud cuckoo land or wherever else it is that people who are in love are wont to mentally retreat to, and Agnes had misplaced her reading glasses. Surprisingly, the only one really making herself useful was Edwina. Every time one of the many papers slid off the bed, she diligently picked it up.

Agnes was a little disappointed. She had expected some kind of breakthrough, or at least inspiration – but far from it. Even if she never would have admitted it, all that data was making her feel tired. If Helen could see her team of experienced investigators working at that very moment, exhausted and intimidated by a pile of paper, she definitely would have needed a couple of tissues again.

But luckily it was only them.

Agnes spotted her reading glasses on the sofa and went to rescue them before someone could sit on them. Bernadette, for example, was a real master in the art of plonking-yourself-down-on-glasses, and Edwina had a few optical aids on her conscience too.

She got the glasses and plonked them on her nose. There, maybe that would make things a bit clearer! She stepped decisively towards the bed and pulled out a random piece of paper. It was a list of employees currently deployed at the Eden – a surprisingly short list. Here was the thing, most of the hotel employees didn't live on-site, they travelled to work from the nearest village. And for that, the coast road was needed.

So, for the moment, the hotel had to make do with the people who were already present on the morning the coast road threw itself into the sea like a lemming.

That was Helen – the manager, a chef, two sous chefs, five waiters, four cleaners, three bartenders, one of which was Max, a yoga teacher, a massage therapist – Lilac, two fitness instructors – Jenny and Pablo, and Frank the gardener.

Agnes frowned. In the absence of a butler, the gardener

would obviously have been a classic candidate. He could have cut the phone line with some secateurs, and then . . .

At that point, her imagination failed her. She had seen the gardener in action yesterday through one of the panoramic windows, his long hair wildly flailing. He was wearing dirty rubber boots and a shirt that had apparently never seen the inside of a washing machine. The idea that someone like that with muddy boots could inconspicuously wander through a hotel like the Eden committing murders seemed far-fetched. For a start, he would definitely have left footprints, rather large ones, and for another, surely one or other of the guests would have seen or smelt him and made a complaint.

Agnes sighed. The gardener could be ruled out.

'You can rule them all out,' said Winston, as if he had read her mind.

'All of them?' That seemed a bit premature to Agnes. If it carried on like that, soon they wouldn't have any suspects at all.

'Well, yes,' Winston explained. 'We'll obviously have to question them still, but if you look at the rotas, you'll see that none of them could have committed all four murders. Especially the murder of Mrs Meyer-Brinks – that was this morning, presumably just after we left the library, and every single employee was working then, in plain sight and always in the company of other employees or guests.'

'Apart from the cleaning lady who found her,' Marshall quickly added. 'She could have strangled Mrs Meyer-Brinks and then found her.'

'In theory,' said Winston. He looked fresher again, more awake, as if he had now digested the information salad.

'But if you look at the statement, you'll see that she was working with a colleague, who was hoovering the hallway outside. That would only have left two or three minutes to strangle and discover her. Is that realistic? I don't think so!'

Winston had once developed a system of communication for the Secret Service that consisted entirely of chocolate bars. If he said something wasn't realistic, it was safe to discount it.

'Maybe they were in it together?' Agnes offered.

'Possible,' said Winston with a lack of conviction. 'But why? These are good jobs here at the Eden. Well-paid in an area where there isn't much else going on economically. If you start just randomly knocking off guests, it's bad for the stability of your workplace.'

'But is it really random?' Marshall asked.

'And are the victims all guests?' Edwina added surprisingly rationally. Oberon seemed to be a good influence on her.

Good questions, without a doubt. Despite that, Agnes lowered the staff list back onto the bed. When it came down to it, Winston was right. The idea that a team of employees was working together to do away with people seemed far-fetched.

The other guests remained the main suspects. But where were the bloody guest lists?

Charlie yawned demonstratively and kicked one of her silk slippers through the room.

Bernadette was sipping a glass of water and looked like she would rather be somewhere else, presumably in male company. That hurt Agnes a bit. Until now, Bernadette had always appreciated a good murder investigation.

Oberon had managed to worm his way out through a little opening in the sports bag and was curiously flicking his tongue in and out around Winston's wheelchair. Luckily Charlie hadn't seen him yet.

Agnes watched the pale snake with a certain envy. Boas like Oberon kept growing their whole lives. She, on the other hand . . . She had to admit that things hadn't been looking good for her in that respect for a while. Nothing budged, and when something did happen, it was in the wrong direction.

Her world was shrinking.

Even she was shrinking, body and mind. Would she ever have turned her back on something like the verger's murder before? Not on your nelly! She would have taken care of it immediately. Instead, she had packed her bags and run away.

Now she had not just one, but at least four murders on her hands. Served her right!

She decisively grabbed another list and squinted at it. Here were all the current guests who had taken part in a behind-the-scenes tour. There weren't very many – the tour clearly wasn't a bestseller.

'Austin Greg,' she read aloud. 'Maggie Bishop, erm, Howard Hope.' Her voice skipped a bit, and she felt the stupid stone in her stomach again. Disappointment mixed with regret. 'Mr and Mrs Frencher, Jack Smith and' – she paused for dramatic effect – 'the White Widow!'

Agnes looked triumphantly around the group. Obviously 'White Widow' wasn't written on the paper but 'Marie de Gurney,' and Agnes had recognised the name.

'I think we should definitely look into this White

Widow a bit more closely,' she declared.

Just then, something clinked. Bernadette's water glass had slipped out of her hand. Water was seeping into the carpet.

'Sorry,' said Bernadette. It sounded like a croak.

Agnes waved her apology away. A bit of water on the carpet really was no big deal. They had other things to worry about after all.

'There, the White Widow!' She pointed to the name. 'Her husband died here three years ago under mysterious circumstances.' That was maybe laying it on a bit thick, but Trudy had implied as much. 'And since then, she comes back every year and lurks about in armchairs with her dog. It's not normal!'

'But then, what is normal?' muttered Winston.

Charlie shrugged, the others looked stumped. They had to admit that none of them had any idea what normal was, especially these days.

'I'm not interested in what's normal,' Agnes said heatedly. 'I'm interested in who's committing these murders! And the White Widow is at the top of my list. She was here when someone died three years ago – and now people are being killed and she's here again. Coincidence? I hardly think so! And why did she do that tour two days ago, huh? She's been here lots of times before – why now?'

'Maybe she's interested in heat pumps,' Marshall offered.

'And maybe she wanted to scope out a suitable location for her next murder!' countered Agnes. The more she thought about it, the clearer it became to her that she *wanted* it to be the White Widow. The woman was creepy with her weird habit of lurking like a spider in armchairs. And she'd threatened her before the ice-cream buffet, hadn't she? Brazen.

'We'll put her on the list,' Winston said.

Now there were already two lists, the list of victims on the napkin and the list of suspects on the recycled paper.

The list of suspects still looked a bit bare.

Nevertheless, Agnes was satisfied for now. They'd made a start.

He hadn't always been called Oberon, far from it. The name was a completely new development, but that didn't bother him. Things came, and things slipped away, that was just what life was like. Names didn't have legs, just like he didn't have legs. Legs weren't necessary. He had shed his old name and his old life like a skin that didn't fit very well anymore, and had leglessly slid his strong, slim body into his new name.

But just like after shedding his skin, he was still a bit sensitive, freshly hatched and vulnerable. He had to be vigilant. *She* was no more, that much was clear. She had slid out of her skin too, but stupidly hadn't thought to get a new one ready in time. Now she was gone, drowned on a whispered word.

Oberon felt a pang of regret.

The origin of the whisper was still causing trouble, out and about on two awkward legs, an embarrassingly clumsy nocturnal predator.

No doubt about it, you had to keep your wits about you. *She* might have fallen for it, but Oberon had immediately sensed the darkness inside. A dark seed, just waiting to find fertile ground and sprout.

If this person shed their old skin, a cold, hard creature would appear. Oberon assumed it had already happened.

He sensed he was by no means the only snake in paradise anymore.

Agnes had switched off the light a long while ago, but Edwina couldn't sleep. Something was preying on her mind. It had something to do with Agnes's investigation, but every time Edwina got close to the thought it rolled up like a woodlouse. It was enough to drive her mad.

If she hadn't been hunting down the wayward thought, she might not have heard the footsteps out in the hallway.

But she heard everything. First, the pleasant, quietly squishing sound of a door softly closing, and then footsteps, a bit stealthy.

Now, they were on a ship, so it seemed completely above board that people would be up and about on the deck, presumably drunk, presumably looking for their cabin. But the footsteps had something secretive about them, and Edwina's curiosity was roused.

She slid silently out of bed, just as Oberon would have done, and flung open the hotel room door.

A shocked squeal.

'Ha!' cried Edwina.

There stood Charlie, frozen in motion, looking like she'd been caught red-handed. She was wearing tight trousers, high heels and a fabulous glitzy jacket that Edwina was instantly envious of.

'What are you up to?' Edwina asked suspiciously.

Charlie peered past her into the room, a look of concern on her face.

Edwina waved to let her know there was no need to worry. The new hearing aid was asleep on the bedside table and Agnes was lying on her good ear, so she couldn't hear a thing. Edwina had tested it out earlier on, first with stupid questions, then by clapping her hands and finally with a teaspoon that she had hit a cup with. Nothing! Once Agnes was asleep, she was asleep.

Charlie stood there like a guilty conscience personified and didn't respond. Edwina raised her eyebrows and allowed herself a bit of time to analyse the situation.

'You're going to the bar, aren't you?' she finally asked with a grin. It was gratifying if she wasn't the only one breaking Agnes's stupid rules for once.

Charlie sighed and slumped against the wall. 'You've got to understand, Edwina! It just can't go on like this!' She groaned. 'I can't stand it anymore! I'm not getting a wink of sleep! I need my beauty sleep!'

And Charlie did indeed have dark circles under her eyes and didn't look recuperated in the slightest, despite all of the beauty treatments. 'She snores!' She moaned. 'She snores like a freight train! It can't go on like this!'

Edwina nodded. She had known for a long time that Bernadette snored, more loudly than all of the others put together. Nobody gave her any credit, but she knew almost everything about her housemates and would have liked to have pointed out to Charlie that she had spurned her room with a virtually soundless snake and voluntarily defected to Bernadette's snoring shenanigans. Now she was getting her just deserts! But Charlie looked genuinely exhausted, so Edwina kept her thoughts to herself.

'So now you're going to sleep in the hallway?' she asked curiously.

'Well,' said Charlie evasively. 'Not exactly.'

Edwina narrowed her eyes. 'Where then?'

Charlie shrugged nonchalantly. 'This is a hotel, isn't it? There's beds everywhere!'

'You want your own room?' Edwina was delighted. Bernadette would take offence at Charlie's moving out, and with that the next argument was inevitable. And the busier the others from Sunset Hall were with one another, the less time they had to moan about Oberon, or to discover the young man in the wardrobe.

'Not a room exactly,' said Charlie, looking at the floor. 'Just a bed. Or maybe . . . *somebody* with a bed.'

'Ah.' Edwina thought for a moment. 'And where . . . ?'

'In the bar, of course!' said Charlie, pushing herself off the wall with some difficulty and tottering off, sparkling like a rainbow.

Edwina wondered for a moment if she should be worried. After all, Agnes had said something about a murderer, and it seemed like Charlie was easy prey tottering about in her high heels.

On the other hand, there were lots of people on board with them, so it seemed unlikely that the murderer should happen upon Charlie, of all people, as he was going about his business. And maybe Agnes was just imagining the whole thing anyway. Edwina enjoyed the investigations just as much as the others, but she knew from experience that at the end of a murder hunt with Agnes, there wasn't always a real murderer awaiting them, but quite often a misunderstanding instead.

Apart from that, it wasn't her problem. While her housemates were living in their fantasy worlds, she had to keep both feet on solid factual ground and concentrate on the mission. After all, important snakes in exile didn't guard themselves!

Charlie was in the company of what was now her second martini at the bar.

Her luck was not in. The guests still in the Sea Lounge were either sozzled or already with someone – in most cases both.

The detox group was shrieking and cackling in a corner like a witches' coven – little wonder really, first just salad and now suddenly the good stuff! They seemed to be the only ones really enjoying themselves, and Charlie would have gladly joined them. Most of the couples, however, were in the process of really locking horns, mainly because one of them was drunker than the other one would have liked.

Charlie observed the situation for a while and inwardly congratulated herself for getting rid of husband number four in good time before retiring.

Then she noticed the chap in the corner watching her with intelligent penguin eyes. A bit portly for Charlie's liking, but neither sozzled nor unattractive. Quite the opposite – he seemed to her to be pleasantly awake. Wide awake. Someone who didn't miss a trick. Charlie tilted her head a bit to show off her cheekbones, still terrific as they were.

'Been stood up?' a voice to her right suddenly asked. 'I don't get it personally. Just leaving such an attractive woman to her own devices on holiday!'

Charlie spun around. Someone was sitting surprisingly close, a man with bushy hair, glinting eyes and round red glasses. An academic type. Charlie had little experience with academics but had always been a little curious where they were concerned.

She put her cheeks into position again and smiled.

'Hello there,' she said.

'May I?' asked the man, even though he was already sitting right next to her. Then he got going. What did she think of the Eden? He himself came every year. Wonderfully secluded and so beautiful and comfortable too. And environmentally aware. It was so important to think about the environment, especially these days.

Charlie tried to suppress a yawn. She had nothing against the environment, not at all, but she currently had other priorities.

The man next to her squinted and seemed annoyed for a moment. 'Excuse me for being so direct, but . . . you really do have gorgeous eyes!' he clamoured.

Charlie grinned. This was more like it!

'Will you look at that!' said her admirer, because that's what he surely was, and let his eyes wander through the room. 'All these couples on this gorgeous evening, and harmony is nowhere to be seen. It's sad, isn't it?' He shook his head regretfully, and Charlie shook hers too, although she was still grinning.

The man leant in towards her. He smelt good.

'I get the feeling that lots of the couples that come here,

well – how should I put it – are in some kind of crisis,' he murmured. 'It's such a shame, isn't it, especially in such a romantic setting. I personally . . .'

Charlie held her hand out towards him before he could go off on another tangent.

'I'm Charlie!'

'*Enchanté*!' cried the man, taking her hand to kiss it, perfectly executed and not too wet.

'I'm Howard. Howard Hope.'

15

BAT

A shrill, piercing sound ripped Agnes from her sleep.

Fire?

Earthquake?

Disaster!

She woke with a start and found herself looking at an unfamiliar room. Strange carpet, a strange recliner and a strange view stared back at her. What was going on? Had she been dumped in a home after all? That really did take the biscuit!

But no, the room was far too luxurious for a home.

A few breaths later, she had got her bearings a bit more. The room wasn't completely unfamiliar, she had seen it recently before, just like the sea having its fun outside her window.

Sea.

Fun.

Luxury romantic eco hotel.

That's right. She was on holiday. That was it! This realisation wasn't accompanied by relief, but a strangely hollow feeling. The Eden might well look like paradise, but there were some issues, that much was clear. Agnes tried to remember what the issues were but couldn't concentrate because there was still an almighty racket.

Before she could think, she had to get rid of that infernal ringing!

It didn't take long for her to identify a little box on her bedside table as the source of the noise.

An alarm clock! Outrageous!

Agnes hit the little box with the palm of her hand. It jumped but carried on going off. Agnes slammed it again, first with her hand, then with one of the many pillows. Finally, at the end of her tether, she sent it catapulting out of the bed.

A final, distorted squawk, then there was peace. It occurred to her a bit belatedly that it wasn't just any old alarm clock that had just given up the ghost, but Charlie's. Charlie had pressed it into her hand yesterday so that she wasn't late. But late for what?

For now, Agnes decided to perform her ablutions, and put her hearing aid and false teeth in position. It was strange and inexplicable, but she could think better with her teeth in.

Once out of bed, she almost tripped over Edwina, who was stretched out on the floor and had taken up corpse pose. What on earth was Edwina doing in her room? Yoga, clearly, but was there more to it? A memory struggled to the surface through the fluff in her head, there had been an argument amongst the housemates – what was it about again? – and now she had Edwina on her hands.

The corpse pose made Agnes think too. It felt like she had spent an inordinate amount of time with people in corpse pose over the last few days. Specifically, a chap without a face and Mrs Meyer-Brinks in the freezer. And neither of them had been taking such regular and relaxed breaths as Edwina!

Agnes carefully tiptoed around Edwina towards the bathroom, in the hope that a bit of soap and cold water would jog her memory. But she was barely in the bathroom when something else jogged her memory, in the sink, tightly coiled, lay a not-all-that-small white snake hissing at her crossly. Agnes was suddenly wide awake. She would have liked to hiss back but took a step back instead, just to be on the safe side. She could forget the cold-water thing for now.

She made sure that at least the shower was snake-free, slipped out of her nightdress, wrestled with the state-of-the-art fixtures and finally managed to get water trickling over her back. There you go! At least there was nothing wrong with the shower. Not too warm, not too cold, water fine and everywhere like tropical rain. Not that Agnes had built up much experience in her life with tropical rain, but this is exactly how she imagined it to be.

She closed her eyes and tried to forget about the snake in the sink. When she opened them again, she noticed something black dangling ominously behind the door.

She gulped.

She recognised the thing hanging limply on a hook like a bat that had been on a hot wash – it was her pre-historic swimming costume! The memory came suddenly and brutally, not like tropical rain at all, more like a tsunami.

She had promised Charlie that she would go to aqua aerobics with her! That's why the alarm clock, and that's why she had forced herself out of bed at this ungodly hour.

What on earth had she been thinking?

But it was too late to rebel against fate. Agnes said goodbye to her rain shower, dried herself with the fluffiest towel of all time and commenced wrestling with the swimming costume. Two legs had to go into two dedicated openings, the chest area with the cups should preferably be at the front, and on the back, there were straps that crossed over. The whole thing was like a dance with a huge, unruly, infinitely flexible squid.

When Agnes finally had the feeling that the swimming costume covered all the necessary places, she felt like she had run a marathon. She sat down on the toilet lid to recuperate a bit.

'You're lucky you don't have to wear a swimming costume!' she said to the snake. Oberon. Yes, that's what he was called!

Oberon looked at her sympathetically but, it seemed to Agnes, also a bit mockingly.

A little while later, Agnes was albeit not up to her neck in the water, but up to her uppermost rib and it was misshaping her swimming costume to an alarming extent.

All around her, women were waving big colourful beach balls. Music was blaring. Agnes considered whether she could allow herself to wave her own ball too – or would the unaccustomed movement be the final straw for her swimming costume?

She felt like a sea horse amongst well-trained seals – wonky, incompetent and fragile. While all the others thrust, squeezed, lifted, or twisted as directed, she just clung to the strategically important strap area of her outfit hoping for some kind of miracle.

But the most annoying thing of all was that Charlie and her chic red swimming costume hadn't graced them with their presence. First, foisting the stupid alarm clock on her, and then just leaving her in the lurch – it really did take the biscuit!

Agnes considered feigning a cramp or a fainting fit before her swimming costume finally gave up the ghost. But she wasn't sure if, with the loud music, anybody would notice, and if it went wrong, she might even be trampled by her overzealous neighbours.

No, she was stuck.

Throwing caution to the wind, she let go of the straps and waved her ball a bit so as not to stick out like a sore thumb. She also discreetly looked around for a way out.

Way ahead of her, in the front row, was the detox group, splashing and twisting their hearts out. Behind them it got chubbier and clumsier. Agnes wondered how much water they were all displacing from the pool. A lot, that was for sure!

The most interesting thing about aqua aerobics was definitely Pablo, the trainer. He was young, dark and presumably the reason so many ladies of advanced years had forced themselves out of bed at the crack of dawn. Agnes hadn't seen a young man in swimming trunks for a small eternity and decided to make the best of the situation. She obediently held her ball as directed to the left or the right or up over her head, and squinted down at her swimming costume out of the corner of her eye as it slowly but surely lost its battle with gravity.

Then she noticed something much lower down. A

shimmer. A refracted, muted glint. There was something near her feet on the bottom of the pool. An image flashed in her mind's eye, the wet woman, dripping and dead in her red dress. Obviously, Agnes hadn't seen her with her own eyes, but Trudy had described the scene very vividly.

Where could someone get so wet near the gym?

The answer was sloshing up and down in front of Agnes in time with the music.

Then it occurred to her that the thing glinting on the bottom of the pool might be a clue.

It was also clear that it would be devilishly difficult to retrieve it. If she had been agile like Edwina, perhaps she could have just grabbed it with her toes and brought it to the surface, but as things stood, the only option left to her was a decidedly risky manoeuvre.

She used to dive, in the sea even. Obviously, that was quite some time ago, but how hard could it be?

Agnes closed her eyes, held her breath and readied herself to sink like a stone.

The music had stopped.

Agnes blinked away pool water.

Her eyes were open again.

The first thing she saw was a mouth surrounded by stubble, enroute to her own mouth.

She instinctively fended it off and had a coughing fit.

Then she felt better.

She was lying somewhere on the floor, that much was clear, and she was sopping wet. Women were standing all around her in swimming costumes. Some were still holding their colourful balls in their hands, and they all seemed relieved that Agnes was coughing and blinking and trying to get up.

But nobody seemed more relieved than Pablo, who had just narrowly avoided performing the kiss of life on Agnes.

'You scared the living daylights out of me,' he said, pale beneath his tan. He helped Agnes sit up. His voice sounded warm and vaguely Mediterranean, and Agnes, whose first instinct was to put up a fight, allowed him to support her back.

'I didn't mean to . . .' she croaked and had to cough again. 'I just wanted to . . .'

Yeah, what was it again? There had been something glinting at the bottom of the pool, and she had made a dive for it like some kind of demented magpie.

Diving down had been surprisingly easy, but just as she was about to reach her hand out for the glittering thing, a heel had come from nowhere and kicked her in the side. After that Agnes had lost her bearings and couldn't remember which way was up and which way was down anymore. Bodyless legs had been stomping all around her, bubbles swirling all over the place. She had tried to cry out, but obviously that hadn't worked, and then everything went dark, as if someone had tipped black ink into the water.

But now she was sitting up and breathing again.

At least that was something!

To top it all off, tears were streaming down her cheeks, as if she wasn't wet enough already. Her body had had enough of her escapades and started to shake violently.

Then all of a sudden, Agnes noticed a chic red swimsuit amongst all the other, rather mediocre ones.

'Agnes, for God's sake, what have you been up to?'

Charlie looked bedraggled and a bit less fabulous than usual, but presumably still far better than Agnes, sitting as she was on the bare tiles wearing a wet bat and shaking like a leaf.

She would have liked to give Charlie a piece of her mind on the subject of alarm clocks, aqua aerobics and not turning up, but her voice was still somewhere at the bottom of the pool and didn't seem to want to return.

So, she made do with reproachfully pointing an equally violently shaking finger at Charlie, but the drama of it was lost because at that very moment Charlie spotted Pablo and struck a pose in her chic red swimsuit.

But Agnes wasn't paying attention to her anymore. Something was in her head, a pang of dread she couldn't quite place yet. It didn't have anything to do with her unfortunate dive though, but with something that was happening right now.

Right under her nose.

Agnes stared at Trudy, who was crouching in front of her, the most worried of all the worried swimming costumes, her eyes big and hazel-brown and obviously kind of hungry again. Agnes wasn't really looking into her eyes, but a bit lower down, at the neckline of her swimming costume.

There, about collarbone height, ran a sharp line, as if it had been painted with a brush. Above the line was a healthy tan, below the line the skin was pale and pasty, just like most English people in the winter.

Agnes's heart, which had only just recovered from the fright in the pool, started pounding loudly again.

The line had reminded her that a person's body can look somewhat different than the attached face. All of a sudden, she knew who the dead man behind the scenes was – it had to be!

And if she was right, then the killer wasn't attacking randomly at all.

If she was right, then Agnes was right at the top of his hit list!

Bernadette leant on the terrace railing and sighed deeply.

The wind huddled up against her, the air tasted of salt and seaweed and rosemary, and gulls screeched playfully. Then there was sun on her face too, warm as a kiss, and Bernadette closed her unseeing eyes and held herself out towards the warmth of the sun like a plant.

She had arranged to meet Jack there, to welcome the new day and capture the sunrise in words, he the colours and play of the light on the water, she the waft of smells and the song of the awakening day.

Bernadette was as nervous as a teenager. It wasn't just eager anticipation. She had decided to discuss certain things with Jack – not just the sunrise, but also his work, his stay at the Eden and a certain Mrs Meyer-Brinks, who would be spending the rest of her holiday in the cold store.

Bernadette was sure he would tell her the truth, but she didn't know what she would then do with that truth.

Something stirred in the pit of her stomach. Hunger, she might have thought before and demolished a packet or two of fondant creams. But now, even the thought of a quite normal breakfast seemed weirdly strange to her.

Was she really the same person who just a week ago

would never have voluntarily skipped a meal?

And if she wasn't, who was she?

Samantha, who'd had sharp edges, and been full of astute, clear thoughts and ideals? Samantha, who would never have cared that her lover was in a questionable line of work?

Lover.

There.

Bernadette felt her cheeks getting hot, but it was too late. The thought had been thought and couldn't be unthought.

Foolish.

She leant further forward and sensed the drop. Although she obviously couldn't see it, she was well aware it was there. It was the cool expanse of a vast space. It was the absence of echo.

Emptiness.

Freedom.

All of a sudden, she heard footsteps behind her, the rhythm as familiar as her own heartbeat.

A hand was placed gently on her back, so naturally, it was as if that were exactly where it belonged.

Agnes was staring out at the sea too. Unlike Bernadette, Agnes could see it in all its glory in front of her, its neat wave formations and the ice-cream hues of the sunrise.

It was beautiful – wild, free and lonely. The sea didn't have any problems with alarm clocks, murders and swimming costumes. The sea knew what it was doing.

She sighed. She had been wrapped up in lots of fluffy towels and deposited in the relaxation room. Charlie had fussed around her like a guilt-ridden and unusually chic wasp, but Agnes had ignored her and looked the other way. She was angry at her friend, too angry for words, but at the same time she found the whole thing a bit uncomfortable. Why did everyone else get on alright with stupid aqua aerobics, while she managed to nearly drown herself within a few minutes?

The truth was, being saved was embarrassing. Unlike in books and films, where people were constantly being saved and cutting a fine figure in the process, a rescue in real life was rather humiliating. Everyone imaginable treated you like a child, rubbing your back unsolicited and shaking their heads pityingly when they thought you weren't looking. Dignity was another matter! On top of that you had to be grateful to your rescuer too, even though you really wanted to tell him where he could stick all of his expertise, stubble and charming accent.

At some point even Charlie had given up on the 'caring', mumbled something about 'catching up on sleep' and left Agnes alone with the sea.

Now she was in a strangely peaceful mood. Warmth was slowly but surely creeping into her limbs again, as the morning sun rose from the waves like a big, glowing exercise ball. Agnes was even starting to develop a bit of an appetite and her thoughts tentatively turned to breakfast.

Only now that the shaking was gradually dying down and her head was clear again – almost too clear, Agnes felt as if the colours around her were brighter, the outlines sharper and things were almost translucent – did she notice her right hand.

Her right hand wasn't resting relaxedly in her towel-covered lap like the left, but was curled up in a fist, so tightly that Agnes could feel her fingernails digging into her palm.

She took a sharp breath in.

Here it was, the cause of all the trouble.

Beyond slowly, Agnes opened her hand, until a golden ring appeared and caught the morning rays.

In the light of the emerging sun outside, it almost looked as if it were on fire.

16

BREAKFAST

'Enchanting view, isn't it?'

Agnes gave a start and wrapped her fingers around the ring. Somebody was standing behind her in the relaxation room. *Howard!* she thought for a joyful moment, before remembering that Howard wasn't a romantic interest anymore, but a suspicious doorway-lurker. And apart from that, the voice behind her sounded different, deep, but also smooth and clear, and a bit wry.

She had heard that voice somewhere before; Agnes was sure of it!

She was too well wrapped up to just turn around, but she peered out of the corner of her eye. She didn't have to wait long. After a few gentle, almost soundless footsteps, the White Widow plopped her portly frame onto the lounger next to Agnes. She really did have a gift for appearing out of nowhere!

'There are lots of beautiful views here, but this one is my favourite!' she said.

Agnes didn't say anything and noticed her heart was pounding away again.

She thought about her list of suspects, which currently

only boasted one name. Had the White Widow seen the ring in her hand? Had she drawn any conclusions? And if she had – were they the right conclusions? She made a fist and felt the ring pressing into her palm, as if it were on fire.

She slid her hand into her lap, in an excessively casual way, to hide it under one of the many towels.

The White Widow looked at her with curiosity and, as it seemed to Agnes, evil amusement. Her gaze wandered over Agnes's hair, then on to the many towels that encompassed her body like a cocoon.

'Aqua aerobics,' the White Widow said with contempt. 'I don't think much of it myself!'

'Me neither,' Agnes quietly agreed. 'Not anymore.'

What did the woman want from her? Hardly to swap aqua aerobics stories! Had she come to finish her off there and then? Agnes lowered her eyes and peered at the Widow's unusually big and strong hands with concern. You could easily think them capable of wielding a dumbbell with deadly force or sending poor Mrs Meyer-Brinks to kingdom come with the help of her tacky butterfly necklace.

A thought struggled to the surface out of the muddle in Agnes's head.

Was she next?

The Widow next to her crossed her legs nonchalantly. She didn't look like a woman who was about to commit a murder.

'You might think I'd hate this view,' she said softly. 'But I don't – quite the opposite.'

Agnes's thoughts wandered off again. *Hate it? Why? It really is an exceptionally beautiful view!* Then she realised exactly what was out there – the cliffs, where the White

Widow's husband had allegedly met his maker, and where just recently an orange hood had done away with a yellow one.

Agnes would have liked to respond with something subtle, but combative, to make clear to the Widow, in a roundabout way, that she could save her allusions, but as usual in situations like this, nothing came to her. This evening in bed she would undoubtedly . . .

She suddenly wondered if she would even survive until this evening. The murderer was following a pattern and had acted pretty swiftly up to now. It was a long time until evening. First, it was breakfast.

Agnes's stomach tightened, whether it was down to nerves or hunger, she couldn't say. Life was short, even a long one like hers, and now, threatened by the White Widow, she could see so many things she still wanted to do.

Have breakfast, for example.

'It's breakfast soon,' she said to bolster herself.

The Widow eyed her with slight disappointment, presumably because she hadn't fallen for her game of veiled allusions.

'In ten minutes,' she said drily.

'Then I really should . . .' Agnes tried to wriggle out of her lounger. There was so much to do! She had to get back to her room and somehow extract herself from the bat swimming costume. Then get dressed, lipstick, rant at Edwina again, because of the matter of Oberon in the sink and also as a preventative measure, so Edwina wouldn't mess around at breakfast.

It was nigh on impossible!

And she obviously then had to catch a murderer, who might be sitting next to her right now admiring the view. She would have to get a wiggle on with the investigation too if she didn't want to end up in the cold store with Mrs Meyer-Brinks. She started to work her way towards the edge of her lounger with little sliding movements.

The White Widow watched for a moment or two, then reached out her hand. At first, Agnes thought the Widow wanted to help her out of the lounger, but far from it! Just as Agnes had made it to the edge, the Widow gently pushed her back into the depths of the recliner.

'Why the rush?' she said meekly. 'I'd like to talk to you about *this*.' Her chin pointed meaningfully towards the cliff's edge. 'This is far more important than breakfast. I thought you were curious.' She leant further towards Agnes and whispered, 'I heard you're a detective.'

She looked at Agnes, her eyes cool and piercing. Agnes ignored her and crawled resolutely towards the edge of the lounger again without saying a word. She wasn't a detective right now. Right now, all she wanted was breakfast, not the crazed confessions of a serial killer. She knew exactly how situations like this went – first the confession and then it was her turn! Over and out! Like many crazed killers, the Widow succumbed to the temptation of confiding in their victims and dishing up any old half-baked explanations, knowing full well that she could silence them afterwards. She could think again!

If only Agnes could somehow manage to get off this lounger, she would have a fighting chance!

'It really is very rude of you to leave while I'm talking to you!' the White Widow complained.

Agnes, who wasn't currently concerned with etiquette, continued to ignore her. She was almost there!

'You have no idea who you're dealing with!' threatened the Widow. 'Be reasonable! Hear me out!' Agnes stopped crawling and saw pure rage in the Widow's eyes. She held her breath and braced herself for something bad to happen.

But nothing bad happened.

The Widow looked at something behind Agnes and swiftly removed her hand. Agnes noticed an odd change cross her face. All of the anger disappeared as suddenly as if someone had pulled back a curtain. For a moment she seemed surprised, then the Widow's expression became flat, detached and almost a bit bored.

'You're right,' she said and eyed Agnes indifferently. 'Tomorrow is another day.'

With that, she gracefully got up from the lounger and now Agnes could also see who had approached from behind, Trudy, who wasn't in a swimming costume anymore, but sweatshirt and leggings, her hair still wet from the stupid aqua aerobics. Relief made Agnes feel wobbly as jelly. As long as Trudy was there, the White Widow couldn't do anything to her!

The Widow seemed to know that too. She nodded politely at Trudy, and the next thing Agnes knew, the Widow had disappeared from her field of vision.

Agnes exhaled, and Trudy plopped herself in the lounger the White Widow had just been sitting in.

'I wanted to see how you were doing after what happened before,' she said without a care in the world, with no idea that she'd potentially just prevented a murder. But what did she mean about before? It took a while for

Agnes to remember – that's it, not even half an hour ago she had almost drowned. The aqua aerobics adventure now seemed a million miles away. Water under the bridge. Now she had already escaped the most recent threat to her life and had definitely earned some breakfast.

'She's a bit creepy, isn't she?' Trudy whispered, after she had made sure that the White Widow really had disappeared from the relaxation room.

Agnes nodded. Trudy had no idea just *how* creepy!

Only now did she realise that she had been scared. Her heart was still pounding like mad and her muscles felt limp and useless, not in a pleasant way like after the massage, but more like someone had let the air out of her like Hettie II.

But then anger prevailed. Fear was for idiots. Fear didn't get you anywhere, especially not when you were hunting a murderer. Nobody could scare her! Nobody, especially not the stupid Widow! Agnes would stop her in her tracks, that was for sure!

'What were you talking about?' Trudy asked curiously.

'About breakfast,' Agnes said truthfully. What they *hadn't* spoken about was obviously much more important, but that was difficult to explain, especially to a simple soul like Trudy.

'Breakfast, huh?' the detoxer mumbled gloomily, absent-mindedly running her fingers through her hair. You could tell that breakfast was a difficult topic for her.

Agnes started to peel herself out of the many towels. She wasn't cold anymore, quite the opposite, she was downright hot, presumably because of all the excitement. A fluffy dressing gown appeared beneath the towels, mercifully covering the unspeakable swimming costume.

'I don't like the way she lurks about everywhere,' Trudy complained, obviously still occupied with the White Widow.

Agnes, who wanted nothing more than to finally rid herself of the wet bat, rush to breakfast and rejoice about her regained life, composed herself. This was in fact an ideal moment to pump Trudy for information about the White Widow!

'What actually happened to her husband back then?' she asked markedly casually as she sat up and tried to shuffle towards the edge of the lounger for the third time that day.

Trudy's eyes lit up.

'Fell off the cliff!' she said triumphantly, as if she were personally responsible for it. 'In broad daylight, on the most beautiful sunny day! Fell, ha! Jumped more like. Or was pushed!' She looked at Agnes meaningfully.

'And you think that *she* . . .' Agnes thought about the orange hood. If pushing someone off the cliff had worked once, it was logical that the murderer would use the same tried-and-tested method again.

Trudy shrugged. 'Obviously nobody can prove it, but if you ask me . . . They were a strange couple; he was younger than her and kind of . . .' She broke off and looked over at the cliffs a bit dreamily. 'In any case, it's weird that she still comes here, isn't it? You would think that if she's innocent, and after such a blow of fate . . . The killer always returns to the scene of the crime – at least that's what I think!'

Agnes nodded, managed to get over the edge and finally had solid ground beneath her feet again. It *was* weird – but it wasn't particularly incriminating.

She got up, a bit sobered. Trudy didn't really know anything. She was just a gossipmonger with a bit of an imagination and a sense of drama. Agnes had hoped for more.

Trudy seemed to sense her disappointment. 'She's worn white ever since,' she said spitefully. 'She never used to wear white and now she wears it all the time. That's got to mean something, hasn't it?'

Agnes nodded absent-mindedly. White, when you thought about it, wasn't a particularly practical colour for a murderer. She thought about the body in the pool pump room. If the killer had been wearing white, it wouldn't have gone off without a bloodstain or two.

Maybe the White Widow had changed before the murder?

That would have been an effective trick. Even in white, the Widow had the rather uncanny gift of melting into her surroundings. In normal clothes, with jeans, jumper and hat – or hood! – she would be practically invisible. Maybe that was the reason for all of the white? Maybe the Widow wore white to throw them all off the scent!

Agnes tried to remember her face. Piercing eyes, short hair, tanned skin. But what else? She wasn't entirely sure she would recognise the White Widow in different colours.

Trudy had got up too and moved closer to her. She wanted something from her, approval presumably or a chocolate bar, probably even both!

Just then, Marshall burst into the relaxation room in full uniform, pursued by the spa lady from the reception.

'Agnes!' he flapped. 'Agnes, what have you been playing at?'

Someone must have snitched and told the others about her mishap during aqua aerobics. And now Marshall was getting unnecessarily worked up. It was embarrassing, especially in front of Trudy.

Agnes felt herself going red and tried to put on a dignified expression. 'I did aqua aerobics,' she said a bit snippily. 'And then I wanted to relax here for a while. But if I keep being disturbed . . .'

The spa woman had caught up with Marshall and was tapping him on the shoulder from behind. 'You really can't wear shoes in here . . .' she hissed. 'I told you that yesterday . . . And stop screaming like that. This is the relaxation room!'

Marshall ignored her and looked at Agnes with such relief that she almost had a guilty conscience. 'I'm fine, Marshall,' she reassured him and reached out both arms to show just how well she was doing.

'There! Still all there!'

By a whisker!

But she obviously wasn't going to tell Marshall *that*!

Breakfast was downright glorious. Everything tasted so good when you were still alive!

Agnes treated herself to a croissant and an apricot pastry, happily ate yogurt with fresh fruit, got some scrambled eggs with herbs made for herself and even tried the porridge. All absolutely first-rate!

Apart from that, for once they were all present and correct at the table and Agnes didn't have to worry that one of them could have met their maker in the meantime. It made a refreshing change. She chatted animatedly with Winston about secret codes, and with Edwina about boa constrictors, and was even gracious towards Charlie, even though after the aqua aerobics incident she really didn't deserve it.

Bernadette, however, was unusually quiet. Love didn't seem to agree with her. Without her usual biting remarks, the harmony at the table was as sweet and thick as the hotel's own honey, and nigh on unbearable.

At least for a little while.

'How did it go yesterday evening?' Edwina asked Charlie. That was unusual because Edwina only took an interest in her two-legged housemates' activities in exceptional circumstances. Four-legged or most recently legless, yes, but two-legged not so much. Now she looked at Charlie curiously.

'A lady doesn't tell!' Charlie declared with dignity.

Agnes's ears pricked up. Anything ladies didn't talk about was worthy of closer scrutiny. 'What happened last night?' she asked. After what she had done earlier, Charlie owed her an answer!

'Nothing,' Charlie mumbled.

Edwina made an indignant sound.

'Well, you know how she snores!' Charlie gesticulated towards Bernadette, who seemed to sink into herself even more. 'So, I just . . .'

'She went to look for another bed,' Edwina explained helpfully.

'Another bed?' Agnes was still none the wiser.

'*Someone* with a bed!' Edwina explained and winked at

Agnes, just like she'd seen Charlie do.

Now Agnes finally understood and stared at Charlie in astonishment. 'You . . . ?'

She looked around the group in disbelief.

Winston had been sitting there open-mouthed for a while and Marshall was blushing.

Charlie shrugged. 'I'm on holiday. What of it? And anyway, at least I got some sleep!'

The truth was, the night with Howard had turned out to be a bit disappointing. And in fact, he had been quite keen to get her out of his room as quickly as possible afterwards. *You should go, darling! What about your husband?* But Charlie didn't have a husband – thank God! – and wasn't thinking about getting out of bed. Even if Howard hadn't been a particularly exciting lover – at least he didn't snore. You had to give him that. Charlie had gratefully fallen into a long-awaited deep sleep, undisturbed by snoring or snakes, and woken up this morning far too late and rushed to aqua aerobics, just in time to witness a lifeless Agnes being pulled out of the pool in her awful swimming costume.

Of course, she was sorry she had stood Agnes up, but the rest . . . it had been an experience at least! Why were her housemates looking at her with looks of such astonishment?

'You . . . *spent* . . . the night . . . with someone?' Agnes asked to make sure she had understood everything correctly. She didn't know if she should be outraged or envious, or just relieved that Charlie was still sitting at the table with them looking fabulous in a dishevelled kind of a way. 'What on earth were you thinking? Anything could have happened!'

'It didn't though!' Charlie said curtly. 'Quite the opposite!' She sighed and bit into a croissant to signal that for her the matter was closed.

But Agnes wasn't finished yet.

'You just go wandering around the hotel at night to meet men while there's a murderer on the loose? Have you lost all sense? Do you still remember the body in the pool pump room, or the wet woman, or poor Mrs Meyer-Brinks?'

Charlie gave herself time to chew. 'As far as we know, none of them wandered around the hotel at night,' she said once she had finished.

'That's not the point!' Agnes cried, so loudly that the people at the neighbouring table looked over curiously. She knew she was overreacting, but first aqua aerobics, then the White Widow and now the thought that Charlie could have ended up in the cold store because of her own stupidity . . . She leant over towards Charlie and wanted to shake her or hug her, but fortunately her hip flagged just in the nick of time and Agnes made do with clumsily, and a bit accusatorily, slapping Charlie on the shoulder.

Her sunny breakfast disposition had been completely ruined in any case.

'It can't go on like this,' she said as soon as she had released Charlie's shoulder. 'We've got to find the murderer as quickly as possible!'

It really was high time! As soon as the killer was caught, Charlie could safely pay men nocturnal visits again to her heart's content; she, however, would be in the relaxation room without a care in the world, and nobody would have to think twice if Edwina and Bernadette disappeared off the face of the earth again.

It suddenly occurred to Agnes that aqua aerobics, albeit a personal failure, had been pretty interesting in terms of the investigation.

She raised her right hand and, in a somewhat inappropriate gesture, showed her housemates her middle finger. The little gold ring she had risked life and limb fishing out of the pool was on her middle finger.

She explained to her housemates all about the ring.

Marshall was aghast.

Winston whipped out his reading glasses.

Edwina congratulated Agnes on her engagement.

'It's obviously a wedding ring!' said Charlie, who had the most experience in such matters. 'It's probably got something engraved in it!'

But before they could examine the engraving, they had to get it off Agnes's middle finger. It had slid easily onto her finger before when she had been scared of the Widow, but now, in the warmth of the breakfast room, after animated conversations and good coffee, it was stuck.

First Agnes tried herself, then Charlie, then Marshall. Then Bernadette nearly ripped her finger off, before Winston finally succeeded with some butter.

Edwina peered at the inside of the ring and squinted. 'There's something there,' she declared. 'Adam!'

It wasn't much, but at least they could establish whether there was an Adam at the hotel.

'And then we'll hopefully know a bit more about the first victim – the wet woman!' declared Agnes.

Bernadette pulled a sceptical face. 'Any one of the aqua aerobics lot could have lost it!' she said, finally showing a bit of interest in the case.

'Lost it, yes,' Agnes conceded. 'But then to not go looking for it afterwards . . . That's a bit unusual, isn't it? I asked at reception – nobody is missing a wedding ring! I'm assuming that's because the owner of the ring isn't able to miss anything anymore – namely, because she's no longer alive!'

'Hear! Hear!' Winston murmured taking his reading glasses off having inspected the ring.

Agnes continued her victory parade. 'Aside from that, I think I now know who the body in the pool pump room could be! And that in turn leads us to how the killer is selecting their victims . . .'

The others looked at her in astonishment, and Agnes allowed herself a smug grin. In actual fact, in a roundabout way, aqua aerobics had been a success after all. It really was quite astonishing what could be achieved if you got up early enough.

She got up, full of vim and vigour, and presumably caffeine again too.

Unlike her, the day was still young, and there was a lot to do!

17

COBRA

Bernadette knew that Agnes and her other housemates were off 'investigating' somewhere, but despite that she went back to her room as quickly as possible after breakfast.

After all, she had made her own enquiries and the outcome wasn't easy to stomach. She needed space and quiet, and above all a place where she, for the time being, was safe from him.

Now she was sitting in an armchair, her face turned towards the sun again, alone and still. At least that's what an observer would have seen from the outside.

It looked a bit different on the inside.

Inside, at least four people had gathered and were having an animated, acrimonious discussion.

There was the old Bernadette who thought that murder was in principle a reprehensible and unpleasant affair.

There was the Bernadette who was hoping against all reason that Jack had nothing to do with the killing spree at the hotel.

There was a rather disillusioned Bernadette who knew this was unlikely.

And even if he didn't, piped up an unsolicited fourth, particularly harsh Bernadette. *If not them, then others. You know what he's capable of!*

And then there was Samantha, who didn't really care either way, Samantha, who could hardly wait to hear his voice and discuss countless sunrises and sunsets with him.

It was a tight squeeze in Bernadette's armchair. She fidgeted uncomfortably back and forth, but the doubts lingered.

She had plucked up the courage and asked him, his hand on her back, his voice still in her ear. She almost couldn't bring herself to say it, but she had finally got it out. Not a direct question about Mrs Meyer-Brinks, of course, that would have given too much away, about her, Sunset Hall and their investigation.

No, she'd asked if he was on a job.

She was greeted by silence in response.

The hand on her back got lighter, like a bird preparing to take flight.

Gripped by a terrible, aimless fear, Bernadette clung to the railing.

Finally, she got an answer of sorts, so quiet that even she, with her bat-like hearing, had to strain to hear it.

'You never used to take an interest in my work.'

'That was before,' said Bernadette, surprised at how tough her voice sounded. 'This is now. Some things change.'

'And some don't!' Now there was some warmth in his voice. Warmth and wistfulness. Bernadette battled the urge to melt like vanilla ice cream.

She stood there in silence and didn't melt, until finally the answer arrived.

'Of course I'm still working.'

All of a sudden, it was too cold to melt.

'How?' Bernadette stammered. 'When? Who?' Even she was shocked at how much his answer scared her. After all, she'd suspected it for a while now anyway, but hearing it from the horse's mouth . . . She wanted to scream, she wanted to cry, and she wanted to throw her arms around his neck.

'No details.' Bernadette felt his fingers touch her hair. 'It's better for both of us that way.'

With that, she thought the matter was settled, but he must have sensed her shock.

'But . . .' His voice was so close, it was as if they were both inhabiting the same space, one person with two souls. 'I'm thinking about retiring. I'm no spring chicken anymore after all. One more job and then maybe . . .'

He fell silent, but Bernadette carried on listening.

A hint of the future hung in the air.

She almost skipped back from the terrace, but during breakfast the reality dawned on her more and more clearly.

Jack was still a contract killer.

And he was on a job.

People were dying at the hotel.

One of them was beaten to death behind the scenes.

Jack had gone on a behind-the-scenes tour a few days ago.

Too many coincidences. Far too many. It wasn't looking good. The only thing that gave her hope was that the murders in the hotel seemed somewhat bungled to her, and Jack was many things, but definitely not a bungler. On the other hand, maybe the murders were meant to look amateurish, maybe that was part of the job . . .

Now, in her armchair, Bernadette made a decision – she could live with the fact that Jack had made his living, smoothly and professionally ending lives.

Somehow.

It wouldn't be easy though.

But if he really was responsible for the faceless man in the pool pump room . . . She couldn't live with that. That was senseless brutality. Rage. A madness of sorts.

If Jack had the man in the pool pump room on his conscience, he wasn't the person she remembered anymore.

If Jack had the man in the pool pump room on his conscience, she would hunt him down.

The decision made her sad, but also brought a sense of relief. She knew where she stood, and once she stood, she stood firm.

Nobody stood their ground more firmly than Bernadette.

She was just about to get up out of the chair to help the others with the investigation – it was so important that nobody made a mistake – when she heard footsteps approaching the door.

Charlie probably, looking for something again. Charlie was always looking for things.

Or Edwina and her stupid snake.

Or maybe – her heart skipped a beat – Jack.

But nobody knocked, and nobody opened the door either.

Silence.

Had she been mistaken?

Then she heard a soft, scraping noise, like something was being pushed under the door.

* * *

Agnes, Charlie, Winston, Edwina, Oberon and Marshall were back at Murder Hunt HQ and it was round two of the battle of the paperwork.

Winston was studying the guest and staff lists, to perhaps find an Adam somewhere, while Agnes was sharing her latest theory, her eyes gleaming.

'At first it didn't occur to me,' she explained. 'Because the body was so pale. But it's the middle of winter. Most bodies are paler. It's only natural. Faces, however . . . People take care of their faces, they're in the sun, and they help it along with creams and stain and the like.'

'Bronzer,' said Charlie, bored.

'Exactly, bronzer.' Agnes nodded. 'Especially if they're vain.' She shot her friend a meaningful side-eye, but it was like water off a duck's back.

'So, I thought about what was logical,' Agnes continued. 'And who was missing. In a nutshell, I am as good as certain that the body behind the scenes is Max the barman. He had access to the pool pump room at all times, it's not at all unlikely that he let his murderer in there himself. And I asked at reception. Nobody has seen him since yesterday morning. His absence just hasn't been noticed yet because Helen sent him into the village on foot, to get help. But has help arrived? No! I'm guessing Max never even left the hotel!'

While she was at reception, Agnes had also dropped a cryptic comment about the pool pump room, and a couple of horrified hotel employees were probably in the process of cleaning it up and depositing the body in the freezer. Agnes was hoping that someone would identify the body by way of his clothing, and confirm her theory.

'But how is the murderer meant to have known who

Helen sent into the village?' Winston asked, looking briefly up from his lists. 'Unless, of course, Helen *is* the murderer. But then why send anyone into the village at all?'

'Maybe the murderer didn't know anything about it at all!' responded Agnes, who had been thinking about it for a while. 'Maybe it was just a lucky coincidence.'

'Lucky for the murderer,' Charlie said gloomily.

'The murderer has been very lucky,' Edwina chipped in and nodded.

They looked at one another. Luck was one thing – but how clever was the killer really?

'Why else would they have done it?' Marshall asked.

Agnes interlaced her skinny fingers. She had to handle this delicately.

'Well, now that we've got several victims, I thought it was about time we looked for a pattern. It's a bit difficult because we know next to nothing about the person on the cliffs or the wet woman, but if we assume that the body in the pool pump room is the barman, then at least two of the victims have something in common.'

'What's that?' Edwina asked.

'Well . . .' Agnes sighed. 'Mrs Meyer-Brinks and Max were both in the Sea Lounge when the murder on the cliffs happened!'

'Just like you!' cried Edwina.

Agnes nodded gravely. 'Just like me.'

Edwina had her doubts. That didn't happen very often and was, she found, a somewhat unpleasant state of affairs. Normally she was so sure of things. While her other housemates were often busy chasing pipe dreams, she knew exactly how the world worked. It was the only way to survive as an agent.

But now she had to admit that maybe her mission was far more complex than she had previously thought. Sure, it was about protecting Oberon, but that might just be the tip of the iceberg. She shuddered. It brought her no pleasure thinking about icebergs while aboard a ship. Heading straight towards disaster – hadn't she seen a film about it once?

What was certain was that the case had many layers, like a cake. Only, unlike a cake, they weren't made of cream, sponge and sugar.

The layers were dead bodies.

It was complicated, and when something in life was complicated, there was normally only one solution – yoga.

She lifted Oberon out of her lap and carried him over to Marshall's bed, where he immediately started rustling about amongst the papers.

Charlie groaned and moved away from the bed a bit, but Edwina ignored her as usual.

Then she was already on the carpet and started to stretch her spine.

Cat and cow.

What was certain was that she had found Oberon in the swimming pool, terribly under-cooled, where a chicly dressed dead body also happened to be floating. It was obvious that there was a connection between the two.

Edwina slid onto her stomach. Cobra.

If she hadn't been so worried about Oberon, she would surely have paid more attention to the body, but . . . she'd been young and blondee, that much was clear, her hair fanning out in the water like bleached exotic coral. Coral die-off. Another one of those eco problems. She had taken Oberon into the relaxation room to warm up, and the next time she had looked in the swimming pool, nobody had been there anymore, no dead body and nobody alive either.

Sphinx.

She had a foreboding feeling that she should tell Agnes about it, but then Agnes would ask awkward questions. Why on earth had she gone off on her own, why hadn't she been a bit more interested in the dead body and above all, why was she only coming out with it now? It was so easy to be critical with hindsight, and Agnes was always big on criticising Edwina.

Upward dog.

No, she would keep it to herself and use her own grey matter to solve the mystery. Strictly speaking, it was actually her job.

Someone had taken the wet woman away, pushed someone into the abyss, then strangled Mrs Meyer-Brinks and bashed somebody's brains out, probably Max the barman. That sounded exhausting. Whoever was behind the killing spree on board must be pretty stressed out – but obviously all of them were now stressed because the internet had disappeared, and nobody liked holidaying with a murderer. Despite that, the killer was probably *even more* stressed.

Downward dog.

And when someone was that stressed, they usually gave themselves away at some point.

Edwina just had to keep her eyes peeled.

It suddenly dawned on her that she did indeed know

someone who was very stressed and acting suspiciously.

He was hiding in her wardrobe, had attacked her earlier and scattered a significant portion of Lillith over the white woollen carpet in the process.

Yet again, Agnes was wondering what was going on in her housemates' heads. Not a lot, obviously.

She was in the process of performing strokes of investigative genius, but her audience was rapidly shrinking.

Marshall had stormed out of the room like a madman straight after her dramatic reveal on the topic of the 'man behind the scenes,' and now Edwina was heading for the door.

Charlie had fallen asleep in her armchair. Oberon was dozing too. Outrageous!

Casting investigative pearls before swine, that's what it seemed like.

The only one who seemed vaguely interested in the investigation was Winston.

He put his lists to one side and gave her a mischievous look.

'There's no Adam here at the hotel. Not on the staff or amongst the guests either.' Winston hesitated. 'But there's an Eve!'

Agnes frowned. 'A bit far-fetched, I'd say.'

Winston nodded. 'I'd normally have said so too. Except . . .'

He pointed towards the bed, where Oberon had made himself at home on a stack of papers and melted masterfully into his surroundings, white on white on white.

Agnes thought for a moment – Adam, Eve and the serpent! And couples often gave each other pet names. Maybe there was something in it after all!

'Who's this Eve?' she asked.

Winston pointed to his list. 'Eve and Frank Ashwood, room 12.'

'Terrific,' said Agnes. 'Let's take a look at the Ashwoods!'

Agnes was standing in one of the by now quite familiar housekeeping stores inspecting the guest photos behind the door.

Marshall was standing outside, armed to the teeth. It turned out that he had rushed out of the room in such a haste earlier to stock up on bladed weapons in the hotel kitchen. Now he was carrying two steak knives and even a small axe in his military jacket, and wouldn't leave Agnes's side.

It was touching, but also kind of annoying. How was she supposed to calmly question people and make enquiries if Marshall was lurking in the background, sabre-rattling? On the other hand, he was normally easily distracted, and if need be, she could always lose him somehow.

Now she took a good look at the Ashwoods' photos.

Eve Ashwood was a striking woman with her ash-blonde hair and fine features. Like someone you could glimpse in the Eden's brochure – draped elegantly over expensive furniture, or eyes closed in the relaxation room or – yes! – in the pool! In reality, the Eden was populated by plump guests on the wrong side of middle-age, and strictly speaking, Eve Ashwood didn't fit in. Too young. Too beautiful. Too slim. Frank Ashwood, however, fit right in at the hotel – chubby, shiny and vaguely pig-like. It seemed completely impossible that the two of them were a couple! They didn't really work as father and daughter either – besides, there was clearly a wedding ring on the hand Eve Ashwood had elegantly placed on her chest.

Agnes mulled it over for a moment, then it dawned on her that the piggish one wasn't Frank Ashwood at all. She had swapped the pictures herself!

She had a quick think, then put the pictures back in their rightful places.

Now it fitted better. There was Eve, and next to her, a good-looking chap with strikingly green eyes and salt and pepper hair, a distinguished, silver fox.

Agnes looked at them both for a while. One thing was for sure, they hadn't crossed her path at the hotel, either in the dining room or anywhere else in the corridors or in the spa – and at a small, intimate hotel like the Eden, that alone was noteworthy. Eve especially would surely have caught her eye, even from afar!

All of a sudden, Agnes thought how well Oberon would fit with Eve – in fact, they even looked similar to each other! It wasn't really a clue, but Agnes still got the feeling that things were starting to come together.

There was a noise coming from outside. Agnes was spooked, braced herself to be caught by Max the barman yet again, and grabbed an alibi chocolate just to be on the safe side. Then it dawned on her that in all likelihood, Max was lying in the cool store. Apart from that, Marshall was keeping watch out there like something out of a mafia film. She was safe. So, she nibbled the chocolate and had a think. Why had she even bumped into Max in the housekeeping store? What had he been doing there? Strictly speaking, as a barman, he didn't have any business there amongst the sheets and towels. The housekeeping stores were set up for the maid service people, so that they could provide the guests with linen, soap and new chocolates whenever needed.

She looked around the room with renewed interest. What on earth had Max been looking for in there? He'd gone unusually pale when he'd caught her in one of these rooms for the first time – or she him! That's what it was beginning to look like! And the second time, he'd been even paler, despite all the tan. Stressed. And he had ushered her out of the room in a far less polite way than was befitting for a guest. What had she done that was so bad? Pilfered a few chocolates, that was all!

Ha! Suddenly, Agnes was certain that the barman had had something to hide, and not just metaphorically, but quite literally there in the housekeeping store!

She must have said the 'ha!' out loud because then Marshall stuck his head in the door and looked around anxiously.

'Everything alright, Agnes?'

'Yes, yes.' Agnes nodded impatiently and dragged Marshall inside.

'I think Max was hiding something in here,' she explained. 'But I don't know what. Or where.'

They started searching, lifting soaps, peering in toothbrush cups and unfolding towels. Nothing.

Every now and then Agnes felt an elbow or a sharp knee. It was a bit of a squeeze for two in the housekeeping store.

Finally, Marshall knelt to look under the shelves. Then he lost the thread and looked dreamily up at Agnes.

'Agnes, I . . .'

Agnes felt uneasy. What was going on? Suddenly Marshall looked like he was about to propose to Agnes.

'I've been wondering for quite a while if . . .' He broke off and looked around imploringly, while Agnes frantically tried to think of a way to get out of the situation. Maybe she should just switch off her hearing aid? It would have been the first time the stupid hearing aid had been a tangible advantage!

'What's that?' Marshall suddenly shouted.

Agnes looked surprised. That wasn't quite the question she had been expecting.

'What's what?' she asked a bit gruffly, but Marshall had already stuck his head between two stacks of bedding.

Then he appeared again and presented her with some kind of metallic tobacco tin.

'Attached to the shelf with a magnet!' he cried. 'That's the badger!'

'Brilliant!' said Agnes, a bit peeved. She was a little miffed, but she couldn't quite put her finger on why.

Agnes and Marshall returned triumphantly to Murder Hunt HQ.

Charlie was now awake again, and Bernadette had kindly joined them. She was pale but seemed somehow more alert than in recent days.

Agnes presented the tin, prised it open and sniffed.

A characteristic smell spread through the room, and Charlie leapt jubilantly out of her armchair.

'Drugs!' said Agnes bleakly.

'I wouldn't call it a drug exactly,' Charlie cried, snatching the tin. 'Well done, Agnes! Where did you get hold of that?'

'From housekeeping.'

'Now that's what I call service!' Charlie beamed. 'Just what I need right now.'

'That's not the point,' said Agnes. 'We think Max the bartender has been dealing hash here at the hotel . . .'

'There's some cocaine too,' Charlie said cheerfully.

Agnes ignored her. 'And now we're obviously wondering if . . .'

'We're wondering if it has something to do with the murders,' added Marshall, who had technically found the tin, but still wasn't getting much recognition. 'Could there be someone here who's prepared to kill for this stuff?'

18

CORE

Edwina made sure the Do Not Disturb sign was still securely on display outside, then she closed the hotel room door and tiptoed over to the wardrobe.

She listened, nothing. Not even breathing and definitely no snoring, as was usually the case when people were asleep. Edwina put the key in the lock and flung open the wardrobe doors. The effect was a bit like when you lift up a rock and throw the life beneath into turmoil.

Mojo tumbled towards her like a woodlouse, and Edwina scrunched up her nose. The air in there was far from clear at the moment. The whippersnapper was now lying on his back, roughly where they had scattered Lillith earlier, and was squinting at her accusatorily.

'What's this all about?' he muttered.

'Surprise!' Edwina crowed, a bit belatedly.

It wasn't a good start for the professional interrogation that she'd had in mind, but you had to let the chips fall where they may, or a young lad in this case.

She sat down next to the whippersnapper on the floor and crossed her legs.

'We need to clear up why you're in this wardrobe,'

she declared. 'It's just not normal. Nobody likes living in wardrobes. Except moths maybe. And you're not a moth, are you?'

She eyed Mojo with renewed interest. Come to think of it, he really did have something mothlike about him – erratic, dishevelled and dusty. A shadow crossed his face. All of a sudden, he didn't just look bleary-eyed, but also bloody suspicious.

'Detox,' he huffed.

Edwina shook her head. She wouldn't be fobbed off this time! 'I found you on the balcony in the middle of the night. Why? How did you get there? Who's after you? Who are you so afraid of that you're willing to spend your holiday in a wardrobe?'

Maybe she should have asked these questions much earlier, but there had always been so much to do, what with Oberon and Agnes, the murderer and all of the meals on board. Better late than never!

She watched Mojo's gaze dart through the room, as if he were looking for something. A way out maybe. But there wasn't a way out because Edwina had locked the hotel room door.

'I can't remember,' he muttered defiantly. 'It's because of the gear. My brain's like a sieve.'

Edwina looked sceptical. There didn't seem to be an awful lot going on in Mojo's brain, it was true. But still . . .'You're still here!' she said. 'You're sitting in the wardrobe because you can remember something!'

She'd hit the nail on the head.

For a moment it looked as if the boy wanted to jump to his feet. Edwina's hand crept towards the corkscrew in her trouser pocket, but Mojo just rolled on his side and pulled up his legs. Foetal position.

'It was very dark,' he said quietly. 'And I really didn't mean to hurt him!'

Agnes had gathered together all of the guest photos from the housekeeping stores and was laying them out in front of her on the table, one after the other, like a game of Guess Who?

There were three piles, not suspicious, suspicious and extremely suspicious. So far, only the White Widow was on the extremely suspicious pile, both the Ashwoods were sharing the suspicious pile, and then Agnes had to create a fourth pile for Mrs Meyer-Brinks, not suspicious and dead.

She had a feeling Eve Ashwood would soon be making her way over to this pile too – at any rate, she was nowhere to be found, and Agnes would be paying her hotel room a visit shortly!

That still left a huge pile of inconspicuous guests.

Howard. Trudy. The married hyena couple. A fat married couple. An even fatter married couple. The other members of the detox group. Bernadette's admirer, the penguin. The rosy chap in pastels with the weird floral cravat . . .

Agnes slid the pile onto the floor and leapt up. Or rather, she tried to leap up. But the chairs in the Eden were low, soft and yielding, so she lost momentum halfway.

She plopped back into the armchair, tried again and then a third time and felt as awkward as a beetle that someone had turned on its back. They weren't armchairs, they were traps!

'What's the matter, Agnes?' Winston asked.

'I . . .' Agnes huffed in frustration. 'We . . . Him!' She tapped her finger on the chap with the floral cravat.

As Marshall pulled her out of the chair, Agnes tried to explain to her housemates why the pastel chap was important.

'He was in the Sea Lounge too,' she cried breathlessly. 'It wasn't particularly full. There was Mrs Meyer-Brinks, and me, and obviously Max the barman. And then there was the chap with the floral cravat too. I didn't give him a lot of thought because it obviously couldn't have been him. But the orange hood must have seen him from outside. And if this is really all about silencing the people who were in the Sea Lounge, then . . .'

'He's in danger!' Winston nodded. 'We've got to warn him!'

'I've got a better idea!' said Agnes. She was finally back on her feet and found herself eye to eye with Marshall, who was looking at her in awe. 'If we tail him and are clever about it, maybe we can set a trap for the murderer!'

'Once more from the start,' said Edwina. The whippersnapper had now given up on the foetal position, and they were both leaning on the wall with their legs tucked up, a bag of peanuts between them. Edwina had discovered them in a little fridge and opened them in the hope of luring Mojo out of his shell. It had worked; he was in the process of telling her a huge amount. Nevertheless, it still seemed a bit muddled to Edwina.

'So, you were in your room late in the evening, and then . . .'

'Someone knocked at the door,' Mojo explained.

Edwina nodded and grabbed herself a peanut. 'And were you expecting anyone?'

'Max from the bar,' Mojo said with a dreamy look on his face. 'He'd said . . . He'd promised me . . .'

'Some gear,' Edwina interjected impatiently. They'd been over this part of the conversation a few times already.

'And was it Max?' she asked, chewing.

'I think so,' mumbled Mojo. 'But to be honest . . . I was a bit out of it, and I'm not quite sure anymore . . . He had one of those jackets on. Like the staff sometimes wear. Orange. But the hood was up, almost completely covering his face. Weird, running about inside with your hood up, I thought to myself. But I wasn't really that interested . . .'

'Priority, gear!' Edwina was slowly beginning to understand what floated Mojo's boat. 'In any case, you thought it was Max, so you let him in. Then what happened?'

'He came in and closed the door. Because he didn't want to get caught with the gear, I thought. But then he just stood there looking at me. Without saying a word. Lurking. And suddenly I knew he wasn't going to give me the gear. I . . . well, I got angry.'

'Just like before,' Edwina said, demolishing another peanut.

'I pushed him,' Mojo said sheepishly. 'He hadn't been expecting that. He fell backwards against the table. I regretted it instantly.'

'Then what happened?' Edwina offered him the bag.

'Then he stood back up,' said the whippersnapper. 'And it was different somehow. Suddenly *I* was scared. That's when I saw the knife.'

'He had a knife?' Edwina asked out of professional interest. 'What sort of knife?'

'Just a knife!' shouted Mojo, 'How should I know? The light was off, but the moon was shining brightly and there was a flash, like in a film. It really did flash . . .' He laughed hysterically and Edwina decided not to pursue the knife topic any further.

'Then what happened?' she asked.

'I just wanted to get away. Somehow, I managed to get past him to the door, but I couldn't open it. I was trapped. And then the knife . . .'

Mojo grabbed his side.

'But you're not injured,' Edwina objected.

'I had this baggy jumper on. Gucci, of all things! The knife went straight through, but only through the jumper. And I was stuck somehow. But then I must have freed myself because I was suddenly standing in front of the balcony door, and I spent an eternity watching it open. Do you have any idea how slowly they open?'

Edwina knew. 'But how did you have time for that? What about the hood?'

'He was on all fours looking for his knife. It . . . it must have fallen somewhere when I broke free.'

'Didn't you consider fighting back?'

'Fighting someone with a knife?' Mojo raged. 'How? With a Biro?'

'For instance.'

'I just wanted to get away. And then the balcony door was finally open, but I couldn't go anywhere because it was such a long way down. I got onto the neighbouring balcony – there was only a dividing screen. And from there to the next neighbouring balcony. But then I ran out of balconies, and I thought, maybe I'll make it one floor down, and I ended up here.'

'And from now on you'd rather stay in the wardrobe!' Edwina concluded.

'Exactly. I shouldn't have tried to buy the gear! It's all because of the stupid gear!'

Edwina frowned. 'And you're sure you were in your room? And you're sure Max got up again? I only ask because Max is a little bit dead now.'

Mojo looked at her aghast. 'I . . . What? Of course it was in my room, how else would I have got onto the balcony . . . dead? What do you mean, dead?'

Edwina shrugged. 'Just dead.'

The peanuts were all gone. Edwina sighed. She didn't seriously think Mojo had Max on his conscience. He probably couldn't even lift a dumbbell like that, never mind . . . How she ever could have believed that he had the makings of an agent, was a mystery to her. She also didn't believe that the figure had been Max. Why would he go around stabbing customers? No, it had been someone who had turned up armed with a knife and evil intent, then locked the door. Was it coincidence that Mojo had been expecting his gear at that moment, or was that something the hood had known and exploited?

Edwina tried to picture the scene, the dark room, the soft moonlight, the silent, masked figure. She was fairly certain that the attacker was the killer that Agnes was also after. How many sinister masked hoods could there be? But if what Mojo had said was true, the killer hadn't gone about things in a particularly professional way. Cold-blooded –

yes. Professional – no. Attacking someone as inept as Mojo with a knife at close range and missing, and then hunting for the respective knife on all fours – that was bumbling! The killer had been lucky that Mojo was of such a nervous disposition! If he had pulled that number on her, things would have turned out differently!

Then there was the question of why someone would have attacked Mojo in the first place. After all, this wasn't a chance encounter; it was a targeted, albeit badly planned attack. Once again, Edwina had the vague suspicion she should tell Agnes about the whole thing. But how would that work without confessing that their shared room was also being occupied by a whippersnapper? Agnes didn't care for whippersnappers and would probably react to the news with a distinct lack of understanding.

Mojo suddenly let out a high-pitched, haunted sound. Edwina leapt up – was the boy injured after all?

But Mojo looked pretty normal, if not exactly healthy, and was staring at his mobile phone in disbelief.

'What's the matter?' Edwina asked and reached for the corkscrew just in case.

'Bullshit!' cried the whippersnapper. 'That's it! Over and out! The battery's dead!'

'There! Seventeen!' Charlie pointed triumphantly at a door.

'We're looking for seventeen A!' Agnes explained impatiently. She looked around. 17A was nowhere to be seen.

Charlie, Agnes, Winston and Marshall had rushed off to find and save the floral-cravat-wearer, and then to possibly use him as bait. But as yet, they hadn't even managed to locate the right room.

Winston suddenly made a triumphant sound at the end of the corridor. Room 17A! There it was!

Agnes hurried after the others. She was sweating. Her hip was hurting again. Their stay at the Eden was clearly an active holiday! Finally, she got there and knocked, while her housemates gathered around her expectantly.

'Just a minute!' shouted someone in the room, and Agnes realised she was impatiently shifting her weight from one painful foot to the other.

Then the door opened, and a plump woman in a dressing gown and curlers stared back at them, expectantly at first, then a bit dumbfounded. Agnes tried to imagine what sort of an impression they made, Charlie in her red kimono, Winston with his woolly hat, Marshall in uniform and her . . . At the moment she couldn't even remember what she had put on after the aqua aerobics saga. The main thing was, it wasn't a swimming costume!

'I actually ordered a sandwich,' the woman with the curlers said uncertainly.

'Unfortunately, we don't have a sandwich,' Agnes explained. 'We're looking for Walter. Walter Ross.' That was what the floral-cravat-man was called according to the photo label.

'Oh, Walter!' The woman was visibly relieved that the Sunset Hall crew didn't want anything directly from her. 'My husband went for a massage. Back in an hour. Or thereabouts.'

'A massage.' Agnes nodded, already on her way to the spa, followed by Marshall, Charlie and finally Winston, who had to turn his wheelchair around first.

There was no time to lose!

But as they pushed open the glass door, their hearts racing, they had a foreboding feeling that it was already too late. The spa reception was deserted, and nobody instructed them to take their shoes off. High-pitched, hysterical screams were coming from somewhere.

'Relaxation room!' said Marshall, who knew his way around quite well by now. Agnes nodded and braced herself for what was in store for them in the serene ambience of the wellness temple.

'You can just charge it up again,' said Edwina stroking Oberon's head. She had collected the snake from HQ and now they were both trying to take Mojo's mind off his phone – and ideally even get him out of the room. Edwina had decided that he had to get out of the wardrobe. So far, she had been lucky that Agnes had been so busy, but it wasn't going to last forever.

'Not without a charger,' Mojo said gloomily.

'But you must have a charger,' said Edwina.

'Not on me!'

'In your room! Go to your room and get your charger. Simple!' Edwina grinned. As soon as Mojo was out of the room, she would lock the door and thus prevent the whippersnapper from establishing himself in the wardrobe again.

But she must have looked a bit too pleased with herself because Mojo eyed her warily.

'I'm scared,' he said finally. 'What if he's still there?'

'Nobody lurks around for days in other people's rooms,'

Edwina responded pragmatically.

The whippersnapper seemed to accept that.

'But he could come back!'

'In theory!'

'In practice too!' the whippersnapper insisted.

Edwina sighed and changed tack. 'What do you even need a phone for anyway? There's no internet and there's no reception here either.' It was a bit like her with the remote control. Since the corresponding television had made its way into the cellar, possession of the remote was only half as much fun.

'It's not about that,' said Mojo. 'I blog every day. I take photos and make little films. I write a diary. And as soon as the internet is back again, everything's going online. Without my blog I'd go mad. Especially in the wardrobe.'

'You don't have to stay in the wardrobe,' said Edwina. Here it was again, the crazy story of the big internet following waiting day after day for news from the wardrobe. Edwina sighed. How someone could go through life with such a weak grip on reality was a mystery to her.

Had it not been so bright and cheerful in the relaxation room, Agnes would perhaps have coped better with the sight. This, by contrast, was a real shock. She could hear Charlie making retching sounds next to her.

'Awful!' muttered Winston.

Marshall was ominously silent.

Walter Ross, the pastel fan and floral-cravat-wearer, whose life had ended in the deepest shade of crimson.

He must have been enjoying the view in the relaxation room after his massage, just like Charlie and Agnes yesterday, when the killer had approached him – likely from behind – and slit his throat – presumably with a knife. Only not particularly skilfully, and instead of quietly bleeding to death, he had crawled around the room.

Someone was screaming in short, sharp bursts next to her.

Charlie threw up almost gracefully onto a lounger.

Agnes turned her hearing aid off so that she could think better.

All hell had broken loose in the relaxation room. Unlike Mrs Meyer-Brinks and Max the barman, the floral-cravat-wearer had drawn rather a lot of attention to himself. There were the spa reception ladies and a dripping-wet, horrified couple that must have just got out of the pool. While Agnes was having a think, the detox folks turned up, still sweaty from their activities in the gym.

The cat was out of the bag. And even if Helen the manager turned herself inside out, there would be no covering up this murder. Agnes wondered if that's exactly what the murderer had intended – or had it just been practical having found the victim alone in the relaxation room? She shuddered on realising that Walter Ross must have been lying in exactly the same chair as the one she had also been deposited in after the aqua aerobics mishap.

A woman was standing right next to her shrieking mutely. It took a while for Agnes to recognise her as Lilac, the massage therapist, green with shock and a million miles away from relaxed.

She was presumably the one who had found the body. Agnes saw a smashed glass at her feet and a few slices of cucumber. Lilac had been about to bring Walter his cucumber water, and then . . . All of a sudden, Agnes became aware of how close they had come to the murderer. The cucumber water was still on the light wooden floor; despite the warmth in the relaxation room barely any evaporation had taken place. They had just missed the murderer, maybe only by a few minutes. It was enough to send you mad!

Agnes pulled a tissue from the depths of her cardigan and passed it to Lilac. If you really thought about it, tissues were one of the most important tools of the modern-day investigator.

Then she reluctantly switched her hearing aid back on. She had to question Lilac and the other people there, in order to get a clear picture of the murder as quickly as possible.

'We've got to get these people out of here,' she said to Marshall and Winston and Charlie, who had now recovered a little.

'And then I want to speak to each of them individually. I'll start with Lilac.'

She sat in one of the treatment rooms with Lilac, only this time she was the one in charge. She had asked the therapist to sit on the bed and was trying aromatic oils out on her, without success up to now. Lilac was sobbing so uncontrollably that she could hardly speak, and now she had the hiccups too.

'Dreams of the Caribbean,' Agnes declared holding a little bottle to her nose.

Lilac pushed the oil away. 'That's too . . . stimulating,' she groaned between two hiccups.

Agnes carried on, emboldened. 'Night orchid!' The

more Lilac thought about fragrances, the less time she would have to think about the situation in the relaxation room.

The next fragrance, 'Forest calm,' finally had the desired effect. Lilac stopped sobbing. Maybe she'd just run out of tears, and her body needed a break before it could start up a new crying concerto.

This was Agnes's chance.

'When did you last see Walter Ross alive?' she asked.

'Eleven-fourteen,' said Lilac without thinking.

'Quite a specific time,' said Agnes.

Lila nodded. Now that the tears had dried up, she actually seemed quite composed. Maybe it was thanks to the 'Forest calm.' 'My next treatment always starts at fourteen past the hour, so I send the previous client into the relaxation room just before. And while the new client is getting undressed, I take the other their cucumber water.'

'And that would be at about . . . ?'

'Twenty past. That's when I saw him . . .' Lilac hiccupped. They were back.

Agnes nodded thoughtfully. A six-minute window. That was tight, but definitely feasible!

'Does that mean the killer must already have been in the spa area?' she asked.

Lilac thought for a moment. 'Not necessarily. *Hic*. There's a service lift. Between the sauna and the pool. It's mainly for staff, but accessible to everyone, so that our disabled guests . . . In principle, anyone from the lobby could quickly . . .'

Agnes made a note. She would have to ask if anybody was seen in the lobby at that time.

'He was so wonderfully relaxed.' Lilac sighed. 'Who would do such a thing? Who's even capable of something like that?'

Agnes sighed. 'That's what I'd like to know too.'

Agnes and her team questioned all of the other people in the spa too, without any different results, however. Nobody admitted to being in the relaxation room, but nobody had a watertight alibi, not even the couple in the pool. Agnes asked Lilac to secure the crime scene. Normally she would have needed a specialist team; instead it was just Marshall armed with a magnifying glass and reading glasses, crawling around taking photos. Winston had started making lists, Charlie found a blood-stained dressing gown in a corner and threw up for the second time, while Agnes sat on one of the loungers having a think.

So that's how it had been done. The murderer had thrown a dressing gown on and instantly been perfectly camouflaged. These gowns even had hoods. It must have been child's play to dart into the relaxation room, and the killer was protected from blood spatter too. No flies on them! Audacious, but not stupid. Agnes was reminded of the White Widow again. Had it been her? Did she still like the view here?

More and more hotel guests were gathering in front of the closed glass door to the spa area, nervously all talking at once and looking sombrely over at the residents of Sunset Hall. The mood was clearly bad, so they decided to slip away in the much-discussed service lift once their work was done.

When they stepped a bit furtively out of the lift into the lobby, they bumped into Trudy, who had taken advantage of the general excitement to get stuck into the apples at reception.

As soon as she noticed the residents of Sunset Hall, she waved them over. Agnes would have preferred to ignore her. Trudy hadn't been with the other detoxers in the gym and probably didn't have anything sensible to contribute to the investigation. But manners won out.

'Hello, Trudy,' she said, tired.

'Well, have you found him?' Trudy asked.

'No,' Agnes admitted and suddenly realised how disappointed she was. They had been so close – and now they were facing another mystery!

'The murderer can't have gone far,' Trudy said and winked. 'And there are a lot of people who must have seen something. If you believe the rumours, most of the guests already know who it was anyway!'

'Really?' Agnes asked, curious despite her better judgement. Could it really be that simple? 'Who was it then?'

'Well, you lot, of course!' said Trudy, grinning and placing her gnawed apple core on the table, where two other apple cores were already waiting.

19

MEALS ON WHEELS

At a loss, Bernadette turned the piece of paper over in her hand, unfolded it and folded it back up again, felt the dull edges and smoothness of the paper. It was a mystery that her hands alone couldn't solve, and it was enough to drive her mad. Obviously, the slip of paper could be something quite harmless, a bill maybe, a wine list or a menu suggestion. But in her heart of hearts, she knew it was a message. A secret message. She thought back to the stealthy footsteps at the door, the moment of hesitation, then the hasty withdrawal of footsteps, an escape almost. Could it have something to do with Jack? Unlikely. Even if the Samantha in her didn't want to admit it, not everything in this world was to do with Jack!

And what sort of idiot wrote a blind woman a message anyway?

Bernadette felt helpless like never before. In the end, she made a decision. She got up out of her chair, grabbed her cane, and felt her way to the door. She should probably have held the fort in the room, while Agnes, Charlie, Winston and Marshall were enjoying themselves out hunting the murderer, but Bernadette had no desire to always hold the fort.

Instead, she stepped out into the hallway and knocked on the neighbouring door.

It took quite a while for Edwina to open up. Bernadette could hear whispering and hasty footsteps – the snake was probably somewhere it shouldn't be again.

Finally, the door opened.

'Yes?' Edwina sounded wary.

Bernadette didn't dither for long, she pushed past her into the room, her cane leading the way.

Edwina made an indignant sound – what on earth had she been up to in there? It really did pong a bit, but Bernadette wasn't the snake police after all.

She held the note out towards Edwina without saying a word.

'I know what you've done!' Edwina read aloud. And immediately protested, 'I haven't done anything!' a bit too quickly and guiltily.

'The note's not for you,' Bernadette explained. 'It might be for me.'

'So, what have *you* done then?' Edwina asked, audibly relieved.

'Nothing!' Bernadette snapped. 'Absolutely nothing at all!'

All of a sudden, she wished she had done more with her life. Had affairs. Gone travelling. Learnt to dance. Set up a choir. Smashed plates. Reconciled with Jack far sooner. What had she accomplished? Grassed up a drug lord and then demolished legions of fondant creams, that was about the size of it!

Suddenly she had tears in her eyes. The note was mean!

'Then it's not for you,' Edwina said plainly.

Bernadette pulled herself together. Edwina was probably right. The note could just as well be for Charlie, or even Agnes, who had only vacated the room yesterday.

The question was, What had one of those two done, and why was it so important that they needed a note to remind them about it?

'Us?' Agnes asked for the third time. 'Why on earth? That's ridiculous!'

Helen fidgeted uneasily back and forth on her chair. She had invited all the available residents of Sunset Hall into her office, then firmly closed the door.

'I personally don't really believe it,' she said. 'But there are a few unsettling observations that I can't simply ignore.'

'What sort of observations?' Agnes asked combatively.

Helen sighed. 'Well, for one, you knocked on Mrs Ross's door and asked after Walter. You threatened her, and the next minute he's dead. It is rather strange.'

'We didn't threaten anybody,' said Charlie. 'We just didn't have a sandwich.'

Helen pointed accusingly at Marshall. 'And you were seen stealing knives from the kitchen!'

Marshall looked baffled at first, then guilty, then he took an upright, military stance and saluted. The knives jangled in his pocket.

'Apparently there's a venomous snake in one of your rooms,' Helen continued.

'It's a constrictor, actually!' Charlie protested, but Helen ignored her.

'And your friend Edwina Singh was seen dragging a body into her room.'

279

Edwina? A body?

'That's ridiculous!' Agnes cried for the second time, knowing full well that unfortunately it wasn't quite as ridiculous as she'd have liked. What on earth was Edwina doing with a body?

'And then there's this.' Helen placed a transparent plastic bag on the desk with her fingertips. Inside was a dumbbell covered in something that now looked like old rust. 'Maid service found this in your room today.' She looked reproachfully at Marshall, who had fallen into a sort of stupor.

'That's evidence!' Agnes raged.

'Evidence, yeah, yeah,' said Helen. 'But evidence of what?'

The residents of Sunset Hall stubbornly refused to say a word. Helen wasn't open to rational arguments, that much was clear. They had done their best to rid the Eden of its murderer problem, and this was the thanks they got!

Helen sighed again. 'As I said, I can't imagine that . . . But you have to admit, it is all a bit strange. And after all, it's not about what I can imagine or not. I'm just doing my job – and I can't ignore the mood here at the hotel any longer. The other guests are scared – and they would definitely feel safer if they didn't run into *you lot* right now. I think it would be for the best if you stayed in your rooms for the time being. I'll obviously get your meals brought to you. If you're hungry, just call reception.'

'What about drinks?' Charlie asked defiantly.

Helen ignored her. 'If you leave your rooms, I can't guarantee your safety here in the hotel. Do you understand what that means? Emotions are running very high!'

'Nobody can guarantee anybody's safety here! That's

kind of the point!' Agnes huffed. It seemed as if in her worry about the strength of feeling in the hotel, Helen had almost forgotten the actual problem. 'What about the investigation? There's a cold-blooded killer running about the place, and you asked us to find him!'

'I asked you to discreetly make enquiries,' Helen said coldly. 'This' – she pointed to the plastic bag – 'is not discreet.'

Then she pushed a button to signal that the discussion was over. The next minute, a particularly big and burly waiter turned up and demanded, with a mute, not so friendly gesture that they follow him. Helen really did mean business!

Suddenly Agnes understood why she was the manager. Beneath all the softness, chirpiness and eco fluff, was a core of steel. The manager's face was tense, but calm. No make-up, but no red blotches either. It was the face of someone who knew what she wanted.

Agnes realised that there was no sense in railing against her decision, and furiously followed the broad-shouldered waiter to her hotel room.

'House arrest?' Edwina was horrified. 'On a ship? How's that supposed to work?'

'Worse!' Charlie groaned, flopping into a chair. 'Room arrest. Apparently, they're going to bring us food, but I wouldn't count on it.'

They had retreated to Murder Hunt HQ, which was now in fact a quasi-prison for investigators, and were trying to get used to the new situation. It wasn't easy.

'Is he still there?' Agnes asked anew. Having deposited

them in their room, the burly waiter had positioned himself not so discreetly in the hallway. There he'd stood when Agnes hung the Do Not Disturb sign, and there he still stood when she took it down again ten minutes later.

'Of course he's still there!' cried Charlie. 'Where would he have gone?'

Nevertheless, Agnes padded to the door again to put the sign back up.

There he stood, no doubt about it.

Agnes shot the waiter a poisonous look and slammed the door shut again.

'We need a plan!' she declared.

'We should drown our sorrows!' said Charlie. 'It's the only rational thing to do in a situation like this.'

'We could try some board games too,' Winston suggested.

'Board games *and* drowning our sorrows!' Charlie insisted.

'What about charades?' Bernadette asked cynically.

'I spy with my little eye . . .' squawked Edwina. 'Something that is white!'

'Oberon!' shouted Charlie and Winston in unison.

Agnes shook her head. 'I don't mean how we should occupy ourselves. I mean how we're going to get out of here.'

Edwina peered through the spyhole and studied their prison waiter. 'He's not that big,' she said. 'I could take him out.'

'Brilliant way of convincing everyone here that we haven't got anything to do with the murders,' Bernadette sighed.

'We just have to wait for the next murder,' said Charlie. 'Then they'll know that it couldn't possibly have been us. Then they'll apologise.'

'The fundamental principle of investigating is preventing murders,' explained Agnes. 'Not waiting for them to happen. Apart from that, I'm probably the next victim. As long as I'm stuck here, the murderer won't lift a finger. Which in turn, doesn't exactly look very good on the face of it.'

'At least nothing can happen to you here,' said Marshall. He'd had to return his knives to the kitchen.

'It's not about that!' Agnes hissed. She was still furious. Demoted within a few hours from partway official investigators to the main suspects – that really was a climb down. The worst thing about it for her, however, was that the murderer was running around out there footloose and fancy-free. There was no guard standing outside his door. Nobody was laying down the law for him. It just wasn't fair!

'Maybe we can catch him anyway,' Winston said, as if he had read her mind. 'We've still got these after all.' He pointed to the paper salad on Marshall's bed. 'We've got data. The murderer is hiding somewhere on these pages. Maybe we can blow his cover from here.'

A murder hunt in a paper jungle – it wasn't exactly Agnes's favourite MO, but it was better than hours of I-spy with Edwina every time. She sighed and rummaged around for her reading glasses.

Just then, someone knocked at the door.

For a crazy moment, Agnes thought it could be the murderer. She opened the door and was ready to go straight for the throat of whoever was behind it. She was in just the right mood!

But it was only Lilac, the massage therapist. She wasn't wearing her spa tunic anymore. Instead she had on the same tasteful dark clothes the other hotel employees wore, and Agnes almost didn't recognise her.

'Sorry,' she mumbled, peering past Agnes into the room. 'The management asked me to collect the documents.'

'Documents?' Agnes toyed with the idea of denying having any documents whatsoever, but unfortunately you couldn't miss the mountain of files on Marshall's bed.

'It wasn't us!' Edwina declared.

'I'm just here for the files.' Lilac obviously had no intention of discussing anything.

It was no good. They had to gather up the documents from the bed and pass them to Lilac in a neat pile. Then they all stood in the doorway and looked on as their last chance to expose the murderer floated away along the corridor in Lilac's strong masseuse hands.

'Well, that's that, then!' Charlie declared. 'I'll order some lunch!'

Contrary to Charlie's fears, lunch was promptly wheeled in, and it was fresh, aromatic and steaming, but that wasn't enough to put the residents of Sunset Hall in a better mood. Locked in their rooms getting meals on wheels – this was supposed to be a luxury hotel, but right now it felt suspiciously like a home. Aside from that, they had to have their meals separately in their respective rooms because there wasn't a table that would have been big enough for them all.

Winston ate slowly and systematically as always; Marshall, on the other hand, wolfed everything down in

record time. He didn't like letting Agnes out of his sight –
and he'd talked Edwina into giving him the corkscrew as
well! How was she supposed to defend herself? But Edwina
would think of something. Edwina was very resourceful
in that respect. Nonetheless, he would rather not depend
on others. He pushed the empty dessert plate away – he
couldn't have said what he'd just eaten – and looked on
with an agonised expression as Winston worked his way
through his main course, pea by painful pea.

Agnes was sitting at the table with an unusually nervous
Edwina and a bored Oberon looking at the steaming soup.
The investigation had gone to pot, and the holiday too.
All that was left was for her to silently sip her soup in her
room. Strictly speaking, the situation wasn't much better
than in a home!

'Do you think he's trying to poison you?' Edwina asked,
wrongly interpreting her hesitation.

'Poison me?' Agnes lowered her spoon. 'Who?'

'Well, the murderer!' Edwina had already finished her
soup and was staring meditatively at her empty bowl.

Agnes shook her head. 'It's not his style. He – or she –
waits until he gets his victims on their own. Maybe he lures
them somewhere. Then he strikes. I think he enjoys watching
them die. Poisoning wouldn't be hands-on enough for him.
At least I'm hoping so.'

'But he can't ambush you at the moment,' Edwina
countered. 'Maybe poisoning is better than nothing!'

Agnes pushed her soup dish away, not because she
really thought it was poisoned, but because something had
suddenly occurred to her. 'If the mountain won't come to

Mohammed . . .' she muttered. 'Edwina, that's brilliant!'

Edwina grinned – delighted, but none the wiser.

'If we can't get to the murderer, then the murderer will have to come to us!' Agnes explained. 'Why should we do all the hard work? *He* should be racking his brains about how he's going to get in here. We'll set him a trap! We'll invite him in. When I'm alone, helpless, as bait – that'll be too tempting for him! He won't be able to resist!'

'Marshall won't like it,' said Edwina sagely.

Agnes winked at her. 'Marshall doesn't have to know about everything, Edwina.'

Bernadette supped her soup, just to have something to do. She wasn't hungry, in fact she couldn't even remember when she had last been hungry. The thought of fondant creams made her feel vaguely nauseous.

She listened to Charlie merrily clattering her cutlery.

Click, click, clap, metal on porcelain, and the kiss of glass on wood every now and then when Charlie picked up or put down her drink.

Maybe the nausea was also because she was essentially locked up there in the room. Bernadette felt helpless. How was she supposed to encounter Jack again and find out if he was involved in the murders at the Eden or not? And did he even want anything more to do with her? The more she thought about it, the colder and sterner the last conversation between them seemed. Maybe he had no desire to be dictated to by her in his old age. Maybe he would leave as soon as the coast road was open again, without so much as another word.

Just drifting apart like that again, without a word,

286

without a goodbye and closure – that would be terrible, worse than anything else imaginable.

And then there was the note. It weighed heavily in her skirt pocket, heavier than you would have expected from a little piece of paper like that. The longer she carried it around with her, the more uneasy it made her feel. She had a bad feeling about it. The note was more than just a bad joke or a misunderstanding – the message meant something; Bernadette was sure of it. But what exactly?

What had Edwina said? That the note couldn't have been meant for her! Bernadette hadn't paid much attention to the issue because of the latest murder and the subsequent room arrest, but now she pulled the note out of her pocket, unfolded it and pushed it across the table towards Charlie.

'This was pushed under our door today,' she said. 'Is it for you? Have you done something, Charlie?'

There was silence on the other side of the table for quite a while.

'I think we should show it to Agnes,' Charlie finally said quietly.

But when they knocked on Agnes's door a little while later, under the suspicious gaze of the burly waiter, it was Edwina who opened the door. Agnes was lying in bed, the covers pulled up to her chin.

'Agnes is ill!' Edwina reported cheerfully. 'We need to find a doctor!'

Charlie groaned. Not that as well!

'I'm faking it!' Agnes declared, as soon as the door to

the hallway was closed again. 'I'm trying to set a trap for the murderer!'

'In bed?' Charlie was sceptical. 'That's a bit unorthodox, isn't it?'

'Where else?' Agnes asked irritably. 'In the bath? In the wardrobe? Unfortunately, I don't have many options right now.'

'Just not in the wardrobe,' Edwina crowed.

Charlie ignored her and held out the note towards Agnes.

'This was pushed under our door today,' she said. 'But we don't know why.'

It took a while for Edwina, under Agnes's instructions, to locate a pair of reading glasses.

Agnes put them on. 'I know what you've done!' she read out loud.

Then she fell silent for quite a while and thought for a moment.

'Your err . . . male acquaintance – was it . . . Howard?'

'You think it's about *that*?' Charlie cried. 'But that was just . . . Ridiculous!'

'It is not ridiculous,' said Agnes, pale and stern. 'It's terribly important. It *was* Howard, wasn't it?'

Charlie nodded. 'But nobody knows . . .'

'Nobody except Howard,' Agnes said quietly.

Then she just sat there, getting paler and paler. The others didn't say a word either, even Edwina. They had never seen Agnes so shaken before.

'Do you want to know who is responsible for the murders of Mrs Meyer-Brinks, Max and Walter Ross?' she finally asked.

'Howard?' Charlie blurted out. 'Impossible. He can't even . . .'

'Not Howard,' Agnes interrupted, her voice barely more than a whisper.

'*Me.*'

20

RAT

'There!' Agnes pressed the receiver into Charlie's hand. Even though the line to the outside world had been cut off, the connections within the hotel were still working.

'You know what you have to do?' Agnes asked sternly.

Charlie rolled her eyes. 'Tell Howard about the note.'

Agnes nodded. 'And then?'

'Listen to what he has to say. And let him say his piece,' said Charlie ungraciously. 'Not that he deserves it.'

'And the rest of you?'

'We keep our traps shut!' Edwina piped up.

Agnes took a deep breath. If everything went to plan, in a few minutes she would know if she was right. *Of course* she was right, she could feel it in her tired bones – but this was too important a matter for her to rely on her bones. If her theory was correct, she hadn't just solved the mystery of the note and three of the five murders there at the Eden, no, she'd also found the killer!

She gave Charlie a signal, and her friend keyed in Howard's room number, which they had found on the back of his photo.

It was ringing.

And ringing.

'Maybe he's still at lunch . . .' Charlie muttered, but at that very moment, someone picked up at the other end.

They listened.

'Howard?' cried Charlie. She didn't have to act upset – she genuinely was in a bit of a state. 'Is that you?'

'Darling!' Howard's warm voice oozed out of the speaker like treacle. 'I was getting worried!'

Agnes realised she was holding her breath. He sounded so genuine. So friendly. So honestly worried. It was disgusting!

'I want you to know, darling, I don't believe this stupid murder story one bit!' said Howard. 'You wouldn't believe what people in the hotel are saying about you all – but obviously you've got nothing to do with the whole thing!'

Charlie rolled her eyes. 'That's not why I'm calling, Howard. Listen, someone sent . . . I've got a . . . someone pushed a note under my door, "I know what you've done!"'

It was clear to see that Charlie would have liked to say more, but Agnes put her finger to her lips and made the international hand-across-the-throat signal just to be sure. Charlie bit her lip and gathered herself.

There was silence on the other end of the line for a moment.

'You too?' Howard finally whispered. 'Oh, darling!'

Charlie opened her mouth to say something, but Agnes shot her a poisonous look.

'And the demands?' asked Howard. 'Did he make demands of you too? The bastard! Whatever happens, I need you to know, I'm completely behind you, Charlie. We'll club together, my darling, I'll take care of the handover. I'll make it disappear; I promise you. You don't have to worry your pretty little head. Your husband will never find out about us.'

'Great,' said Charlie drily and gave Agnes a look. She nodded encouragingly. 'And, err, what money? There was nothing about money on the note.'

'They contacted me too,' Howard explained. 'Someone was watching us, darling. And now he wants money, otherwise he'll tell your husband everything. Shocking, I know. What a thug! A real gentleman would never . . . But I . . . I wish I could pay it on my own, but there's obviously not a cash machine anywhere here, and unfortunately, I've only got five hundred.'

'Five hundred?' Charlie asked indignantly.

'So, if you could contribute, my darling . . .' Howard warbled. 'I'll talk to him, but I fear he won't be fobbed off without some cash.'

'Of course not,' Charlie said gravely. Agnes gave her a signal and she hung up.

Then it was silent in the room for a while.

'He wants money,' said Edwina in astonishment. 'What on earth for?'

'What a rat!' said Bernadette.

'But why . . . ?' cried Charlie. 'And how did you know that . . . ?'

Agnes was still sitting silently on her bed digesting what she had heard. Having a suspicion was one thing, but having it irrefutably confirmed was a completely different matter. How was it possible for Howard to sound so warm and convincing and concerned, while simultaneously . . .

The phone rang.

Charlie picked up the receiver, listened briefly and then disconnected it. She left the receiver on the bedside table.

'There we have it,' Agnes explained. 'Howard is a con artist. He carries on with married women here at the hotel – or women he thinks are married – seduces them and then fabricates this blackmail story to get money out of them. He tried it on with me too . . .'

Even the mere memory of it made Agnes blush with shame. How could she ever have thought that Howard was a nice acquaintance?

'He didn't with me!' said Edwina, offended.

'Believe me, it's better that way,' Charlie comforted her. 'You really didn't miss much. He wants money? Ha! He can wait until he's blue in the face!'

'So far, so bad,' said Bernadette. 'But that's got nothing to do with the murders.'

Agnes sighed. 'Unfortunately, it does.'

'But Howard . . .' cried Charlie. 'He's too much of a coward to even blackmail people directly. He uses some third person as a pretext! A wimp like him would never . . . !'

'Howard isn't the murderer,' Agnes explained with a heavy heart. 'But he's the catalyst. Howard – and me!'

Nobody said a word, not even Edwina, and even Oberon seemed to be following the proceedings with an unusual interest. But maybe the mention of rats had just made him hungry.

'Howard is a shrewd fraudster,' Agnes continued. 'He realised that the Eden wasn't so much a hotel for romance, but a hotel for repairing the romance. The guests are overwhelmingly wealthy older couples, and many of them come to the solitude here because something is going awry

293

in their relationship – he even explained that to me himself! He carries on with as many married women as possible, and as soon as they have done something compromising, he pushes an 'I know what you've done' note under their door. I even saw him do it once – only I didn't know what he was doing then. If the lady herself finds the note – great! If the corresponding husband finds it, that's also not a problem, after all, the message is a bit vague!'

'But how does Howard know which door is the right one?' Agnes looked into the spellbound faces of her female housemates. For once, she couldn't complain about a lack of attention.

'That's easy,' she continued. 'There are housekeeping stores that have photos of all the guests with their relevant room numbers. It's clear on first glance who is staying in which room. Howard exploited that. And it had probably been working wonderfully, until . . .' She gulped. 'In short, I was annoyed about the pictures. So, I just swapped a few of them around.'

Bernadette made a noise not dissimilar to that of Hettie II being blown up. She had understood what Agnes was getting at. The others just looked at her expectantly.

'Because I swapped the pictures, Howard pushed a note under the wrong door,' Agnes explained. 'The *murderer's* door!'

The penny had dropped for Charlie, and even Edwina, too.

'Imagine, you've just pushed someone off a cliff, and all of a sudden, someone slips this note under your door. You don't think about affairs. You obviously think that someone saw the murder and is trying to blackmail you!

And who's in line for that? Only the people who were in the Sea Lounge at the time of the murder. So, the killer started to eliminate them, one by one.'

'All apart from you!' said Edwina.

Agnes nodded. She felt dreadful. It had only been a stupid prank, a bit of rebelliousness because she'd been irritated by the smooth efficiency of the Eden. But the prank had already cost three people their lives.

'The good thing . . .' Her voice broke, and she tried again. 'The only good thing about it is that I didn't swap very many pictures. And that in turn means that *he* is our new prime suspect!'

She pulled out Frank Ashwood's picture and laid it in front of her on the bedcover.

There he lay, with silver hair, twinkling eyes and a smile as practiced as it was winning, the murderer they'd been looking for all this time.

'Who is it?' Bernadette huffed.

'His name's Frank Ashwood,' said Agnes. 'And I've never seen him before. That alone is suspicious.'

Bernadette slumped, again not dissimilar to Hettie II. 'Good.' She seemed relieved.

'Why is that good?' Agnes hissed. 'I wish I could get a better idea of him. It's driving me mad! He must have gone completely underground after the first murder . . . we do know one thing about him though,' she continued. 'He wasn't here alone. He booked the romantic package, with her.'

She laid down a second photo. 'That is Eve Ashwood. She could . . .'

'That's the woman in the pool,' cried Edwina. Then she

clapped her hand over her mouth, but it was too late.

Agnes narrowed her eyes. 'The body in the pool? You recognise her? You saw her?'

'Well, yeah,' said Edwina. 'Not really. Hardly at all. Maybe a teeny-tiny bit.'

'And you didn't tell us?'

'I had to take care of Oberon,' said Edwina defiantly. 'He was undercooled. He needed help!'

'*That's* where you found Oberon?' Agnes delved deeper. 'In the swimming pool? With the dead woman?'

'She's dead, is she?' Edwina muttered. 'That means I can keep him!'

'Slowly things are beginning to fit together!' Agnes's eyes were gleaming. She was too excited to get annoyed about Edwina's priorities.

'That's how it must have started. He' – she stabbed her finger on Frank Ashwood's distinguished brow – 'drowned his wife in the swimming pool. Maybe he hid when Edwina came in, or he came back later to dispose of the body. Then, something happened out on the cliffs.' Agnes frowned. What exactly had happened on the cliffs remained a mystery. Had Frank Ashwood disposed of the body? It wasn't entirely out of the question, although Agnes still thought she'd seen two living people. Who could the second person have been? Who was missing from the hotel? 'Whatever happened out there, it's the reason for the murder of three more people.'

'Why on earth did he drown her?' Charlie took the photo of Eve Ashwood in her hand. 'I mean, that really is an exceptionally beautiful woman.'

'Beauty doesn't protect you from murder,' Agnes

snapped back. 'The usual, maybe. Jealousy. Infidelity. How should I know?'

In her experience most murder motives were fundamentally banal. Greed or fear, hate and jealousy, sometimes desperation too. In the cold light of day, nothing about it was particularly deep or compelling. The true reason wasn't often in the external circumstances, but in the murderer themselves, in a disposition and a coldness, in a darkness of the soul.

She inspected the photo of Frank Ashwood more closely. The darkness of his soul wasn't discernible. What sort of person was he? What was going on in that handsome head of his? What made him tick? In any case, one thing was clear, he was starting to enjoy murder.

'Maybe we should ask him,' Edwina suggested.

'Out of the question!' Charlie hissed. 'If you're right, this guy already has five people on his conscience. We're staying away from him! We're not asking him a single thing!'

Agnes opened her mouth to protest.

Just then, there was a knock at the door.

They all gave a start, but it was just the woman from room service who wanted to tidy up the remains of the meal. When she spotted the pictures on the bedcover, she smiled.

'Beautiful couple, huh?'

'Do you know the Ashwoods?' Agnes asked hastily.

'Well, yeah, know is maybe a bit much, but I obviously noticed them. You don't get a good-looking couple like that here every day.'

The woman eyed Agnes and the others with pity, and

more than ever, they felt like a motley crew.

'When did you last see them?' Agnes asked as casually as possible.

The woman stacked plates on top of one another and narrowed her eyes. 'Strange. I don't even know . . . Quite a while ago. They put the sign out, and you know what that means.' She winked.

He killed her, and now he's in the process of creating one blood bath after another. That's what it means, thought Agnes.

'The Do Not Disturb sign?' she asked.

'Exactly. Bit of a shame really. He's a very generous tipper.' The woman had completed her plate stack and had a dreamy look on her face. Frank Ashwood had obviously made a good impression on her. 'But thinking about it, two days ago, I saw the two of them heading out for a walk. Like love birds. Completely understandable too. They're on their honeymoon as far as I know. We put a fruit basket in their room.'

'In hoods?' Agnes asked.

'Sorry?'

'Well, did they have their hoods up when they went for their walk?'

'Of course. It's unusually cold for the time of year. And it's supposed to get even colder, you know? The next thing we know, we'll have snow!'

'How can you be so certain it was Frank Ashwood then?' Agnes delved, to avoid a longer speech about the weather.

'I'm certain it was him,' the woman said hesitantly. 'Something about his posture . . .'

She broke off. It suddenly seemed to dawn on her that she wasn't dealing with normal guests, but potential criminals under room arrest.

'Did they have those outdoor jackets on?' Agnes wasn't letting go. If someone had seen Frank Ashwood with the person in the yellow hood, he was as good as convicted! 'An orange one and a yellow one?'

The room service woman peeked warily out from behind the stack of plates. 'I don't really know what that's got to do with you. Frank Ashwood is a loyal guest, and I don't wish to . . .'

'Orange and yellow?' Agnes insisted.

The woman lowered her eyes and made her way to the door with her plates. But the door had fallen shut, so she had to interrupt her escape, and stood there a little helplessly with her hands full of crockery.

Agnes heaved herself out of bed, padded to the door and put her hand on the knob. 'Orange and yellow?'

'Orange and yellow,' the woman reluctantly admitted.

Smiling contentedly, Agnes opened the door. But at that very moment, the woman spotted Oberon, who had made himself comfy on a chair. In all the excitement about Howard and Frank Ashwood, they had forgotten to hide him.

The woman didn't scream, but she dropped the stack of crockery and scuttled away through the open door.

Marshall was sitting at the table staring at his empty plate, empty glass and a corkscrew, which was lying somewhat forlornly on the table – useless since they had obviously had water. The water bottle was still standing there half empty, Marshall couldn't find any wine anywhere though.

The sight of the corkscrew unsettled him. He had this feeling that he had to get away immediately, go somewhere, do something, but he didn't know what.

He'd got used to just doing nothing in situations like this, which unfortunately weren't that unusual, until it came back to him what was going on.

But this time, doing nothing didn't feel right. Not at all.

'Exquisite!' Opposite him, Winston had finished eating and was dabbing his mouth with his napkin. 'You can say what you like about them, but they can definitely cook!'

Marshall, who couldn't remember his meal, nodded noncommittally.

Winston yawned. 'Time for a nap, I'd say, since we're stuck here anyway.' He put down the napkin and rolled over to his bed.

Stuck? Why stuck? Marshall didn't dare ask.

One thing was certain, he didn't want a nap. While Winston pulled the covers up to his chin, he grabbed the corkscrew and stuck it in his uniform jacket pocket. Fail to prepare, prepare to fail.

They had just picked up the final plates, shards of crockery and leftovers from the floor when there was another knock at the door.

'*Now* they come! Once we've already cleaned everything up!' Charlie flung the door open in a rage. 'This isn't my idea of service!' she hissed.

But it wasn't the room service woman standing there, but Trudy. The burly waiter peered angrily over Trudy's shoulder, but obviously didn't dare intervene.

'May I?' asked Trudy.

Charlie nodded. 'We had a little mishap,' she muttered.

'More than one, according to everything I'm hearing!' Trudy stepped into the room and looked around curiously. Luckily, Edwina had banished Oberon to the bathroom again after the latest slip-up, so everything looked deceptively harmless.

'So, room arrest, huh?' Trudy slammed the door in the waiter's face.

'Unfortunately,' said Agnes.

'You've missed quite a bit,' said Trudy chirpily. 'There's a lot going on out there. Rumours upon rumours. They're saying the murder in the relaxation room wasn't an isolated incident. Apparently, there's been a whole spate of them. And guess who it was?'

'Us,' said Bernadette drily.

'Correct!' Trudy plopped herself down on the sofa. 'They're saying you're working as a team. Contract killers. Proper romantic!' She grinned. 'They're also saying you've got a venomous snake here in your room!'

'He's not venomous,' cried Agnes, irritated by all the stupid rumours. Did people have nothing better to do? But if you were stranded in a hotel, scared of a serial killer, you probably really didn't have anything better to do than speculate.

'They're saying that you've . . .' Trudy pointed at Edwina, 'got a body hidden in your wardrobe!'

'Lies!' squawked Edwina.

'And even though they all agree that you must be behind it, everyone's scared of everybody else. Go figure!' She shook her head in bewilderment. 'Lots of people are choosing to stay in their rooms, but a few people have also barricaded themselves in the Sea Lounge. They've got a password. The password is *quinoa*.'

'Key what?' asked Edwina.

'Key *noir*,' Bernadette coached her.

Trudy ignored them. 'Today the knives ran out at lunch because everybody's trying to arm themselves somehow. With butter knives! Just imagine!' She laughed and fished a knife out of her tracksuit pocket. 'I obviously got myself one too. Better to be safe than sorry, huh? But the best part is that they've cancelled all of our training sessions and nobody's checking what we eat anymore. So, that's what's going on.'

She leant back and eyed first Agnes, then Edwina, Charlie and Bernadette. 'Don't worry, I don't believe it was you. What an idiotic idea! I don't think they should be holding you in here. I think you should be out there finding the real murderer.'

'I think so too.' Agnes sighed. 'But they've put a waiter outside our door.'

Trudy nodded with a serious expression on her face. 'That's why I'm here.'

A little while later, Agnes stuck her head out into the hallway.

Empty.

Trudy had promised to distract the waiter for a few minutes, and indeed, he was gone!

But they had to hurry.

Agnes had decided that if they didn't want to be recognised, they had to go their separate ways. Together they were conspicuous, alone on the other hand, old ladies. The place was swarming with old ladies. Who could tell them all apart?

She plucked up the courage and stepped out into the hallway, waved at her friends again and gave them the thumbs up. Then she made her way towards the lobby. It was dangerous, yes, but at her age practically everything was dangerous, getting up, bending over, getting out of the shower.

But if they managed to get some kind of tangible proof that Frank Ashwood was the killer, they could mobilise the hotel staff and make a combined effort to immobilise Ashwood. Until then, Agnes would have to go it alone.

The hallways were deserted and didn't have anything warm and homely about them anymore. Someone had turned the lights right up, presumably to create a feeling of safety. The opposite was true. Even the nice smell seemed to have vanished. Instead, she could smell something she knew all too well, fear.

Agnes's heart was pounding as she crept through a glaringly illuminated labyrinth, like a hesitant rat, with a sinister sense of foreboding.

21

ROOM 12

By now, Agnes knew the octopus-body of the Eden quite well and had a clear idea of where room number 12 was located. Nevertheless, the corridors of the hotel suddenly seemed strange to her. Somebody had switched off the tinkling raindrop music. The Eden was as still as the grave. Agnes's footsteps echoed. Her heart pounded loudly through the corridor. Organically formed stone sculptures and orchid arrangements made ominous shadows on the walls, and for a moment she was completely disoriented.

Then she pulled herself together.

Frank Ashwood's room was in the third of the four corridors and was either accessible directly from the lobby, past the Sea Lounge, or on a little detour through the spa area on the lower ground floor.

After a moment of brief hesitation Agnes plumped for the route through the lower ground floor. That way, she didn't need to cross the lobby, and the probability of bumping into Helen or one of her waiter henchmen was reduced. Her hip wouldn't cooperate with a wild chase, that much was clear.

She stepped into the lift and pressed the spa button. As the lift made its way on its little journey, she scrutinised herself in the mirror on the back wall. She looked small, smaller than she remembered, dry and somehow muddled. A lost old woman, not a detective hunting a murderer. Before she could decide if she was actually completely out of her depth or just particularly artfully camouflaged, the lift door opened with a cheerful chime.

Agnes gave a start, then warily peered out into the spa area. It was quiet at any rate, absolutely dead. She summoned the courage and stepped out of the lift, not a second too soon. It made a mocking sound and wafted away upstairs again, in a hurry it seemed to Agnes, as if it wanted to get out of there as quickly as possible.

She couldn't blame it. Completely deserted, the spa area had an eerie feeling about it. She clutched her walking stick and headed off, past the reception, deeper and deeper into the oppressive mugginess of the former wellness oasis. Eventually, there were only a few steps left to get to the service lift, and from there . . .

Something brushed her shoulder. She almost screamed.

Just a plant!

Onward!

She felt like an explorer, penetrating the deepest depths of the jungle, a protein-rich snack on two legs, well-hidden monsters eyeing her with interest. All of a sudden, she wished the spa area wasn't quite so . . . dead.

Her footsteps clacked unnaturally loudly on the sandstone floor.

There was the door where she had received her first – and presumably also last – massage. Agnes tried to remember the feeling of warm relaxation and didn't succeed. Her heart was pounding too loudly, but it didn't matter. She was almost . . . She just had to get past the . . .

For some reason, she hadn't banked on the glass doors of the relaxation room.

She briefly glanced inside, and then couldn't look away again.

Obviously, they had taken poor Walter Ross away, presumably to the cold store, where it must now be pretty tight, but the relaxation room still wasn't a very nice sight. Agnes could hazily make out the sea through the window behind, blue and carefree, light years away.

She tried to concentrate on that, but she didn't really succeed.

Before, when she had only been seventy or so, and still a bit overconfident, she'd tried keeping chickens at Sunset Hall. Why not? She had plenty of space, the eggs tasted much better than the ones in the shops, and the hens were pleasant and surprisingly outgoing companions.

Then one day, the fox had come, and afterwards the hen house had looked a bit like the relaxation room did now.

Agnes shuddered.

What was she doing here? Wouldn't it have been wiser to barricade herself in her room with a butter knife like the other guests? Was she really in the process of hunting down the person who had created all that carnage in the relaxation room?

But someone had to do it. She had ignored the verger's murder and let her hair down. She wouldn't let that happen again – she owed herself and the world that. Keep growing until the bitter end, that was what it was all about, she'd learnt that much from Oberon.

Suddenly she was certain, the spate of murders in the hotel might have started for practical reasons, but it wasn't just about doing away with witnesses anymore. He was having a whale of a time.

Suddenly, she heard a clatter. Not overly loud, just as if someone had tripped on a bucket or maybe a chair, but she could have sworn it had come from here on the lower ground floor.

There was someone there!

She wasn't alone!

The next thing she knew, Agnes was already standing in the service lift, her heart pounding, frantically pushing the close door button, her eyes glued to the hallway. How she had made it there so quickly was a mystery to her, but the main thing was that she was there, and the main thing was that the lift doors closed before something came along the corridor and scuppered her getaway.

Getaway, and not the romantic kind.

That was the way the cookie crumbled.

The doors finally shut. The service lift sighed deeply, then jolted into motion, and Agnes hovered upwards. It was only one floor, but she felt like she'd escaped from Hades. She stepped out into the lobby, disappeared behind one of the big ferns and briefly caught her breath.

The reception area was deserted, but Agnes could hear agitated-sounding voices. Time to get moving again. The good thing about an adrenalin rush like this was that nothing hurt anymore, nothing at all. She waited briefly until her knees weren't quite so wobbly, then rushed down the corridor, fear spurring her on, towards room 12.

Edwina had already made good progress on the way to room 12. She was wearing the blonde curly wig from her agent kit and had borrowed a glitzy jacket from Charlie. Nobody would recognise her with that on! Nobody!

Not that there had been much opportunity to be recognised up to now. But as she passed the Sea Lounge and tried to turn into the lobby, she suddenly found herself in front of a barricade of stacked-up bar stools.

Two middle-aged men were waiting in front of the barricade, a scrawny bald one and one more rotund with limp grey hair stuck greasily to his neck. Neither of them had noticed her yet because they were looking the other way, over the stools into the lobby.

Edwina joined them and peered into the lobby too. What were the two of them waiting for? The lobby was empty, but Edwina saw some people sitting on the other side of the glass doors, in the Sea Lounge, who seemed to be eyeing one another with mistrust.

She soon got bored of spying on them.

'Nothing to see here!' she said.

The two men spun around. Edwina had seen them both before, presumably in the restaurant or at breakfast. She peered out from beneath the fringe of her wig and grinned at them kindly.

'Nice day for it,' she said politely. Although she didn't think much of small talk herself, she had learnt that a few meaningless comments about the day or the weather quickly put people at ease.

This time, however, her line didn't have the desired effect.

'How could you say such a thing?' said the man with the limp hair indignantly. 'This is an absolute crisis situation! We're sitting ducks! It's a matter of life and death!' He shuddered.

'It can still be a nice day for it,' Edwina insisted, straightening her wig.

'Who even are you?' the bald one asked sternly.

'I'm . . .' It occurred to Edwina just in time that she was incognito. 'I'm Hettie!' She beamed. If she had to be someone else, then Hettie!

'I've never seen you here before!' said the bald man.

Edwina shrugged. What the man may or may not have seen really wasn't her problem!

She decided that that was enough of the pleasantries and started climbing the stack of bar stools. The bald man grabbed her by the arm.

'We can't just let you run around here like this,' he said. 'Don't you know there's a murderer on the loose? At least one! Maybe even a whole gang of them!'

Edwina tried to shake off the bald man's hand, but he wasn't letting go.

'Freddy,' moaned the rotund man with the hair. 'Is that really . . . ?'

'Of course it's necessary!' snorted the bald man. 'Nobody gets through here. Those are the rules! It's about all our safety!'

'But she's only . . .' The hairy man pointed dismissively at Edwina. His greasy curls quivered. 'And apart from that, she didn't come from the other side!'

309

'Rules are rules!' cried the bald man. 'It's completely irrelevant which side you come from!' He'd talked himself into a rage and was going an unattractive shade of red.

Edwina thought for a moment. Obviously, she could have ridded herself of the rule fanatic with one targeted kick. But then her cover would have been blown, and Agnes had absolutely unequivocally said that they had to act inconspicuously. After all, it wouldn't be any use turning up at room 12 with a pair of barricade-builders on her tail. So, she allowed herself to be dragged down from the bar stools and led into the Sea Lounge.

'I really must be getting on,' she said politely.

'Not without the password!' the bald man insisted.

Edwina thought some more. Hadn't Trudy said something about a password before? It had something to do with locks, didn't it? And French colours.

Lock *noir*?

Code *rouge*?

Cordon bleu?

Agnes had arrived at room 12 and was kicking her heels. The door itself looked completely innocent. It was made of dark wood, just like all the others, the room number shone in brushed metal. The handle boasted a Do Not Disturb sign.

It was silent behind the door.

Agnes's heart on the other hand was beating more vigorously than usual.

Where was Edwina?

They had made quite clear arrangements, they would

separate and make their own different ways to room 12 and wait for each other there. Then they planned to infiltrate the room together (how was still a mystery to Agnes, but Edwina would surely think of something) and either question Frank Ashwood or (ideally) search the room for clues in his absence. After that . . . who could say?

Charlie and Bernadette should each hold the fort in their own rooms and if they weren't back within half an hour, alert Winston and Marshall. Then she would hopefully be rescued somehow, and could brace herself for a thorough dressing-down.

It was a risky strategy, but just sitting in her room waiting for the murderer to think of something clever didn't seem a very attractive prospect either.

She stepped from one foot to the other and listened into the corridor with the help of her new hearing aid. There was nobody to be seen or heard. Nevertheless she had the uneasy feeling that she was being watched.

Where the hell was Edwina?

Edwina had made herself comfy in one of the armchairs in the Sea Lounge and was being interrogated. It wasn't going particularly well. It was blatantly obvious that neither the curly haired man nor the bald man, nor any of the other guests, had any idea how to lead a proper interrogation.

For example, you didn't offer the subject a comfortable chair, along with maybe a selection of nuts to nibble on, and a nice sea view – no, you put them in a small dark room on a stool and shone bright light in their eyes. This, however . . .

Edwina was finding it hard to concentrate. She missed Oberon, and being incognito was getting boring.

The red face of the bald man appeared in front of her. He said something far too loudly for her liking. Maybe he was hard of hearing?

'What are you doing here?' he asked, not for the first time. 'Where are you going?'

Edwina looked at him pityingly. You never just asked what you actually wanted to know. Anything but that!

'I was on my way to yoga!' she said defiantly.

'Now? Today?' cried the curly haired man in dismay. 'In a situation like this, you're thinking about yoga?'

Edwina explained to him that this was exactly the right time to be thinking about yoga. Yoga was practically made for situations like these. After all, it helped to find inner peace and tranquillity at times of crisis, to breathe deeply, reduce fear and to recognise the beauty of the moment, even if the bigger picture maybe didn't look quite so rosy.

Yoga was an inner journey, an alternative to the outside world, an affirmation of life.

Meanwhile, a group had formed around Edwina's armchair, and they were all ears.

Agnes wasn't exactly appreciating the beauty of the moment just then. She was still standing at the door like an idiot, and her hip pain was fighting its way through the adrenalin rush to the surface. Shame.

No Edwina in sight, and with every extra minute that Agnes stood around like a fool, the chance of someone, like the murderer, spotting her increased.

Apart from that, she was wondering how they were

312

even supposed to get into room 12. There were no keyholes to pick with hairpins, instead the lock was activated by a hotel card, but not just any card, only by a specific card.

Or maybe not?

Agnes rummaged around in her jacket pocket. Before she aborted the mission and returned to her room humiliated, to spend the rest of her days lecturing Edwina, she could at least try her own card, couldn't she?

There it was! She leant on the door and pushed the Do Not Disturb sign to one side to get the card into the correct position. It wasn't easy at all, and then . . .

Click.

Before she could even get her card anywhere near the sensor, the door slid open a crack. It hadn't even been closed properly. Once again, Agnes felt like a fool. Stupid enough to stand at a closed door – but an open one . . .

Now what?

Should she wait a bit longer for Edwina? She had made a promise to her housemates that she wouldn't go in alone. But here she was, on the go and alone. Those were the facts. And whose fault was that? Definitely not hers!

Maybe she could risk a quick look, so that the mission and all the risks she'd taken downstairs hadn't been for nothing.

A quick look or two couldn't hurt, surely! Apart from that, Ashwood was bound to be out and about in the hotel somewhere, ready to ambush her; he certainly wasn't bargaining on her turning up in his room. Under the right conditions, the lion's den could be the safest place for miles around – Agnes had once read something along those lines . . .

She pushed the door open a little more and listened. Nothing. Then she bravely stepped inside, and pulled the door shut behind her.

The Ashwoods' room was considerably bigger than the one she and Edwina were sharing. There weren't just individual armchairs, but a sprawling, sumptuously curved suite, a driftwood table with an orchid arrangement, a sunken bath – Caution, Trap! – and a bed where you probably had to arrange marital activities in advance – top right behind the third pillow!

But Agnes's envy was short-lived.

In marked contrast to the other spaces in the Eden, it was cold there, unnaturally cold, so icy cold that even the body in the bed had pulled the covers up to its chin. At least that's what it looked like.

Agnes cautiously stepped closer and looked down at the small pale face amongst the sheets. The wet woman, no question. They met, at last!

Of course, the wet woman wasn't wet anymore, but you could tell that she must have been wet by the way her hair was stuck to her head. Apart from that, Eve Ashwood's pale skin and the delicate facial features were unmistakable. She even looked good dead. A pale hand lay elegantly on the sheets and was holding something. A white orchid, already a bit limp from the cold, and from having been broken off.

Frank Ashwood hadn't pushed his dead wife off the cliff then.

He had laid her out, and with a certain care and tenderness.

That threw Agnes a bit. Was this really the same killer

who had so heartlessly done away with poor Walter Ross in the relaxation room just a short while ago? On the other hand, dead was dead, and the fact that Ashwood had dragged the body out of the pool and hid it in his hotel room obviously spoke volumes.

Suddenly, Agnes understood why it was so cold in the room, Ashwood had left the balcony door open, presumably so that the wet woman didn't start to smell quite so quickly.

There wasn't the slightest sign of him, luckily. Maybe he was hiding somewhere behind the scenes or in another room, or he'd even left the hotel to break off on his own? An athletic-looking chap like him might stand a chance!

Agnes realised she didn't want him to simply go on the run. She wanted to catch him. She wanted to bring him to justice, for his crimes obviously, but also in part because he had ruined their romantic eco holiday.

Just then it dawned on her that there was a good reason for the murderer not to just go on the run. The reason was her, Agnes Sharp, the last witness from the Sea Lounge.

Her heart was pounding. What was she doing here, alone and unarmed in a murderer's room?

'Where are you?' she whispered into the cold room.

Who are you?

Her breath hung in the air like a question mark.

22

CHAMPAGNE

'What's the time now?'
        'Five past four.'
'Still?'
'Yes. Still!'

Charlie shifted about in her chair, completely on edge. Bernadette had started pacing back and forth like a tiger in a cage. An overweight tiger with a white cane. It was very noisy. Bernadette seemed to be thinking too. Deeply alarming!

'Sit down!' nagged Charlie. 'Toing and froing isn't going to make the time pass any more quickly!'

It was now quite some time since Agnes and Edwina had gone off. Another ten minutes, then they would have to tell Winston and Marshall. Charlie was dreading it. She could just imagine it, first the horrified looks, then the panic in Marshall's eyes followed by silent reproach. After that, they'd run around like headless chickens, and launch into some kind of improvised plan. And without Agnes, who was normally responsible for planning, the whole thing was practically doomed to fail.

Charlie groaned.

'What time is it now?' Bernadette asked, relentlessly pacing.

Resigned to her fate, Charlie glanced at her watch. A gift from her first husband – he'd actually been quite sweet, especially compared to husband number two.

'Six minutes past four.' She sighed.

'Six minutes past four already?' Bernadette stood still and frowned. 'I think Agnes and Edwina are in trouble.'

'We're all in trouble.' Charlie groaned. 'Especially when we fess up to Marshall.'

Bernadette tapped her cane on the floor, deep in thought. 'Maybe we don't have to fess up to Marshall at all,' she said. 'I mean, what can he even do without any of his guns, apart from maybe have a heart attack? And who would that help? Definitely not Agnes!'

Charlie's ears pricked up.

'Have you got a better idea?'

'I do actually!' A worried expression crossed Bernadette's face, and Charlie immediately suspected that the idea had something to do with Bernadette's secret admirer. And why not? The man could make himself useful – and anything was better than admitting to Marshall that they had just sent Agnes and Edwina into the killer's lair like that.

Bernadette was already at the door, listening outside. Charlie joined her, then peered into the hallway. Nobody there! Whatever Trudy had come up with, it really had distracted the waiter!

'The coast is clear,' she hissed.

Bernadette nodded and was already out of the door. 'Wait here!' she whispered. 'I'll be back as soon as I can!'

Charlie opened her mouth to protest, but Bernadette

had already disappeared round one of the soft curves of the corridor, surprisingly quickly and surprisingly soundlessly.

Charlie gazed helplessly after her.

Wait! she wanted to shout, but loud shouting suddenly seemed inappropriate, risky even. She was confronted by a great and vaguely menacing silence in the corridor. Charlie shuddered, hastily shut the door and put the safety catch on.

'Rats deserting a sinking ship,' she muttered, mostly just to do something about the silence. She was reminded of Oberon, who presumably also had rats on his mind, albeit for different reasons. Edwina had dragged him into the bathroom with some words of warning before her departure.

That was it then. Alone with the snake! Charlie had always feared that sooner or later it would come to this. And that wasn't even her biggest problem. She was a sitting duck in the room the murderer thought Agnes was in and wasn't even armed with so much as a butter knife! Why hadn't she thought about that sooner? Probably because Bernadette had been making such a racket the whole time!

Charlie dragged one of the chairs over to the door and pushed it under the handle. There! Nobody was getting in! Nobody! But what about the window? She hastily drew the curtains and was toying with the idea of taking her chances with the devil she knew rather than the devil she didn't, and barricading herself in the bathroom with Oberon, when she heard a dull thud pretty close by.

The sound went through her like ice.

What if the murderer wasn't trying to get into her room?

What if he was already there?

* * *

Bernadette rushed through the hotel's corridors, her cane leading the way, and the cloud of determination that had surrounded her at the start, was slowly petering out. What had seemed like a damn good idea just a moment ago, was beginning to look like a smoke screen.

She wanted to see Jack again, that was the truth of the matter!

And obviously he would be able to help her save Agnes.

Providing Jack wasn't the murderer, but Agnes had been fairly certain that it had to be this Frank Ashwood, and Bernadette had decided to believe her.

So far, so good. That was the cunning part of her plan.

The less cunning part consisted of her first having to find Jack, without any eyes at all, in a hotel, where everyone now suspected everyone of murder. Not a very nice situation to be in.

And she didn't even know his room number!

Bernadette stopped to listen. Why was it so damn quiet? There were distant sounds of the sea and a gentle humming, that presumably had something to do with the heating or the air conditioning.

Nothing else.

Or maybe – breathing?

She clutched her cane and strained to hear. Now she was certain, somebody was breathing, not far away at all, discreetly but just about discernible nonetheless. Bernadette racked her brains. The fact that the breather wasn't addressing her, or raising the alarm didn't bode well. She must be just before the Sea Lounge, roughly where the corridor got wider and then opened out into the lobby. Maybe she would make it to reception, where with a bit of luck they would recognise her and escort her back to her room. Not a very illustrious prospect, but in the given circumstances, not altogether unattractive either.

Bernadette hastily strode on, her cane leading the way still.

On the first few steps, everything was going well, but then, to her surprise, her cane hit something hard.

She could feel metal and wood in all directions. Chairs maybe, higgledy-piggledy?

Stacks of them.

She tried to push against them, but the chairs didn't relent.

Charlie had looked under the bed, behind the sofa, in Agnes's wardrobe and, taking her life in her hands, she looked in the bathroom, where Oberon was lying in the bathtub surprisingly peacefully, fast asleep.

Nothing.

Then only one possibility remained. She was now fairly certain that there was somebody in Edwina's wardrobe. Every now and then an audible gentle rustling came from there, once even a kind of suppressed cough. Another one of Edwina's animals, she'd thought at first, and knowing her housemate, it was probably a scorpion or a tarantula called Titania. But animals didn't cough. Or suppress coughs at any rate.

For a while, Charlie contented herself with staring warily at the wardrobe doors, then she couldn't take it any longer. Murderer or no murderer – she had to know who was in there! She looked around for a suitable weapon and finally plumped for the champagne bottle from the minibar. It fitted nicely in her hand.

Brandishing the bottle, she approached the wardrobe. Open the door and then whack the occupant over the head as quickly as possible, that was the plan. Simple and effective! Her hand inched towards the handle. Finally, she grabbed it and pulled . . .

'Haaaaaa . . . !'

In the middle of her war cry she realised that a few things weren't quite going to plan. For one, the wardrobe door wasn't opening. She shook it with all her might. She could forget the element of surprise now. For another, due to all the shaking, her grip on the neck of the bottle was loosening, and her weapon plummeted to the floor. Luckily it consisted of soft wool carpets, so not much happened to the precious champagne.

After a while, Charlie gave up on the shaking to give herself a breather.

'It's locked!' said a voice from the wardrobe.

'I know that!' Charlie hissed, by now completely miffed. First all the excitement, and now this! The voice didn't sound particularly dangerous, more young and a bit dozy.

'Edwina put the key on the chest of drawers,' the voice said helpfully.

Charlie looked up. Indeed, there on the chest of drawers lay a key that looked like it would fit.

'Why should I open it?' she cried indignantly. 'If Edwina locked you in there, then there must have been a reason for it!'

'I'm not saying you should open it,' the voice explained rationally. 'Just that you can if you want to. You just seem to want to get into the wardrobe, that's all . . .'

You couldn't really argue with that. Charlie didn't say a word, overwhelmed. She felt betrayed. Was this some kind of trick? She could just as well leave the door locked – disaster averted! The wardrobe seemed extraordinarily solid to her.

But her curiosity was getting the better of her. She sauntered over to the chest of drawers and grabbed the key. Should she? Or shouldn't she?

To hell with it! She had to know who was in the wardrobe!

'I'm going to unlock it now!' she declared. 'And I'm armed!'

'Cool!' chimed the voice from inside the wardrobe.

Charlie put the bottle close at hand next to her on the floor and put the key into the lock.

'I'm going to unlock it now!' she repeated to give herself courage.

'Knock yourself out!' the voice encouraged her.

Bernadette tripped, but then caught hold of somebody's hand.

Big, warm and dry.

'Bar stools,' murmured a voice close to her ear, 'Stacks of them. Some idiots piled them all on top of one another. Quite silly to build a barricade here, if you ask me, particularly when you don't know where the person you're barricading yourself from is.'

Even before she had processed the information, she sensed her body relaxing.

'What else?' she whispered, so as not to show her sense of relief.

'There are lots of people busy doing yoga in the Sea Lounge. So busy that it hasn't occurred to anybody to man the barricade. So, if a certain enchanting lady wanted to get to the other side, it would be a definite possibility.'

'I want to get to the other side,' Bernadette admitted. What she really wanted was a moment or two alone, just the two of them, so she could finally melt away like ice cream. But unfortunately, there was no time for that now.

She heard a few stools being moved, then the warm hand zigzagged her skilfully towards the lobby. Straightaway, Bernadette sensed the space in front of her opening out, widening.

'Is there anyone here?' she asked.

'Just a dog,' Jack whispered. 'And it's asleep.'

Bernadette let him carry on leading her, presumably behind one of the ferns that she'd involuntarily made the acquaintance of earlier. She decided to allow herself an ice-cream moment.

Life was short, especially now, and some things had to be done at least once, before shuffling off this mortal coil.

Edwina had started slowly, with breathing exercises and seated meditation, but most of the people in the Sea Lounge were at their limit with a simple tree balance. One woman was groaning and rubbing her ankles, and the chap with the hair unceremoniously toppled over – in a vaguely tree-like way, admittedly.

The rest were wavering and wobbling precariously.

'It's easier if you fix your eyes on a certain point,' Edwina explained, one foot in the air. She stood there like a young birch, graceful and effortless.

'If you close your eyes, though, it's much harder . . .'

She closed her eyes to spare herself the sight of all the wobbling bodies around her. In principle, she had nothing against teaching other people a bit of yoga, especially people who were as in need of it as the nervous Sea Lounge visitors, but right now she had other things on her mind. She had to find Agnes, search room 12, catch the murderer, and then get back to Oberon as quickly as possible. The snake was bound to be missing her already!

There was an audible plopping next to her, and Edwina reluctantly opened her eyes. Her yoga pupils had obviously tried it out and closed their eyes. Now they were falling about and tripping all over one another, holding on to one another for dear life.

In the general chaos, Edwina suddenly had a brain wave.

'Key *noir*!'

She tore the wig off her head, leapt over a fallen yoga beginner, crossed the Sea Lounge, opened the door, scaled the barrier and rushed towards room 12.

A man in the wardrobe! Edwina's wardrobe!

Charlie couldn't quite believe it. She wouldn't have put much past Edwina, baby elephants – absolutely! Tarantulas – every time! Men – less so! But the facts spoke for themselves.

Hats off to her!

The man was more of a boy really, stick thin and badly dressed, and he whiffed a bit – but at their age you couldn't afford to be picky.

Charlie and the young man from the wardrobe were already in the process of becoming firm friends. First, they shared the bottle of champagne, and now the lad was charging his much-loved phone with the help of her cable.

It turned out he was a vlogger. He made a living by putting little videos of himself on the internet – and not even *those* kinds of videos. Just videos about his everyday life, music, clothes (oh, God!) and beauty products – and he looked like he hadn't set eyes on a single beauty product for a very long time. Would you believe it?

He'd filmed little videos at the hotel too, most recently even in the wardrobe. Charlie obviously didn't ask how exactly he came to be in Edwina's wardrobe. She was a lady, after all.

'Actually, I'm going cold turkey!' the lad admitted without being asked. He had introduced himself as 'Mojo,' but Charlie didn't believe for a second that it was his real name.

'Cold turkey!' she huffed with contempt.

'It was actually quite alright,' Mojo explained. 'But then my nan forced me to come to this hotel, and there's just nothing going on here! It's like watching paint dry!'

Nothing going on! Charlie polished off the rest of her champagne. Mojo had missed quite a bit while he'd been in the wardrobe!

Agnes had gone through the Ashwoods' room with a fine-tooth comb without coming up with anything particularly noteworthy. She had found a kind of crate with a heat lamp – proof that Oberon had indeed belonged to Eve Ashwood – but as far as the murder case was concerned, it didn't really get her any further. In the bathroom, she had discovered not only two toothbrushes leaning harmoniously against each other, but also an empty packet of sleeping tablets. Interesting. But apart from that, the couple's possessions were a veritable textbook example of chic minimalism. Nothing there explained why Ashwood had suddenly decided to bring his new marriage and his wife's life to an abrupt halt and to carry on committing murders to pass the time.

Or was it this very emptiness that betrayed him, the complete lack of personality? If only Marshall had been there, or Winston, or at least Edwina! One of them would definitely have had an idea, and even a stupid idea was sometimes enough to help the investigation along. Where the hell was Edwina?

For a moment, Agnes felt such a sense of exhaustion that she would have gladly lain down with Eve Ashwood, covers up to her nose, done! She had been right as far as the wet woman was concerned. Frank Ashwood had claimed his place at the top of her list of suspects, and yet it seemed like she wasn't getting any closer to the truth.

What was she missing?

And what now? What next?

She should at least sit down for a moment.

She lowered herself onto the edge of the bed – despite Eve's dead body, there was still a lot of space – and enjoyed the softness of the mattress. There! Just do nothing for a bit. Above all, no thinking. She realised how tired she was. There she sat in an ice-cold luxury hotel room in the middle of nowhere, next to a dead body. And this was supposed to be a holiday? The cold reminded her of Sunset Hall, and she allowed herself a slice of homesickness. If you were going to hunt a murderer in arctic temperatures, then preferably in your own four walls! At home she would have known the killer and the victims personally. She would have been able to get a better picture of them and not just with stupid photos . . .

It occurred to Agnes that she was staring at something on the floor. There lay the skeletal remains of a bunch of grapes, slightly reminiscent of a finger, seemingly pointing at something, just like a finger would. There, slid half under the bed, was something she had missed before.

It was a small, rectangular piece of paper. Like a photo . . .

If it was a photo, then it was obviously the wrong way up. Just like bread, photos always fell on the butter, or photo, side. That had to be a kind of law of nature. Agnes tore herself away from the mattress with a sigh and began the complicated, painful process of bending down. At first, her fingers had difficulty grabbing the photo – was it because of the cold? – but then she managed it, squinted for lack of her reading glasses and focused.

There was Eve Ashwood, her modesty covered only by Oberon and a kind of glitzy belt. For a moment, Agnes was taken aback by how flawless Eve seemed from head to toe. Only then did it dawn on her where she was sitting, on a man's knee – and the man quite clearly wasn't Frank Ashwood!

Agnes exhaled sharply and watched a little white cloud surreptitiously drift away from her. Here it finally was – motive! Not a nice thing to be confronted with a picture like that on your honeymoon – that could definitely make someone lose control for a moment and drown wifey in the pool!

But she immediately realised that something in that

thought didn't quite ring true. Eve Ashwood hadn't been spontaneously drowned – she was still wearing a bedraggled red evening gown and most certainly hadn't been wearing it for a swim. Somebody must have dragged her into the pool first! A risky undertaking and completely unnecessary, after all, there was a generous bath in the room.

And there was another interesting question, where had the photo come from? Who had leaked it to Frank Ashwood? A blackmailer? Was Howard maybe at play again?

Agnes shivered.

It was time to go.

Ashwood could come back at any moment, and if he found her on the edge of the bed, he'd make short work of her, that much was clear.

Maybe she should just close the balcony door? It wasn't exactly environmentally friendly to let the cold into the hotel, and her stay at the Eden had made her considerably more environmentally aware. It wasn't just about yourself – it was about the penguins too! After all, Eve would soon end up in the cold store, and unlike with Hettie, it didn't matter if the cold chain was interrupted or not.

Agnes padded to the glass door and looked out onto the generous terrace. Obviously useless in this weather. Daylight was already beginning to trickle away at the horizon again, and the sky hung over it like lead. And there, on one of the loungers, something had got caught, it was fluttering and flapping in the wind as if it were alive.

Something yellow.

A memory stirred in Agnes, first hesitantly, like a freshly hatched brimstone butterfly, then with greater vigour.

She quickly stepped out onto the terrace and grabbed the yellow flapping thing. It was a little bag made of light material, weightless almost. An empty case. Agnes was sure she had never seen it before, but the memory stirred even more vigorously. Then it spread its wings, and Agnes understood. It was one of those bags for storing down jackets. Agnes knew that because Edwina had a jacket like it with a bag, and was constantly losing the blasted thing. Bag hunting was a popular social activity in Sunset Hall, particularly in the winter, just like carping on about the food, and moaning about the weather.

All of a sudden, Agnes sensed movement behind her. It had been foolhardy to let the room out of her sight. She spun around, but there was nobody there. Nevertheless, something wasn't right. It took a moment for Agnes to realise that the automatic balcony door was moving, and slowly, but inexorably closing in front of her very eyes.

She dropped her walking stick in fright and hobbled towards the door, but she was too late and, in her haste, collided with the glass like an overgrown fly. She thought she could make out a figure on the other side of the glass, but as she screened her eyes with her hand in order to be able to see better, all she saw was the hotel room door closing.

Drat!

The bag worked itself loose from her hands and drifted past her out to sea, a little speck of colour amidst the broad expanse of the ocean. Agnes watched it go. It was a very distinctive yellow, lemony and aggressive, and she had seen it before just recently – also out in the cold, also at sunset.

And suddenly she understood what the yellow bag meant.

Everything went black for a moment. Her feet were like blocks of ice. In shock, she sank down into the ice-cold embrace of one of the loungers.

Frank Ashwood had indeed been out and about on the cliffs that evening – but not in the orange hood.

He had been in the *yellow* hood!

That changed everything! Agnes had been wrong.

Again!

And now she would pay the price with her life.

Buoyed by yoga and the feeling of superiority that always ensued when she watched other people practising their asanas, Edwina rushed through the lobby.

She was content with her little outing. Now to quickly solve the murders with Agnes, and then she could deservedly return to Oberon.

Someone shouted something in the distance, but Edwina didn't listen. She had already crossed the lobby and was in the corridor where room number 12 should be, according to Agnes's description.

Now she just had to . . .

She stopped. No Agnes far and wide – and she'd promised to wait for Edwina! But – and this was even more surprising – there was no room number 12, at least as far as Edwina could see.

Someone had removed all of the numbers – only the screw holes were still visible – and a whole host of bare doors stared mutely back at Edwina, each one just as blank as the next.

23

THE SEAGULL

A sharp pain in Agnes's brow jolted her awake.
Her eyes shot open.

Grey wings and a waft of sea and decay clipped her face, then she saw the snowflakes, an endlessly gentle, endlessly silent swirl. Snow! The room service woman from before had been right! But it wasn't the snowflakes that had woken her.

It was the gull.

It was sitting just an arm's length away from her on a snow-covered bistro table, a scheming look in its eye. Seen at close quarters, it wasn't a friendly bird. A strong, curved beak pointed in Agnes's direction; piercing carrion-eating eyes stared at her calculatingly.

Carrion.

They hadn't quite got to that point yet!

Surprised at the amount of snow covering her knees, thighs and chest, surprised also by the silence, Agnes looked around.

She was sitting in a lounger on the coldest terrace of all time. It was dark on the other side of the glass door, but in one of the rooms above her there must be a light on.

Agnes, snow and seagull were shrouded in a gentle glow. Snowflakes appeared out of the darkness, glowed golden and descended towards her. It was hypnotic. Her eyelids were getting heavy again.

The seagull sat on the edge of the pool of light, in silent anticipation.

If Agnes fell asleep now, she probably wouldn't wake up again. That was what the seagull was banking on.

But in its overzealousness, it had saved her life for the time being. It was up to Agnes to do something with this gifted life.

She tried to get up.

Even under ideal circumstances, it wasn't easy to free yourself from a lounger like that, and now, exhausted and frozen stiff, it would be even more of a struggle for her. Agnes tried to support herself on the armrest, but her hands weren't gripping properly. The cold, probably. Oddly enough, she didn't feel cold, it was more like her body wasn't really there, as if she were just dreaming it. That gave her an idea.

She folded herself forwards, in order to crawl out of the lounger on her hands and knees. Her sensitive knees on the cold, hard ground – normally it would have hurt like hell. But her dream body complied without complaint, and Agnes found herself on all fours again. Her hands left imprints behind in the freshly fallen snow.

Success! She had made it out of the chair, but her new position wasn't exactly ideal either. She crawled over to the terrace railing, so that she could pull herself up. The seagull looked on, disillusioned.

Agnes's fingers were still good for nothing, but she

managed to get an arm over the railing and pull herself into a more or less upright position with her elbow.

There! She was standing up! Wobbly and exhausted, but undeniably upright. She leant on the railing and watched the glowing clouds of breath leave her body in quick succession. Lost warmth, puffed away, gone forever.

The sea had to be down there somewhere, but even the sea was silent.

The seagull saw Agnes standing up, squawked a lament, plainly disgusted, and flew up into the air. The next moment, it had disappeared.

That was one way to leave the terrace, but was there another one too, one better suited to a flightless creature like Agnes? She couldn't stay there, that much was clear!

It dawned on her that she was hunting a murderer. It was going terribly. She had allowed herself to be tricked, lured out onto the terrace and locked out, and all that without managing to establish the identity of the killer.

That was probably what annoyed her the most.

And something else was disappointing, she'd been wrong! Again! Frank Ashwood had been in the yellow jacket, not the orange one. That meant he wasn't the murderer. He was the victim in the yellow hood!

That obviously offered a very good explanation for why he hadn't been anywhere to be seen over the last few days. But other than that, it didn't explain very much. Why had someone gone to so much effort to kill the Ashwoods? Had they been chosen at random? Did the killer just want to kill as many people as possible for his own edification? Was he a blood-thirsty lunatic without a plan?

No, it couldn't be that simple. Everything had started

with Eve and Frank Ashwood, and then the murderer had set about systematically silencing witnesses. He was a blood-thirsty lunatic *with* a plan.

How on earth had he – or she – managed to lure Ashwood to the cliffs shortly after he had fished his dead wife out of the swimming pool? There had to be a connection there, but Agnes couldn't see it.

It was clear that answers to these questions weren't to be found on the terrace, especially not when her brain was in the process of turning into a block of ice.

She had to get out of the cold, as quickly and straightforwardly as possible, otherwise her investigating days were over, forever. Agnes didn't know what scared her more, the prospect of her imminent demise or the humiliation of leaving the case unsolved.

Why was nobody coming to her rescue? Where was Edwina? They all knew exactly where she'd gone. She'd planned everything so meticulously!

Where was the Sunset Hall crew?

Agnes started to shake like a proverbial jelly.

'Again!'

Charlie was nibbling on a packet of cashew nuts from the minibar and having a lovely time watching little videos on Mojo's revived mobile phone.

The concept was always the same, Mojo went somewhere (to a shop or a restaurant), tested things out and was rude to everyone present. Objectively, it wasn't exactly anything particularly original, but Charlie had to admit that the videos were an absolute scream.

Mojo breezed through the finest of shops in ripped

jeans and frilly shirts, sniffed handcrafted perfume samples, licked lipsticks, stuck his finger in gateaux and made inappropriate looking flower arrangements. It was refreshing.

'And they just let you in?' Charlie asked.

'They don't just let me in. They *invite* me!' Mojo explained, blasé. 'They pay me! It's my job!'

Not for the first time, Charlie wished she was young again. Sure, you had to grapple with affairs and husbands, but you could also get paid for making fun of everyone and his dog on the internet. What a wonderful time it was to be alive!

But for her, it was obviously too late to conquer the internet – or was it?

Her finger carried on scrolling, from one video to the next.

Suddenly a less glamorous scene appeared. Mojo was sitting there in a basic T-shirt, complaining about the food, and was pale even for him. He showed a small room with mustard-coloured wallpaper and a nice view of a park.

'That was rehab,' he explained.

'Testing that out too?' Charlie asked sarcastically.

'I'll test anything out.'

Charlie nodded. Life was a long succession of testing things out, and as long as you saw it like that, you couldn't go far wrong.

'And how was it?'

Mojo shrugged. 'As long as you can make something of it, it's okay.'

That was an interesting approach. Charlie carried on scrolling, deep in thought. In one of the next videos

Mojo was suddenly walking through familiar climes, past the rounded reception of the Eden, along the corridors towards the spa area.

'That hasn't been edited yet!' Mojo protested.

Fascinated by the fact that Mojo's test drama was now playing out amidst familiar surroundings, Charlie waved dismissively. The video showed the relaxation room and the treatment rooms. Mojo fingered fresh towels and massage stones and was finally escorted to the exit by a furious spa woman.

The next clip showed him on the way to the Sea Lounge. A waiter opened the glass door for him and smiled. Then the camera made its way to the bar. Mojo was shown spirits, sniffed corks, and surprisingly took a quick swig straight out of one of the bottles (whisky, judging by the shape of the bottle).

The person manning the bar took the bottle away in disgust and looked around in desperation. A second bartender joined them – Charlie recognised Max, who was now sharing the cold store with the other murder victims. She sighed nostalgically. The camera zoomed back and forth between them, then it made a complete 180 and showed the astonished faces in the Sea Lounge. There was the pastel-suit-wearer – now in the cold store; a couple with pointy features, who were just leaving – not in the cold store; and Mrs Meyer-Brinks, who didn't look up from her book once – cold store. Agnes wasn't there yet.

Then the camera panned farther, past the glass door back to Max who was trying to gain control of the situation with an authoritative stare.

Fin.

'That's the last one.' Mojo sighed. 'It's just the wardrobe after that.'

Charlie was about to give the phone back to him when something struck her like slightly delayed lightning.

Orange and yellow.

Agnes had gone on about it until the cows came home. She clicked on the bar video again.

Door open. Sniffing bottles. The swig. General outrage. Then the pan past the lounge door.

Charlie paused the video. On the other side of the glass door, you could undoubtedly make out two figures in hooded jackets.

One orange. One yellow.

They were holding hands, or sleeves, and the orange jacket was in the process of leading the yellow one past the door of the Sea Lounge towards the lobby. There was something urgent about the way they moved, it wasn't a stroll, more of a stride, as if they were struggling against an invisible force.

Charlie let the video run. When they were both almost past the door, the orange hood turned and looked straight into the Sea Lounge.

Charlie paused the video again and zoomed in.

Then she zoomed out again.

And in.

Impossible!

It couldn't be!

Agnes was stuck on the terrace. Nobody was coming, nobody could hear her cries, the Eden's soundproofing was

337

far too good for that. Nevertheless, she had now come up with a solution of sorts for her current temperature issue.

But as was usually the case, the solution brought new problems along with it, and if she didn't want to freeze to death right there, without having achieved anything, Agnes would have to hurry. There was a big, round wooden structure on the right-hand side of the terrace that she hadn't been able to make head nor tail of at first. A viewing platform maybe? An unsuccessful art installation? But now, the thing had started to make a muted hum, and the occasional gurgle, and it dawned on Agnes that it might be one of the much-vaunted hot tubs. She had marvelled at the things in the hotel brochure with a mixture of fascination and amusement, oversized round bathtubs for outside that, according to the brochure, were made for toasting each other with organic sparkling wine and looking deeply into each other's eyes. Why you needed a tub full of water to do that remained a mystery to Agnes.

But that was by the by. The key point was this, hot tubs were hot!

If she managed to get into the tub, the risk of freezing to death was over for now.

Agnes circled the tub like a wary, but hungry wolf. Unlike in the brochure, there was some kind of cover on this specimen, but Agnes could hear water sloshing underneath. The cover was attached with straps. It had to come off!

Agnes's clumsy ice fingers fumbled around with the buckles for a small eternity, but she managed it in the end.

The cover was surprisingly light to lift, maybe because

she was pulling at it with a strength born of pure despair.

A cloud of white steam billowed towards her.

She dipped her finger in the water, but quickly pulled it out again.

How hot was this water exactly?

Initially she imagined just warming herself on the tub like a fire, but she quickly realised that wouldn't be enough. A strange fatigue overcame her. The shaking had stopped, and actually she felt quite composed and at peace. The world seemed far away, and somehow not particularly important.

You didn't have to be on the go all the time.

You could also just . . . stop.

If it hadn't been for her curiosity, the gnawing desire to still solve the case, or at least look the murderer in the eye, Agnes probably wouldn't have made it into the tub.

But she gathered herself.

She took off her shoes, tore off her cardigan and skirt, and then climbed the small platform in her petticoat and blouse. The snowflakes swirling around her gave up the ghost in the hot steam.

Agnes looked down at the gurgling water.

Once she was in there, she was stuck. But what was the alternative? Just freeze to death? She wouldn't give the murderer the satisfaction. And she could forget a rescue from the outside world too for now. If everything had gone to plan, her friends should have been there a long time ago. But clearly something had gone awry in there. Agnes sighed. She couldn't take care of everything.

Enough with the thinking!

It was actually quite simple, hot tub or death.

She held her breath to be on the safe side, and slid into the water, toes first.

But straightaway, she knew she had made a terrible mistake – that wasn't water, it was fire, she was sitting in a blazing pot that was scorching the flesh from her bones.

Was she in hell already?

Why?

She tried to remember what she had done in her life that was so terrible that she had deserved a place in hell.

Then the fire scorched that thought away too.

There was a knock at the door and Marshall, who had already been feeling restless for a while, rushed to the door. Surely it was Agnes with a plan. Agnes always had a plan.

That was one of the many things he liked about her.

But as he flung open the door, Charlie was standing there, rather unsteady on her feet, holding a mobile phone in his face.

'There! *That's* the killer!'

It took a while for Marshall to locate his reading glasses under Winston's instruction, then he took the phone again.

Charlie stepped into the room, dragging someone behind her, but Marshall barely looked up.

He stared at the face beneath the orange hood in astonishment.

'*Her*? Really?'

'No doubt about it,' Charlie explained. 'The problem is, Agnes doesn't have a clue! She suspects this Ashwood chap . . .'

Marshall frowned. Why was that a problem?

'Somebody should tell her,' he suggested. Charlie laughed nervously, and behind him Winston was already getting ready to go, or better put, ready to roll, with his woolly hat and garish blanket.

It took a while for Marshall to get the whole story out of Charlie. Agnes hadn't been in her room for quite some time. She was out and about, hunting the murderer. Only she was hunting the wrong person.

Edwina and Bernadette had since done a runner too. The only one who had been dutifully sitting in his room like an idiot the whole time was him. Marshall toyed with the idea of a tantrum but decided against it.

No time. No energy.

They had to do something fast!

He hastily threw his jacket on. Medals clattered.

Somebody tapped him on the shoulder. A young lad in black, who Charlie had apparently found in a wardrobe – but he must have misheard.

'Yes?' Marshall snorted.

'I'd like my phone back, Grandpa,' said the wardrobe kid. 'And I'm coming with you, if that's alright!'

Agnes was sitting in the hot tub having trouble distinguishing between the present, past and future.

Just now, her mother had warned her not to eat too many biscuits (so what? Agnes could eat as many biscuits as she wanted, she was an adult after all!), then her boss tore a strip off her because of a typo, and now a faceless killer in an orange hood was hovering over her.

Even the seagull was back.

Agnes squinted through the plumes of steam.

Which part was real?

Everything, she decided. Just not all *now*.

She could place her mother and her boss firmly in the past, the seagull was clearly in the present, simply because Agnes's subconscious would never ever have gone to the trouble of imagining it.

And the murderer in the orange hood? Future, Agnes decided, near future even. She may well have escaped freezing to death, but now she was sitting like a shrimp in a hot pot. It was only a matter of time until the murderer realised that plan A hadn't worked and moved on to plan B – drown Agnes in the hot tub. At least then she would catch a glimpse of him. It wasn't a great comfort to her.

In any case, she didn't feel like the flesh was being scorched from her bones anymore. Her body had got over the drastic temperature change – it was a miracle she hadn't had a heart attack – and she had to admit that a hot tub like this also had its good points. With the snow still fluttering down on her, it was nothing less than picturesque and surreally beautiful.

She watched the snowflakes melting on her hand and tried to enjoy her time in the tub. After all, these were probably her final moments on the planet. She should probably make the best of it. Agnes listened inside herself, and to her surprise realised that she wasn't scared of dying at all. Other things scared her, yes. Pain, illness, the prospect of a home – anything but that! Death, on the other hand, seemed a relatively gentle affair.

The truth was, Agnes didn't really believe in it.

The older you got, the further away and more unlikely

your own demise seemed. Statistically speaking, you may be rapidly heading towards it, but in practice, you already had a lot of life behind you and hadn't died yet. Day by day, it had continued, despite any threats. If Agnes had learnt one thing in the course of her life, it was that death was giving her a wide berth.

But as she looked up from the melting snowflakes, she realised her luck had run out. A figure was standing on the terrace, white on white, as if she weren't really there, looking straight at Agnes.

24

LADDER

Bernadette was back on cloud nine.

It was nice there!

Here was the thing, you could think about things until the cows came home, go round and round in circles, but sometimes a simple kiss was enough to bring clarity to the situation.

Crystal clarity.

Bernadette leant contentedly on Jack's shoulder. The shoulder had changed over the years, had become softer and rounder, but it was still the right shoulder.

That's what it was all about!

Something tickled her ear.

'Why did you do it?' murmured Jack. 'Why did you betray the boss?'

Bernadette raised her head. She'd obviously seen this question coming, sooner or later. Maybe it was better that it came sooner.

'My brother,' she said. 'He had my brother on his conscience!'

She felt an old pain stirring inside her like a seed sprouting, still alive after all this time. Her little brother with the soft hair, the beautiful voice and the big plans, dead in a public toilet like a rat. Overdose. Bernadette had never really believed it.

'Your brother was no angel,' Jack said softly.

'No,' she replied, suddenly furious, 'but he was my brother! The boss thought he could do what he liked to us. What's a blind girl going to do about it? He was wrong!'

'Clearly. But it was an accident, I think.'

Bernadette shook her head frantically. 'That's the point. I think I realised back then that it wasn't an accident. Not at all. All the murders and power struggles, the violence. The boss always acted like he was a nice guy really, as if they were all regrettable coincidences, but the truth is, it was at the very heart of it. If you deal drugs, you're dealing in death. I didn't want to deal in death anymore. That's why I went to the police.'

'I would have stopped,' said Jack. 'Any time.'

'They wouldn't have let you stop.'

'We could have had a life together.'

'But it would have been the wrong life.' Bernadette felt light. Words she had been carrying around with her for years tripped off her tongue. It had needed to be said, and now it was said. No regrets anymore, no false remorse, no excuses.

You had to see things for what they were.

'You're still working, aren't you?' She could still feel the kiss on her lips, warm and somehow bitter. She wanted nothing more than to remain silent and enjoy this new feeling of lightness, but her mouth foolishly carried on speaking. 'Who are you here for?'

She felt a hand stroke her hair.

'For you, of course.'

Edwina didn't know what to do.

Where was Agnes? Already in room 12, or had she fallen by the wayside somewhere? And what now? Should she sit tight, look for Agnes, or go it alone?

Sitting tight was boring, so Edwina plumped for making sure that everything was alright in room 12. But where was the blasted room? She stared inimically from one door to another. Which one was the right one? She tried a few handles to be on the safe side. None of the doors opened, and they didn't have sensible locks that could be picked either. Edwina had witnessed a door being kicked in a couple of times, but she had never tried it herself, and the solid wooden doors of the Eden were definitely not for beginners.

She would have liked to talk to Lillith, or Oberon, or at a pinch even Hettie II, but stupidly none of them were around.

Eventually, Edwina decided to lightly kick one of the doors, just playfully, as a test. Practice made perfect.

She aimed, took position, made a run-up and . . .

'I'd leave it if I were you . . .' said a voice behind her.

Edwina spun around.

A podgy man was standing there very properly dressed, looking a bit like a penguin.

Edwina paused and made out she hadn't just run into a door. She kicked the air a few times and then did a few half-hearted stretches, but she wasn't fooling the penguin man. He might look friendly and perhaps a bit boring, but she knew straightaway that that wasn't the whole truth.

There was something about the way he stood and spoke and looked at her. Poise, intelligence, maybe even something like charm. And he knew exactly what she had in mind. The penguin man was a consummate professional!

Edwina stopped with the stretching, and eyed him with curiosity.

'Why?' she asked.

'Well,' said the man. 'It's my door, and I'd really appreciate it if it stayed in one piece. Especially since there's a murderer on the loose.' He gave a wry smile.

She carried on peering at him. 'What's deep and shallow at the same time?' she asked. It was a test.

'The sea,' the penguin answered without hesitation.

Edwina nodded at him in acknowledgement and was just preparing to try one of the other doors when she sensed movement at the end of the corridor.

There were footsteps, clattering and the squeak of wheels, then a familiar jangle. She could hear Charlie's excitable voice, and Winston's calm instructions. Before she knew it, half of her housemates were hurtling round the corner. Winston had a hotel brochure on his lap and was reading it like a map, Charlie was pushing the wheelchair. Marshall was leading from the front.

To her surprise, Edwina saw that even Mojo was in on it. Following the others, his arm stretched in front of him holding his phone like a talisman. Charlie must have somehow got him out of the wardrobe. Respect!

Marshall came to a halt in front of Edwina, his medals jangling.

'Where is she?' he snorted. Obviously, he meant Agnes. Marshall always meant Agnes.

'In room 12,' said Edwina, although she was in no way certain. When Marshall had gone as red as that, it was a good idea to give him a quick answer, before he went even redder.

'And where exactly is this bloody room 12?' he cried.

'That's the question,' Edwina said, crossing her arms.

Winston looked up from his hotel brochure and smiled. Just the kind of puzzle he liked!

'Well, if we assume that the numbering follows the same principle in all of the other corridors, and know from our own corridor, what that principle is, and if we further assume that these are rooms eleven to fifteen' – he paused and pointed to a sign on the wall on which '11–15' was written – 'then we know . . .'

He counted the doors like in a nursery rhyme.

'That is room 12!'

Winston pointed at the door behind Edwina. That easy! Edwina was annoyed that she hadn't thought of it herself. She turned around, sized up the door and went into warrior pose. Now she knew which door was the right one, it would be easier to kick with force.

But before she could get going, the penguin man stepped forward. Up to now, nobody had paid him a lot of attention. He was one of those people nobody noticed – until it was too late.

'I think there's a more elegant way of doing it,' he said and whipped out a plastic hotel key card.

'You've got the key to room 12?' Edwina asked warily. Was this Frank Ashwood? If so, he really had aged in the last few days!

'It's a master key card, like the ones the staff here use,'

the man explained. 'Very useful and very easy to get hold of if you know how. The murderer probably has one too.'

Edwina still looked sceptical, so the man introduced himself as 'Jack,' offered them all his hand with the utmost of respect, and then elegantly passed the card over the sensor. The door clicked open, and cold air wafted towards them.

'Agnes! Agnes!' Marshall stormed past them all into the room. Continued shouts of 'Agnes' revealed that he hadn't yet struck lucky.

Edwina followed him, then Charlie, then Winston.

Mojo, still fixated on his phone, stood in the doorway.

Charlie found a switch and flicked the light on.

'Oh my God!' she screeched, but it didn't have much to do with God. There lay the woman already known to Edwina from the pool, very beautiful, but dead as ever. There was a weird bath sunk into the floor and – Edwina stepped closer in interest – a big crate with a heat lamp. In the crate there were a few stones around a shallow water bowl. Edwina grabbed the bowl and a few stones and put them straight in her pocket. Oberon would be so happy!

Marshall had started flinging open wardrobe doors.

'She's not here! She's not here!' he cried in alarm.

'But she *was* here,' said Jack. He'd entered the room too – Edwina hadn't seen him come in – and was pointing at the glass door and the terrace beyond it.

There, only just in the beam of light, lay a shoe, half-covered in snow. It was a typical Agnes shoe with a wide, round snout and a little square stacked heel, too comfortable to look elegant, and too elegant to really be comfortable.

'Oh my God!' Charlie cried again and started pressing the buttons next to the terrace door. Before she found the open button, the light went on outside. Edwina could see swirling snowflakes, a kind of steaming witch's cauldron and footprints, big ones and small ones, in the process of being erased by the falling snow.

An angry-looking seagull was sitting on the terrace railing spreading its wings.

Once again, Edwina wished she could speak to animals. This hopping mad seagull was sure to know exactly where Agnes had disappeared to.

Agnes had imagined her last minutes on this earth differently.

Calmer somehow.

More dignified.

The White Widow hadn't immediately drowned her in the hot tub, which she now found to be pleasantly warm, but first put her finger threateningly to her lips.

'Just as I thought!' cried Agnes, because, in her situation, she really could do without being told what to do.

Her voice was a thin crow that got lost in the night.

The Widow came closer and looked around shiftily.

Agnes, ready to put up a fight, or at least a token offering, braced her toes against the wooden bottom of the tub.

But the White Widow surprised her. Instead of shoving her into the water, she grabbed her under the arms and pulled. Agnes, who had positioned herself for a downward force, shot out of the water like an overzealous fish. The Widow was pulling her out of the tub! Why was she doing that? Agnes thrashed around half-heartedly, but was too surprised to effectively defend herself, as the White Widow dragged her towards the railings.

She was trying to push her into the sea! That was kind of her specialty after all!

Agnes baulked, but the White Widow was not deterred. She said something, but Agnes couldn't hear her. The cold was back, and all of a sudden, her body seemed to be completely and utterly occupied with breathing. In. Out. In. Out. Keep going!

Then they were already at the railing, and the White Widow passed her a snowy bundle. With some difficulty, Agnes recognised her cardigan. Suddenly grateful, she grabbed it. The wool thing wouldn't be particularly warming in its current state, but at least she didn't have to die half naked. As she wrangled with the sleeves, to her surprise, the Widow folded a section of railing to one side. Agnes saw that behind it a fire ladder led down the wall, maybe not into the abyss, but into the Eden's leafless wintry garden.

Was this how the Widow had got onto the terrace?

The murderer waved at her from the ladder to follow her. Was that supposed to be some kind of joke? Had the woman ever seen how painfully she moved, even under optimum conditions? She was a million miles away from ladder climbing.

On the other hand . . .

On the other hand, Agnes was enormously relieved that the White Widow hadn't just pushed her into the sea. She obviously wanted to take her somewhere else, and any delay could mean that someone came to Agnes's aid. Maybe there would even be the possibility of escaping on the way?

So why not try her luck with the ladder?

Despite the adrenalin coursing through her veins in the face of her impending demise, Agnes would never have made it down the ladder on her own. But the Widow literally gave her a helping hand, and somehow, she managed it.

After a brief nail-biting moment, Agnes suddenly had solid ground beneath her feet again and looked around, disoriented. To one side, a row of dark glass windows looked at her, on the other there was a deceptively gentle incline. Between the two, a snow-covered path led past the hotel. The Widow grabbed her arm and resolutely dragged her along next to her. In the darkness, she seemed to glow like a ghost in her white clothes.

Agnes couldn't feel her feet anymore.

Or her fingers.

Her nose was on the way out too.

They made it to a glass door that was ajar.

The Widow flung it wide open and tried to manoeuvre Agnes inside.

Agnes, who in the meantime had realised that they must be on the level of the spa area, resisted with the last of her strength, despite the tempting warmth pouring out towards them.

All of a sudden, she was dreading the spa area. She remembered the heat from before all too well, the eery silence, and obviously Walter Ross and the relaxation room. Not like that! Not her! Come to think of it, she was quite picky when it came to how she died, but of course it wasn't easy getting that across to the White Widow.

The woman quickly managed to get Agnes through the door, despite the resistance. The sticky mugginess left Agnes breathless. The Widow pushed her mercilessly along a corridor.

Past the treatment rooms, where Agnes had experienced

her first massage, past the pool, where just that morning she had performed her foolhardy diving manoeuvre, past the relaxation room, where . . .

Agnes closed her eyes.

It might not be her whole life flashing before her eyes, but at least half the holiday. What could possibly save her? What had she missed? There must be a connection somewhere between the Widow and the Ashwoods, one in the past.

It became clear to Agnes that she should have focused on the past a lot sooner. The Eden, especially at this otherwise rather quiet time of year, was full of regulars. She should have concentrated more on the regulars, the repeat holidaymakers, all of the ones who had potentially been there three years ago. Might Ashwood have witnessed the Widow committing her first murder? Had he been blackmailing her?

But why wait three years to get rid of him? Did it have something to do with him getting married, maybe?

They had stopped again, and Agnes felt herself being leant against the wall. She opened her eyes wide and saw that the Widow had left her and was now trying to open the fire door to the staircase. It was a heavy door, and the Widow was having a little trouble. She looked a little the worse for wear from the climbing antics, the cold and the wet. Her face was bright red, which made her eyes look even bluer, her clothes – well, currently she was more of a grey widow.

Agnes wasn't leaning very comfortably. There was something uneven on the wall, and when she had a look, she saw that the offending article in her back was a lift button. Where there was a lift button, there usually wasn't a lift far away!

Agnes looked. Correct, right next to her!

And the lift was waiting.

Just as the Widow had finished propping the fire door open, Agnes quickly stepped into the lift and pushed the button, holding her breath.

Up! Now, please!

The lift made a co-operative ding that to Agnes sounded like angels singing, and she could still make out the Widow looking at her with an expression of boundless outrage through the closing doors.

Then she hurtled upwards.

Once on the ground floor, Agnes quickly got out of the lift. She had no idea where the energy was coming from, but the thought of the White Widow likely rushing up the stairs right now, was definitely a motivating factor. Agnes looked at the fire door next to her. The White Widow could turn up at any moment. She had no time to lose. She had to . . .

A mop was leaning in the corner, presumably left behind by one of the housekeeping ladies. Since the hotel had been in a state of murderous emergency, nobody was doing any cleaning anymore.

Agnes wedged the mop under the door handle. It wouldn't hold for long, but a little while maybe.

Then she hobbled away as fast as she could.

She didn't quite know how she had found her way back to her room, but clearly her subconscious knew the hotel much better than she had imagined. She found her key card in one of her cardigan pockets, opened the door and stepped inside, relieved beyond measure. Against all the odds, she had made it. Now hopefully someone would soon take care of her – and if she was lucky, it wouldn't be Edwina.

'You're not going to believe what's just happened to . . .' croaked Agnes, then stopped.

Something wasn't quite right. There was nobody there! Hadn't they made a crystal-clear promise that . . . An empty champagne bottle was lying on the floor, with two glasses next to it. Oh, Charlie! But Agnes was far too tired to get worked up about it. She was alive, and that was all that mattered. And she was standing just a few feet from her bed. That was a cause for celebration, wasn't it?

She closed the door behind her.

Widow secure?

Hopefully!

Now to bed . . .

The route seemed surprisingly long and arduous, but finally it was there in front of her, the bed, a dream of white fluff and forgetting. Agnes knew that she should really get out of her wet clothes, but she didn't have the energy.

She sank into the pillows as she was. Covers pulled up to her nose.

The shaking receded.

She closed her eyes, exhausted.

When she opened them again a moment later, or maybe quite a while later, someone was sitting on the side of her bed eating an apple.

25

APPLE

Agnes squinted up at the figure.

It wasn't Edwina, or Charlie, and definitely not Bernadette.

Something about the figure unsettled Agnes, but it took a while for Agnes to realise what it was.

The colour.

Orange.

The figure was wearing an orange jacket, but the hood was pushed back, and you could make out a head of scruffy blonde hair.

Agnes tried to get up. Everything hurt.

The figure must have felt her moving. She turned to her and smiled.

Trudy! Just Trudy! At first, Agnes felt a sense of relief, but a strange unease ensued.

Why Trudy? What was *she* doing here? Something wasn't right. If only things in her head weren't so cold and stiff! Everything was numb and dull, even her thoughts.

She tried to sit up again. Without success.

'Most people die in bed,' said Trudy cheerfully. 'Did

you know that? Statistically speaking, beds are the most dangerous place in the world.'

Agnes didn't like the way she was smiling.

'I actually wanted something different for you,' Trudy continued. 'A bit of fresh air. A bit of drama. But here we are!'

She put her apple core on the bedside table, and Agnes gasped for air. Her numb brain was finally picking up pace, and she *saw* . . .

The bare grape stalk in the Ashwoods' room!

All the apple cores near the lift – they could have told Agnes that Trudy had already been there for quite a while, just a few seconds' lift ride away from the bloody relaxation room! The murderer had literally left behind a trail of mutilated fruit, and Agnes had been too pig-headed, too fixated on the White Widow to see it. Come to think of it, her interest in the White Widow had started with Trudy! In her prattling, scatty way, Trudy had directed her attention to the Widow from the very beginning!

'What nobody tells you when you start murdering is just how stressful it is.' Trudy sighed. 'Constantly on the hop. You never have time to approach the whole thing . . . a bit more mindfully. Everything's always chop-chop . . . But this' – she patted her hand on the bed – 'nice and cosy with a bit of time for a chat . . . lovely, isn't it?'

Agnes nodded. Chatting wasn't bad. Far better than dying at any rate.

She couldn't help but look towards the hotel room door.

'Don't worry,' said Trudy. 'They're all looking for you in room 12, of course. I took the room numbers off, you know? Quite easily done. Your own room is the last place they would think of. We're safe here for now.'

Safe was relative. Agnes's thoughts were racing.

Trudy was the murderer! No matter how harmless she looked, she had the Ashwoods, Mrs Meyer-Brinks, Max and Walter Ross on her conscience – and soon her too, Agnes! Hard to believe, and yet . . . Agnes realised that she hadn't just swapped Ashwood's picture back in the housekeeping store, but also Trudy's, but she hadn't thought for a moment that it could mean something . . . When someone seemed exclusively interested in calories, you just didn't think them capable of all these murders.

'But how . . . ?' Agnes stammered. 'Why?'

Trudy took a sweet out of the pocket of her orange jacket and laid it next to Agnes on her pillow.

'Service to the end,' she said, and smiled. Agnes wanted to back away but didn't have anywhere to go. 'I used to work at the Eden, you know? Not a great job. You're supposed to constantly make the guests happy, but most people just aren't made to be happy, and when they realise that it's not working despite all the food and the wellness treatments and the view, they take it out on you. But I did make one of them happy!'

'Ashwood?' Agnes asked.

Trudy waved dismissively. 'Frank came later. But first, there was Harry . . .'

She was miles away, and the dreamy look on her face jogged Agnes's memory.

'The White Widow's husband?' she guessed.

'Harry.' Trudy smiled. 'We had a few beautiful hours together, but then his guilty conscience got the better of him and he didn't want to be happy anymore. You can't just let go of happiness like that, that's what I think. It's – a crime!'

'So, you killed him?'

Trudy ran her fingers through her blonde hair. 'Of course not. Not *killed*. Just . . . gave him a bit of a shove. I didn't mean it, not really, but, anyway . . .' She shrugged. 'Then he fell. And if I'm honest, I felt better afterwards. Obviously, I was horrified – and scared to death that someone had seen me – but underneath it all I felt good. And nobody saw a thing. It was so easy . . .'

'But the White Widow was suspicious?' Agnes deduced. Her brain seemed to be working again. It was thinking flat out, not just about the murders that had been committed, but how future murders – amongst them her own – could be prevented.

Trudy pulled a face. 'She knew straightaway that it wasn't suicide. Not Harry – they had probably just made up. What a load of tosh! And she hadn't quite believed the thing about the accident either. Nobody's fool, the Widow.'

'She knew *someone* had done it,' said Agnes, nodding. 'But not *who*.' Now her brain was back in action, she felt a bit better. Her old curiosity had been stirred, and it at least looked like she still had a bit of time left to solve the mystery of the deaths at the Eden. Trudy was obviously in no rush to continue her murder spree. 'She probably suspected he'd had an affair. And now she regularly returns to the Eden in the hope that the killer is a creature of habit too. And she's right!'

'I'm not a creature of habit!' Trudy protested.

'And Ashwood?' asked Agnes.

Trudy's eyes flashed with rage, and Agnes decided not

to provoke her anymore. Nevertheless, she wanted to get a few more pieces of information out of her before it got down to the nitty-gritty.

'The thing with Frank was different! Completely different!'

And yet, he's lying at the bottom of the sea too, thought Agnes, but she kept it to herself and looked enquiringly at Trudy.

'Harry was nice. Frank was *wonderful*. He made *me* happy! He first came here two years ago, completely on his own, and just sat there with his phone most of the time. To start with, I just felt sorry for him. We had wonderful chats, and for the first time, I thought . . . He came back again and again, and then all of a sudden . . . Nothing. They even fired me because of him!'

Agnes tried to make a sympathetic face. Of course! An ex-employee doesn't need a behind-the-scenes tour. An ex-employee knows all of the routes and routines in the hotel – that's how she succeeded in committing the murders in quick succession without being caught. But why exactly, Agnes still didn't understand. It might be that Ashwood had dumped her, but that wasn't the end of the world after all.

'I even followed him to London,' said Trudy. 'But it was too late. He'd already met the snake.'

'Eve.'

'The snake,' Trudy repeated with a stony expression. 'It's all the snake's fault!'

Agnes nodded pensively. For Ashwood, it had just been a holiday romance, Trudy had hoped for more. Things like that happened all the time, but in this case the spurned ex-lover had an obsessive streak and she already had her first murder under her belt. It wasn't going to end well.

'And you couldn't just let it go?' she asked plainly.

'How?' cried Trudy, in genuine surprise. 'It was about *happiness*! Mine and his! That snake wouldn't have made him happy. Not really. Not in a million years. I tried to find out as much about her as possible. And believe me, I found a lot!' Trudy laughed unpleasantly.

'I started to write her little notes telling her everything I knew about her. But she just didn't want to hand him over!' Trudy's fingers ripped up invisible scraps of paper in the air. If you looked closely, behind her seemingly down-to-earth façade, every now and then you could see a flicker of the abyss, a lack of genuine feeling. A lack of empathy. Instead, childish emotions swirled like snowflakes.

That was obviously bad for Agnes. She would have liked to negotiate somehow, brought the senselessness of Trudy's actions home. But how did you negotiate with a black hole?

Trudy laughed her thin, brittle laugh again. 'Then a colleague called me. Ex-colleague. Supposedly to see how I was, but in reality, she obviously just wanted to rub it in, what a cow. Frank had booked the Eden again! The romantic package! For his honeymoon!' The murderer balled her fists. 'He'd gone too far. How could he? How could he do that to me?'

'A little insensitive,' Agnes agreed and started considering escape possibilities anew. Or if not escape, then at least defence. She was pretty sure she wouldn't even make it out of the bed, and definitely not quickly enough to get away from Trudy. But maybe she could at least hit her with something – or throw something?

'He wasn't supposed to get away from me like that!' Trudy rebelled. 'Not like that! I wanted to throw a spanner in the works! So, I scraped together my savings and booked a room. Unfortunately, they only had the stupid detox package left!'

So, Trudy hadn't really been fasting voluntarily. No wonder she was constantly hungry.

'And nobody recognised you?' asked Agnes.

'Nobody!' said Trudy proudly. 'Dyed my hair, different hairstyle, changed my name a bit. Some chic sportswear. Apart from that, as soon as you pay, you're a different person!'

'And then you packed your bag, and off you went to Cornwall to kill them both.'

'Of course not!' cried Trudy. 'I'm not a monster, you mustn't think that, Agnes! I just wanted to make sure that their honeymoon wasn't all plain sailing. I wanted to . . . *spice things up a bit*. That was all.'

'Like the serpent in paradise,' said Agnes.

Trudy frowned. She didn't seem to like that comparison. But eventually she nodded and looked searchingly at Agnes. 'And what did the serpent in paradise *do*?'

'It . . . it told the truth!' cried Agnes.

Suddenly she understood.

'*You* showed Ashwood the photo of Eve. The one with, err, the snake and . . .'

'Not Frank,' said Trudy. 'The whore! She used to turn tricks, you know? Exotic snake dancer – my foot, everyone knows what that means! She obviously didn't tell Frank that. When Frank was having a massage, I just knocked on her hotel room door and showed her the picture. She

362

needed to know that I'd rumbled her! I suggested she do a vanishing act.'

'And she *did*.' Agnes sighed. 'In the pool, dosed up on sleeping tablets, forever more.'

Trudy shrugged. 'Totally over the top. She could have just packed her bags, instead of drowning herself. But no, she had to create drama. Depressive through and through. She would have thrown in the towel sooner or later anyway, if you ask me. All just a question of time. But Frank didn't take it very well. He pulled her out of the pool and howled and howled and didn't get it at all. "Put your jacket on," I said. "We're going to the cliffs. A little walk and everything will soon look different."'

'But everything didn't look different?' Agnes assumed.

'There was no doing anything with him,' said Trudy. 'He just didn't want to accept it. I'm still here, I said. I've been waiting for you. But he just laughed, this weird, hollow laugh . . . Nobody laughs at me like that. Nobody!'

Trudy herself laughed a weird, hollow laugh. Then she looked down at the sheep's wool carpet at her feet, but in her mind, she was standing on the cliffs reliving Ashwood's fall.

'It obviously wasn't what I'd imagined, but afterwards . . . I felt so free! Free as a gull! Freer even! I didn't need Frank anymore! I didn't need anybody! I had solved my problems for myself. Obviously, I was waiting for the guilty conscience, but it didn't come.' Trudy looked triumphantly at Agnes. 'Ever!'

'Instead, you got the note!' Agnes reasoned.

Trudy nodded with respect. 'Maybe you're not such a bad detective after all.'

'The note made you think that someone had witnessed

Ashwood's murder. And the only people it could possibly have been were those in the Sea Lounge at the time. So, you went about silencing them, one by one.'

Trudy shrugged again. 'To be honest, it was quite a shock. I came away from the cliffs in good spirits, a spring in my step like I hadn't felt for a long time – and then that! I was shocked to my core. Harry in broad daylight, nothing. And now this, despite the dark and the hood. At first, I thought it was the weird young lad with the phone. I paid him a little visit, but to be honest, I was nervous . . . some things demand a certain level of poise, you know? Some things have to be conquered first.'

The expression on her face changed abruptly, and she grinned from ear to ear.

'Shall I let you in on a secret, Agnes? Without the detox group, I'd never have managed it.'

'Oh?' Agnes didn't really know what to say to that. Best to stay silent and look interested. Looking interested had already gained her at least a quarter of an hour's extra life.

'The detox group isn't just about fasting and sport,' Trudy explained. 'It's also about your mindset. *Find yourself! The universe will take you exactly where you need to be! Be true to yourself! You can do anything you put your mind to! You deserve only the best! Follow your dreams! You have the power within you to solve your own problems!* And so on. What can I say? They're right. The universe brought me to the right place at the right time. I found myself. I can do anything I put my mind to! And I solve my own problems!'

A shudder ran down Agnes's spine. Trudy was a psychopath through and through. It was a mystery to

Agnes how someone could be merrily chomping away on apples and grapes and ice cream, and at the same time . . .

Ice . . . There was a cold lump on Agnes's side. She carefully felt beneath the bedcovers for it – sure enough! She hadn't just been imagining the lump! Her fingers found something hard and cold, something round in her cardigan pocket. It was the apple she'd pocketed at reception what felt like an eternity ago, because despite meticulous denture care, she couldn't bite down with force, no matter what the adverts claimed. After its time on the terrace, the apple, much like herself, was frozen solid and was only slowly defrosting.

A heavy, hard, cold object.

Agnes allowed herself a wry smile.

She had a missile.

Trudy was far too fixated on her inner journey to self-liberation, self-discovery and murder to notice Agnes's change in mood.

'And the constant hunger pangs!' she continued. 'That hunger made me realise for the first time that I'd actually been hungry my whole life. That it was about time I satisfied my hunger! All the tales they tell you about guilt and regret and conscience – all lies. None of it's true at all!'

'Not for you,' Agnes whispered.

'Not for me!' Trudy grabbed one of the pillows and fluffed it up in a practised motion. You could tell that she had once worked in a hotel. The look on her face changed again, subtly, but unmistakably. The silence said the rest.

It was time for Trudy to realise her own potential once again.

It was time for Agnes to die.

* * *

Oberon wasn't in the best of moods. First, being sniffed at by an impertinent four-legged creature, growled at and humiliated, and now boredom in the bathtub again!

He'd had enough of the bath and the heat lamp, the sink and stupid lying around, he needed variety. Maybe he should conquer a lovely viewing point or devour something? A rat maybe, or even a rabbit? That would show the sniffer who the real master hunter was! Definitely not that four-pawed creature!

He slid out of the bath, across the floor, towards where he could feel a draught. There it was again, the crack he had successfully passed through once before. He crept over soft, white ground, to lie in wait in the shadows of the bed once again.

He didn't have to wait long. Something was moving back there, but to his disappointment, Oberon realised that it was legs again. There was a real plague of legs in these climes!

Only these weren't just any legs.

Oberon could taste it in the air straightaway.

He could identify tones of vanilla, skin and sweat, and – just beneath it, barely covered by soap – a slight predatory whiff of hunger.

The legs of the whisperer!

The legs that had taken *her* life in such an unpleasant way!

That those impertinent legs dared to just roam about under his nose was a barefaced cheek!

Oberon was a constrictor through and through, and he was well aware of that fact. Strangulation was his guiding principle, his nature, his passion, but at that moment it didn't matter. In that moment, rage prevailed.

He let out a warning hiss, opened his snake mouth as wide as he could and bit into the ankle in front of him with all his might.

Far above him, someone screamed.

The ankle thrashed about all over the place.

Oberon managed to hold on for a bit longer, then he was flung into a corner. Never mind! He tasted blood.

Triumph!

The legs of the whisperer did a furious little dance, then they turned towards the bed again.

Through some kind of miracle, Agnes had managed to fend off the pillow, but now Trudy had her by the neck. She was in the process of banging Agnes's head against the bedpost, when she suddenly let out a scream. Her grip loosened, and she hopped through the room on one leg.

Agnes squinted. Her head was swimming, and it was difficult to see clearly. But this was her chance! Trudy was finally far enough away to throw something at!

Agnes wrenched the cold apple out of her pocket, squinted and tried to take aim. Trudy was moving a lot, but then, she stood still and bent over to inspect her ankle.

Now or never!

Agnes lunged, took a deep breath and, with all her might, flung the apple towards the back of Trudy's lowered head. Luckily, she had experience in throwing balls thanks to Brexit, so it was a clean shot.

The apple hit Trudy's skull with a satisfyingly loud crunch, and the murderer looked up for a moment with a look of surprise, then toppled over sideways.

'I solve my own problems!' Agnes muttered, sinking back into the pillows in exhaustion.

The Sunset Hall crew had looked everywhere.

First, they had picked up Bernadette, who oddly enough had been in Jack's room, then they'd gone downstairs to the spa area, where the footsteps in the snow had led. Under Jack's expert guidance they had managed to avoid any barriers and unpleasant encounters with hotel guests and staff, and had gone over the spa area with a fine-tooth comb.

They looked in the pool and the treatment rooms.

They checked behind the scenes.

They even ventured into the relaxation room.

Marshall shouted.

Bernadette listened.

Winston thought.

All without success.

Agnes was nowhere to be found.

Instead, they found the White Widow in the stairwell. She was unusually red in the face and also on the lookout for Agnes.

It turned out the Widow had been shadowing Trudy and found out that she had locked Agnes out on the terrace and decided to save their friend. But Agnes obviously didn't want to be saved and had run off at the first opportunity.

'Honestly, I wouldn't have thought her capable of it!' cried the White Widow. 'I mean, she was sopping wet and pretty worn out. I just wanted to get her to safety!'

'And where is she now?' cried Marshall impatiently.

'Definitely not safe!' said the White Widow gloomily. 'I wouldn't put anything past that fitness freak!'

'Where would *you* go?' Charlie asked Mojo, who was still trailing along behind them filming, shouting 'cool' or 'wicked' every now and then.

Mojo looked up from his phone for a moment and shrugged.

'In a wardrobe, I think.'

'But not just any wardrobe!' cried Bernadette. 'She'll go where she feels safe!'

'And where does she feel safe?' asked Jack.

'With us, of course!' said Bernadette. 'And where does she think we are?'

'In our room,' mumbled Charlie. 'Like we promised!'

Marshall had already stormed off, and the others followed him right up to Agnes and Edwina's hotel room door. It came to light that Charlie had forgotten her key card. Edwina never had her key card with her, on principle, and for some reason, Jack's master key card wasn't working.

It was the first time in her life that Edwina had kicked a door in, but under Jack's expert guidance it had gone like clockwork.

They rushed into the room.

There was Agnes, in bed, her forehead bloody, pale and wet, but irrefutably alive, her eyes sparkling feverishly.

And there was Trudy, unconscious on the floor, a bump on her head and an angry Oberon around her neck.

Edwina knew that although Oberon was still young, his constricting skills were far beyond his years.

26

WRAPPED UP

'She's tough, you've got to give her that.'

Agnes opened her eyes wide and saw that a torment of spectres had gathered around her bed. The White Widow with her blue eyes, the brat, and the white snake, and even the orange hood. The corgi, the penguin man, Bernadette and Edwina in her glitzy glad rags.

A nurse leant over her.

Agnes felt a rising sense of panic.

Was she in a home?

She groaned and tried to pull the covers over her head, but it didn't work.

Somebody was tightly holding her hand.

Marshall. If Marshall was holding her hand, then things couldn't be that bad.

Agnes squinted and looked more closely.

The White Widow didn't look threatening anymore, she looked exhausted, wet and relieved. She had put the corgi on her lap and was absent-mindedly stroking its head.

Oberon the snake was cheerfully flicking his tongue in and out. It looked like the two creatures had made their peace.

The brat wasn't wearing dark eye make-up anymore and was smiling at her.

And it wasn't Trudy, the serial killer, in the orange hood, but a bearded stranger wearing a high-vis vest. A construction worker! That could mean only one thing, the road had been repaired. They weren't cut off anymore, and someone else could take care of all of the mayhem in the hotel.

Agnes sighed with relief. It was only the nurse who was still bothering her. If the woman thought she could patch her up that easily, she was very much mistaken!

Agnes's head was pounding, as if a descent of demented woodpeckers had, well, descended. She touched her forehead and could feel a bandage. Too late then. The patching up had already happened. And something else occurred to Agnes, she was warm, and she was dry – not to be taken for granted these days.

'You should rest,' said the nurse sternly.

Agnes huffed and tried to sit up. If she'd learnt anything in the last few days, it was this, a romantic eco hotel was good for many things, but definitely not for resting.

The nurse gently pushed her back into the pillows.

The construction worker chap grinned at her warmly and shuffled out of the room with his hands in his pockets. Agnes would have liked to do the same, but she didn't have the strength.

'There's some news, Agnes,' said Charlie, who was standing at the foot of the bed and up to now had been hidden by the construction worker.

'Trudy has been arrested,' said the White Widow.

'She's still alive,' said Edwina apologetically. 'Oberon

371

is still a bit young to suffocate someone after all. But she's got a bump on her head. Bigger than yours.'

'She confessed to my husband's murder,' said the White Widow. 'And a few other things too.'

'She distracted the waiter with a butter knife to the eye,' Bernadette added. 'But he survived.'

'From today, all of our drinks are on the house,' said Charlie. 'But I think we're leaving anyway.'

'Howard has been caught,' said Edwina. 'He tried to escape, but the people in the Sea Lounge intercepted him. They found blackmail notes on him, and photos of the bald man's wife. Topless.'

'Now he's got a black eye,' Charlie explained with satisfaction. 'And they arrested him too.'

'The ship has docked,' cried Edwina. 'We're back!'

'This is Jack,' said Bernadette, squeezing the penguin man's hand. 'He was trying to kill me, but now we're getting married.'

'And I'll spend my sunset days online,' Charlie declared, as if she were going to move in, the whole kit and caboodle. The brat grinned at her encouragingly.

Agnes gulped. That really was a lot of news. All you had to do was rest your eyes for five minutes, and when you opened them again, the world had turned upside down! Bernadette – getting married? And Charlie on the internet? Were her housemates in their right minds?

'And the police are here,' said Winston with a tinge of regret. 'As soon as you feel better, they'd like to talk to you!'

* * *

372

'Once more from the start,' said the police officer.

It had taken a while for the nurse, who proved to be a real dragon, to allow the police to talk to Agnes. Agnes's job was first of all to get her strength back and consume an unholy quantity of the hotel's own herbal tea. The rest of the time was taken up with trips to the toilet due to the fluid balance.

But getting her strength back didn't suit her.

She was over eighty. She could pour tea down her neck for months on end, and it still wouldn't look overly good as far as strength was concerned. And apart from that, the murders were still going round in her head. Trudy, the cake demon – a five-time murderer? Really? Why hadn't she seen it coming? Why hadn't her gut feeling, which used to be so dependable regarding such matters, sounded the alarm?

Maybe it was down to the fact that Trudy didn't see herself as a murderer, but just as someone solving her own problems. The murder of the White Widow's husband maybe really had been a partial coincidence, and when her conscience didn't stir afterwards, killing as a problem-solving method had become a more and more attractive option. When it came down to it, Trudy was convinced, now as ever, that she was actually a nice person. Just pragmatic. Pragmatic enough to lure Max into the pool pump room under false pretences and bash his skull in with a dumbbell. Pragmatic enough to rather bumblingly slit Walter Ross's throat at some point between his massage and his cucumber water. So pragmatic that she had decided, at the first opportunity, to lock Agnes, who she thought was really kind after the cake incident, out on the terrace of room 12, and leave her to freeze to death. But the hot tub and the White Widow had thrown a spanner in the works!

'How did she know that you would be in room 12 then, Miss Sharp?' the police officer asked. He was a little slow on the uptake.

'She knew because she'd practically sent me there,' Agnes explained impatiently. 'She came to mine, probably to see if there was an opportunity to do away with me. I was right at the top of her list, you know? And since Howard was still pushing his stupid notes under her door, she thought I had something to do with it. Howard was enormously lucky that she didn't catch him with the notes. Then a black eye would have been the least of his worries.'

Agnes allowed herself a moment to picture Trudy and Howard meeting. Two predators exploiting the weaknesses of the people around them. Only Trudy had been a shark, and Howard a little fish.

But the police officer still looked confused, and she explained further, 'When she was in my room, she quickly realised she couldn't do anything. We were all together, you see.'

'Almost all,' said Marshall accusingly.

'Almost all.' Agnes sighed. 'So, she decided to make sure I left the room. It didn't take much. Nobody likes being cooped up, do they? When she saw the photos of Frank and Eve Ashwood on the bed, she knew that I was getting close – just not quite close enough. It wasn't hard to guess what my next step would be. So, she took out the waiter and then lay in wait in room number twelve. She made sure the door wasn't closed properly, and I walked straight into her trap. As soon as I stepped out onto the terrace, she saw her chance. I think, deep down, she prefers those kinds of murders. A little shove here, press a button there. Clean. You see, she's not particularly good at the more hands-on stuff.'

The police officer shook his head uncomprehendingly. 'I still don't understand it – all those gruesome murders, all because of . . . And the killer – she seems so *normal*. When you speak to her, she makes out you're making a mountain out of a molehill. And yet . . .' He broke off. He suddenly looked young and helpless, and Agnes felt a wave of sympathy for him. An inexperienced whippersnapper trying to make sense of the labyrinthine fabric of the world.

She leant forward and comfortingly patted the police officer's knee. 'Some people just don't have any compassion. No conscience,' she explained gently. 'It's hard to tell if they come into the world like that, or if something makes them that way. But most of them lead pretty normal lives. A bit cold, maybe, rather unfeeling, but they keep to the rules. But when one of them breaks the rules and does something terrible, and realises that it doesn't bother them . . . That's how monsters are made, I think. And maybe the worst thing of all is that they don't even know they're monsters.'

The police officer nodded, went to write something down, but then decided against it.

He opened another page in his notebook.

'According to my notes, in the end the killer was neutralised by a snake?' he said and looked around at them all in disbelief. 'Have I understood that correctly?'

'There is no snake,' Edwina said quickly, placing a

375

protective hand on the sports bag next to her.

'No snake,' confirmed Charlie. 'What nonsense! Agnes took out the murderer with a frozen apple.'

Agnes watched as the police officer crossed out the word 'snake' with a look of relief.

The residents of Sunset Hall cast conspiratorial glances at one another. They were all behind Oberon the super snake, who in all likelihood had saved Agnes's life with his bite and youthful suffocation attempt.

After that, the questioning must have got a bit boring because Agnes dozed off. When she opened her eyes again, she was alone in her room. Or almost alone. On the other side of the bed, she spotted two pointy corgi ears, and sitting in the armchair next to her, inconspicuous as ever, was the White Widow.

Only she wasn't white anymore, she was wearing jeans and a grey jumper. Her blue eyes looked piercingly at Agnes.

Agnes got a little fright.

The last time they had been alone together, she had been fighting for her life. *Against* the White Widow, she had thought. With hindsight, it turned out they had been on the same side.

Now she was a bit embarrassed. How did you speak to someone you'd recently wrestled in a hot tub? Agnes didn't know.

Finally, the White Widow spoke up.

'I wanted to say goodbye,' she said. 'I'm leaving, and I'm not coming back, view or no view!'

Agnes nodded. She could understand that the Widow had had enough of the Eden.

'Thank you,' she said. 'For saving me and everything . . . If only I'd known . . .'

The widow sighed. 'If only we'd all known . . . But now we do! That's something anyway!'

Agnes smiled weakly. The ice had been broken. 'How did you know I was on the terrace? I've been wondering that this whole time.'

The Widow shook her head. 'I didn't know. But I recognised her, Trudy! Finally, after all that time! When we were both sitting in the relaxation room and she joined us – she has this way of running her fingers through her hair, and against the light, when I could only see her silhouette, I suddenly knew that she had to be the manager from back then. Just like that! And then . . . The rest wasn't very hard to work out. She was just Harry's type! I've been coming here for years in the hope of finding any little detail, something that I'd missed up to then. And suddenly it all made sense! Obviously, I didn't have any proof. So, I tried to tail her. It wasn't easy at all, and obviously she was wary. Unfortunately, she caught me a few times. But I saw her disappear into room 12. And shortly afterwards, you turned up. I wanted to warn you, but you wouldn't have believed me . . . And then you were already in the room, and the door was shut. So, I tried to get onto the terrace from the outside to see what was going on. And then you were sitting there in the hot tub, and well, I wanted to get you out of there before Trudy came back. Save at least one person, I thought, even if it wasn't Harry . . . A shocked old lady – how hard could it be?' She laughed drily, and Agnes looked sheepishly to one side.

'Sorry,' she said. 'I didn't know . . .'

The Widow waved the apology away. 'Water under the bridge. The important thing is that Trudy has been caught. And that's down to you! And your apple, and the snake!'

Now the Widow laughed again. She had a surprisingly pleasant laugh.

'Well,' croaked Agnes, lowering her eyes. 'Maybe. Thanks again.'

'My pleasure,' said the Widow.

They shook hands and Agnes even dared to stroke the corgi between the ears. Then Marie stood up and went, not white anymore and only a little bit widow still, off into the future, alive and free.

The corgi followed her on its little legs, but at the door it turned around towards Agnes again and gave a friendly wag of its tail.

Agnes waved back, with a smile. If you thought about it, it really had been a very special holiday indeed.

27

HEAT LAMP

'Hello there! Hi! Roll up! Welcome to Charlie's Wacky World of Wonders!'

Charlie ignored a groan behind her and waved manically into the phone's camera.

'So, this is where we all live. Sunset Hall. Fabulous! The good life, dear readers. Listeners. Viewers.'

Charlie had got ahead of herself a bit and was filming in the lounge, where in age-old fashion, the residents of Sunset Hall had gathered around the fire complete with blankets, coats and hats. There were now a few strategically placed heat lamps from the internet as well.

This morning they had received a big 'well-being package' from the Eden and were in the process of lighting scented candles, trying on bed socks and nibbling on biscuits. Agnes had been presented with a super fluffy dressing gown as well, with agnes embroidered on it in red letters. She had put it on straightaway for warmth reasons. There she sat, white and fluffy, visibly content with herself and the world.

'Yes. Err. So, this is where we live!' Charlie repeated, at a bit of a loss. She panned to Winston, who was snoring, and then quickly continued, on the lookout for an attractive subject. Marshall was at least wearing uniform and had a halo because of the heat lamp behind him.

'Everything okay, Marshall?'

Marshall saluted.

'We've just come back from holiday,' Charlie explained. 'Luxury romantic eco hotel. A last hurrah!'

She zoomed in on Agnes.

'Have you made a good recovery, Agnes?'

'Excellent,' said Agnes from out of her dressing gown, pointing her thumbs, albeit not upwards like they had discussed, but sideways, thumbs to the left. You could still see the outline of a nasty bruise on her forehead. Charlie quickly panned away.

'And this is Edwina.'

'And Oberon!' Edwina declared.

Oberon the super snake was currently living in a removals box illuminated by lots of heat lamps – until the terrarium that had also been ordered on the internet arrived. All the residents of Sunset Hall envied the constant warmth.

'He's grown already!' Edwina declared, holding a handful of Oberon up to the camera.

Charlie took a step back, just to be on the safe side.

'And this is Lillith!' Edwina reached for a tin and started to undo the lid. 'We lost a bit of her, but she's not angry with us anymore!'

Charlie made a hissing sound and Oberon eyed her with sudden sympathy.

The camera moved away from Edwina before she could get the lid off and went looking for something more internet-appropriate. 'We live here on the outskirts of an idyllic village and are enjoying our sunset years to the fullest,' Charlie continued with iron determination.

The camera found Jack and Bernadette, who were snuggling on the sofa, exchanging some rather sloppy kisses.

Charlie groaned, tapped the red button and stopped recording.

'We're not enjoying our sunset years *that* much.' She moaned. 'At least not on camera. We'll go again in five. Maybe like we discussed for a change! Cuddles yes, kissing no!'

'Have a biscuit!' Winston advised her, but Charlie treated her housemates with disdain. She looked out of the window, out into the wintry dead garden.

Somebody was standing at the gate,

A hooded figure.

Well, in this weather nearly every figure was hooded.

Charlie put her phone on the table and checked her hair in the mirror.

Perfect as ever!

Then she stepped out into the hallway to greet the visitor.

If they were very lucky, it was the plumber!

If they were less lucky, maybe it was the murderer who had the verger on his conscience and was still up to no good in Duck End.

Maybe even both at the same time.

Thanks to the scented candles, a wonderful hay fragrance suddenly filled the air. Charlie smiled. They lived in Charlie's Wacky World of Wonders, and anything seemed possible.

ACKNOWLEDGEMENTS

Thank you to . . . my agent, Astrid Poppenhusen, for her hard work and constant support . . . my German editor, Claudia Negele, and my publisher, Grusche Junker . . . Amy Bojang for her delightful translation and for being a pleasure to work with . . . my US publisher Soho Press – special thanks to Rachel Kowal for her keen eye for detail . . . the team at Allison & Busby, my UK publisher – special thanks to my editor Lesley Crooks . . . Steffi, Camilla, Werner and Susi, Tanja and Martin for being my 'test readers' . . . Rumi for her moral support . . . Theo Holroyd for some really eye-opening insights into the world of the blind. (One of the things we discussed was how he feels about the many visual metaphors pervading our language.) . . . Rob & Fyo, for being home.

LEONIE SWANN's debut novel, *Three Bags Full*, was an instant hit, topping the bestseller charts in her native Germany for months. It has since been translated into 26 languages. She lives in Cambridgeshire.

@_leonieswann